1620

Mayflower
a novel

HOLLY BLAIKIE

Cover Artwork:

De Windstoot – A ship in need in a raging storm, by Willem van de Velde II, 1707

Judith and her maidservant with the head of Holofernes, by Orazio Gentileschi, circa 1608 (altered for thematic purposes).

Page of William Bradford's original *Of Plymouth Plantation* circa 1647

ISBN 978-1-7770386-0-1

To Sarah, Liam and Jeffrey

Nautical Time Keeping

00:00 – 04:00	Middle Watch
04:30 – 08:00	Morning Watch
08:30 – 12:00	Forenoon Watch
12:30 – 16:00	Afternoon Watch
16:30 – 18:00	First Dog Watch
18:30 – 20:00	Second Dog Watch
20:30 – 24:00	First Watch

Passenger List

William Bradford
Dorothy Bradford

John Carver
Katherine Carver
Desire Minter
John Howland – servant
William Lathan – servant
Roger Wilder – servant
Dorothy 'Anna' – servant
Jasper More

William Brewster
Mary Brewster
Love Brewster
Wrestling Brewster
Richard More
Mary More

Edward Winslow
Elizabeth 'Beth' Winslow
George Soule
Elias Story
Ellen More

Isaac Allerton
Mary Allerton
Bartholemew Allerton
Remember Allerton
Mary Allerton
John Hooke – servant

William White
Susanna White
Resolved White
Peregrine White
William Holbeck–servant
Edward Thompson–servant

Stephen Hopkins
Elizabeth 'Lizzy' Hopkins
Constanta Hopkins

Giles Hopkins
Damaris Hopkins

Oceanus Hopkins
Edward Doty – servant
Edward Leister– servant
John Tilley
Joan Tilley
Elizabeth Tilley

Ed Tilley
Ann Tilley
Henry Samson
Humility Cooper

William Mullins
Alice Mullins
Priscilla Mullins
Joseph Mullins

Myles Standish
Rose Standish

Samuel Fuller
William 'Billy' Butten

Edward Fuller
Mrs. Fuller
Samuel Fuller

John Billington Sr.
Eleanor Billington
John Billington Jr
Francis Billington

Francis Eaton
Sarah Eaton
Samuel Eaton

Christopher Martin
Mary Martin
Soloman Prower
John Langemore

Francis Cooke
John Cooke

John Crackstone Sr.

John Crackstone Jr.

Thomas Rogers
Joseph Rogers
Thomas Tinkner
Mrs. Tinkner
A son (unnamed)

John Turner
2 sons (unnamed)

John Rigdale
Alice Rigdale

James Chilton
Mrs. Chilton
Mary Chilton

Richard Warren
Moses Fletcher
Gilbert Winslow
John Goodman
Peter Browne
Thomas Williams
Degory Priest
Edmund Margesson
Richard Bitteridge
Richard Clarke
Richard Gardiner

John Alden
John Allerton
Thomas English
William Trevore
Ely

*Andrew Weston 'Prince'

_____

* Not actual passenger

Table of Contents

Asunder

July 27, 1620
Delfshaven Wharf, Holland

*D*orothy roared his name into the crowd. "William!" Her cry shattering like a breaker on the shoal. The busy wharf clamoured with their congregation members, and sailors, yet William was nowhere to be found. She rehearsed what she would say to him with the doggedness of the town clock, her only companion through the sleepless night. She refused to yield to the chaos around her. Time was running out. Clasping her son's small hand in her own, she pushed forward into the human squall.

Jonathan tugged and pointed to the *Speedwell*'s sails. Folds of canvas luffed and billowed round their loosening bounds, forming clouds in the morning's pale sky.

"Why wouldn't that sailor let me on? Daddy could have made him," Jonathan said, peering up at her through a tangle of limbs. "Mama? Mama, what's wrong?"

Dorothy knelt to embrace him. Her son's face was red with heat, the air close between them.

"Just don't let go of me, no matter what," she breathed. "Promise?" Her plea quaked in time with the wharf beneath them.

"Promise."

Like the tide's ebb on bare ankles, the brush of silk skirts tugged her toward the ship. She tacked between passing bodies until, at last, her eyes found William.

"Quickly now, child."

She jumped as a heavy mooring line came to life beneath her feet. A pair of sailors struggled on its other end to coax it onto the *Speedwell*'s main deck. Over the channel the *Mayflower*, their companion ship, awaited their arrival.

She had to convince William.

To ignore what was right, to ignore every natural impulse and be a good wife, as Pastor Robinson insisted, would break her. It would mangle her inner workings, like the gears of a clock prevented from ticking. What William wanted would destroy her.

"Owww, you're pinching!"

"Sorry, baby."

A pair of arms encircled her waist and she stiffened at the sound of the voice in her ear. Bridgette Robinson pressed a wet kiss to her cheek. "I'll miss you Dorothy and pray for you every day while we wait for word. You needn't worry." She smiled at Jonathan, spreading her palms in invitation. "Shall I take him and let you get things settled?"

"No." Dorothy pulled him into her skirt and looked beyond Bridgette, anxious not to lose sight of William's dark wispy hair.

Bridgette dabbed her cheeks with lace. "I hear the Master is ready to sail and . . . look at me, crying again," she sniffed. "We'll find each other in a few minutes, dear soul, and have our final goodbye."

Dorothy nodded absently and resumed her press through the crowd, Jonathan still enveloped in her skirt.

William was bent forward listening intently to old Moses Fletcher and the Chiltons. He wasn't looking at her, but she sensed that he knew she was there.

The words stuck in her dry throat. Her tongue felt too large for her mouth. The words, those words she had taken such care to assemble, that she had marshalled to represent her, now refused the purpose she had given them.

Forgetting everything, she blurted, "He *must* come. He *must*."

"A moment, dear. I'm sorry, Moses, what were you asking?" William smiled warmly and pulled her and Jonathan close.

"Are you sure about this, William? Have we made the right choice to … emigrate?" said Moses, emotion pooling in his milky eyes. "I sold all we had."

Mr. and Mrs. Chilton gripped his arm, speaking in turns, "Will we be safe aboard that ship? It seems so small a ship."

"Pastor Robinson and Deacon Carver secured the ship," William said. "My role was mostly in arranging our patent to New England. The Pastor can reassure you. He's just over there."

"But you're one of us, William. Nothing fancy. If you say we'll be free of persecution, well, I just want to tell you, we'll follow, we'll trust the ship," said Moses, measuring out his words.

Dorothy smiled politely, as was her duty, stifling her inward scream. They were running out of time.

William took Moses by the hand. "I can assure you, God is with us. We *will* be free, as New England is our Canaan." He gave Moses's bony shoulder a squeeze and then excused himself.

Her eyes pulsed. She held Jonathan's head firmly against her hip and covered his exposed ear with her palm. With the other, she drew William's neck down and pressed her cheek to his.

"We must bring him. I can't do it, William. I can't leave our son behind. On top of everything, you've made me lie to him."

She started to cry. It was happening too quickly now. The volume of voices rose around her like a flooding tide aiming to trap her.

"It's arranged. He can't come. Not yet. It's too dangerous."

"I can't leave him. I'll stay behind," she whispered, her voice strained and jagged. "Don't do this to us, William."

"Al'board!" boomed over her head. Her knees weakened. Jonathan began to wiggle free.

"Let's go, Mama. I want to see the ship."

A thick sob escaped her throat. "William?" she pleaded, no longer whispering.

"Come on, Mama," he said pulling her by the skirt.

She stooped and lifted him in her arms, smelled his golden hair, felt it soft on her cheek and kissed his little face. "William, he *is* coming. We can borrow the clothes he needs from Mary Brewster's son." She held him tighter.

"Mama, you're squeezing."

"Here, give him to me," said William.

"No. You can't take him from me. Don't do this, William."

The embarkation swelled, dragging her forward. She had to make it to the ship with him in her arms.

She saw Bridgette and Pastor Robinson looking at her with their heads tilted, gentle expressions on their faces. A hammering started in her ears. She pressed backward against the crowd, but William was behind her, blocking her escape.

Bridgette's hands encircled Jonathan's chest, pulling him from her. He screamed.

William dragged her up the gangplank.

"Stop! No! This can't happen!"

She slithered from William's grasp. She was on her knees crawling back through the forest of legs, catching hold of them randomly, dragging herself toward Jonathan's cry. William caught her ankle and she kicked. A hand caught her bodice and hauled her upright. Fifteen feet away, Jonathan's face was red. He arched his body trying to get free of

Bridgette's arms. He reached for her. Begged for her. Bridgette backed away, melting into the crowd.

"Bring him to me, damn you! Don't betray me."

"Mama! Mama!"

God won't allow this. Surely God won't allow this.

"I'm coming Jon! Mama loves you. I'm coming!"

Secrets

*D*orothy dabbed at the sweat on her brow and wondered again whether her prayers had caused the near sinking. If so, God was on her side, not William's, not the congregation's. Every day the *Mayflower* bobbed at anchor and the *Speedwell* sat in dry dock, it cost them money they didn't have and provisions they couldn't spare. Any day, a decision may be made to turn back.

While moored at Southampton, she had tried but failed to convince William to send her home. She'd been trying all week here in Dartmouth too. The more reports she overheard of the failure to find a leak, the more convinced she was that God had, indeed, arranged this second chance. What could explain it otherwise? She'd seen the water rising in the hold with her own eyes. The ingress had been rapid enough to force them into Dartmouth soon after departing Southampton. Strangely, now, they could find no leak, even when they ought to have found a gap the size of a rabbit hole.

If this was God's plan, what did He want *her* to do now? Begging William wasn't working and waiting for the congregation to come to a decision was costing precious time, time that could have been spent with Jonathan in her arms. He would be reassured of her love for him. He would know that she hadn't abandoned him.

With a handkerchief pressed to her nose, she skirted crouched sailors applying pitch to the deck and steadied herself on the rail. The oily black ooze mingled with the smell of fish being cleaned along the wharf.

It was better than being below. Down there, the air was molasses, thick and dark. Scattered everywhere were trunks, bedding, platters and spare boots. After only a fortnight, belongings littered the 'tween deck like lumps of seaweed tossed on a storm-battered beach. Worst of all, weaving in and around the debris were busy, doting mothers, their children by their side.

Her eyes drifted along the quayside. The *Speedwell* lurched as water flooded the dry-dock. They were re-testing for leaks.

She heard footsteps and turned. Desire leaned on the rail beside her.

"Better? I saw you dash above. You looked upset."

"Yes."

In the act of raising an arm to smooth her hair in the breeze, Dorothy noticed the lace on her cuff was crumpled and lowered it again. She noted, that Desire, as usual, looked impeccable with her fresh face and neatly tied dark curls.

I am the normal one, despite how I look. It's this ship, this voyage, being torn from your child that is madness.

"I can't go with you," Dorothy said. Her eyes scanned the shore as her mind ferreted out escape routes to Holland.

How does God intend for me to do this?

Desire patted her hand and gave her a sympathetic look.

"Why have you come on this voyage, Desire? You didn't need risk your life on this dream. There was no one to force you."

"There's nothing left for me in Leyden. The Carvers are my guardians and apart from them I have no family and no prospects for marriage among the congregation left in Holland. So . . . I had no more choice than you. Besides, Deacon Carver has assured me we will be safe. I trust him, and God, to protect us. Isn't it our duty to work together to accomplish God's great will for the freedom of His congregation?"

Dorothy examined Desire curiously. She was eighteen and beautiful – but still unmarried, an orphan, perpetually homeless and without suitors. Life had tried to teach her its cruelty, but she was a poor student. In the crystal blue eyes staring back at her she saw only solicitude, selflessness and a steady optimism.

Dorothy restrained herself from telling Desire what God could, and could not, be counted on to do. She needed God on her side more than ever right now.

Dorothy removed her ruff and fanned her neck. "Can you loosen my stays? Sleeping in that cabin is like being trapped alive in a coffin, each wave hitting the hull like a spade of dirt rapping the lid."

She turned her back and fumbled with the ties until Desire took them from her. The younger woman loosened lace after lace, releasing the pressure around each ascending rib.

"Should we be doing this right here, in front of the sailors?"

"They've no business with what we do. They are like servants."

"You shouldn't speak the way you do. About the ship and coffins. You're just being morbid. I find the lapping of the waves soothing and you'll soon get used to the bunks. I can't tell you how many beds I've slept in since Mother and I lost Father, and then after . . . . "

Dorothy squinted at Desire, the rising sun a bright halo around her.

"I meant it when I said I'm not coming. I'm going back to Jonathan – one way or another."

"You can't."

"I have to." Dorothy turned squarely toward Desire. "You could have helped me get off the ship, back in Holland. You could have helped me get off. You stood above me and let them pin me to the deck."

"What could I have done, Dorothy? I'm sorry. But, what could I have done?"

"Anything. You could have run to get Jonathan for me. Pushed them off. Taken my side against William. You were my friend."

"Were? Don't you see, I couldn't have. And William is your husband. You're bound by duty to obey him. And how was I to wrestle Jonathan from Pastor Robinson – he's my Pastor."

"You must see how I feel."

"Look," Desire pointed, "there's William on the dock with Elder Brewster. I'm sorry, Dorothy. I am. I need to get back to help with the meal."

"Yes, go. You can't help doing what you're told."

The light from the blue eyes faltered for an instant. The remark bit deeply.

August 20th – Afternoon Watch

Everything had changed. It was just after mid-day and she held William's arm as they sauntered up Lower Street. He had insisted they walk toward Bayard's Fort, to catch a glimpse of Dartmouth Castle. While at the Fort she had let her tears flow and this time William finally promised to make things right. Every few steps she gave a skip and squeezed William in gratitude. God *was* with her. William had relented.

Away from the river the street sprouted a few teetering residences that leaned toward one another across the narrow cobble lane. She caught her reflection in a window. The light brown hair and a joyful green dress, wavered and flowed like the frond of a willow. William's outline was as rigid as the spine of a book. How glorious that she'd managed to bend him at last. She quickened her pace. There was packing to do. William needed to make arrangements.

A tall, white-washed building, criss-crossed and supported by stout black beams, stood on the corner just beyond. A brightly painted sign swinging above the door read 'Bayard's Cove Inn'. As they neared, William nodded at the locals curiously pressing their faces to the rounded bay windows on either side of the door. He opened the door for her. She hadn't expected they would stop. She was more surprised, not long after, to be gazing through the diamond-paned windows of a second-floor room, their purse nearly empty.

She studied William's reflection in the glass as he turned down the covers of the bed and removed his boots. Having paid handsomely for a private room, William clearly expected, or hoped, to spend the afternoon locked in her amorous embrace.

There wasn't time for this. They shouldn't be here. She turned and watched him. Before getting in that bed, she needed a promise that he was sending her home. She couldn't remember now if he had actually said those words. If this room was what he meant by *making it right*, he was mistaken. Knowing his gentle temperament would not yield if she let her feelings boil over, she pinned a sweet expression to her lips. William patted the bed. She was aware of how many cares he had on his shoulders from the congregation. But hers should be first.

Surely he did say he would. He would send me back.

Her shadow wavered for a moment within the elongated diamond shapes shimmering on the floor, then it stretched out, met his and was engulfed.

He buried his nose in her hair and then smoothed it behind her ear. She hated to defy him, but husband or not he . . . he had taken from her, her very reason for being.

"William, you are sending me back, are you not? This is my last chance. You promised."

"What are you talking about, my dear? I've made no such promise . . . we've settled this. What's gotten into you?" William bent to plant a kiss on her cheek.

She dodged it. "But you promised! I've no faith in this voyage. Do you not sense it? We'll be torn apart at sea and drowned. I'll never see my baby again if you force me back on that ship. I cannot go. It's not safe." She searched his face for understanding. "I had a dream I was being swallowed by icy water."

"You've just been overwhelmed by the conditions aboard. A night of privacy here, away from all the others, will make all the difference. I'll have some food brought up and we can sit together on the bed."

"You aren't listening! My poor Jonathan needs me and there is still a chance I can get back to Leyden with the help of our friends." Her hands gripped and tugged at his as she tried to make him realize what this meant to her.

"I keep seeing his arms outstretched for me as the ship pulled away. I hear his desperate cry, pleading for me not to leave him. I'll never see him again if I set foot back on that ship for New England. I am sure of it. Please, dear William, have you no remorse for what you are doing to me and our son?"

A shutter closed behind his eyes. Her chest began to heave. "You said you would!"

She recoiled at the sound of laughter cutting through the boards at her feet and hated the happy people below for their indifference. How could there be joy anywhere when her world was falling apart?

"Dorothy, my dear, God will protect us and guide us. Just as He has shown that we are doing right by supporting us through all of our previous troubles, he will continue to ensure our safety."

Her face slackened and her head hung forward. She wilted. The life slipped from her slender neck. He wasn't listening.

"We shall have Jonathan sent to us as soon as we have shelter built," he assured her, "and surety of being able to feed and clothe him. He is only four-years-old, and such a thin child," soothed William, "I'll not risk he sickens and spends his childhood as feeble as I did. He'll be heartier when he's grown."

Her heavy head swung like a pendulum. Silent moments ticked by.

"If we had brought him, would it not be worse, Dorothy? Must we watch him suffer the terrors of the sea and the hunger that already pinches us?"

She looked up. Burning eyes fixed on him as she launched a fresh assault. "If the conditions are as bad as you say, what help do you think I will be? You endanger me. Do you care less for your wife than you do for your son? My place is with him! I am his mother. Who better to care for him and see he grows strong than me? We can both come to you when all is settled."

She allowed him to take her hands, feeling at last, from the softening expression on his face, that she was making headway. His large fingers stroked her swollen knuckles, stinging the cracked flesh.

"Surely there are friends here who can shelter me until the Church in Leyden can raise alms to bring me back to Holland."

"No. There are few here I can trust and all of them are watched by the Crown. I won't leave you to an uncertain fate."

"But you will *take* me to one."

"I love you. You know I do. I wish I could let you stay. How am I to reassure others of the safety and importance of our mission if I admit it's too perilous for my own wife?" William said tenderly.

"The Spanish are at war with the Dutch and if the Spanish take the city then what we've suffered so far for our beliefs will be as nothing. Our congregation in Leyden is shrinking. It is one thing to ask our friends to care for Jonathan – it is another to ask them to care for you. What would you do to eat, clothe and protect yourself without me there? All we have is invested in this. Besides, the work ahead can't be harder than what we're used to. We will be free from oppression and the whims of the world at last. God wants this for us."

"I understand what you are saying, truly I do, but *my* place is with Jonathan – and *my* world was a few narrow blocks and our own warm settle. We had a good life!"

She tugged her hands from his grasp as he coaxed her toward the bed.

"Things are expected of me," he reminded her, "Carver, Isaac, Edward, Brewster and I have been instrumental in this. I can't risk our hard work, and the expenditure of so many families' savings, by showing I've lost confidence."

"It is *my* misfortune to be married to such an important figure."

She pinned her hands to her sides to thwart William's repeated attempts to recapture them. The consoling expression on his face fuelled her anger.

"Do you see these calluses? How chapped and worn my hands are from all the hard work I do for our family? Where are your calluses, William? Your only calluses are the matching ones on your thumb and forefinger. The only thing you scour are your books. You read and debate and give speeches, but do you understand? I am paying the real price. Your *child* is paying the real price. This is all just a mission to you. There are real dangers, real pains, real toils."

"Of course I know there are real dangers. What has gotten into you? You've been a temperate and obedient wife for seven years. Don't chastise me for my scholarship! Was I not a successful silk weaver in Leyden? I provided a good income. That income paid for this room."

William stepped back, his nostrils flaring. He leaned against the small table. "We are so close to freedom for our people. All we need do is set sail. But you want me to jeopardize the respect I've worked so hard to win. I need to be an example to them. I've made promises. I *will* deliver them to freedom and a bountiful life. You must stop thinking only of yourself and see that we need to do what is best for the whole."

She launched herself at him, slapping at his chest. "How can you sit in council with John Carver and discuss the dangers of the seas and the lateness of the season and know all that has happened with the merchant investors withdrawing their support, and still want to proceed yourself? What if God is telling us by all these things that we are wrong? Do you not see it? And the leak!"

A scarlet tide rose up from William's collar. She wondered if she had gone too far. Uncertain of what he might do or say she stepped back a few paces until she bumped the edge of the bed.

Laughter bubbled up from the taproom below.

A fresh wave of exhaustion washed over her. His resolve began to press her down. She stayed on her feet, resisting the force of his will. But she was flagging – without his consent, what could she really hope to do? With quiet determination she whispered, "I cannot do it, William."

She'd heard stories of the Virginia Company's ship lost on the American Coast – all but 50 of the 180 passengers dead from flux and lack of fresh water. Drowning in the icy depths was not the only death she feared. Surely fleeing on land, even alone, must be safer. "I cannot do it, William," she repeated, louder this time. She began to shake.

He threw up his hands. "I don't want to lose my temper. I think it best if I leave. I have a meeting."

She turned away, throwing her words to the rafters, "Go! Go to your *meeting!* You don't care about me or Jonathan!" William picked up his boots, ducked under the lintel and closed the door behind him. Relief flooded her shaken body. She could not bear to listen to his hollow arguments another minute.

She groped for the long slender bedpost behind her, willing it to keep her upright long enough to hear his footfall on the stairs. The hall remained silent. Her eye alighted on a roughly stitched tapestry. A golden chariot pulled by four giant hippocampi charged foaming waves, with Poseidon and his wife Amphitrite riding abreast; Poseidon at the reins. Its colors gradually bled as her eyes filled with tears.

August 20th – Afternoon Watch

At the foot of the stairs William ran into Robert Cushman.
"I was told I'd find you here, William. A word if I may?"

William grimaced. Robert's supposed illness seemed to come on suddenly as they put in for repairs. Perhaps he could sense the congregation's animosity toward him.

"I have something important to say." Robert removed his hat and wrung it as he spoke, "I have decided not to proceed on the voyage. I volunteer to remove myself and my family from the passenger list. Stronger more able-bodied men may go in my stead."

"It is too late for that, Robert," said William. He sucked in his already narrow frame and pressed himself against the wall to allow two barmaids to pass with steaming plates of mutton. His stomach groaned.

Robert cleared his throat. "I fear that I am dying and this may be the last I see of you, dear friend. Please don't think ill of me. My heart and soul have always been with the congregation and I wish you all the protection and love of our Creator."

William stepped past Robert. He had no interest in mollifying him. Especially in his present mood. "God go with you and your family," is all he could manage.

Robert caught William's sleeve, concern etched on his face. "I must in conscience share with you a word of warning, as I will with the others who have a hand in securing the success of this venture."

William tugged his arm free and, resigned, bade Robert follow him.

"I'm on my way to meet with Carver, Isaac, Edward and Brewster. If you would share your warning with all of us, come along. There's been ill will toward you Robert. I confess that I myself harbour some still for your actions on our behalf."

William softened on seeing Robert's expression. "But I won't be parted from a fellow brother on bad terms. If you're willing, come and answer our complaints."

Lower Street was crowded with merchants and women doing business. Straight ahead, at the end of the narrow street opposite the inn, William could see rough men busy at the docks. For a brief moment, nostalgia seized him. He turned left into the bustling crowd, into the scents and sounds of his homeland. He needed a break from the worries of the ship. Robert was right behind him, but he spared him no notice; he was too intent on avoiding the muck that collected between the uneven cobbles, stepping from stone to stone as if fording a stream.

The warm smell of bread emanated from the shop door on his right and mingled with the sharp odours of the tannery opposite. The bright, woven fabrics of the tailors and the shining metals of the chandlery lent an element of summer festivity to the town.

The fading din of the streets woke him from his thoughts. Reaching the end of Lower Street, he turned right, crossing to an inn situated just beyond the last moorings. He waited for Robert to catch up.

The inn was a broad two-story establishment lurking beneath a heavy-set brow. Less than fifty years old, its timbers were already so bowed it was a wonder the upper windows could open, so askew were their frames. It was like something seen through a thick and wavy bit of glass.

As he stepped across the lintel, the bright green of Isaac Allerton's tunic drew his eye. He and the others were huddled round a table in the back corner. William snaked his way through a Bacchanalia of sailors, standing, lounging and leaning on every available surface. Robert lagged somewhere behind him.

He tugged at the damp lace of his collar, nodded to the others and held up two fingers to the barman's wife. Robert appeared and sat down beside him.

Carver, Isaac and Edward Winslow pushed their chairs back and started to rise.

"Has Brewster been held up?" asked William, motioning them to sit.

"He's keeping out of sight. The pursuivants are still looking for him. News of the congregation's arrival will have travelled by now." Carver glanced at Robert. "I didn't think we would see you this evening, Robert. I heard you were unwell," he said acidly.

"I regret to tell you I will be remaining behind."

Chair legs scraped the sticky floor.

"Of course you want to remain behind," said Carver, his white beard quivering. "You told the Adventurers, as our investors so bravely call themselves, that we would work seven days a week for seven years without a day for rest, improvement or gain. You agreed to alter our original agreement without asking us. Now you have decided it's too hard a bargain for yourself and you seek to leave us. Because of you, because I wouldn't sign what you agreed to, Thomas Weston at Southampton threatened that we must stand on our own. Does he speak for the rest of the Adventurers?"

With his invitation, William had intended for Robert to clear the air. But the angry mood at the table caused him to doubt whether he had the stomach for it now. His mind was still with Dorothy, a few blocks away.

Robert spoke up. "My dear brethren, I bear your discontent and dislike of my proceedings, as well as I may. You can see the weakening effect it has had on me. I will repeat, however, that without my consent to the terms, there would be no voyage."

Robert took a long swig of his beer before continuing, "Thomas Weston agreed to our original terms and took our money, but he did so before the rest of the investors had seen or agreed to them. When one of the investors withdrew his 500 pounds, the rest threatened to follow suit if the agreement was not altered." Robert threw his hands up helplessly. "What was I to do?"

"But the new conditions are too harsh," Carver said, narrowing his eyes.

"That matters little right now," broke in William. "We need to know whether they will be provisioning us with food, seed, and implements come spring. Ought we tell the rest of the congregation the risk we run?"

Robert spoke again. "We've already spent the Adventurers' investment on the terms of the altered contract. I'll travel to London to assure them you are still with them. It is in their interest, is it not, that you should prosper and send back wealth to repay them?"

"Stop talking of that damn altered contract. And there is no 'we' where you're concerned," growled Carver. "With your change of heart, you won't be a slave to repaying it, like the rest of us."

"Because we didn't sign the contract, we don't have rights to settle the land. The patent is in their name. And yet we can't turn back. Everything we ever owned is spent," said William.

"We'll ask Brewster. He's the legal man. In my mind, the King has issued the patent and we shall occupy the land. I don't intend to turn back, whatever the legality," said Carver.

"Carver is right," Robert declared. "The greatest risk is not the lack of patent to the land, but the lack of help you will receive if the Adventurers abandon you. I am happy to die here rather than bear witness to the evil and grasping of hungry persons."

"You aren't dying any more than I am, Robert," Carver huffed. "We won't tell the others. This stays between us, or there will be mayhem. Carry on as though everything is as it should be. There is no alternative."

Edward Winslow leaned his thick forearms on the table and laced his fingers around his sweaty tankard. "Let's not blame Robert. Thomas Weston is responsible for this *and* for our leaving so late in the year. Instead of searching for a ship, he sat on our money until we were nearly starved back in Leyden. He intentionally waited until we were desperate. Desperate enough to sign anything he wanted. What storms now await us because of it?" Edward slammed his tankard down hard on the table.

Isaac lowered his voice, "Have we had any recent contact with the Adventurers, other than through Thomas Weston? How do we know he acts on their behalf?"

"He has been plain with me about each investor's feelings. I trust him. He has our holy mission foremost in his mind and will not desert us…you," Robert stammered, forgetting his recent departure from the group.

"If there is any chance we no longer have a contract and patent to settle, then we must send a letter to the Adventurers now, before we depart. We will offer to work longer than seven years if they will bend on their conditions. We need them more than they need us," said William.

"Nonsense," spat Carver. "They will want to collect on their investment. They won't abandon us. There is no need to abide by anything other than the first agreement I personally signed with them."

"Gentlemen. Stop arguing. If we don't remember the special bonds we have with one another, what will become of this voyage or the purpose upon which it is founded? All depends on our bond," said Isaac solicitously. He offered Robert his hand.

Robert's balding head shone beneath a few wisps of greying hair. He appeared to have aged decades since beginning work on their behalf three short years ago.

William downed the rest of his beer. "I forgive you, Robert."

"Thank you," Robert said quietly, savouring this small recovery to his reputation. Hesitant to sour it, but nonetheless emboldened, he broached the real reason he was before the group. "Gentlemen, I have further reason for disquietude. We've made a mistake appointing Christopher Martin Governor of the *Mayflower*. He keeps our people trapped onboard. He says they will run if he does not. Perhaps they would – he has so abused them. His friend, John Billington, is as much trouble."

Robert stood and placed both hands squarely on the table. "As you know, William, we only appointed him so that the strangers he represents wouldn't accuse us of partiality. Now he and his followers will bring ruin to your colony, if they don't prevent its creation entirely." He dropped dramatically into his chair.

William had dealt with Martin already and knew that Robert's warning was not frivolous.

"Thomas Weston did us a second disservice by bringing these unruly and ignorant men into company with us for the sake of profit," said Edward, a renewed flame of discontent taking hold of him.

"Thank you for bringing this to us, Robert," said Carver. "I'll speak to Mr. Martin this evening and see what can be done."

William's body relaxed the moment Carver volunteered. An earlier incident with Martin had shaken him. When the two groups – the congregation and Weston's English recruits – first met in Southampton, Christopher Martin had all but pushed him overboard to earn a laugh.

Although Martin caught him by the jabot and pulled him back at the last moment, William was humiliated, unable to avenge himself against the larger man who enjoyed such easy physical advantage.

The memory was fresh and unpleasant. William rose to take his leave. "You are ever a friend to us, Robert, and working for our common good. How fortunate it is that we've remembered it. Good evening."

August 20th – Afternoon Watch

Dorothy sank to the floor as William's footsteps faded from the stairwell. Rough knots and splintered wood bit into the bare flesh of her knees. She buried her face in the musty blanket and tried to pray, but only tears came. Her heart broke for Jonathan. Despite the thin walls she called out in great heaving sobs, her anguish purling along the rafters.

William would be disappointed in her loss of control, but who at the inn would mention it? They could whisper amongst themselves. She was beyond caring.

The bitterness of her tears gradually subsided and she became aware of the sounds below her, the pain in her knees and ankles, the coarseness of the blanket, the smell of smoke and sausage from below and the gradual relaxation of her own breathing. Without moving, she opened her eyes and watched the dust swirl in grey eddies against the dying light.

When the pain in her knees became unbearable; she stood, then sat on the edge of the bed and examined the spacious room for which William had traded their last remaining coins. Its extravagance meant nothing compared to Jonathan. The thought of him pulled her under again. She cried out to the emptiness, pleading for him. The weight of her powerlessness bore down on her, curling her sideways on the bed. She was nothing; had nothing. As William had pointed out, without his help she had nowhere to turn. She would be towed away, out to sea, by a current she was helpless to resist. What then? Struggle to keep her head up? Or acquiesce and let the enormity of her impotence and grief take her under one final time?

She did as she had originally intended and got down on her knees to pray.

Dear God, what more can I do? Am I to set out alone, penniless? Or am I to join William? Will you bring my son, safe, come spring? Tell me the way.

When she finished she realized her mind was set. She watched through the window for a time and then paced the room, disturbing nothing but the motes swirling behind her.

A second inspiration came to her. She quickly collected her few possessions from the desk by the window and left.

Nearing the wharf, she tucked her hair under her cap and, in spite of the warmth still lingering in the late afternoon air, pulled her mantle closed. Under the leering gaze of the sailors, unmistakable in its intent, her resolve faltered. Fearful lest it fail entirely, she quickened her pace to outrun it.

Coming around the bend in the seawall she caught sight of the *Speedwell*. Dread of re-boarding the vessel welled up inside her like the seawater that had nearly sunk it two weeks earlier. It wasn't a sinister ship in appearance, nor was it beautiful, like the *Mayflower*. It was a working ship, purchased to remain with them in New England for fishing and exploration. It was unremarkable, but it was poised to take her away from all that was familiar. And from Jonathan.

At the base of the gangway she took a deep breath and renewed her vow. *Trust in God.*

By helping those she envied most, God would look favourably on her.

As she grasped the hatch to the t'ween deck, she noticed Mary Brewster looking out over the far rail. It was tempting to offer her room at the inn to Mary. She was a kind, and once beautiful, woman. Now at almost fifty, greying hair and a slight stoop spoke to her hard life. How she kept up with two young children – Love, nine, and Wrestling, just six – was a wonder. To that burden, she'd added the care of two of the More children; bastards forced onboard at Hampton by their cuckolded father, Sir Samuel More.

Insensitively, William had asked Dorothy to look after one of the More children: another failure to put her feelings above the needs of the congregation.

No, Mary and the youngsters would appreciate the room, but there were others in greater need.

Descending the ladder, she found Sarah Eaton and Suzanna White sitting together. A shaft of light shone on them through the hatch above. Sarah nursed her one-year-old son, Samuel, looking on him with such adoration that it made Dorothy's heart clench anew. Suzanna amused her five-year-old son, Resolved, with word games. Giggling, the boy skipped around her. Clearly uncomfortable with the increasing bulk of her pregnancy, Suzanna made only half-hearted attempts to catch him.

Dorothy looked for Lizzy and her little girl. Lizzy Hopkins was also pregnant and she thought it best to offer the room to all three women.

While she was deliberating, Lizzy waddled into the light with two-year-old Damarus clinging to her hem. One hand smoothed down the front of her skirt, the other swung the latrine bucket.

"Fifth time in three bells that I've had to use this. The baby is pressing down on my bladder without relent. And speaking of bells, is it necessary, do you think, for us to know the time so frequently? I can sleep though four bells but above that I'm woken every half hour 'til the sounding of eight," sighed Lizzy.

The ship's watch was responsible for ringing one to eight strokes at each half hour within each of the day's six, four-hour-long watches. Still unaccustomed to the constant activity aboard, even at anchor, everyone was suffering from a lack of sleep.

Moved by Lizzy's sunken eyes and obvious discomfort, Dorothy burst into tears again. "I confess I've been ignoring what you three and all the others, of course, have been enduring."

She studied the three women. Their heavy physical burdens made her arms feel emptier.

"William hired a room for us, but I can't keep it. You three should take it instead. You've humbler and nobler spirits than mine." Joy and excitement bubbled up between them.

"I would be grateful if you would," she continued. "We can send word for your husbands to meet us there. If they think it unwise, then at least we'll have stretched our legs and gotten some air."

Together, the three women embraced her. Little Samuel, squished between, churned his legs, unhappy to be interrupted in his nursing.

"What is this? Have I missed a cause for celebration?" Desire said, stepping out of the gloom, her curls glowing in the half light.

"Dorothy has just invited Sarah, Suzanna and I to take her room at the inn tonight," said Lizzy excitedly. She clapped a hand over her mouth. "I'm sure she would have asked you too."

"You needn't worry about me. What a kind gesture."

"I suspect Desire would not come anyway," said Suzanna, giving Desire a meaningful look. "Don't protest Desire. I've seen you looking at Deacon Carver's servant."

"I have not been." A blush rose to Desire's cheeks, her normally high color attaining a new brilliance. Agitated, she made a show of straightening her bodice. "Besides, he's *my* servant now that I'm the Deacon's ward. It's immoral to think of a servant that way and you shouldn't dare suggest it."

"Desire wouldn't do anything improper," said Dorothy tonelessly.

"Oh, leave her. He's a good looking, healthy young man. I'm sure you've all noticed. Who can blame her for doing the same?" said Sarah, shielding Desire and taking her hand. "You can walk with us if you like."

"I would come, thank you, but Katherine's trusted me to buy some heavy wool and I've left it late already."

"That has reminded me of something," said Dorothy. "Here's the key. The inn keeper knows of the arrangement. You had better hurry."

August 20th – First Dog Watch

John Howland, the Carver's bond servant, stood outside the shop surveying its interior. His clothes marked him as someone common, attracting little attention. He glanced down the lane. Baskets of blooms overflowing with scent were hung about the woollens shop and the millinery down the way. Over the rooftops opposite, he caught a glimpse of rolling hills, patchworks of summer gold trimmed in emerald green. The hills wrapped themselves round the shoulders of both Dartmouth and Kingswear across the river. It was a pretty place to be waylaid. He turned his eyes to the interior of the shop and watched Desire's nose crinkle. She was trying to decide between two colors of cape for the children. The view was as lovely within as without.

Two women exited the shop, arms linked, and gave him a wide berth. The younger flicked her eyes at him approvingly.

"Master Bishop will surely fleece the young lamb and more the powers to 'im. We gets what we can from these for'ners. Double they're payen – an' they's none the wiser," said the older, pulling the younger in closer and laughing.

He watched them go and then uncrossed his ankles, taking notice of the activities within. The shopkeeper's wife was now draping Desire in silk while Mr. Bishop held a mirror and smiled encouraging.

Fleecing? They were leading a lamb to slaughter.

With a nod from her husband, the wife instructed Desire to hold up the silk while she retraced the well-worn carpet to the counter. Returning, she grasped Desire's Diadem cap with the arthritic fingers of one hand and began lifting it from her head, a new, expensive replacement ready in her other.

Desire's own hands shot up and the silk slithered down her body to land in a coil at her feet. She stepped daintily backward, careful not to mark the crimson draping, then pressed herself to the counter, one small hand still clasped protectively to her head.   Behind her, Mr. Bishop signalled for the silk to be gathered up and brought for inspection.

There was a movement to John's left and he knuckled his forehead to a gentleman opening the door for his wife. Before the door closed, he made up his mind to go in. He would not let the shopkeepers take advantage.

The scent of women, and women's things, overlaid the scent of dyed wool. He felt out of place at once, not having had cause to come into such places before.

Desire was pointedly saying, "the heavy wool, only. Three-and-a-half yards of the black and but two of the red".

She caught sight of him and frowned. Her foot tapped and she looked very much like she wished to scold him, but didn't want to appear unmannerly in front of the shopkeepers.

"Beg your pardon, Miss Desire, but Katherine will be waiting for us and she wished me to carry the wool for the capes.   I'll take your purchases."

"We haven't quite finished, John.   Good heavens though, I forgot about Katherine. Please wait outside for me again. I'll be through in a moment."

"If you are nearly finished I can wait here and take your parcels directly."

"No, I am quite all right. Please wait for me in the lane." She turned and smiled stiffly at Mrs. Bishop. "I am so sorry about this," she said.

He couldn't stay without making a scene, so he slowly made his way to the door. He wasn't sure what to do to prevent them from overcharging her. He didn't know the usual price of the wool, but could only assume they were charging double.

She followed him out a few minutes later and handed him the parcels. Her lips compressed in a firm line of disapproval.

"I think I may have dropped something inside. Pardon me while I check," he said.

She gave him a curious look. She began to speak, but he missed what she said as the door clicked shut behind him.

"Mr. Bishop, sir, you have overcharged the mistress and I will have you correct the account right away, if you please," he said in his most clipped tone, squaring his shoulders.

"I never."

"You have. Through some error, you have charged her double."

"Says who?"

"I do. If it's not corrected, you will have gained double today, but lost quadruple tomorrow. I will spread word aboard ship that you are not to be trusted. In fact, my word will be carried to both ships. Do you know how many aboard the Mayflower are in need of heavy winter cloaks?"

Mr. Bishop stood his ground and tapped his fingers on the counter. "I have all day," he said, smiling.

John stood his ground. The money Desire parted with was almost the Carver's last. He knew that.

He stepped closer to the counter and leaned forward. He towered over the squat little man. Mr. Bishop's chin wobbled a little as he swallowed.

"Think of how much you will lose, Mr. Bishop," he said. "While you do, I shall browse." He began to slowly unwind the ribbons stacked to his right.

Mr. Bishop's short fingers stopped drumming, darted forward and brought the spinning spool to a halt.

John reached to the left and began picking the broaches out of the felt-lined display. He examined each one and laid it on the countertop. Mrs. Bishop swept them up and started re-pinning them. John turned his attention to several bolts of silk stacked by the mirror behind him. Moving from the counter, he gave Desire a reassuring smile through the window and swept the ground with his eyes as though searching for something. He lifted a bolt of rose silk and, rotating it, unspooled the fabric onto the floor like a ribbon of honey. Mr. Bishop stomped around the end of the counter.

The elegant couple still waiting to be served edged toward the door and left the shop.

"That wasn't my color. Shall I try this one instead?"

He glanced at the window again. Desire looked worried standing on the street by herself.

He picked up a midnight blue velvet. "I shall stay until your honesty recalls itself, Mr. Bishop." He unwound a sheaf of the velvet.

"Stop."

"When you are ready to settle up, we will carry on with our errands."

"Mrs. Bishop, settle the balance," Mr. Bishop said gruffly, pointing at the cash box with a wobbly finger.

"We needn't," she said, shaking her head and not moving.

"Do it!" He turned an apoplectic expression on John, "And you'd best tell everyone we treated you fair – 'cause we did."

John collected the coins and slammed the door shut behind him. Mr. Bishop, at the window, chased him with a scowl.

Desire was unsettled. "What were you up to in there? You made an awful mess. You shame me, not knowing how to act in such a shop. You aren't to touch the fabric yourself," said Desire. She awaited his explanation and apology.

"Ah," he said, opening his palm. "Mr. Bishop realized there was a mistake in the charge. Put this in your purse." Her pride was too important to him to admit the truth.

Desire opened her change purse obediently and he slid the coins in. She cinched it shut and waited. "Well?"

"Well, we had better get on. Katherine will be concerned if we're much later." He stepped out into the cobbles and motioned for her to go ahead.

She stayed rooted to the spot, hands back on her hips.

He shrugged and started down the lane, her brown paper package draped over his arm. He imagined for a moment that she might be appraising him and stood taller at the thought.

August 20th – Last Dog Watch

William stepped nimbly over the cobblestones, retracing his path to the inn. His spirit was light despite the mention of Christopher Martin. It was right they forgave Robert. It was right that they strengthen the bonds of love that must tie them together. Tomorrow, he would go with Carver to see how the repairs to the *Speedwell* were coming. If all was well, they could leave the next day. Feeling freer, he yielded to curiosity, pausing to glance in each shop window until at last he reached the end of Lower Street.

The inn was cozy and inviting. He hoped it would extend to his reception from Dorothy. Perhaps tonight he would be able to wrap her in his arms and make love to her in private one last time before leaving. There were untold dangers ahead, he knew, but should they be blessed with another child…

He took the stairs two at a time.

Reaching the landing he heard chatter coming from their room. It made no sense. The key turned easily in the lock and he lifted the latch.

What he saw would have felled him had it been full light. His mind grappled with it, tried to make sense of the bare flesh before him. Mouth agape, his mind spinning furiously, he felt a tide of red flood his features for the second time that day.

Lizzy Hopkins was standing naked in a small wash-basin, rag in hand. Reacting faster than he, she sunk low, attempting to submerge herself in the ankle-deep water. Thin arms flew in a vain attempt to cover both her breasts and her belly, the flesh on her body goose-pimpling with the fingers of chill thrust in through the open door.

As both she and William were shocked into gaping silence, the rest of the room erupted into cacophonic animation. Sarah, in luxuriant repose nursing little Samuel, shrieked and rolled half-off the bed, setting Samuel howling. Her breast popped from his mouth and hung exposed as she tried, one-handed, to right herself and stop from falling to the floor on top of him. Suzanna leapt from the chair, the laughter of a half-told joke rising to a scream, as she rushed to shield poor Lizzy from view. Two-year-old Damarus, asleep in a blanket by the window, sat bolt upright, surveyed the scene with bleary eyes and howled.

William yanked the door shut. Stunned in to confusion, he prayed until he was calm enough to speak.

He knelt before the door. "Please forgive me … but Dorothy? Where is Dorothy?" he said with an unmanly squeak. He firmed his voice. "Ladies, please forgive me any harm I've done to your honour. I shall not think on this scene again. There's been some confusion, and the fault is all mine."

He would have to tell their husbands and make a formal apology. His stomach began to seethe. This, on top of the trouble they were already dealing with. *Was that Lizzy Hopkins? Her husband one of the strangers boarded from London? Please may he be an understanding man.*

He turned to go and then remembered he still had the key. "Dear sisters, please don't be afraid, I'll slip this key under the door and then you'll be safely locked in and undisturbed." He pushed the key under the door, the silence in the room seeming to grow louder as he retreated.

Bracing his still shaken body against the timbers of the hallway, he made his way to the stairs. The door opened behind him. It was Suzanna.

"Brother William, please know you are forgiven. We're quite recovered. Though ashamed at having been caught so, we've resolved that nothing more need be said. The voyage ahead will no doubt cause us to have need of each other at various times and in poor circumstances. We must be able to look each other in the eye." To prove her word, she caught and held his eye, then added, as an afterthought, "And you will find Dorothy aboard the *Speedwell*."

William fought back exhaustion. Despite Suzanna's declaration that all was forgotten, he had sought out both William White and Francis Eaton to apologize. Only after informing Stephen Hopkins of his trespass at the inn would he return to the solace of Dorothy's company. He waited on shore for the lighter that would row him to the *Mayflower*.

His bowels churned. He especially liked Stephen Hopkins.

A remarkable man, Hopkins was becoming something of a legend among the passengers. Not only had he made the Atlantic crossing before, he had survived a shipwreck on the Island of the Devils in the middle of the ocean. He'd lived on the deserted expanse for ten months before managing with the other survivors to build a new ship and set sail for Virginia. Hopkins knew the conditions awaiting them and had proven he had both the fortitude and the ingenuity to tackle them.

William could not afford to fall on the wrong side of such a man.

The bobbing lantern of the rowboat grew nearer.

"William! What are you doing here?" said Carver, startling him out of his thoughts.

"I've an errand aboard the *Mayflower*. Something unfortunate I'd rather not share at the moment, if you don't mind, John," said William, keeping his gaze on the approaching boat. The swell would not help his anxious stomach.

"Well, no point both of us going over," said Carver. You know how Katherine can get when she has a meal waiting. You wouldn't mind speaking to Martin, would you? Since you'll be there? Just as good coming from you – we both know the same about the whole business, after all."

"I would really rather not, John. Besides, as the Governor of the *Speedwell*, you'll be talking to him on equal terms, Governor to Governor," said William, sweat beading his brow.

Carver slapped him across the back. "Lack of a title never stopped you from taking charge, William. It's in your hands. Here is your boat. Hop aboard and I'll see you back on the *Speedwell*. I can always count on you, William."

"Really, I'm not fit…"

"I'll see you on the *Speedwell*," Carver's voice echoed off the cobbles.

William accepted the sailor's help boarding the lighter and huddled in the stern.

I can't do this. Please may I find Stephen first and may Martin not be onboard.

He shuffled across the broad deck of the *Mayflower* toward the open hatch of the t'ween deck where the passengers were housed. The now familiar smell of sweat and urine assaulted him as he ducked his head below.

His hand on the ladder met a solid body. Soloman Prower, Christopher Martin's stepson, leaned against the ladder, grinning at him with an impressive display of broken teeth. He was forced to remove his hand to finish his decent.

"Soloman. Good evening," said William, tipping his head slightly in an effort to disguise his annoyance. "Your father's not here tonight, I ho – imagine?"

"He's over there," said Soloman, indicating a group of men playing dice and noisily shoving one another.

Stephen Hopkins wasn't among them.

"You haven't seen Stephen Hopkins have you?" said William. Telling Stephen about the inn now seemed like a social call compared to talking to Martin.

"Haven't seen him. Not sure who he is, neither."

"Good for you, Soloman, for not joining in the dicing. God doesn't approve of gambling."

Soloman gave a short laugh, the corner of his fat lips twisting upward, "It's not that, Sir. Me Dad's appointed me to watch the ladder in case any of them families try to take their stuff and sneak off. I was in the King's Watch – didn'ya know? I's to make sure at least one of 'em is left behind, as 'surity, if they should want to go ashore for anything."

William stiffened reflexively, then with difficulty relaxed the look of disapproval twisting his features. He glanced over Prower's shoulder at the homely scene of women and children, talking quietly together and preparing food in the dimly lit common-way.

Perhaps he should have eaten something before coming to improve his temper. Resigned, he began a cautious approach toward Martin, as one would approach a snake. The snake hadn't yet noticed.

"Gentlemen?" he said, trying to sound casual. "Martin, a word, please, if you will?"

He backed up a few paces to indicate they should step away from the group for more privacy. Martin shifted his weight and gazed at him with slow calculation before approaching.

Sweat prickled William's upper lip. He made a subtle attempt to stretch but could not match Martin's height.

"Come to take part in the game have you? What was your name again?"

"William. William Bradford." He kept his eyes steady.

"I'll guess you *would* take part, but you've nothing to wager, hey?" Martin winked at his companions and, getting a chuckle, puffed up a little more.

"I've come to discuss complaints I've heard against you, *Christopher*," he said, deliberately using his Christian name. It seemed right to do so – he hadn't had a lot of experience with this kind of confrontation, but he sensed it was how he should begin.

Martin's face darkened. He took two heavy steps forward, bringing himself so close that William could feel the heat of Martin's breath.

He steadied himself. His belly was cramping fiercely now.

One of Martin's companions stood and took a step. William vaguely remembered him as John Billington. This wasn't going well and so far he had said almost nothing.

Martin's eyes were slits. "How dare you? I'll hear no complaints! Your people are waspish and discontented. I've been made Governor of this ship and you have no right to come aboard and tell me how to do my own business."

"It's just that we have heard – "

"You are an ungrateful lot! Did I not spend all my time in Southampton purchasing provisions for you? Hmm? And as for your planters, if I didn't keep tight watch on them that's here, I have no doubt they would go complaining to the Adventurers – crying that they would sooner have satisfaction for their investment than make the journey." Martin pointed his finger at him and began to stab the close air between them.

William spoke over Martin in an effort to get a word in. "Seek forgiveness from God, Christopher, and from the men who elected you to govern. Look out for them on this voyage. Seek not to raise yourself above them and exercise tyranny." His words didn't seem to be having an effect, but he continued, "Furthermore, let any who wish to remove with their families, thinking they are unfit or unwilling to continue, go with the blessing and good wishes of the rest. We are neither imprisoners nor enslavers."

"What would you do without your fishers and wool carters and the like? And their wives who will dress their meat and keep them warm?" Martin paused here to look over his shoulder with a leer as if to ensure his audience was still with him. They whistled, nodding their heads in unison. Martin snickered with confidence, "I've no yoke around my neck to your bloodsucking merchants. I'll work the land and sea for my own profit and it matters not to me how many we be."

William didn't mean to do it. It was reflex. Pent-up anger. Mid-jab of Martin's finger he grabbed the digit and twisted. Momentarily, Martin's arm twisted with it. And then recovered.

The punch landed square across William's jaw. Before he knew what happened, he was on the deck and Martin and Billington were above him, laughing. He looked around and felt a shame that was intensified by boyhood familiarity.

He tried to recover some of what was left of his manhood and pushed himself up.

Billington's boot landed square on his chest. Not hard. Not hard enough to break anything. Just hard enough to grind him down. The women on the other side of the ladder were looking at him sympathetically, ready to come to his aid. So much the worse.

"Hey! Get off! Do you know who that is?"

William looked over his brow. Stephen Hopkins towered over Martin.

"That's William Bradford. He is the reason we have our patent. You're not fit to shake his hand Martin, nor you, Billington. Remove yourselves!" demanded Stephen. "Go!" For a moment no one moved. Martin turned his back, breaking the tension.

A neatly dressed, good looking man beside Stephen extended his hand. William clasped it gratefully. The stranger dusted off William's coat and offered him a handkerchief.

Stephen turned to the concerned faces watching, "Is that the kind of man we want to lead us," indicating Martin with a wave of his hand, "a man that attacks another half his weight in stone?"

Stephen steered William and the stranger away while his words settled on the spectators. "William, Andrew Prince, cartographer. Andrew, this is William Bradford." Stephen bent over a pot on the brazier and offered William a cup of broth.

"You'll have a bruise," said Stephen.

"Maybe two," said William. "Stephen, I've wronged you. I'm a man faithful to my wife."

August 21st – Middle Watch

Dorothy crossed the river to Kingswear just after dark. She was cold and her bundle of clothes bit into her shoulder. No matter what, she wouldn't return to the ship nor to William. She walked as fast as she could. By now, William would likely have learned from one of the other ship's Masters that she begged them for passage to Holland.

They mostly laughed at her. No way of paying. One did not laugh. Instead, he offered to take another form of payment. When she stumbled off his ship, he cackled that even what she had to offer would not have been enough.

She felt for the edge of the road with her toe and sat down on the bundle to save her dress from getting damp. The sweat beneath her bodice cooled, making her shiver. Her stomach suddenly cramped. She dashed a few feet further from the road, pulled up her skirt and relieved herself.

There was nothing to wipe with. She started to cry.

She grabbed bunches of grass and balled them up, trying hard not to get her hands dirty. Afterwards she picked up the bundle and started again, making sure to keep the crunch of the road under foot.

She had no plan, besides not returning. If she found another harbour, she could ask for a ship going to Holland. If she could find a fellow reformer, asking quietly in the next town, she might be able to enlist help getting word back to Pastor Robinson.

She stubbed her toe on a rock and swallowed a curse.

She passed one cottage after another before fields surrounded her again. The moon emerged from behind a cloud and illuminated a large oak tree not far from the road. She reached it, threw her pack down and laid her head against the gnarled, uneven trunk. Curling herself around her hollow stomach, she hoped for sleep.

August 21st – Forenoon Watch

"That will be two pence, Sir."

"What?"

"She didn't have the fare and said as how I could find you to recover it," said the ferryman, leaning on his oars within arms reach of the wharf.

William dug into his purse and his finger fished around, swimming between three small coins in a sea of velvet. "When I find her and confirm your assertions, I'll pay her part."

The ferryman gave him a narrow look and took the final stroke.

William was frantic. He hadn't slept. His throat was hoarse from shouting her name. Last night they asked everyone they saw for word of Dorothy, but by the time he'd finished on the *Mayflower* and had been rowed back to shore, the majority of the townspeople had returned home and the other rigs had raised their gangplanks and tied their lighters. Carver urged him to return to the ship for the night, but he took a lantern, walked to the fort and into the hills, disturbing the church wardens. At dawn, he got news of her attempt to board a ship to Holland. The ferryman confirmed he'd taken her to Kingswear.

The road forked immediately at the wharf. He surveyed the high road, which wound steeply to the right, heavy with houses and then looked straight ahead along an isolated country road. She would have taken the country road.

Four hours later, on the verge of turning back, he spied a small frame, hunched under the weight of a large bundle, shuffling along the roadway. The figure passed from the light into the shade cast by a small copse of trees. He strained his eyes. Recognizing her, he didn't know whether he wanted to embrace her or throttle her. He quickened his pace until he was within easy hailing distance.

"Dorothy! Stop. This is madness."

She began to trot. The pack bumped up and down against the back of her knees.

"Dorothy stop!"

He broke into a run and, catching up, snagged the bundle with one hand. She released it, the bundle falling to the road between them. His momentum was too great and he tripped over Dorothy's abandoned load, nearly pitching headfirst onto the roadway. She sprinted ahead and he watched her go. She sobbed and clutched her side.

"I'm turning around and taking this with me," he said.

She didn't stop.

"Come on Dorothy, this is senseless."

She was shuffling now, wounded.

"I know you can see reason. I'll count to ten and if you aren't following me I'm coming to get you."

She turned around, seeming to recognize her foolishness. He relaxed. When she was upon him he reached out his hand to offer her support for the walk back.

She bent over and placed both hands on the road. Suddenly straightening, she launched a flurry of rock and dust at his face.

"I'm never going with you! Give me my things."

She pulled at the pack. William hung on, clearing dirt from his eye with his free hand.

"Foolish woman! Do you know what you've put me through? Carver got word last night we were ready to sail on today's tide. You've probably delayed us an extra day!"

"Don't shout at me!" she yelled, tugging at the bundle. "You should have left. You will still be leaving tomorrow without me."

"I correct myself, you're a selfish fool. You think only of what you want and can't see that everyone on that ship is making sacrifices too. They are doing it so that others can have a better life and the congregation can survive. You dismiss the fact that you've delayed them and cost them more time and money. Meanwhile they are worried for you and know *damn* well I can't leave without you. Even one of the strangers is out helping to look for you."

He wasn't a very strong man but she wasn't a very big woman. If he had to carry her, then so be it. He wrenched the bundle away from her and wound its knot round his wrist. With his free hand he scooped her up round the knees and tossed her over his shoulder.

"How dare you!" she said. She forced her knees into his back to break his hold.

He almost dropped her. Readjusting, he slipped the knot of the makeshift pack further up his arm to free his second hand. "I dare because you are my wife. I'm not going to see you turn yourself into some kind of beggar . . . "

She screamed in his ear and he wanted to shake her.

". . . over a crazy idea that the ship is going to sink. You'll never see Jonathan this way. Admit it. You'll starve yourself. What were you planning to do? Sell your dresses for food?" He winced, "Prostitute yourself for passage to Holland?"

She deflated in his arms and her weight seemed to double. He knew he'd broken her. The thought gave him no pleasure.

"Come on, we're going back."

She struggled against him one more time, clawing at his back, breaking the skin, but he had a firm grip now.

"What kind of mother leaves her child," she sobbed.

The Letter

*J*t was a stellar day. Arms swung in graceful unison as the crew raised extra sail, the sheets rising in time to their exertions like stage curtains on opening night. Soon the freshening wind billowed them with purpose, driving both the *Speedwell* and the *Mayflower* before it. The speed of her ship, as it reeled alongside the beautiful *Mayflower,* was so thrilling that Dorothy trembled in William's arms. He enveloped her tightly as she leaned over the rail, mesmerized by the crystal sparkle of spray arching like angels' wings from the *Speedwell*'s prow.

Without taking her eyes from the spectacle, she shouted into the wind, "Can you promise me we'll be safe?" Her red-rimmed eyes turned to him, strands of hair coming loose in beating waves across her cheek.

"You've nothing to fear. You can see it there. The ship cutting through the dark surface of the water reveals its true nature. It's nothing but shining jewels of light."

He was proud of her for accepting the plan he had so carefully laid out for his family. She broke down only briefly this morning, but understandably, as they cast off and the renewed realization that she wouldn't see Jonathan for a year washed over her. But she came around. He knew she would. In their seven years together, she had grown used to dealing with setbacks and always encouraged him to see the positives.

"Dorothy, to look on your face reminds me daily of the beauty of God's works." He lifted a strand of her nutmeg hair from her lips and tucked it behind her ear. "Your lace cap is likely to go flying and join those jewels if you're not careful," he teased, pulling her in closer and resting his chin on top of her buffeting chapeau.

On deck behind them, the older children chased one another around the main mast, weaving between busy sailors oblivious to the shrieks and teasing taunts of the game at hand. Katherine Carver, lifted by their energy, still felt the need to settle them and moved in with a warning. William nodded as she passed.

Over on the opposite rail Edward Winslow's two servants, both still in their late teens, were looking very serious. They fixed their gaze on the retreating grey mass to the east – all that could be seen of England now. Their ship seemed to grow smaller as the land retreated.

William refocused his attention. Something had changed. A sailor snapped at one of the children for nearly tripping over a coiled line. Carried on the wind from the bridge above him, he heard fragments of a report to the captain. "Leaking….pumps cannot maintain…time still to come about…".

Kissing Dorothy's head, William steered her from the rail and asked her to wait out of the wind. Carver must have sensed something too, for they met each other mid-deck.

"I just overheard one of the crew say the ship is leaking again. We should speak to the Master," grumbled William.

"Best we get up there," replied Carver, pulling his short, snowy beard to a point. Above him Master Reynolds paced the upper deck and shouted orders, urging his sailors to move faster.

"What is it now?" demanded Reynolds, as the pair approached, his tone suggesting little interest in the answer. Carver opened his mouth to speak. "I'm in the middle of a situation," barked Reynolds, "and if you don't want to get wet you'll stay out of my way."

"That is just it, Reynolds," said Carver, "you may be the Master of the Ship, but we are her owners."

"Her safety depends on me at present, Mr. Carver, Mr. Bradford. I'll ask you to get out of my way," rebuffed Reynolds, "and for God sake put an end to that caterwauling."

They turned together. The main deck was in an uproar and at the centre was Dorothy with her arms raised to the heavens.

"We failed to heed you, oh mighty God. We shall perish in the freezing depths! Keep us from suffering and watch over my child. Keep him safe. Keep him safe. We await your glorious resurrection and deliverance from this terror."

The other women surrounded her like spokes on a wheel, fervently praying and moaning as they moved around her. Dorothy's terror was proving infectious.

"For pity's sake, stop her," said Carver, "she'll have them tossing themselves overboard if she convinces them we're sinking."

"We are sinking," William pointed out evenly.

"No worse than before."

"She's scared, that's all," said William.

He dropped to the main deck and waded into the sea of women surrounding Dorothy. "Ladies, it's just another small leak. Master Reynolds has all well in hand, I assure you." Reaching Dorothy he swept her into his arms, burying her face beneath his cloak and softly hushing her.

"Go below, Dear," Carver said to Katherine, settling a kiss on the silver crown of her small head, "and let the others know to move things that might get wet and then come above. There's nothing to fret about."

"Let's all remain calm. Perhaps Carver can lead us in a *quiet* prayer," said William. Thankfully, with Dorothy's wailing suspended, the others regained sobriety. The cessation caused William to stop and think of his own feelings. *Angry* . . . that's what he was. *Angry and frustrated. Another problem. God had his reason, but what was it?*

Dorothy was inconsolable. She was mumbling into his doublet, making it hard for him to hear Carver. He pulled her aside to keep her from disturbing the others.

"Dorothy, it's just a leak, like the last. Promise to stay strong. I'm needed, but I can't leave you when you're like this, can I?" Using his thumbs he wiped away her tears.

"It *is* a sign. Do you believe me now? God is telling us to turn around. It was wrong to leave him. You know that."

"Hush. Take Beth and Desire's hands and sit here out of the way. You can see you're the only one in a state."

As he approached the men gathering by the starboard rail their eyes lifted in unison.

"Looks like it's serious enough to warn the *Mayflower* we're in trouble," said Edward, eyeing the new signal flags that had sprouted from the *Speedwell*.

They were thrown against the rail as the ship suddenly came about.

"That is it!" huffed Carver as he turned on his heel and headed unsteadily for the Master's deck. William followed.

"I demand to know the situation, Sir," shouted Carver at Reynolds. The *Speedwell* continued to come about, heeling over hard as the wind shifted its attack. William faltered slightly, then spread his legs to brace himself. Carver arrested a certain fall with a quick grab of the railing. But Reynolds had regained his calm, his body flowing to meet the ship's changing posture. He was Master here.

"We are putting for England," said Reynolds calmly, "the ship is leaking again and *if* we are lucky, we will reach the nearest harbour before she sinks. And that is no jest."

William stared at Reynolds. There was so much he wished to say, to argue, but none of it mattered, none of it would hold back the water. He approached his friends. Their faith had been tested so many times already. How would they take this?

The nearest harbour was Plymouth. They dropped anchor not more than a nautical mile from where they had set out that morning. Twice now the *Speedwell* had been checked and trimmed with nothing found amiss and twice she had to return with leaks so severe her Master feared she would be lost. As William expected, this further complication was seen by some, as it had been by Dorothy, as a sign from God that they must turn back. These families, many of them strangers to the congregation, elected to stay in England. How could they risk a voyage already so late in the season, one beset by so many ill tidings?

He drew up agreements for the *Speedwell* to be sold to redeem shares for their Leyden friends returning to Holland. As he laboured under yet another unexpected administrative burden, he received whispers that Dorothy was trying to arrange passage among their friends. He wasn't surprised. But it hurt, nonetheless. He could understand a mother's need to be with her child, but Dorothy failed to appreciate how much he was relying on her. He couldn't do this on his own – not with so much at stake. Whenever his courage and self-belief faltered, she had always been there to help him, strengthen him, to make him feel worthy; she had always seen him as a better man than he saw himself. He needed this now more than ever, given the great challenges ahead. The truth of it was he needed her as badly as they all relied upon the *Mayflower*.

September 6th – Forenoon Watch

Dorothy squeezed along the length of one of the *Mayflower*'s cannons and peered through the gunport. Below, William and her friends were saying their final goodbyes to those returning to Leyden.

She shimmied out from behind the cannon and sat on a stool. Next to her, Andrew Prince, her temporary guard, scribbled busily on his parchment. She watched the slow efforts of two ants climbing the trunk supporting his desk. They crested the oak ledge as Prince dipped his quill. Without looking, he reached over with the opposite hand and crushed one ant and then the other, wiping his thumb on the edge of the table.

She examined the small space Prince had made his own. Men travelling alone weren't allotted a cabin, so he'd claimed this narrow space between Stephen Hopkin's cabin and the elderly Chilton's. The improvised desk was its only furnishing. Dorothy's eye roamed the clumps of rolled parchment and folded letters suspended from the inner walls by straps of leather; the arrangement like a riot of sails in a crowded harbour.

Restless, she returned to the gunport. William glanced up, saw her and nodded. Her face ignited with renewed irritation. How dare he leave her captive to a stranger.

She strummed her fingers over the parchment rolls as she returned to her seat, inadvertently setting the armada adrift.

"Keep your fingers off of those!" Prince snarled, rising from his chair. "Know your place, woman."

"I just …" She sat and spun her back to him. What would he do if she got up right now and marched over to the ladder?

"Sir, there is someone with a letter for you on the dock. He says he must deliver it to you personally."

Dorothy looked over her shoulder. A hefty sailor, his thin shirt unable to restrain the heaving roll of fat around his midsection, stood uncomfortably before Prince. His eyes remained glued to floor at Prince's feet.

"What is your name?"

"Harlock, sir."

"Harlock, I need you to make sure this woman doesn't leave the t'ween deck. Stand guard at the top of the companionway until I return and I shall pay you three farthings."

"Very well, Sir." Harlock stuck out his hand, his gaze now raised eagerly.

"I don't have it on me now, but I will note the debt in my journal. You can do me other services." Prince withdrew a small brown leather booklet from his pocket and made a show of noting the amount. He replaced the booklet and sidled between Dorothy and the end of the desk. His thigh caught the pile of parchment he'd stacked to one side and sent several sheaves sailing to the floor.

"Pick that up," he said to her, "and don't leave that stool till I return. Practice doing as you are told. I don't need you confounding business between your husband and me.

When he was gone she looked around the common-way. It was quiet aside from a few passing sailors. She left the parchment where it had fallen and moved again to the gunport. She watched as Prince stepped off the end of the gangplank to shake the hand of a tall figure wearing an oversized neck frill before striding off together down the quay. She saw Prince accept a folded parchment and study it.

She made a point of sending the armada to sea one more time before retaking her seat. She idly scanned the parchment on the floor, catching the name Thomas Weston on one of the fallen sheaves. With her toe, she deftly moved the letter nearer and picked it up.

Dorothy's heart began to race as she read.

Beloved brother,

You shall be handsomely rewarded. It has pleased God to stir up ye hearts of our Adventurers upon hearing of ye dealings at Hampton. I have begun in secret petitioning ye counsel for a second patent which shall be in both our names, in addition to the sum agreed. It is paramount you stir up disfavour toward ye Adventurers and assure ye lead council with you that I will stay true and provision them in the Adventurers' stead. I have purchased a ship. They must be convinced to fill it with skins and other trade upon its arrival according to ye original agreement, with promise that provisions will come within the next ship. If it is too late and their hearts are turned from me, weaken their bonds and promote that which will ensure their failure. We will have our revenge on ye Adventurers for ye turn they have done me and ye insult given you by John Peirce. If ye company are verily starved and have lost all order and good direction we shall have ye better hand to deal and make ourselves rich.

God be with you, and all brotherly affection. A fishing vessel will carry you to Virginia where we shall meet again.

Tho: Weston.

Dorothy hastily picked up the remaining letters and dropped them on the desk, shuffling this one to the middle. Her fingers shook. She couldn't sit down. She rushed to the port and looked for Prince. The blood pounded in her head. This man was no Prince. He was a Weston.

She craned her neck and spied the others coming aboard. There he was, beside William, striding up the plank in good humour. She returned to her seat but couldn't stop fidgeting. Then she remembered the letter Prince had been writing when interrupted. She leapt up as voices wafted along the upper deck and quickly scanned Prince's erratic script, trying to imbibe its meaning. She froze. She read William's name. Prince planned to use him.

September 10th – First Dog Watch

Dorothy pulled the basin closer and hung over the edge of the bunk. She convulsed in another empty wretch. Four days now. At first, she had fought her sea sickness, but long since yielded to each involuntary spasm, praying it would be her last. She wiped her face, sitting up as William's rolling laugh tumbled through the common-way beyond.

"Dorothy, you will never guess. John Carver has been elected the new Governor of the *Mayflower* – by large majority. And I, I have been elected assistant Governor. What do you think of that? Andrew Prince proposed me."

"I'm very proud of you," she said weakly.

He kissed her cheek. "Have you been sick my dear?"

"Just a little." Her eyes set on William's. "Don't trust Mr. Prince. Believe me. I know what I saw."

"He doesn't even look like Weston, for one. He has been very supportive of us and me in particular, for another. You likely didn't understand what you were reading. I'm not going to challenge him on it and risk our friendship. I'll look a fool. He is a cartographer, not a saboteur."

"I know what I read. And although I am mad at you over Jonathan, I will not have someone use you, or any of us, to destroy our chances altogether. Why would I make this up? We have to survive this or I'll never see Jonathan again."

"I'm not saying you are making it up. It wasn't right that I left you onboard with Mr. Prince when the rest of us said our goodbyes. I was wrong to do it. I just couldn't risk you running off again when we were so close to sailing. Now you resent the gentleman because of it. That's my fault, not his.

The Hold

*S*unshine kissed Desire's bare feet in the warm lee of the forecastle. Lost to the world, she was stitching up a tear in a child's shirt. A pair of scissors was passed to her from the side.

"Thank you," Desire started, her reverie breaking like a whitecap upon the *Mayflower*'s hull.

Dorothy didn't respond. Desire snipped the errant thread and placed the scissors between them, respecting Dorothy's continued silence toward her.

The gloomy area 'tween decks was too crowded for sitting and stitching, let alone letting the children run. While each family and married couple was granted space for a crudely constructed cabin along the hull, the single men slept in the long central common-way on bedrolls. The bedrolls and associated linen had spilled about like flotsam, claiming even more of the meagre space. Combined with the odours of vomit and sweat, it was a relief to be on deck.

Beth arrived soundlessly, settling beside Dorothy and resting her head in her lap.

Dorothy stroked her hair.

Lizzie Hopkins and Suzanna White, their fingers as pregnant as their bellies and useless for stitching, took turns holding Sarah Eaton's son Samuel, allowing Sarah to mend a pair of breeches.

The children wove around, over and under obstacles on deck like a school of fish capering in a reef.

"Mother Katherine, do come and sit down. You'll wear yourself out chasing and worrying after the children," Desire said, squinting up through the slits of her fingers.

"Fiddle!" Katherine exclaimed. "They might fall overboard with all this running about. Those railings aren't nearly high enough! I can't stand to think one might trip on a rope or a cleat and fall right over. I won't relax until there is solid ground under our feet."

Mary Brewster stood up and shook out the back of her skirt. "I'll worry over my four. We will each worry over our own. You needn't run about clucking like a mother hen. You won't get a stitch of knitting done."

Katherine delegated most of the knitting and mending to her servant Anna. Needles, to her, were merely an excuse to join in gossip.

Katherine crossed her arms, "Well, if you don't appreciate what I am doing. "

"You know we're grateful, but we can all keep an eye," placated Mary.

Desire was only half listening, her ears drawn instead to John Howland. He was busy telling his friend John Alden, the cooper from London, a joke, almost tripping over the details in his race to the punchline. His laughter at his own jape was infectious and Desire smiled. Despite the fact that he had behaved badly in the woollen shop, he was so very amiable.

Still, he was a servant. Her servant.

His looks, his bearing, the fizzle she felt deep within when he was near, all of it threatened to make her forget the social distance between them. But it was a distance she was duty-bound to accept. Living in such close quarters made it increasingly difficult. But she *must* remember it.

A shadow fell across her lap and she glanced up, the rush of blood to her cheeks and the unguarded wickedness of her thoughts still kissed her lips. Katherine hovered above. She prayed not to be reprimanded in front of the others. And then, as though nothing had happened, Katherine said, "Well, I guess I'll stitch," and she sat, patting the billows of dark blue silk ballooning around her and looking for her basket. "Oh fiddle! I've left my needlework stored in the chest and it's in the hold."

"I'll go fetch what you need," said Desire, grateful to get away and compose herself. What private machinations were taking place behind her guardian's eyes, she couldn't tell, but she feared she would soon find out.

The 'tween deck was quiet. She paused at the foot of the ladder to savour it. Dust motes drifted up around her in the haze. Muffled bleats and clucks from the small livestock pen in the prow added to the serenity, taking the bite out of her guilt. At peace again, she wended her way aft through the scattered belongings toward the lower ladder.

Despite the damp and the chill, she had managed to retain a healthy glow to her rounded cheeks. Some of the other women, she'd noticed, were losing their color. She mused that Katherine was starting to look more and more like a frilly white forest mushroom. She smiled to herself at the comparison as she carefully felt for the last rung on the ladder.

The hold was cave-like. She felt her way along the passageway waiting for her eyes to adjust and imagined Dorothy as the spindly, brown-capped

variety and Mary Brewster as a stout red and white toadstool. "No, no",
she said to herself, "those are poisonous and Mary is....OHH!"

There was a sudden movement just inches from her face. Startled, she
lost her balance. Her shoulder struck a beam as she slipped and she cried
out. But it wasn't pain that suddenly wrapped itself around her bowels as
she stood again, but fear. Fear of the pungent smell in the darkness, of the
hot breath lapping at her. A sailor.

The sailors shared a unique odour beyond the unwashed funk that she
and the others had acquired. She was accustomed to the patina of oily
hair and body odour, laced with smoke, cooking and vomit. But the
sailor's stench was a concrescence of years aboard ship. Theirs was a
recipe so much bolder in the making – sour sweat, festering gums, tar,
bilge water, dried ejaculate, urine – that she did not need eyes to know a
sailor lurked beside her in the dark. The scent, a solid miasma filling and
occluding her lungs, rang every alarm in her body. Her fear crystallized.
They were alone.

"What are you doing down here, Darling? Come to have some fun,
have you?" The lid of a barrel snapped shut and a gasp of vinegar briefly
freshened the air between them.

"You surprised me. I thought you were one of the men," he chuckled.
"It'll be our little secret you caught me in the barrel." His white orbs
slowly expanded in the dusky light, "If it isn't the prize I've been eyeing
for weeks, the girl of my *desire*. It is Desire, isn't it?"

The hot reek of his breath on her face was unbearable, yet she was too
afraid to look away. Neither could she draw air enough to scream. A
greasy hand shot from the darkness, slithering around the back of her neck.
Fingers toyed with a lock of her hair unwound by her fall.

"You know what the penalty is for stealing? They keel-haul you. I
don't relish having the flesh torn from my bones by thick barnacles, nor
drowning in the process. You won't tell anyone I was here, will you,
Dear?"

"Get away from me," she said, barely able to hear her own voice.

"Come now girl, you aren't as pious as you pretend to be. You've been
watching me. I've seen it. This trip doesn't have to be without its
pleasures." He twisted the lock of her hair and gave it a sharp yank that
made her cry out.

"That's right, Desire, squeal. I like 'em lively." He was breathing
heavily, fat quivering along the length of his torso in anticipation. Taking
hold of her with both hands he drove her back against the bulkhead.

Her head snapped against hard oak and the pain awakened her to the
peril of her situation. She tried to scream again but her lungs only forced

out a whisper, "No – no, please no." Tears fell from her eyes with the force she couldn't muster for her words. "No, no, no," she repeated hoarsely. She couldn't think. Panic blinded her. His rough hands roamed her body, squeezing her midriff, pinching her breasts. His filthy body swayed back and forth against her, smearing her clothes with his filth.

He grew more urgent. Stoking her hair he cooed to her, "Hush now pet. This isn't going to take long. They named you right didn't they?" His tongue flicked out and she heard her name coated in oil and lust, "*Desire*." His hand reached lower. "You tell anyone and all my mates are going to want to share you, huh? You're all mine now, don't forget it. Fresh … and you won't tell, will you, *Desire?*"

He was pulling her to the floor. She struggled to stay on her feet, locking her knees, pulling his fingers from her shoulders. Her legs suddenly buckled and she fell hard against the planking. Her mind finally unseized as the fight welled up inside her. Her voice grew stronger, angry. "Stop!...Don't!...Help!"

"Oh I'll help you, and I'll help myself, pet." His fingers dug into her leg as he worked to shimmy her skirt up. She battled to keep it down.

"Heeelp! Help me!"

September 22nd – Afternoon Watch

Dorothy put down her needlework and stretched her legs. She leaned back to catch the sun on her face. To her left, Beth's needles chattered as she worked, the tick, tick, tick of a metronome. To her right, Katherine encouraged little Ellen More to play with the other children. But Ellen was reluctant, a tenuous smile creasing her features as she fiddled with the beading on her shoe. She was a pretty, fine-featured child with waves of long chestnut hair and round brown eyes that shimmered as though holding back tears. Dorothy wondered if Ellen felt she needed to be a mother to her younger siblings, or whether, as Katherine had said, she just needed permission to be happy.

Ellen's brothers, Jasper and Richard, were having no trouble enjoying themselves with the other children. Hair blowing wildly about them, they leaned into the wind, stumbling forward between the gusts with shrieks of laughter.

They'd been torn from their mother by her cuckolded husband, the man they thought their father, only to be abandoned by him on the gangplank of the *Mayflower*. It sickened Dorothy, but something was holding her back from caring for them as Katherine, Beth, and Mary did. She resented them. They were here and shouldn't be, yet Jonathan was absent. The injustice broke her heart.

"We can't replace your own mother, of course," said Katherine, lifting Ellen's chin, "you miss her terribly."

Tears dropped in Ellen's lap, spreading web-like through the silk of her fine dress.

Katherine kissed the top of the child's head.

Dorothy wondered how Jonathan was feeling, whether he could run and play happily. Whether he was loved.

Ellen suddenly stood and charged into the wind, arms straight at her side, fists closed tight. There was no mistaking the smile.

"If love is what the children need they will have it from us," murmured Beth.

"I can see why Desire is grateful to be your ward, Katherine. You've a generous heart," said Dorothy.

"Speaking of Desire, where is she with my needlework? Daydreaming, likely," said Katherine. She bent forward, signalling the women to move closer. "I think John Alden could make a fine suitor for my Desire."

"What of Gilbert, my brother in-law?" said Beth, knitting her brows. "It's practically arranged!"

"Oh my, yes, Gilbert," said Katherine distractedly, looking across to Gilbert, Edward's brother, draped against the rails, his face pinched with smug distain. "It's just, Mr. Alden is a *cooper*."

"But he's not a member of the congregation," pressed Beth. "Who would Desire prefer?"

"Your loyalty is admirable, but Deacon Carver will determine what is best for her," said Katherine, patting Beth's hand before it was withdrawn.

Dorothy didn't feel particularly forgiving toward Desire. Her defence of the men in Leyden and her support of William's decision to leave Jonathan behind stung of betrayal. But, looking at Gilbert, she couldn't stay silent, "Desire may not care, having waited so long for an arrangement, but I should like to have been asked my opinion when it was my turn, however young I was."

"But you are happy with William."

"Yes, but what if I had not been?"

"The church always knows best," pronounced Katherine. "Deacon Carver will personally ensure Desire makes the most beneficial match available."

"I'm sure Katherine knows best," said Beth with acerbity. "I'm going below again to lie down." Beth rose unsteadily to her feet. "I can make it on my own. Please don't trouble yourselves."

"See what Desire is doing when you're down there and send her up with my needlework," said Katherine.

September 22nd – Afternoon Watch

Quaking floorboards rocketed pain into Desire's lower back. He suddenly released her.

Her eyes adjusted enough to make out shapes wrestling close at hand. Grunts, thuds and curses exploded around her.

A sudden kick, deep to her stomach, drove the air from her lungs. She spasmed, arching backward before curling inwards, a fish floundering on a line. Her mouth gaped until she could snatch a breath. Not enough, before the grunting, whirling, many-limbed beast pummeled her shins and crushed her toes.

How many were there? Were they fighting over her – or for her? *Oh God, help me.* Clutching her chest, she pushed herself backward along the deck, feeling for an opening into which to press herself. She gulped the stale air, tasting the salt in her tears, the mucus flowing in a torrent from her nose.

The vibrations at her back abruptly stopped. Scattered sounds regrouped into words. "I know you, you cur! Get off!"

"Anyting 'appens to me and the ot'ers'll come for you. Food for fish, tha' wha' you are."

A heavy form lurched down the corridor. She caught sight of the bloody and pocked features of the sailor known as Harlock. He fell against the ladder, stumbling up its rungs, one arm cradled against his chest.

She heard heavy breathing near at hand. Then a thick voice, flat, even, "I am coming for you." The figure moved toward her, sweeping its outstretched arms through the inky gloom. She was backed against a pair of crates. Delirious with fear, she imagined squeezing herself into the slim space between them. Her breathing was too loud. She caught it. Held it. But her next breath only emerged louder.

"Come out, you're safe now, he's gone."

He was closer. She had to draw her legs in or he would walk right into her. She lifted her heel and tried to bend her knees soundlessly, one and then the other.

He heard the rustling of her skirt and bent down almost in front of her. "It is only me, you're safe. Who is there?" He reached toward her, groping the darkness. The crate behind her wouldn't yield any further. Sensing him on the verge of touching her, she screamed and kicked at him, churning her legs and forcing him back, heels thudding against him.

"Stop, stop. It's John Howland. Whoa there, I'm here to help you." Her heels slowed and then moved toward the searcher uncertainly, experimentally.

"John? John? Is it really you? How do I know it is you? Move back. I don't believe you." Her voice was shaking, and so was her body. It didn't sound like John.

"Well, if you can tell me who I've rescued I can endeavour to prove myself," he said.

She wasn't sure if she should speak. Tentatively she whispered, "Desire, I'm Desire." She hated her own name; she would never hear it in the same way again. The taunting, foul smell of her attacker tainted the syllables. He had dirtied it, the way he had dirtied her.

"Well then you have made it easy for me." His voice smiled with care. "Crimson silk brings out the color of your lips, but I say you would have looked better in the blue velvet I spilled on the floor. Blue brings out the color of your eyes. I won't touch you, but come with me, if you aren't hurt, into the light of the hatch and let your eyes prove to you what your heart can't trust."

He backed up slowly toward the hatch then stopped when he realized she wasn't following. "Are you hurt? How much did the filthy swine hurt you? Oh Heaven…was I too late?"

"I can't move…I can't, I can't seem to get up." Panic crept into her voice. "I'm so cold and my legs are shaking. I can't move." Desire couldn't get her feet under her.

"May I come closer? I just want to help you. It is me, Desire. You can trust me," pleaded John. "Can I not help you?"

"Retreat into the light so I can see you. You don't sound like John," she quavered.

John walked to the end of the corridor as quickly as he could and then turned to face her with hands outstretched in a gesture of supplication. She gasped. The reason for the guttural sound of his voice revealed itself in the bloody mess that was now his nose.

"Oh John, forgive me. I didn't mean to do it to you." Desire reached her arm toward him in invitation and apology but he couldn't see it. "Help. Get me off the floor. Get me away from here."

He rushed to her side and lifted her easily in his arms. "Let's get you to the ladder and then I'll help you up. Did he hurt you badly, Desire?"

"Please don't use my name. It's vulgar," she whispered.

"Nonsense. Let's just get you some air and we can talk about it." Reaching the ladder he cautiously lowered her legs to the deck. "Can you stand?"

"My legs are like water. I can't lift them," she said, starting to cry again.

"Sit down then, in the light, and we'll rest. You can tell me what happened and then forget all about it. You're safe. He can't hurt you now." He held her hands as she lowered her bottom to the first rung of the ladder. He sat back on his heels facing her, but immediately she fell forward into his arms, dissolving in tears.

"It was so terrible, John, the…the smell of him." She shuddered and buried her face in the soft fabric of his shirt. John's rich scent washed through her nose and she took her time letting it swirl through every chamber, pooling in the deep, dark corners so that no remnant of the sailor's odour could remain.

"And . . . he said things to me. He told me I was all his and that if I said anything they were all going to hurt me."

"Did he do anything to you?" asked John, choked with feeling.

"No … yes … he, he dug his fingers into me." Her cheeks grew hot. She clenched her teeth to trap the awful reality of her words, but still they escaped. "He tore at my bodice . . . tried to lift my skirt. He … ," her voice grew small, ". . . my breast."

September 22ⁿᵈ – Afternoon Watch

John looked down, instantly regretting it. Her grease-smeared bodice hung open on one side, revealing a snowy mound already discoloured with a bruise. He seethed, imagining a noose being thrown around Harlock's neck. He needed to get Desire up the ladder and back to the women.

Who, though? She seemed particularly friendly with Dorothy and it might be better if Dorothy handled this rather than Katherine – at first.

He couldn't have Katherine interfering before he had a chance to discuss it with the other men.

"Safe. You're safe. You did right, defending yourself so admirably." He stroked her soft hair and then caught himself, worried Harlock might have done the same thing. He was impatient to act, but desperate to stay and watch over her. She was trembling now with her tears.

"Well, do you think anyone will notice my new nose? Does it improve my looks?" he said, hoping to take her mind off her own injuries.

"Oh John, you have such a beautiful face. What have I done to you. I am so sorry. I wouldn't have kicked you if I had known it was you. I was just so scared."

"Ahh. I see. No. You didn't do this," he said, drawing a circle around his face, "this was courtesy of the fat whelk, Harlock. But, don't worry, I gave him worse. He won't bother you again." Pulling Desire closer to him and hitching her up a bit, he spoke softly into her hair, "I promise to keep an eye on you. And no going anywhere alone again. Agreed?" His heart was pounding. He shouldn't be holding her like this.

"Agreed. I think I can stand now," said Desire, some firmness returning to her spirit. "I'll try the ladder. And, John, please don't tell anyone. I am so ashamed. I couldn't bear it."

There was no one in the common area of the 'tween deck. He steered Desire toward the capstan and motioned for her to be quiet. Then he carefully peaked into each cabin. He found Beth lying on her bunk, head hung over a basin. He tiptoed back to Desire and whispered she should join her.

With Desire settled, he grabbed a handkerchief from his bedroll and gingerly wiped his face. A searing bolt of pain shot though his nose when he brushed it with his thumb. He abandoned his efforts. Desire was still his priority. He needed to find Dorothy. He hoped she could keep a secret. Only then would he tell Deacon Carver and Elder Brewster of the attack.

He looked up to see Dorothy descending the ladder. *Thanks be to God.*

"You're just the person I need," he said stepping back and quickly turning his head politely away.

"Oh? I was just coming down to check on Beth. Sea-sickness, again," said Dorothy with sympathy, as she placed her foot on the deck. Her eyes widened when she looked at him.

"Something's happened. I've put Desire in Beth's cabin –"

"Desire? Is she like this?" said Dorothy, indicating his face and starting for the cabin.

"No. Wait." He rushed ahead to block her way. "A sailor . . . Harlock . . . attacked her." He lowered his voice. "I fear the worst might have happened if I hadn't heard her scream. She is badly shaken and her bodice torn. Look after her."

"What am I to do? Shouldn't we get the doctor?"

"She doesn't want anyone to know, but she will trust you. Please, can you clean her up? I need to speak with Deacon Carver, but no one else can know."

"But, we're not – "

"Just stay with her and raise an alarm if any of the sailors come down." John left Dorothy standing open-mouthed as he leapt for the ladder, fuelled with purpose.

Desire was his responsibility. Her heart had beat against him like a kind of delicate bird. Her eyes, so full of fear, awoke in him a tenderness deeper than any he had ever felt. He would do anything for her.

September 22nd – Afternoon Watch

Every eye focused on his swollen and still bloody proboscis. He had done his best to wipe away the mess before approaching and interrupting the Deacon's meeting, but the bleeding wouldn't stop.

"What the sweet juniper happened to you, John?" asked Edward Winslow, yielding the floor to him. "Weren't you standing by the rails talking to John Alden just a quarter of an hour ago?"

"I'm sorry to interrupt, humble brothers, but I must speak with Deacon Carver and Elder Brewster alone, and perhaps William Bradford." John tipped his head back and shifted uncomfortably from foot to foot.

"Well, what is it John? As your employer I demand you stop fidgeting and tell me what trouble you've gotten into," said Carver. "Look at you. While you were getting your face knocked in I was giving a sermon on the importance of avoiding violence – on showing patience and love to those who might try us. If you'd been here, you might have saved yourself this gruesome result." He gave a disapproving sweep of his hand from John's brow to his breeches.

"I beg your pardon, as my employer and my Deacon. And may God forgive me. But, I pray you let me explain in private please, Sir." He bowed his head. "It is a delicate matter."

Carver nodded toward Brewster and William and they followed him to the relative privacy of the opposite rail.

John surveilled the nearby sailors before recounting the incident. He leaned in close to prevent his voice carrying as he told the story, starting with his decision to go below for a warmer doublet.

As the tale progressed, Carver's eyes narrowed and a vein boiled to the surface of his temple. He raised his palms halfway through the explanation as though he could not bear to hear more.

John kept going, if only to reassure them Desire was safe.

As he finished William grabbed him by his collar, hard enough that he feared it would tear. "Are you sure she's untouched?"

"Yes. I found her before anything happened," he said, peeling William's fingers off.

"She's just a child – an innocent," said William.

"She's a young woman, really," John interjected, needlessly.

No one spoke. William turned and looked out over the waves. "We have to sail with this cockroach of a man for a while yet. If we don't go to the Master, Harlock will think he can attack us with impunity."

Brewster grabbed William's sleeve. Andrew Prince joined them.

"I couldn't help seeing the state of your servant's face, Carver. You say it was a sailor, William. I may be able to lend advice. You're absolutely right by the way, what you said."

"It is a private matter," said Carver and Brewster together.

"You can't let these sailors have any rope. You do, and they'll make you a noose."

"Thank you, Mr. Prince. We will converse in private now. If we need anything further of you we shall ask," said Carver.

Prince bowed. "I meet with the Master regularly to discuss my maps. I can mention the incident on your behalf, if you wish. No, no don't protest. It is no trouble. I believe so heartily in your cause that anything I can do to ensure its success, I shall do."

"Thank you, Andrew," said William.

They huddled closer together as Prince withdrew. John wasn't sure if he was meant to leave as well, but he remained. He needed to see a result. The sweat from his earlier exertions had saturated his shirt and the wind was biting. Uncontrollable shivers moved in waves up his body and into his jaw.

"We need to keep this between ourselves. If the others think their wives are in danger they may act rashly. We don't want to bring the wrath of the sailors down upon us," said Brewster

"I still believe the Master should be told," said William. "You heard what Andrew said."

Carver drummed his fingers on the rail. "If he is told, he'll have no choice but to publicly whip Harlock. When he announces the crime, Desire will be ruined." He stopped drumming. "No, we can't inform the Master. Mr. Prince doesn't know the full story."

"But Harlock can't go unpunished either, Deacon," urged John.

Carver massaged his beard. "We'll pray." He lifted his face to the Heavens. "Join hands with me and ask for guidance."

They stood hand in hand in silence, the wind whistling between them, until Carver spoke again, "What say you, each of you?"

John spoke first, "Desire's honour must be protected above all, but Harlock must pay for this. How, I don't yet know."

"I think we should follow the Deacon's earlier advice and guide the sailor to repentance," said Brewster solemnly.

"Exactly, answering violence with violence will only damn our souls," said Carver with a shake of his head.

William was sceptical. "The serpent will not be so easily shaken from that man's prodigious flesh and I won't have any further, or greater, harm come to the women. With all the work and planning still to be done, the four of us can't be as vigilant as necessary." He stamped his feet, hugging his arms tight to his body. "Where is Harlock now, for instance?"

"John, we will handle this," said Carver. "Accept my apologies. What you did was honourable. More than that, the young woman you saved was my responsibility. You're a faithful and reliable servant."

As he bowed his head and stepped away he heard Carver continue, "In majority we are agreed the Master cannot be told. And Desire's marriage needs to be arranged. As soon as possible."

Warning

September 22nd – Afternoon Watch

*D*orothy found Desire on her knees alternately praying and weeping in Beth's cabin. She knelt and wrapped an arm around her shoulder, giving it a gentle squeeze. Desire winced but otherwise didn't acknowledge her or falter in prayer.

Dorothy saw under her hand a purple shoulder marked with violence. There were scratches on her forearms and her bodice was ripped, its verdant embroidery fraying along the torn edge. Her hair fell in long hanks around eyes swollen with shock.

"The men won't let him get away with it," offered Dorothy.

"I don't want anyone to know. It's my fault. I shouldn't have gone down alone." Desire covered her face and rocked forward and back.

"Are we not to walk twenty paces from our cabins without a chaperone? This isn't your fault," said Dorothy. "What kind of world are we now in that a man who is basically a servant can attack you? He will be punished. Don't you agree, Beth?" said Dorothy, looking at Beth whose head was lolling over the edge of the bed.

"It has to stay a secret. Gilbert can't know," said Desire.

"Well . . . no. He can't. So you can't be seen like this." Sitting back on her heels, Dorothy leaned in and tried to catch Desire's eye. "We need to get you out of this dress and into a clean one. Which trunk is yours in the Carver's cabin?"

Desire turned her head, staring blankly.

"You are going to be fine, Desire. I am going to do everything in my power to make it so. But you have to help me get you cleaned up."

Desire's sluggishness frustrated Dorothy's sense of urgency.

"Desire, which one?" she demanded, a little unkindly. Thinking aloud she said, "We need water to wash your face and arms."

Dorothy stood and moved to the doorway, trying not to tap her foot with impatience. At any minute someone could come below.

Desire's words fell listlessly from her lips, "Green trunk. Yellow dress."

Dorothy walked quickly to the Carver's cabin and, looking around to be sure she was alone, ducked into the dim chamber, feeling blindly for Desire's trunk. Finding it, she removed one dress after another, bringing each into the light to examine its colour. Her heart raced with the fear of discovery. After three failed attempts to find Desire's choice she decided a rose dress would do and quickly stuffed the others back into the trunk. She heard a creak in the passageway and scrambled to look between the curtains. She was still alone. Her heart now hammering in her ears, Dorothy walked briskly down the corridor, the dress balled up in front of her.

"It's me. I've got it," she whispered, pulling the curtain open and stepping inside. Desire and Beth cowered in the corner. An intense odour, a mix of fresh urine and filth, stopped her like a solid force. "Desire, what is…"

Fingernails raked Dorothy's scalp, wrenching her neck back. A seething voice spat in her ear, "You won't tell anyone. I warned them and I'll warn you. If anyone hears, I'll find each of you and afterward you won't be able to walk. Got it? You and your pious murmurings – God can't save you."

She twisted her head slowly to the right, working against the vice-like grip on her hair. She looked up and saw scaly folds of skin contorted into a gargoyle's grimace – a face of pure malice. Harlock. Pockmarks blackened with crusts of blood. Eyes bloodshot, bulging. She was so close she could see the fissures in his lips pulsing open as he spoke, raw gashes dancing before her. The foul heat of his breath was overpowering.

He let go suddenly and Dorothy stumbled back, clutching the curtain for support.

"Dorothy!" Desire leapt and reached for her.

"Get down, trollop!" Harlock's paw shot toward Desire, a feint, ending near her nose.

Behind him now, propelled by a rage composed of all the hurt this voyage had brought upon her, Dorothy swung her leg at the back of his knee. Harlock buckled momentarily. Then his fist came around.

September 22nd – Afternoon Watch

Beth's voice was urgent, but Dorothy could barely hear it.

"She is white. Her mouth is bleeding."

They were shaking her, making it harder to hear.

"Dorothy. Dorothy. Wake up. Oh dear God help us, help her."

Dorothy opened her eyes as vomit exploded from her nose.

Beth lifted her against the bunk and wiped her chin.

Desire was shimmying into the rose gown, her stupor now gone.

No one spoke.

Beth tipped a small amount of water into a wooden cup and wet the corner of a fresh cloth. She daubed at the black smudges on Desire's face and chest and then dipped the cloth again. She turned to Dorothy and cleaned the blood from her face.

"Hold this to your lip," said Beth.

Everything was grey for Dorothy. Her arms were heavy. She couldn't feel her hands. She kept the cloth obediently to her chin like a child after a fall.

Beth looked from her to Desire.

"Desire, sit and I'll do up your hair. We must do as he says. We can't tell anyone. Act normally," cautioned Beth. All traces of her seasickness had vanished. She briskly removed Desire's cap, re-twisting and pinning her curls.

"Dorothy, I will help you onto the bunk in just a moment. I think we should all lie down and feign sleep until we can gather our wits."

"I can do it myself."

"No, you're in no state … oh, Dorothy, your tooth!"

Dorothy's tongue darted around her mouth, stopping in panic at the gaping hole beside her top front tooth. Her fingers flew to her mouth. It was gone. "Help me! It must be here somewhere!"

She pitched forward, sweeping her hands back and forth over the floor boards. Beth and Desire followed.

"Here," said Desire. She held up the tooth by its bloody root.

Dorothy grabbed it and pushed it back into place. It fell out. Beth took it from her, lifted her lip and forced it in as hard as she could, bringing tears to Dorothy's eyes. "Now hold it."

Dorothy pushed on it and clamped her teeth together.

"How are we going to keep this a secret now?" said Beth, looking at Desire for answers. "Keep the cloth to your mouth Dorothy, you're dripping."

Dorothy wiped tears from her cheek and returned the cloth to her mouth.

Beth picked up Desire's dress from the corner. Bringing it to her nose she recoiled. Terrified by Harlock's arrival, Desire had wet herself. "We might be able to rinse this before anyone comes down," she said.

The curtain parted behind her, making them all jump. "Beth dear, how are you feeling?" asked Edward.

Beth's shoulders slumped in relief. She dropped the dress and ducked out of the cabin, throwing herself in his arms. The curtain was redrawn.

Dorothy and Desire looked at each other nervously.

Beth's words chased each in a nervous rhythm, but she said nothing to give them away.

A rustling against the outer cabin wall told Dorothy that Beth was gathering her skirts to sit. Her voice was level again.

"Is that our beer ration? I missed my ration this afternoon," said Beth.

"Take it dear. I'll finish whatever you don't want." Edward's solid form slid down beside Beth, his boots scraping the deck.

Their secret was safe.

"I'm so sorry," said Desire.

"It wasn' your faul'." Dorothy said through the finger holding her tooth. She extended her free hand to Desire, drawing her closer. Making sure she wasn't dripping blood, Dorothy leaned her forehead against Desire's and looked into her eyes. "It wasn' our faul'." They sat, hand in hand, waiting for the tears to stop.

September 22nd – First Dog Watch

William ducked his head and followed Carver aft, down the narrow corridor leading from the 'tween deck to the gunroom. According to the sailor hired to stay with them in New England, Mr. Ely, they were likely to find Harlock loafing here. The dark gunroom was not a place William would choose for a confrontation. They'd have no lamp-light owing to the gunpowder.

Sulphur snaked up William's nose as he cracked the door. He coughed.

Carver pushed past him, threw the door wide and in a confident, booming voice announced, "Time to come out, Harlock. We'll have a word."

Having searched the ship fruitlessly for an hour William was surprised when Harlock lumbered forth from the darkness. William held up his Bible. He'd selected a few passages.

Carver spoke, "You have committed a grievous sin against one of our gentle and godly lambs and you will answer to God for your crime. In our presence we ask that you beg forgiveness of God for your trespass. Save yourself a terrible doom." Carver raised himself to his full height. His head brushed the beams.

Harlock laughed, "She was sweet and plump . . . and didn't your God give me a pecker so I could enjoy myself where I might." He enjoyed the shock. "Forgive me Lord," he bowed, "for not using it more."

Two other sailors peered around the doorway.

"You go too far, Harlock!" said Carver, ashen.

William felt as Carver looked. "Blasphemer!"

"You will answer for your wickedness. God will smite you down," Carver intoned.

"Here before God, on the Holy Bible, beg forgiveness. Cast the serpent out, for you are wholly infected," implored William, holding the Bible like a shield as he extended it toward Harlock.

"You pious little Bible-worshippers." Harlock ripped the Bible from his hand, threw it to the deck and stamped on it. "That's what I care for your Bible and your God. There is no God!" chortled Harlock. "You are so prancing with your love and worship. A duller waste of life I've never seen. You don't even have cock enough to stand up to me when I throw it in your face."

William hurriedly picked up his wounded Bible and dusted it off.

Snickering, Harlock turned to his friends. They smiled uneasily. Some sailors were non-believers, others were of varied faiths. All feared the Master, if not the Lord.

"God sees you, Harlock. Not only has the serpent twisted within you, you have made him a nest there. You are warned. The Almighty is stronger than any man. Fear Him!" said Carver.

Harlock stared over William's shoulder to something beyond, then beckoned the sailors. They charged down the narrow passage straight toward him and Carver. William braced for the impact. The three men slipped past, avoiding contact. Perplexed, William turned. The reason for their hurried retreat presented itself in the form of Andrew Prince, standing at the end of the corridor.

"Everything well?" asked Prince.

"Yes. Well," said Carver. He locked eyes with William and nodded. They would have to talk later.

September 22nd – First Dog Watch

Dorothy stared at the boards between her bunk and the Whites' cabin. She could see glimpses of Suzanna waddling back and forth collecting pots for dinner. When Suzanna left she resumed worrying over her tooth. Her mouth ached and the tooth still wiggled in its socket. It wouldn't stay without her help. Hunger gnawed at her but she couldn't go out like this. And how was she to eat?

"Here you are," said William.

"Where haf you veen?" said Dorothy, reluctant to remove the finger and cloth from her mouth.

"What? Where have I been? I suppose you know about Desire. John said he left her with you and told you what happened. Carver and I have been hunting for Harlock. We spoke to him directly, rather than going to the Master. Are you sick? Lying down in here?"

Dorothy swung her legs out over the edge of the bunk and brought her head into the light. She removed the cloth from her mouth slowly, unsure whether she was still bleeding. The tooth wiggled and she quickly pushed it back in place.

"He did this to me," she said, starting to cry again.

"Who?" William dropped to his knees, examining her swollen lip.

"Harlock. He came into Beth's cabin, warned us not to speak. He hit me."

"What! He came back? Was Desire there too?"

"My tooth came out, William. It won't stay in. I have to hold it."

"Oh, Dorothy," he said, hugging her, "it will be fine. It will heal. Don't worry."

"You have to do something, William. He warned us not to tell anyone, but I'm afraid. Can't you tell the Master? The Master will do something."

"We can't, darling. Desire's reputation will be ruined. You wouldn't want that, would you? It's important Desire make a good match and this would spoil her chances. She doesn't deserve that."

"But William, what about what he's done to me?" she said, her voice rising.

"He won't be back. We've warned him and this will be the end to it. Trust me."

"I trust you to keep me safe. Surely I mean more to you than Desire's reputation."

"Of course you do. We are handling it. From now on you must stay with the other women. And do not let the children out of your sight. Now, come, please, and have a bite to eat. You can't hide in here." He took her hand.

"Do I have your word you will keep this quiet?"

Dorothy looked at William, her finger on her tooth. "Yes."

September 22ⁿᵈ – Last Dog Watch

William lowered Dorothy to a spot near the warm belly of the brazier. Carver sat across from them, his eyes closed. Katherine was fussing, tucking blankets around him and rubbing his feet. Around them the *Mayflower* rose and fell in time with the sea, her passengers now sufficiently inured to her motions.

"Anna, bring the platters for William and Dorothy," ordered Katherine. "I didn't see Dorothy preparing your dinner so I took the liberty of making extra," she said to William.

"Thank you," said Dorothy.

"Twas no bother," Katherine said with a wave of her hand. But her eyes lingered on Dorothy's swollen lip. "Have you begun arranging Desire's marriage, dear?" asked Katherine, turning to Carver.

"I haven't had a chance yet, but we will do so shortly. Isn't that so, William?"

William swallowed and nodded.

Katherine said, "I have some thoughts on it, Dear."

Carver leaned close to Katherine. "This is a decision the leaders of the church shall make together. It is a matter of delicacy and complexity. I cannot propose a suitor on the strength of your thoughts, although I'm sure, my love, they are well reasoned."

Dorothy got to her feet. William started to follow but she shook her head and narrowed her eyes. He turned quickly to see if Carver and Katherine were watching. Both looked away. Katherine lifted a steaming pot from the brazier.

"I've a broth here if ye'd like some, Dorothy? I notice you haven't touched your platter," said Katherine, not looking up.

"No, thank you, Katherine. I don't feel hungry."

William tried coaxing a smile from Dorothy, but she stepped around his outstretched hand.

"Come and eat something, my wren," he said.

"I can't," she said stonily.

"Excuse us," he said to Carver.

"William, tarry a little and finish your supper. We have much to discuss," said Carver.

William kissed Dorothy's cheek and watched her until she disappeared into the cabin. He followed Carver to the foot of the ladder.

"I'll get right to it," said Carver flatly. "I want your opinion. Besides Gilbert, what of Peter Browne or John Goodman as suitors for Desire. They're fit and thatching will be a useful trade."

"But what trade will either have once the thatching is done. Besides they're never parted, both with their dogs. I fear the whole business could spark rivalries and jealousies between them," replied William.

"What of John Alden? Coopering is a better trade than thatching. And, I saw her looking at him favourably this morning. If we can make the best match, and make her happy in the process, I will do it. She deserves it, poor thing," said Carver.

"Alden is a stranger. We do not know his faith. It would be better for her to marry within the congregation. That means Gilbert, and Gilbert already expects the match."

"It won't be hard to ask Alden his faith. There aren't many eligible men on this ship and I won't have one of the other girls making a better match than our Desire."

They were silent for a minute, each musing on the choices. "A cooper will do well. Alden's quick-witted and intelligent. Whether Gilbert or Alden, neither will refuse. Desire is a striking beauty, pious and of good upbringing. You'll have my support when we meet formally, if this is how you want to proceed. As you know, though, Edward, as Gilbert's brother, will be insulted should Alden win the prize," said William.

Resilience

*D*esire stared at the curtain and let the emotions roiling her – guilt, fear, humiliation – carry her like a craft adrift on a confused sea. She had no compass, no experience to help her deal with the events of today. But she had encountered enough obstacles in her life so far, to have learned one thing. *Move. Keep moving. Someday, the seas will yield.* And so she charted her course. Harlock be damned, she would not founder because of him, at least within the limits of her own power.

Besides, all she had suffered was fright, along with a few bruises and scratches. She was intact. God could help her conquer her fear and shame. She would repay him by staying strong. She dropped from her bunk and stepped into the common-way.

The women chatted while scrubbing pans. Desire sat down next to them. She made little conversation, wondering if the day's events had somehow marked her. She answered questions about her supposed seasickness as vaguely as she could.

Glancing around to confirm that everyone was behaving normally and no one was staring, she caught John Howland's eye. An unfamiliar surge of emotion splashed through her, strong enough to rattle the platter of cold fish she was holding against her knee. He stood by the capstan polishing a pair of boots, his face glowing with warmth and sympathy.

She didn't turn away. Instead, she dropped her focus to his nose and back, trying to convey what she hoped he would understand as an apology. While their eyes conversed, everything and everyone disappeared. They remained locked together by mutual understanding until his friend John Alden approached and put a hand on his shoulder. The spell was broken.

Desire returned to the world around her, guilt dousing the afterglow of her exchange with John. Had anyone noticed their silent communication? Katherine was busy fussing over Ellen and her siblings. Mary Brewster was speaking to Mary Allerton about a young woman named Priscilla.

She risked a quick glance towards her rescuer, now sharing a laugh with John Alden.

She owed him her deepest gratitude. He had worked by her side for weeks, accomplishing small tasks for her benefit as well as the Carvers'. Had she even thanked him? He slept outside their cabin, ate his meals with them, yet she was only now truly recognizing him for what he was: not a servant, but a man. He was chivalrous and brave. More importantly still, she could trust him.

A powerful revelation struck her. Harlock, the attack, the rescue – God had intended for what happened today to bring them together.

Glancing up again, she saw him watching her. Katherine called her name and she immediately dropped her gaze.

"Desire, child, I should have come looking for you when you didn't return with my needlework this afternoon. Can you forgive me?" she asked earnestly.

"Of course Mother Katherine. Forgive *me*." To avoid further explanation she affected an interest in her supper. "Did you retrieve these rations for me, Katherine? I'm sorry I wasn't there to help with the meal."

"John brought them up from the hold this evening when we realized you were resting," said Katherine.

Her next bite of herring and peas never tasted better.

"You look very happy this evening," said Katherine. She gave a knowing nod toward the two Johns, still deep in conversation. "I'll do my best."

"Oh, yes, yes, thank you, of course," Desire responded, thoroughly confused.

Mary Brewster clapped her hands. "I have a happy surprise for you, Desire. We have met, and do think you will admire, the very lovely Miss Priscilla Mullins. She is only two years your junior and, although a stranger, she seems a very suitable friend. She'll be joining us soon and may bring her mother along for introductions. Aren't you glad?"

Mary's smile held a hint of triumph; she had trumped Katherine in arranging the visit and demonstrated her prowess in mixing with the other passengers.

"Oh, I'm very pleased. Thank you for your thoughtfulness." Desire forced a smile, hoping to disguise her nerves. The day had been extraordinarily difficult, she wasn't sure she could muster the enthusiasm to meet someone new. And the ship continued to deliver reminders that she was still in danger. Not the dangers of the incalculable ocean around her, but of the threats near at hand, the perils waiting in the *Mayflower's* dank, fetid spaces. Malice lurked in dark passageways, passing sailors trailed *his* scent. How was she to make scintillating conversation in such a state?

But then Priscilla arrived, wearing an emerald green dress, not yet spoiled by life aboard ship. Her golden hair was pulled high, revealing slim, arched brows rising above dancing blue eyes, the same color as her own. On a ship so crowded, and with so few women her age, Desire couldn't believe they had not yet spoken.

"How do you do?" she curtsied to Priscilla.

"I do very well, now I have finally met you. You've had such an exciting life, full of adventures and intrigues. You must share them all," said Priscilla, breathless with excitement.

Desire was taken aback. *What did Priscilla mean?* "Oh . . . surely you have me mistaken," she stammered.

Desire looked around for a suitable place to sit, like a hostess surprised by a visitor at the threshold of her untidy sitting-room.

Priscilla motioned to the capstan, which offered a little more room.

Not wanting to be disagreeable on their first meeting, Desire assented, although this would take them right under the nose of the two Johns.

"I confess I don't know to what you are referring," said Desire in a whisper she hoped Priscilla would likewise adopt.

"For one, I heard that you were once the ward of a man who was arrested in your parlour, right in front of you!" said Priscilla, in a volume that made Desire wince.

She hushed her with a flutter of her hand.

"He was no criminal. He was a great man, a gentle and noble propagator of the faith. He was only arrested for printing religious truths." Desire thought back sadly to Thomas Brewer, his reputation unjustly sullied, his life ruined, for the simple crime of promoting good worship. "You wouldn't call William Brewster, Mary's husband, a criminal would you? He, too, was charged as Thomas was. Mr. Brewster simply had the good fortune to escape in time."

"Did your mother's husband really give you an extravagant allowance?" Priscilla continued, ignoring the finer points of the story in a rush for the next sensation. "What was it like to have all that money to spend? Your dowry must be impressive."

"Priscilla!" Desire whispered curtly, "You are too forward. And what lies you have been told."

"Well, did your benefactor not give you a great sum of money?"

"He paid for me to go away. To be cared for elsewhere," Desire's voice faltered, thick now with sorrow. "That was it. And when Mother died, the allowance stopped." She looked around, hoping to make her excuses and leave. Priscilla's company was proving tiresome.

"I can see I've upset you. I'm sorry."

"You have upset me. You've done nothing but bring back sad memories."

"I get nervous. I always say the wrong thing when I'm nervous. Can we start again?" Priscilla eyes pleaded with her, reminding her of her own vulnerabilities. She couldn't refuse.

They talked of other matters and twice Priscilla managed to make her laugh. She learned that Priscilla's father was a cobbler. She had a younger brother onboard and two older siblings that stayed behind in Dorking.

Eventually, the conversation came back to marriage, as it always did.

She steeled herself, but quickly relaxed as it became clear that Priscilla's only intention was to discuss every eligible man on the ship.

"Whom do you think Governor Carver will choose for you?"

Desire remained silent. Before today, the question of marriage had mattered less. In truth she had been as a piece of flotsam on the tide, steered in a direction that was not of her design. Each the same as the other. Today's events had altered her, tearing her ambivalence away just as Harlock had torn her bodice.

"John Goodman and Peter Browne are very handsome, do you not think?" whispered Priscilla.

"They are handsome but they are so together that the woman who marries one will be getting the pair – and serving them both the rest of her life." A giggle erupted. Desire hid it quickly behind her hands.

"And Gilbert Winslow?"

"Shh. It's assumed, yes," said Desire.

"John Alden?"

"Priscilla."

"Well?"

"He isn't a member of the congregation. Father Carver wouldn't even consider him." Desire smoothed the silk across her knee and glanced sideways. "Let's talk of other things," she whispered.

"No, no, first answer me. Whom would you most wish to marry?"

"I must marry whom the church wishes me to marry. But I trust in God. He will guide Father Carver in his choice," said Desire quietly.

Priscilla wiggled her brows. "I would take my pick of either John Alden or John Howland."

Desire could feel a flush rising up her throat.

"Why aren't you married already?" asked Priscilla

"It's impolite to ask such a question of someone with whom you share such a brief acquaintance," reprimanded Desire.

"Honest question. Not impolite," said Priscilla, still looking at her expectantly. "How are we to enjoy a full acquaintance if we don't share each other's confidences?"

"My father was arranging for my marriage before he died, but mother was too ill before her death to settle things. My opportunity died with her and the gentleman took another bride. You know the remainder."

Priscilla's face fell in sympathy. "That's terrible. Did you love him? How tragic to have your fiancé marry another woman."

"You needn't be so dramatic. I didn't love him. I didn't know him. I believe, now, that God had better plans for me. A better match." Unconsciously she glanced at John Howland, then caught herself, relieved that Priscilla's eyes did not follow.

"If you're expecting to marry a nobleman in New England, well, I think you'll find they're in short supply on this ship."

"I want to know and respect the man to whom I bind myself, that's all," blushed Desire. "Enough about me."

While she had been anxious for the two Johns, standing no more than six feet away, not to overhear their conversation, she was aware of Priscilla's frequent glances toward them suggesting the opposite intention. It seemed to Desire that Priscilla had aimed her little attentions towards John Alden, but she couldn't be sure they hadn't landed upon John Howland as well. She was relieved when Katherine called upon them both to deliver evening tea to the single men.

September 22nd – First Watch

The routine creaks and groans of the ship changed as the evening wore on, causing John to dig his heels into either side of his bedroll. The sea stiffened. As winds howled across the deck above, he could feel the vibrations of the rigging shivering in response. He leaned into the boards of the Carver's cabin at his back. Only inches away, on the other side, he knew Desire was preparing for bed.

It was dangerous, but thrilling, how badly he wanted to turn his head and sneak a peak at her through the cracks.

How could he stop himself from thinking of her?

She and Priscilla had probably talked of her arranged marriage to warn him of his position and of hers. He couldn't be considered with the other men – he needed to stop thinking of himself as a candidate. His circumstances had changed and he had better get used to them. If only he had met her while a scholar, before he'd been forced to indenture himself, they might have fallen deeply in love. Knowing Carver as he did, he knew Desire would never be free to marry outside of her class.

He scratched his shoulders against the rough wood. He owed it to Desire to want the best for her.

He heard a hard thud from her cabin. He pulled in his knees and began to rise instinctively. "Is everything alright in there?" he said.

"Yes."

Katherine hustled past him, parted the curtain narrowly and slid inside. He heard murmurs, then felt the boards press against his spine as Desire lifted herself onto the top bunk, the wood releasing a gentle sigh under her weight. For a moment it seemed as though their energy was shared. It hummed back and forth through the long grain of the wood. He closed his eyes. He was touching her.

Conspirators

"*D*orothy, we have to talk." Desire pulled Dorothy aside from the dish washing. Katherine kept everyone busier than usual while the men were conducting a meeting above deck. Only a handful of men remained below with them.

Dorothy dried her hands and handed the towel to Beth. "What is it?"

"In your cabin," Desire whispered.

She followed Dorothy in the tepid light, closing the curtain behind before joining Dorothy on the bunk.

"I was delivering tea to Mr. Prince last night," Desire whispered. "He was talking with Christopher Martin. They took no notice of me and I plainly heard Mr. Prince promise to support Mr. Martin if he would disrupt the meeting today. He said he knew something about William, something that might hurt him."

"What?" Dorothy gripped her elbows to control the trembling of her hands.

"I don't know. I couldn't linger."

Dorothy burned inside. "It's too late to warn William. The meeting has started. I know Mr. Prince has ties to Thomas Weston. William dismissed it, but this is proof he means us harm. I don't think Prince is even his real name. I think he is Andrew Weston."

"I can make sure I am the one to deliver all of his meals and tea. He has men coming and going all day. I'll pass on everything I hear."

"He has letters on board. I've read parts of them. If we could find them and show them to William or to Deacon Carver, perhaps we could stop him." Dorothy grew excited, happy she was no longer alone. "How though? He's sure to keep them hidden."

"We can do it. We must get those letters!" Desire caught Dorothy's excitement. "I'll do everything I can. I'm not afraid. Not if it will protect the congregation." Desire grabbed her and pulled her into a tight embrace.

Dorothy squeezed Desire in return, feeling her friend's heart beating fast against her own. The heartbeat was strong, but all Dorothy could feel was Desire's vulnerability. This was her friend's very essence throbbing against her. A dove clasped in her hands. How could she ever have doubted Desire? She wanted to protect her, guard her. Love welled up inside her. "Be careful," she whispered into her hair, "Prince isn't what he pretends to be."

Desire pulled away and searched her face, "Your tooth? How is it? Your lip is still swollen."

Dorothy shook her head. "It'll be fine."

The risk involved descended upon them. They both felt its weight; reality dampening the shared frisson of excitement.

"Desire, listen to me, you don't have to do this."

"I want to. I owe it to us all. It's our duty toward God."

"True. Although perhaps not the duty God and the Church intend for us to perform. Yet, we have just as much reason as the men to want the plantation to succeed. More. If it doesn't prosper William will not send for Jonathan. If it fails, we shall starve, no differently from the men."

Rendezvous

*D*esire plunged her hands into the shallow basin of cold brown water and glanced over at Prince's desk, now unmanned. Dorothy accepted a platter from her and distractedly towelled it dry, eyes fixed on the same target. Prince tidied the scattered parchments, filing them into the leather pockets suspended from the narrow walls of the gunport. Mary struck up a song and she and Dorothy joined in, turning back to look at one another across the basin.

"Pardon me, ladies?"

Gilbert was suddenly beside her.

"I'll have a moment with you, dear Desire," said Gilbert, taking her elbow and directing her down the corridor several paces. She still held a dripping mug.

"When you are my wife, I wish you to behave more somberly. Your gaiety is attracting attention. And if you wear your hair a little more thus …" He reached up and smoothed the top of her hair back straight from her face. She pulled her head back, the memory of Harlock's touch still raw. "… you will not have these curls tempting other men. And your neckline …"

Dorothy took the mug from Desire's tight fingers and stood beside her. Gilbert kept talking.

"We've been discussing safety and it occurs to me that your behaviour must be plainer on the whole, especially since, if you are to be my wife, your behaviour will be a reflection on me. You will do things entirely differently, as I should not be expected to put myself in danger, rescuing you from harm that is entirely avoidable on your part."

"Let's hope you shall never have to do so," said Dorothy. "Come, Desire, we need your help."

Desire looked stiffly over her shoulder and watched as Gilbert strode toward the hatch, forcing his way past John Howland, who was deck-bound with a pair of heavy buckets.

"Excuse me a moment," said Desire.

September 23rd – Forenoon Watch

John was so startled at the gentle touch on his sleeve that he almost dropped the buckets of night soil. His heart leapt to his throat. Desire's eyes seemed impossibly blue.

"Can I help you carry that, John?"

"Certainly not." He was shocked she would offer such a thing.

"Well then, what makes you better than me, that you are worthy of it and I am not?" she teased.

"I'm a servant and well you know it." Shame thrust its mark across his cheeks and he had to look away. "You are superior to me in station and grace."

He put a foot on the ladder. And then took it off.

"It's just that sometimes I look at you and forget that we're anything but a man and woman, as God created Adam and Eve," he said hurriedly.

He risked looking at her. Her colour intensified. Her eyes met his and the air between them fairly crackled with the fission of silent confessions. Then he remembered himself. The foul stench of the buckets returned.

"I'm indentured for two more years," he said, dropping his eyes to the buckets. "Forgive me for speaking like that. I had no right."

"No, you have every right. You're not just a servant, at all. And your speeches don't offend, if they're authentically spoken. In fact, I would welcome such entreaties from you – and more. You rescued me. Your character is nobler than any man's onboard. All that was my station died with my parents and I . . . " Desire looked down.

"You what?"

She shook her head. "I risk offending your high opinion of me – that is if you have one." Her eyes widened. "Oh dear, I didn't mean to imply that you must."

Her flattery was making him uncomfortable, not for its brazenness – he welcomed it – but for its cruel effervescence. Nothing, after all, could come of it. They both knew their place.

The buckets grew heavy and the struggle to hold them as far away from her as possible, while not removing himself an inch from her side, began to tire him. He feared one might drop at her feet. "I must bring these above." He looked around for the first time since she'd approached him. Dorothy and Beth were watching them from the far end of the passage.

Once again, the harsh reality of his situation returned. "Shouldn't you be with the ladies?"

"I won't be missed for now. May I come with you, John, even if you won't let me carry one of the buckets? I would love some fresh air."

"No. I'm sorry Desire, but you have to stay here with the other women. We've been instructed to guard you while the other men are at the meeting. You'll have to stay."

"Guard us? Oh. Would I not be safer with you?"

The question's plain intent rocked him like a blow. Its intimacy, its presumption, and her, dare he think it, devotion to him? She could not be any clearer. Was it just a latent reaction to Harlock's attack or was there something in her eyes, in her manner, that made her open to him. Just to him. "Please don't," he pleaded. "Can you not see it's hard enough for me . . . knowing my position."

The note in his voice caused her to draw back.

"You must not. You, you can't Desire, that's all."

"May I speak with you later then? I only want to discuss what happened yesterday. You see, I can't talk to anyone else about it."

"Yes, I suppose so."

"It will have to be somewhere we won't be overheard."

"That won't be easy," he said as he climbed, leaning into the ladder, his hands occupied with the pails. Three rungs from the top, his toe caught.

He teetered. The buckets sloshed.

He righted himself and swung the buckets forward to the deck with a thud, their momentum propelling tiny showers of slop which rained on the deck around him.

He looked down. It had been close. Desire was looking up with a pretty smile on her pink lips, unaware of the danger. *Lord, she is beautiful* is all he could think as she waved and walked away.

September 23rd – Forenoon Watch

The morning meeting on the upper deck was becoming raucous. With every point raised, ten more germinated. Edward's pen skittered across the parchment.

Debate raged over the size and number of fresh water sources sufficient for household use and irrigation. The shortage of fresh water on the ship had made everyone unusually sensitive to its importance. Scouting parties would need to be given specific direction so that none of the necessities would be overlooked.

William eyed Christopher Martin warily. Martin's expression alternated between bemusement and haughtiness as he leaned against the rail at the fringe of the gathering, his body language signalling indifference to the meeting's subject matter.

"I think we can move on," said Carver. "Myles Standish would like to discuss the defensive positioning of the town."

Myles strode to the front and the group fell silent. He was no missionary, no farmer, no humble man of God. He was a soldier, a warrior. Their worlds could not have been further apart. His frame was easily twice that of the other men; his movements were deliberate, ominous in their efficiency.

"I will train each of you in the proper care and use of your muskets." Myles punctuated his opening remarks with a few jabs of his meaty fingers in their direction. "We will practice our swordsmanship. Today, however, we discuss our defences. It is crucial we have a high vantage point on which to position our cannon, ideally with a view of all surrounding countryside as well as any approach by water. As for –".

There was a disturbance in the crowd. William leaned in to whisper to Carver, "It's Martin, deciding to join us after all."

Carver nodded and stepped forward to intervene, then retreated. "I think we should allow everyone the chance to speak."

Myles didn't yield the floor, regardless. Martin strutted like a cock before the group. He lifted his arms repeatedly, reinforcing the resemblance. "Have you heard enough? Did you come here for the promise of a meager share and seven years' toil for your overlords in England? I was a thriving merchant in England. I'm not content with a few scraps. The new world ahead is vast and unoccupied. Why settle for a pebble when we, as the first, can have mountains. What can stop us from taking as much as we want? Wake up peasants! We aren't in England anymore. Do you think the King, his Bishops and his Magistrates have power to watch you still? We are free to be wealthy, powerful men."

Carver's face turned crimson. "Our patent is for New England and we've made contracts willingly with our backers. We made those agreements in good faith, regardless of their imperfection and incompleteness. Furthermore, the King has provided the patent and you will be held accountable under English Law, sir."

"Those who side with me will have their own law. I say we have the right to more than is laid out in that contract," shouted Martin, trying to rally support from the agitated men. "Besides, the contract was unsigned. You have no contract!"

That was enough. William stepped past Carver, occupying the space between Martin and his audience, Bible in hand. "We did not undertake this exodus to live in a lawless society governed only by greed and a lust for supremacy. You are tempting these men into a life of anarchy, of violence – verily a Dante's inferno. You may have drifted far from our course, but I won't stand quietly while you solicit others to follow you."

Martin laughed. "*You* won't? Their will is their own! I invite any man to join me in continuing to Virginia where we can live as free men instead of slaving for the Adventurers. There we shall have a proper chance to prosper. Is it a sin to want better for one's family? To be raised out of the squalor and toil that so far has served only to hasten a meeting with our maker? I'm a godly man, but the fearful chains of servitude that bound me in England have no weight upon me here! Follow me and you shall know what it is to be truly free!"

If Martin expected his exhortations to sway them, he was mistaken. The others eyed him, silent and reproachful.

"There is no support for you here, Martin," said William.

"You elected this man above me?" Martin gaped at the crowd incredulously, poking William in the chest. "This man lied to you." He gave William a disdainful look. "He's given you false hope – did you not hear me before? You have no patent for New England!"

"What does he mean, William?" said Moses Fletcher. "William, correct this ingrate – we have a patent, do we not?"

William sighed. Why Moses, he thought. The man most loyal to him, most trusting. A wave of guilt washed over him. Why had he kept the trouble with Thomas Weston and the patent a secret?

"We have a patent and a contract," said Carver. "We argued over a few points, all in our best interest, and we have sent a letter to the Adventurers reassuring them of our continued goodwill. It will be signed by them shortly and they expect us to proceed as planned. As for a contract, the King has issued the patent for New England giving us full right to plant ourselves there. You in the congregation know full well why we can't go to Virginia. It's the reason we undertook this voyage in the first place."

A cacophony assaulted William's ears as congregants shouted their concerns. Carver shouted back, but in truth, William knew Carver's response was only muddying the matter. Once again Martin had shamed him. A part of him could accept being physically overpowered by the man, but to be whipped by the very achievement for which he was proudest in this endeavour – the negotiation of the patent – was too much. He felt drained. He ran his fingers through his hair. Intellectually and spiritually he was a member of the inner circle of the church. The negotiation of the patent had cemented his belonging and proved his leadership. Yet here he was, feeling exposed and naked before the men who had entrusted their lives and families to him.

William held his head high, trying to make eye contact with those closest to him as he eased his way through the crowd. Though they had quieted he knew they now had suspicions. He had to make a quick decision as he nudged past the last man, whether to take up a position on the rail or go below in a dramatic exit. Martin was gloating. William decided he couldn't leave. It would only make him look more guilty. He turned to face the crowd, legs apart, hoping to affect an air of approachability. Behind him, his hands turned white as they gripped the railing.

Prince ignored Martin, who was hoping to catch his attention, and approached William with hand extended. William took it gratefully. "Well done, William. I think you and Carver have won the day against Martin and his faction. A true purpose faithfully executed will always trump the shallow pursuit of wealth and power. "

William smiled, but it felt like another lie. Carver hadn't been entirely honest and he hadn't corrected him. This was a temporary reprieve at best. What would remain of his reputation when Moses and the others discovered the truth about their predicament?

September 23rd – Afternoon Watch

John Howland tried to break away from Edward and Brewster once news of the morning meeting had been shared. Ordinarily, he would have been happy to listen to these interesting and influential men, but when their discourse switched to talk of old matters in Leyden, his mind drifted. He wondered where he could be alone with Desire.

In truth, he had been singularly preoccupied with Desire since she had proposed speaking with him in private. He wondered now whether, by the word *private*, Desire meant *alone*, or just out of earshot of the others. Would she not be terrified to be alone with another man given what happened just yesterday? Yet he wanted so badly to be with her again that he immediately dismissed the concern.

William startled him from his thoughts, putting a hand on Brewster's shoulder to interrupt the conversation.

"I've just come from the Master's," he said in an undertone that John could nevertheless hear. "I wanted a private word after the meeting, to make it clear he isn't to take direction from anyone but Carver or myself regarding our plotted course."

"Of course," said Brewster. "We don't want to suddenly find ourselves in Virginia."

"Harlock was up there, giving me the evil eye." William shook his head. "The effrontery of that vile man! He fashions himself some kind of hawk and me his prey."

"Yes, a worse example of God's creation I have never seen," agreed Edward. "But, William, regarding Martin's interruption . . . we must write that letter to the Adventurers and send it back with the ship. Especially now that Carver has said we already did so. Truthfully, William, we should have settled the contract long before leaving Dartmouth."

"Yes, I agree," said William. "Have you a fair hand, John?" he said, turning to him.

"Yes," John replied, his mind intent on catching Desire's attention.

"Well, we'll speak to Carver about having you make some copies."

"Thank you, I'd be pleased," he said distractedly.

He moved to where he could catch her eye.

She excused herself and floated toward him. Her face lit up. She was about to speak when he came to his senses. They couldn't be seen leaving together. He dropped his smile and nodded toward the ladder. If they were lucky, it would now be quiet on deck.

Speaking as quietly as he could, his head down, he whispered his hastily arranged plan. "I'll go first, bring a cloak and follow. Starboard side, toward the bow. You'll find a cache of barrels there – meet me behind them."

September 23rd – Afternoon Watch

Desire lowered her head and kept walking, a brief touch on his cuff signalling that she understood. She held her breath, hoping for stealthiness, but the blood coursing through her seemed to run so fast and so loud that surely others could hear her. She was taking an extraordinary risk, one that put John in peril as well. But to be with him, free from prying eyes, nothing else mattered.

She watched surreptitiously as John took the lower rungs of the ladder.

The chatter continued, everyone voicing their views on the morning's business. She tucked her gloves under her cloak and ambled toward the ladder. She wanted to fly to John so as not to lose a second of time with him, but that would attract attention. Near the ladder she stooped as though checking her shoe, took a quick look to be sure Katherine wasn't watching, and then nonchalantly reached for a rung and began climbing.

"Miss Desire, I think you ought not to be going up there alone," came a small voice from below, just as she was about to step onto the deck. She froze, turning slowly to see her speaker, then thawed with relief. It was young Will, the Carvers' other servant.

"Oh, I'm not alone. I'll be perfectly fine, Will. Thank you for your concern," she sang down.

"Beg your pardon but I didn't see anyone with you. The men say that the women aren't to be left alone." Will fidgeted, nervous at contradicting his superior, even if she was only the ward of his employer.

Desire worried that he would go and inform Carver if she ignored him. She glanced to starboard to see if she could see John, but he was hidden. "Oh dear, Will. Come up and see for yourself if you must," she said with as much confidence as she could.

"Well I reckon that I must, miss, or I'll be in trouble for letting you go." Will muttered and shook his head as he climbed the ladder, no doubt conversing with himself on the foolishness of women.

Reaching the top he looked around. "Miss Desire, there's no one here to accompany you. I'd appreciate it if we could go back down now."

"Well, Will, now that you are here I am accompanied and truly do need some air." Searching for a solution to the new problem of how to rid herself of little Will, she decided to walk to the railing in hopes John could rescue her. "Let's do a circuit of the deck before going below again. Shall we?"

"I shouldn't be up here myself. I'm going to be missed about my chores."

"I won't keep you long Will and I would be very grateful. There isn't much air below and I do like to feel wide open space about me, being packed in so tight all the time." Desire reached for Will's hand and pulled him with her.

John spotted her as soon as she reached the rail. When he saw that she wasn't alone, his smile sagged. He approached nonetheless, feigning surprise at seeing them.

"It's good to see I'm not the only one taking some air. How is it you are up on deck, Will?" asked John, ruffling his apprentice's hair.

"Miss Desire wished to get some air and I had to come with her seeing as how she can't wander about on her own. She won't come back down," said Will, with a tone that suggested John should talk sense to her.

John ignored the hint. "I'll watch over Miss Desire and you may return to your duties. I have a bit of free time and she will be perfectly safe with me." John bowed dramatically to Desire. "Would that be acceptable? You needn't fear you're putting me out."

Taking her cue she said, "Yes that would be very much appreciated. I needn't keep Will any longer in that case. Thank you John, and thank you Will, for your escort and worry." She turned toward the rail ignoring them both. Will abandoned her reluctantly to John.

The crew working the deck had more important matters to attend to than their passengers' secret liaisons. As soon as Will's head disappeared below the hatch, John grabbed her hand and pulled her into a small space between the barrels and the railing. They were just close enough to the forecastle to be out of the wind.

Laughing about their little play, they lost all shyness and she abandoned the pretences concocted for the meeting. They were closeted together in the alcove, their hands still joined. At first, she wanted nothing more than to look at him, their eyes both alight with discovery. Then an urgency came upon him as much as her, their fingers intertwining, squeezing, then decoupling only to travel up each other's wrists and arms, each new territory a revelation. They pulled each other closer.

Time stopped in their small world, untroubled by the dull routine of seafaring taking place around them. She spoke softly, moving her gaze from his eyes to his full lower lip, "Despite everything that happened yesterday, I have hardly been able to think of anything but you ... and how wonderful it felt when you held me."

John searched her eyes, leaned forward, hesitated, pulled her infinitesimally closer, then hesitated again.

"Desire, you are so beautiful and graceful and the kindest being I have ever met," his voice was tight with suppressed need. "You can't know how much I want to hold you again. But ..." His body trembled.

"But what John? Do you not like me? If you say you don't, I'll tell you I can see the truth in your eyes. I have so little time to tell you what I'm thinking. Who knows when we'll be able to see each other alone again?"

"Desire, I do want to hold you. I want so badly to hold you . . . and kiss you, but I can't. You know what I am. You shouldn't be here with me. We can never marry. Not while I am nothing to Carver but his servant. Two more years. It's too much to ask you to wait, but if you did, I would prove myself to you. I'm an educated man, Desire. I had greater prospects once and it is only through misfortune, like your own, that I find myself as I am now. I will prosper, and I will make a good husband to you, then, but Carver will never allow this. This will ruin you."

Her eyes stung with the rejection. She wanted to slink away knowing how much, and how wrongly, she had exposed her feelings. Unexpected boldness possessed her to keep speaking. "Do I get no choice in the matter? If not, then I won't wait for what I may never get."

She leaned forward and kissed him before he could pull back or protest. At the touch of her lips on his he did neither. He stilled. He breathed her in. Her lips parted and hovered against his with invisible energy. She tried to commit his smell and taste to memory. And then, like two poles of a magnet, their lips locked together with a crushing lust. She met his urgency with equal intensity, with a need to go deeper, to be pulled by a will beyond her own, past their lips and tongues until they were wholly inside each other.

Reluctantly, in time, they parted. Each thrilled with excitement. Guilt, too. Desire flushed at her own brazenness.

"We had better go down before someone comes," she said, looking around for the first time and realizing that they might have been seen. "We should go together," she said, squeezing his fingers. "Will likely told someone you were watching out for me."

"Little did he know it was me from whom you needed watching," he said, dazed.

Invitation

"William, I can't tell you how I know, but Mr. Prince is responsible for Mr. Martin creating the disturbance today at the meeting," said Dorothy.

"You are set against Mr. Prince." He patted her hand. "You needn't be. I'm sure he feels badly for that first day. He should join us for tea, perhaps tomorrow, or the next day, and you can see for yourself how he values our cause."

"No, William. He means us harm. I can't prove it to you, yet, but he does. Did Mr. Martin not try to undermine your arrangement with the Adventurers or turn our friends from New England? Why would Mr. Martin do this? What would he gain? Mr. Prince put him up to it."

"Martin bears us an ill will that began even before the loss of his Governorship. A man like him feels out of place among men with love for each other. He doesn't understand sacrifice for a higher purpose. Greed and jealousy made him do it."

"Mr. Prince mustn't come for tea. You mustn't trust him."

William waited for Prince and Stephen Hopkins to finish their conversation before approaching Prince at his desk. The man was popular. William felt lucky to have his support.

Prince stood and shook Stephen's hand in parting. He shuffled some papers and was reaching to pull a map from the wall behind him when he spied William waiting patiently. "William, a pleasant surprise. What occupies you today?"

"I thought it might be nice for you to join Dorothy and me for tea this evening."

"That is a fine offer, thank you indeed."

"She has it in her head that you are not our friend. She holds it against you, I'm sure, that I asked you to watch over her in Plymouth. She thinks you are behind the foolery Martin caused the other day. It's preposterous. It would be nice to repair things between the both of you."

"I am pained to hear that she thinks ill of me. Of course we must work to dispel such a gross error in perception. How sad she cannot see that I am doing just the opposite. It is you whom I support. When I overhear others speak against you, I remind them how critical your role was in engineering the patent, with Thomas Weston's help, and that he and the Adventurers must be relied upon. All hope for the plantation's survival is lost if you are not united."

"It's clear to all that you are with us. I thank you for it. Dorothy will see it too," said William, newly energized by Prince's support. He leaned against the cannon and looked over the growing number of parchments swinging with the motion of the ship. The steady back and forth had worked to unfurl one of the rolls, which was now poised to fall. He reached up to secure it.

"Come look at this, William," said Prince, brusquely steering him to the desk, "This is a map of the New England coast and New Amsterdam. You are proposing to disembark somewhere along here, are you not?" He passed his finger over the area just north of the Hudson.

"Yes. I have not seen this map before. I should like to study this more."

"It's still crude. I shall work my way along the coast adding detail. Now tell me, how would Dorothy come up with such an idea?"

The rapid shift in the conversation tripped up William, who was still poring over Prince's map, studying the markings indicating rivers. "She . . . this is extraordinary! Surely these lands will prove abundantly fertile."

"William, where did Dorothy come up with this notion that I am not to be trusted?" pressed Prince.

William finally looked up from the map. "She won't say."

"You don't suppose she is plotting the failure of the venture, herself? She was desperate to get home to your dear child."

William's eyes had fallen to the map again, but he suddenly looked at Prince in full. The impossibility of his question now exerted a far stronger gravity on his attention than the intricate spiderwebs spreading from the Hudson.

"I say plotting. Wrong word. I mean hoping for, of course, as there is nothing she could do to affect its success or failure either way," smoothed Prince. "Turning you against me may just be her attempt at a plan, seeing how helpful I could be to you."

"Oh, I don't think Dorothy could be capable of anything like that," he said. "She is just protective of me, that is all. Speak to her. She will see how earnest you are."

September 24th – First Dog Watch

"Desire, wait. I'll help you feed the animals and collect the eggs," said Dorothy. She took one of the baskets from Desire's hand and stepped over the lip to the prow. The ship rolled and Dorothy fell against the starboard wall of the narrow corridor.

"I've heard something new about Mr. Prince," said Desire. "He is trying to get a copy of the letter that John is transcribing. The one the congregation will send to the Adventurers."

"How did you find out?"

"He's been asking what it will say and where John will be scribing it."

"Hmm," said Dorothy. She pushed the goats gently to the corner of the pen and raked the damp straw through the lower edge of the netting.

Desire pulled fresh straw from the bail and scattered it.

"You must tell Deacon Carver. Will he believe you?" asked Dorothy.

"And let him know I'm spying? Interfering in men's business? No. He treats me as his own daughter."

"Then there is no one we can trust who will stop Prince."

"I can trust John. He can tell Father Carver."

"Remember, he is the Deacon's servant first, not yours. You can't depend on his loyalty," said Dorothy, reaching under a warm hen and gently retrieving an egg.

"But, I can."

The surety in Desire's voice gave Dorothy pause. She laid the egg in her basket and looked at Desire. Something was different with her, but she didn't know what.

"Desire, I want to ask … Deacon Carver and the rest of the council are arranging your marriage. William is meeting the Deacon again tonight if the seas don't worsen. Have they chosen Gilbert? Is it him?"

The ship plunged forward and Desire grabbed Dorothy's arm for support as she pitched ahead. "It may be. Gilbert acts as though it is. But, I haven't heard."

"Can you love Gilbert? Answer me plainly."

"What does it matter? I will have to marry him." The prow fell and the goats bleated in response. Desire's heels lifted.

"Can you love him?"

"No! I dread it. I pray that God guides their choice."

They both grabbed the netting as the prow fell sharply into another trough. The seas were building.

"Then it must not be him," said Dorothy. "I know what it is to be broken by the rules of the Church." A wave of impact vibrated through their feet. "The Deacon and Elders know nothing, or care nothing, of our needs!" The ship groaned, collecting itself before falling heavily against the sea once more. "I will get Jonathan back, but if you marry Gilbert he will rob you of all joy and spirit. You will never recover it."

"How can I go against them?"

"Follow the word of the Bible. You believe in the resurrection. God is with you." The roar of the ocean was deafening. Dorothy raised her voice. "William has said many times that man's understanding of God's word is incomplete. How can our husbands and fathers pretend to know everything that is right when your heart is telling you clearly they are wrong?" Desire moved closer to the wall to hold a shackle for support. Dorothy stood where she was, feet planted. "You once judged me for fighting to be with Jonathan, but can you see now that we have to rely on ourselves, and each other. We must act, even if we can't do it openly. We must be the current beneath this ship, and change our course unseen."

"I don't want to disappoint anyone," said Desire.

"I don't want you to disappoint yourself."

Desire's voice rose above the groan of the ship. "Nor do I."

September 24th – First Dog Watch

"Katherine, do you want the eggs?" asked Dorothy.

"It's too rough to pickle them tonight. When you collect your rations Edward will put them somewhere safe."

Dorothy swayed toward the hold, almost bumping into Prince as he approached his desk.

"Sit, Dorothy."

"I have to get below," she said trying to edge past him.

"Sit down." He smiled and extended a long, smooth hand toward the stool opposite his.

Warily, Dorothy acquiesced.

"Your husband says you don't trust me and that perhaps we should get to know each other."

Dorothy looked around for William.

"Please, relax."

His hand fell on hers before she could withdraw it. He pressed, grinding her palm into the wood. His eyes smiled.

"This can be a *quick* visit. Tell me how you heard of my conversation with Mr. Martin?"

"Did you speak with Mr. Martin?" She looked him in the eye and smiled pleasantly back.

"You're not looking so pretty these days. I hear you had an accident."

He waited, nibbling at the nails of his other hand.

"Dorothy, who has been telling you tales? With whom are you allied?"

His hand pressed harder, splinters pricking her palm. The *Mayflower* was both pitching and rolling now, her movements unpredictable. The pain in her hand made Dorothy queasy. But she was unbowed. *Let him hurt me. Let him push harder. He will not see me beaten.*

Prince crossed his legs, maintaining the pressure on Dorothy's hand. "Harlock passes my desk every now and then. He's a big fellow isn't he?" He spat out a cuticle. "He likes women, more than I do. I don't trust them." He twisted his wrist, bolts of pain shooting up Dorothy's arm. "They require lessons in obedience. I can make things uncomfortable for you and the people you love. Mine is the upper hand."

She didn't try to hold it in. Happily she yielded to the urge, leaning across his desk for better effect. His flailing hands were too late – the vomit hit him square in the chest.

"Make your excuses to William," she said, wiping her mouth. "The invitation for tea is withdrawn."

Courting

*T*he *Mayflower* rhythmically rose and fell. Overnight the seas had laid down, the roar of their attack in the night reduced to melody. So great was the change from only hours earlier that it was as though the Atlantic herself needed respite. Desire hung back from the brazier and sorted through her provisions while waiting for Deacon Carver to finish his conversation with John Alden. Eventually the Deacon stood and patted John Alden on the back. Mary swooped in with her pot of water and set it to boil. The common-way was crowded this evening.

Desire plunked her basket down and extracted an onion. John Alden sidled up next to her.

"May I help to fetch anything?" he stammered.

"We have everything we need, thank you."

He knelt and watched her peel the onion. She smiled and reached in front of him to pass Katherine's servant the salt beef. "Will you soak that, Anna?"

"If there is anything at all that needs doing, please, just ask," Alden said.

"Thank you, Mr. Alden. It isn't necessary, as you know. We don't mind preparing the single men's meals."

"You are a generous woman. I truly appreciate it."

She tipped her head at him and sliced into the onion. He stood and moved behind her.

Onion sliced, she glanced over her shoulder. Alden was still there, hovering. He gave her a knowing, unsettling wink. She turned away quickly and needlessly reworked the onion. Had John told him about the kiss? Was he teasing her?

Anna shooed him off, needing more room around the brazier. Desire sent her a grateful look.

With the onions and beef finally simmering, Desire leaned back and crossed her legs. Dorothy joined them at the brazier. She looked exhausted.

"I'll ask John tonight," Desire whispered.

Dorothy squeezed her hand.

September 30th – Second Dog Watch

Alden's expression niggled at Desire as she stacked the last of the clean dishes. When she finally she sat down with Priscilla at the capstan she was determined to ignore Alden, who lingered nearby and cleared his throat.

"Did you hear William and Dorothy arguing again?" asked Priscilla, recapturing her attention. "Everyone's been whispering about it. She's obviously been hit in the mouth. Her lip is still swollen."

"It wasn't William. Is that what they're saying?"

"Well, he did lie about there being a patent," said Priscilla. "I'm not sure he should be the Assistant Governor."

Alden coughed loudly; they turned to look. He raised his hand in greeting. "Are you both well this evening?" he said, stepping forward.

Desire nodded before turning away, intent on resuming her conversation with Priscilla.

Priscilla continued to watch him over her shoulder.

"Shame on you, Desire. He wanted to talk and thought you invited him to do so. The poor man. Look at him, embarrassed, wondering if the other men witnessed his blunder. I feel for him."

Priscilla concluded her remonstration with a pinch on Desire's arm and, getting to her feet, tossed Alden a smile. "We are very well, sir. It is you we must worry about, with that cough of yours."

He was grateful. Eyes reignited, they wolfishly swept across Priscilla's stomacher and up her slender neck. Priscilla stretched taller. Desire stood and elbowed her.

"My cough is nothing that a kind smile from a beautiful young woman won't remedy. And, now that I have that, I can leave you both in peace as you are clearly enjoying each other's company." He was speaking to Desire, but sliding his eyes sideways to Priscilla.

"You needn't go. We must meet formally. I am Priscilla Mullins and this is Desire Minter."

"And I am John Alden, at your service, both of you. Desire and I spoke earlier," he said raising his eyebrow and bowing to her.

"Yes," she said with a curtsy.

"You must both call me John. After all, we've only each other for company until another ship joins us; a small party on the edge of a vast wilderness. We're bound to be close friends, perhaps more, before long.

Desire coloured with irritation.

Priscilla batted her eyes and piped up before Desire could answer. "It is very daunting and yet very exciting when you speak of it like that, John. I never imagined I would be part of such a great adventure, one of the first to populate the new world. Who knows what we shall really find there. Does it scare you at all Mr. Alden – I mean, John?" Priscilla tittered. "You seem very brave."

"You suggest the peril will be all his and the novelty all yours," said Desire to Priscilla behind her hand.

Priscilla gave her an annoyed look.

"I have no doubt we shall discover many queer customs and environs," agreed Alden. "As for fear, I have none. God is with us in this quest. And all that shall come he has already prepared us for. Isn't that right, Desire? Isn't that what providence suggests? Why should we be afraid?" Alden crowed.

"I am afraid," said Desire quietly. "It is sometimes God's will that we shall die, whether we are doing his work or not. And God forgive me, but I am not ready to leave this world for the next."

"No one is going to die," said Priscilla, vexed at the effect of Desire's morose tone on their pleasant conversation. "Just look at how prosperous Virginia has become."

There was an awkward silence. Desire looked behind her to see who might have overheard and then tugged at Priscilla's sleeve. They shouldn't be talking to Mr. Alden like this. If Katherine or Gilbert noticed, she might have to stop seeing Priscilla altogether.

John Howland appeared over Alden's shoulder, a broad smile on his lips that Desire knew was hers and hers alone. Her tension melted.

"Alden, my friend, what have these two ladies got you talking about? Needlework? The latest dress fashions likely to be popular in New England this year?" He gave her a mischievous wink.

"As a matter of fact, we were discussing how important bravery will be, given the many dangers ahead. Were we not, Miss Priscilla?" said Alden, giving John a playful shove. "And Miss Desire and I were just becoming acquainted with each other's beliefs."

"That's not fair, Mr. Alden. You imply we have different beliefs. And perhaps we do. I believe in the reformed Church and I practice according to the true written word of the Bible. I simply meant I have no wish to die before I've had more of this life. I've seen too much death already," she added.

John leaned toward her. She badly wanted to take his hand.

"Alden, you're too careless with a woman's feelings. Pardon us ladies, but I must drag him away for a minute," he said bowing to Priscilla, and then to her.

She held his gaze as long as was seemly and then, half-turning to Priscilla, made her excuses to leave. Begging tiredness. She turned to look at John. "It is my turn to check the livestock tonight. I'll need your help, if Katherine doesn't have any other duties for you, if you please." Addressing him as a servant seemed so unpleasant, but she would make it up to him.

"I'd be happy to. Come and get me when you're ready." John turned and motioned for Alden to follow.

Instead of lying down as she had suggested she must, she sat next to Katherine by the Brazier. She knew Priscilla would see her, but when it came to following through, the thought of spending more time in the dark and cramped space of her bunk was unbearable. It was far preferable to watch John and count the minutes until she could be with him again.

"Desire, lean close," said Katherine with a sly smile. "I've overheard Father Carver's plans," Katherine winked.

"I saw you speaking with John just now and the feeling you have for him is plain," said Katherine seriously, taking her hand.

Trepidation mingled with confusion. Katherine's expression was at odds with the crime Desire knew she had committed. She couldn't defend herself if she had been seen kissing him.

"It's John they are considering."

Desire blinked, trying to take it in.

"You look relieved. I thought it would please you. I care about you like you are my own daughter."

"Isn't he beneath me? I thought for certain you wouldn't approve."

"Father Carver thinks his future prospects will be very good. But, don't let on that you know until he tells you himself. I'm not supposed to know."

"I couldn't be happier, Mother Katherine. I am in disbelief. I can tell you now, I would not want any other. I feel as though I've known him all my life." She couldn't stay still. Bouncing onto her heels and squeezing Katherine's hands she looked over at John with a bursting heart. How could this really be happening?

"It's early still. John must agree to the match as well. Remember not to be too forward until things are formally agreed upon. You may need to rely on other suitors. Now, sit down. You're creating a scene bouncing around like that. You've too much vigour." Katherine pulled her to the deck and handed her the mending.

"And I was so worried you'd say he was beneath me, but you can see he isn't," she said, still in disbelief that life could be this fair.

September 30th – First Watch

"Katherine, I'm going to feed the animals. It is my turn," said Desire nonchalantly. The seas picked up again while she waited for John.

"Oh dear, it's too rough. You should have gone earlier. We'll have to ask one of the men to go instead."

"I'm perfectly fine going, besides, I want to check the goats. I noticed yesterday while milking that one had injured his leg. Someone else won't know which one it is," she pleaded.

"Well, I don't feel right about it," hesitated Katherine.

"John could come with me – and he could lift the feed and straw."

"John? Alright. John!" called Katherine. "Where is John, Anna?"

"I'll go and fetch him, Mistress Carver."

John Howland was back almost immediately, walking quite steadily despite the sawing of the deck. "What can I help with Katherine?"

"Will you please go with Desire to feed the animals? One of the goats is lame. Don't take too long and be sure she doesn't get hurt."

"I certainly will. Are you ready Miss Desire?" John said naturally.

She took his arm and felt his rapid pulse beneath her fingertips. She floated beside him like a county dancer in a rhythm to match the rise and fall of the deck. When she stumbled, his arm would encircle her waist and she felt him close. She was in ecstasy over the possibility of soon being Mrs. John Howland. Her whole life had changed. He would protect her and she would care for him. She would never be alone again.

"I wasn't going to let anything keep me from being with you again," she said, a coy smile playing on her lips. He lifted her hand to help her over the sill to the prow. "Why didn't you say anything to me earlier about us?"

"I didn't want Alden and Priscilla to read my feelings too plainly, to be honest. If I hadn't pulled Alden away, I might have taken you in my arms, seeing how miserable you looked," whispered John.

She stopped and braced one arm against the wall of the narrow corridor. "I don't care if they know. I love you, John. I'm certain of it."

He lifted her chin and searched her eyes in the orange lantern light. "You don't know what you're saying. It thrills me to hear it, but be careful. We might be overheard." He pulled her further into the shadows. "I need to hold you, just for a moment, Desire." He pulled her close, breathed in the smell of her hair and brushed his cheek lightly against it. "How is it that before I kissed you I was content to only look at you and listen for your sweet voice? Now, my arms ache to hold you and my lips – my lips, cracked and bruised, can only be healed by the very thing that wounded them."

When he let go, she took both his hands and walked backwards. The goats skittered as they approached.

"I want so badly to be yours," she whispered.

A black shape suddenly appeared behind John. She stifled a scream and John turned at once to shield her. The shape stumbled forward, bounced off a stout beam and into the weak light from the corridor.

"Beth!" she exclaimed in relief.

"Mrs. Winslow? Are you alright?" John let go of one of Desire's hands and lunged forward to take Beth by the elbow. "Steady."

"What are you doing here?" said Desire, hand held to her chest.

"It's my turn to feed the animals," said Beth.

"It's mine." Desire grabbed her by the other elbow and then stepped sideways to catch her balance as the ship plunged forward again and rolled to port.

John cocked his head. "Can you make it back to the common-way without me? You're both unsteady. I'll stay and feed the animals."

"I . . . yes I can," said Desire.

She took Beth's hand and cast a winsome look over her shoulder.

"I just have something else I have to tell John first. Wait here. Hold the beam."

She stepped drunkenly back into the manger. "John, remember what you told me about Prince? Tell Deacon Carver. Prince may be Thomas Weston's brother. He's acting against us. Will you?" She wanted to kiss him.

"Go now, before she is suspicious."

"Desire?" Beth called.

"I'm just showing John which goat is lame." She took John's hand. "I love you," she whispered.

"I love you," he whispered back tenderly. He cocked his head. "Wait. What are you doing involved in such dark business?"

Kiss and Tell

*D*esire placed the tray of porridge on the clear space between Moses Fletcher and Richard Warren. She kept a steady eye on Prince. He and Harlock were deep in conversation, just out of hearing.

"Take this Moses, dear. Careful it's hot still." She kissed the top of his head. "I put in extra raisins for you." She had a soft-spot for him. The damp had seeped through his bones and washed the colour from his skin. He shivered and held the hot bowl to his chest.

"We should move you somewhere else. It's so drafty here," she said.

"I'll keep. Thank you, Darling."

She handed Richard his bowl and tipped her head to him.

At Prince's desk, Harlock's head bobbed up and down. Prince inscribed something in his brown leather booklet before snapping it shut and tucking it into his waistcoat. Harlock backed away and turned for the ladder with a grin on his face.

She lifted the platter. Prince was next.

"Your porridge, sir," she said. No raisins for him.

"This side. Place it here." He arranged the parchments to make room.

A sliver of light illuminated his desk. It issued from the porthole, which opened onto the hard, grey waves parting reluctantly alongside the *Mayflower*'s hull.

"Are you not cold?" she asked. "A sailor has neglected to seal the porthole as required."

"No. I want it open."

She deposited the bowl carefully into the space he'd dug in the mountain of paper. "Thank you . . . Desire?" He reached his arm behind her and squeezed her bottom. She straightened and moved back to the front of the desk. Her platter shook and she cursed it.

"Hold there. You'll drop that."

"I'm fine." But he had already scooped the platter with its remaining three bowls out of her hand."

"Come sit."

She was about to protest, but glanced down. A document with the name 'Adventurers' clearly visible lay unfurled before her. She sat. "I'm dizzy, sir. That is all." She brought her hands to her temples, rubbing them slowly while hiding her eyes from Prince. She quickly scanned the paper, her eyes alert for anything of import.

To ... worthy Adventurers,

My own conscience ... will testifie, y^t my end in sending this letter is to protect ye joint investment of the Adventurers. There is much prejudice against you ... whereof ye greater part of ye planters have agreed, to make excuse and send no lading until they receive from you further provisioning and ye rest of the companie from Leyden, for whose cause this bussines .... They plan by means of an article in ye agreemente to breake of their joynte stock with the Adventurers, once they have received − "

Prince yanked her arm from her temple and twisted her wrist. "Do you read girl?" He dragged her up and pushed the platter into her arms. "Do you read?"

"No."

"Don't lie, now. You were reading my letters." His eyes bored into hers.

"I was admiring your pretty hand. That is all."

He spun her around and pushed her away.

He snapped his fingers and a sailor ran from the far dark corner. The sailor jostled her as he passed and her heart drummed. She looked back at him in fear, but after a quick word with Prince, his baggy pants and bare feet were already disappearing up the ladder.

October 8th − Afternoon Watch

"ORDER YOUR MUSKET!"

Even though he knew it was coming, the ferocity of Myles's command startled William. The older boys in front of him jumped as well, and were now exchanging embarrassed smiles. William stiffened to attention, musket erect against his right leg, his left hand grasping the hilt of a sword dangling from his waist. The women were doing the laundry on the other side of the deck and Dorothy, running up and down from the 'tween deck, would be back any moment. He hoped she might see him.

Myles moved through their ranks.

"SHOULDER YOUR MUSKET!"

Chaos ensued as barrels swung left and right, grazing heads, narrowly missing eyes.

"Watch your fellows!" Myles bellowed. He lowered his voice, slowly placing his own musket against his shoulder and cradling the stock in his hand. "This is how I want you to carry your musket on the march. Never tip it back, you may end up blowing your brother's head off behind you. Point the muzzle up at the sky.

"ORDER YOUR MUSKET!" Half of the men ahead of him resumed their starting position. William swung the butt over to his right hip, left hand gripping the barrel. He felt sorry for the men that had blundered. Silence stretched out along the deck and Myles' shadow followed.

"ORDER YOUR MUSKETS!" Myles looked directly at the musket perched firmly against William's hip. William suddenly realized he had assumed the wrong position and clumsily tossed his musket back down against his right boot. There was a simultaneous commotion ahead of him and Myles walked on.

"Now, PORT YOUR MUSKET!"

In spite of his blunder, William was enjoying himself. For the first time in his life, he felt he must be cutting a gallant figure. He turned his head to scan for Dorothy, but she had yet to return.

A clatter erupted to his right. He turned to see Carver's servant Will Latham bend to pick up his musket, almost as long as the youth himself. Beside him, Stephen Hopkins' son Giles was wilting under the weight of his weapon.

George Soule and Elias Story, the two older teens William had noticed on their first departure from England, were listening very intently and having no trouble at all. A good thing, he thought. They needed young, agile defenders.

William started. Myles was still talking, demonstrating how to prime and load the musket. He was halfway through the procedure. A wave of anxiety passed through William, the prospect of forgetting all of these instructions in battle and perhaps blowing his own hand off sobering him instantly. There were more steps than he remembered. It had been a long time since he had held a gun.

"I need to borrow your matchlock," Myles said to John Howland. "Mine's a snaphance – a flintlock. I see you have a snaphance Alden – good man. I assume you can shoot."

"Yes sir." Alden grinned broadly.

William wondered if Prince was a good shot. He had excused himself from the practice session, claiming he didn't need it. Instead, he would discuss maps with the Master. William was happy Prince wasn't around to see his misstep. His support mattered.

"Now measure the exact amount of charge using this pan here." Black powder sintered from the mouth of Myles' pouch as he demonstrated.

"You would now light your wicks," he continued. "Leave a long wick if you need to be ready, but your foe is not yet in sight. If we are in the heat of things, the wick will be short, here, in front of the hammer arm holding it. Just long enough to swing forward and hit the priming pan." Myles pulled the pipe from Moses Fletcher's mouth and lit the wick on the borrowed matchlock. He got a laugh and paused to enjoy it.

"Take aim. Steady yourself, left foot ahead of right."

BAM! The report rocked William. The women gave startled screams and then laughed.

October 8th – Afternoon Watch

"Quickly, climb down to the hold with me," said Desire, shifting the rolled linen to one arm and pulling Dorothy by the hand.

"Let's go to the manger instead."

"No. We might be seen together, or overheard. Mr. Prince isn't drilling with the others."

Dorothy resisted.

"It's important."

They left the washing at the mouth of the hatch. The cold air in the hold pimpled Desire's skin. The ocean vibrated beneath her feet. Only the occasional thump of a shark broke the constant burble of the waves. Neither she nor Dorothy let go the ladder. Dorothy peered at her anxiously though the back side of the rungs.

"He caught me reading a letter on his desk. He suspects me. We can't be seen together from now on or he'll know for sure I'm the one watching him and telling you everything. The letter, addressed to the Adventurers, is meant to prevent our receiving supplies as promised. If they receive it they may break off with us entirely. The Deacon and William must see it if we are to convince them of Prince's perfidy."

The light disappeared. Desire tipped her neck back. Three faces stared down at her. Prince kicked the roll of linen and sheets. Shirts and petticoats rained down on her. "Go," she whispered through the rungs and backed away.   Dorothy disappeared into the shadows behind the ladder.

Desire backed into a crate.   Prince, Harlock and a second sailor she did not recognize descended the ladder at a surprising speed, surrounding her.

Dorothy made a sound.   Prince turned.

"Come on over here too, darling.   There is no sense hiding.   You can't go anywhere that I can't find you."   He pulled Dorothy by the elbow and stood them next to each other.   Desire took her hand and held it tight.

"Deacon Carver tells me that you teach the children.   Is that so Desire? It seems to me you would have to be a good reader to do that."

"I don't."

"Give them a kiss, Harlock, Jobe.   Take your pick.   Take turns, if you like."   Prince stood back and grinned.

Desire tugged Dorothy and together they lunged for the ladder. Harlock swung his meaty arm out and thrust them back against the crate. His wet lips crushed Desire's before they could articulate a scream.   Eel-like his tongue darted out, probing her warm mouth.   His teeth struck hers clumsily.   And then he was off and the other yanked her hair back. Muffled sounds beside her told her Dorothy was receiving the same.

"Come on, dogs.   You've had your fun now."   Prince roughly shouldered both men behind him.   "I hope," he snarled, "that you have learned your lesson.   No spreading lies with those lips, now.   That's not what the lips of young women are for.   Now, thank these men, for their instruction."   He bowed and followed the attackers up the ladder.

Desire grabbed Dorothy, sobbing.   They stayed like that for several minutes until, shakily, they shuffled toward the ladder and lowered themselves onto the scattered linen.   Desire rested her brow against Dorothy's and cried again.

"They can just do this to us! I want them cut apart.   I want to . . ."

"We're going straight to the Master," said Dorothy.   "We'll see they're punished.   We'll tell the Master about Prince.   And, you will tell Deacon Carver what you read.   These lips *will not* be silent.   There is more going on here than men lustful of our dignity.   If the Adventurers are turned against us, they won't resupply us.   We will starve.   And my Jonathan will never come."

October 8th – Afternoon Watch

William listened to the women singing while he polished his musket, his gaze steady on the long horizon.   Occasionally he chimed in with a few verses, but in truth he was many miles away.

Dorothy emerged from the companionway empty-handed. Many of the women were already laying their clean linen on the deck to dry.

Desire, red eyed and puffy-faced, was close behind her. Dorothy looked at him and motioned for him to follow. She was also red-eyed. Breaking from his reverie, he smiled at her, confused. *Why is she at the Master's door…?* She was knocking. *Why is she knocking!*

William jumped to his feet.

Prince opened the door wide and then barred the doorway with a long roll of velum. He smiled at the women but said nothing. The Master looked on quizzically from behind his table. William was mortified.

"I am so sorry Master Jones, Andrew. I confess I am not sure why they disturbed you."

"We are here to complain," said Dorothy, her elbows locked with Desire's.

"Please accept my apologies," interjected William. "This won't happen again. Come, Dorothy. You know this is not proper." He tried to steer her from the door, but she and Desire pushed the velum out of the way and rushed to the Master's desk before he could restrain her.

"Mr. Prince, your sailor, Harlock, and another sailor just accosted us in the hold. It isn't the first time. Tell them, William. We don't care if the Master knows the truth. This time, Mr. Prince cornered us and had the sailors pin us down and take turns kissing us in a beastly way. William, my tooth is loose again. They hurt us. We will have them punished. We need to be protected."

Prince guffawed. "The Master can vouch for my whereabouts. When was this supposed to have happened? I've been here for the better part of the hour and only briefly went down to the 'tween deck for another map."

The Master looked amused rather than angry. William hoped that meant he would overlook this break in protocol.

"You are a liar, Mr. Prince. You are working against the congregation and we know it. William, you must believe me, over him. He means to turn the Adventurers against us and rob us of any chance of supply," said Dorothy.

"Now stop Dorothy. You can't be calling our friend Mr. Prince a liar. Of course I believe some of your story," said William.

"Are you raising this as an official complaint against the conduct of one or more of my sailors, Mr. Bradford?" said the Master.

"I think we must involve Governor Carver, who is also the young lady's guardian, before we decide what should be done. Something should be done. I must believe my wife regarding Harlock," said William, sweat prickling his brow. "Who was the other sailor, Dorothy? What did he look like?"

Dorothy wrapped her arms around Desire. "He was thin, his hair hung over his face. I can't remember any particular feature. Maybe his teeth. He had long teeth. It was dark."

"His name was Jobe," said Desire.

William recognized the description as the sailor that was with Harlock in the gunroom. The hair stood up on the back of his neck. She was telling the truth. He would take pleasure in seeing Harlock's skin flayed. The punishment was long overdue. Perhaps he was wrong not to come to the Master with their earlier troubles. As for Prince, Dorothy wasn't usually this spiteful.

Carver came up behind him, his face a question.

"Ah, now that Governor Carver is with us, the women need to leave and we can discuss the incident," said the Master, coming round from behind the map-strewn desk to gently lead Dorothy and Desire to the door. William hoped Dorothy wouldn't resist.

The Master closed the door. He generously offered them a tip of whisky from the sideboard as William repeated the assertions of the women. Despite the gravity of the story, he took pleasure in the drink and the gentlemanly manner in which the Master received them. He hadn't enjoyed a proper spirit for months.

"William," said Carver, "perhaps we should have a word in private before we discuss what is to be done. Outside, perhaps?"

"Do we need to? Can we not trust everyone here?"

"I think it best, all the same. Desire is my ward."

They slipped out the door and Carver closed it behind them. "William, how much do you really trust Prince? I've been hearing some disturbing things that cause me to doubt him."

"He has shown us nothing but support. He has offered to help carry our letters on his return. He has helped quell rebellious talk from Martin and Billington's camp. I trust him."

"Hmm, I think we should be wary. As for the women, Desire's marriage remains unsettled. If the sailors are punished, we must strive to preserve her independence from any proceedings."

"You mean we are to say only Dorothy was attacked? Then all will know I couldn't protect her. What does that say about my character?" William paused, looking defeated. "It damn well says what is true, doesn't it? *Again* I wasn't there. I'm hopeless. You saw me at musket practice. I'm not capable of anything."

The door opened. "Gentlemen. We've agreed on a punishment. Don't worry. I made recommendations with your interests at heart," said Prince. "The Master trusts my opinion. No need to come back in."

"What?" said Carver, angrily. He looked at William, avoiding Prince's gaze. William felt he should say something.

"What is the punishment to be? It is imperative that the identities of Desire and Dorothy not be revealed. Desire, especially, is to be kept out of it."

"The matter is complete," Prince said sweetly. "The crime won't be made public. The sailors will do extra duties for a full fortnight. They will learn their lesson and no harm will be done to the reputations of the innocent. The Master wanted otherwise, something a little more public, but it would have left a stain − not only on the deck."

"It is not enough," Carver grumbled.

"No. But, I appreciate you thinking of the women's welfare, especially after Dorothy's accusations. It shows your character, Andrew," said William.

The Storm

"*D*orothy, I can't discuss this anymore. We did what we could. Prince actually had the Master punish Harlock and his accomplice in the manner most likely to protect your name. You have him all wrong."

"Can you search his belongings? He has a letter there, proof that he aims to communicate behind your back. He is Thomas Weston's brother. His name isn't even Prince. You've been fooled. Confront him. Have him show you all of his correspondence."

"That is preposterous. Are you trying to turn him against us?"

"I am your wife. You should be taking my word over his."

"Shh." William poked his head into the common-way.

"Seas are picking up," hollered a sailor. "We're closing the hatch on the next bell. Master's order. All passengers below Anythin' you need, best get it. Douse all fires and lanterns. We'll be in the blackness 'til at least tomorrow, longer if the seas stay a boilin'."

"Well, we best prepare for this weather." William kissed Dorothy's forehead. "I'm going to help secure everything. Go carefully and retrieve some tack. We don't know how long this will last."

William said a short prayer for their safety, adding a postscript that Harlock not be among the sailors locked down in the t'ween decks with them. The seas would be ordeal enough.

Carver hollered from across the room. "It may not be safe for those bedded in the common space to remain so once they close the hatch. Find room on the floor of a cabin, where you can wedge yourselves in." He assigned single men and boys to various cabins and enclosed spaces. "Someone has to go and check on the animals! Has anyone done it?"

William had completely forgotten about the livestock. Their bleating and squealing suddenly registered. They needed to be netted in tight.

Carver swayed down the common-way ordering the tying down of various possessions and the lifting of bedding.

Dorothy pocketed her knife. She went straight across to Katherine's to collect the tack that Anna was handing out, then lingered, waiting for Prince to check the ropes binding his desk and trunks, and then disappear into the Chilton's cabin beyond.

The light dimmed to almost nothing as the lanterns overhead were extinguished one by one. She squeezed between the cannon and the wall. All of Prince's leather straps with their maps and parchments were gone. She didn't have much time. She mentally rehearsed the number of steps from here to the opposite side of the common-way and counted the number of doorways back to her own cabin, just in case.

Withdrawing the knife, she sawed the nearest rope and felt a snap. She crouched as low as possible and cut the ropes securing Prince's chest to the walls, and the cannon he shared space with. She could only reach one side; from the other, she would be visible to everyone still clearing the aft half of the deck. She cut the rope securing the lid to the trunk and then see-sawed back across the heaving deck, praying it would be enough.

The hatch above her clicked shut as a voice bellowed, "We're in tight. Clamped 'til it's safe to open 'er."

October 9th – First Dog Watch

Before the light was gone, John checked once more on Desire. She was still there, curled on the deck just inside her cabin door. Little Will and the More children had been lifted to the top bunk and were packed tightly together down the length of the bed, their heads at the outer edge.

A hush fell, punctuated by the movements of a few stragglers feeling for doorways and stepping on fingertips.

Whispering loud enough for everyone to hear, Katherine admonished Carver to finally come into the cabin and settle on the bunk. As he entered, he asked hoarsely, "Is everyone in?"

John answered calmly, "I'm behind you sir. Everyone's in. The five children are up on top. Little Will on this end. Anna is near the hull and Desire near the door. I'll settle on the floor myself and use the door frame for support." He waited until he knew that Carver had climbed into the bunk with Katherine, then knelt next to Desire and reached for her hand.

A warmth like whiskey moved through him when she held it close to her breast. Their eyes had met so frequently in the last hour that it was a relief to finally hold her. Exhausted, Desire's tears anointed their joined hands. With his free hand he stroked her curls until she calmed. The darkness created a cloak for their tenderness and their bodies rejoiced under it, communicating unapologetically. When he lifted her onto his lap he didn't think of his servitude or the impossibility of their future. He only considered how much he loved her – and what a relief it was to have her all to himself.

The swells deepened, spreading terror and sea-sickness throughout the ship. The *Mayflower*'s erratic pitching, the violent crashing of waves against her beam, the high-pitched screams in the tortured rigging, all worked to heighten the primal fear surrounding them. It was as though the black ink of night was conspiring with the endless, heaving Atlantic to threaten them all with oblivion. Some prayed; some cried; some wept.

But he was lost in Desire and she in him. Her head rested on his chest. She traced the lines of his thigh with her fingertips. His own nausea had evaporated, replaced with an overwhelming fascination. He marveled at the shape of her body, the softness of her skin, the naturalness with which their fingers intertwined and mated.

Anna, wrapped in a blanket, stayed tucked into the outer hull. She only occasionally interrupted them by reaching out to squeeze Desire's ankle. Each time, John feared Anna would take her from him, a theft of precious seconds, or worse, that she might discover their dangerous proximity.

The terror of the night drove him like a whip, quickening his need for her. As it built, they grasped and hungered for each other in a frenzy of passion so desperate he wanted to consume her, and be consumed. When she bit his lips and pulled his hair he didn't cry out.

Occasionally they slept and upon waking would begin again, reassuring each other they were still alive.

He was so intoxicated by her that he didn't notice the swells diminishing. When the hatch above unexpectedly flew open and daylight rained upon them, they flew apart, suddenly as aware of each other, and their sin, as Eve with the juice of apple on her lip.

The fresh light proved as blinding as the dark. Their secret was safe.

October 10th – Forenoon Watch

The *Mayflower* continued to plough the waves in heavy seas, but the tension in the rigging ebbed. The worst had passed. A handful of sailors stepped down the ladder carrying armloads of fresh beer.

Blinking at the sudden light, William raised his eyes to the square of leaden sky above, then lowered them to survey the storm's carnage. His friends shivered on the floor, knees curled tight to their bodies. Debris – scattered linen, plates, tools, kegs – lay everywhere. Nothing was where it had been. Nothing was dry.

He spied the More children holding each other in prayer. His chest tightened with emotion and he shuffled toward them. The touch of his hand on Ellen's head summoned fresh tears, washing away the bravery and resolve she had fought all night to keep. He sat and pulled the foursome into a broad hug, reclining slightly so they could lie their tired heads against his chest.

Around him, the women began to search for dry clothes for the little ones, rifling through trunks now haphazardly littering the common area. His own clothes chafed with damp and salt.

The renewed activity of the crew, along with the fresh air from above, offered a fragile illusion of reprieve. Katherine, her back straight, slowly wandered among the men and boys who had emerged from the cabins only to crumple on the wet deck, still weak from seasickness. She prodded them to rise and help wring water from their soaked bedding. Once she managed to invigorate them enough to begin helping themselves, she moved on. Some, still retching over basins, were far from ready.

William accepted a ladle of beer from one of the sailors and mumbled his gratitude.

"It's me, sir. Mr. Ely"

"I'm sorry Ely, it's been a hard night. Please make sure Dorothy gets some. She's in our cabin still," said William, nodding in her direction.

"I did, sir. Don't worry, she's in the stern helping with clean-up."

"I doubt she is, Ely, but thank you all the same."

William leaned back, rested his head against the wall and closed his eyes. The four children gathered on either side of him assumed the same posture. He might have fallen asleep, but a familiar snicker made him snap awake.

Harlock ambled toward him, cursing and laughing at the wretched state of the passengers. Behind him lurked a pair of sailors, one of which was the thin faced demon with long hair draped across his face.

Harlock pretended to trip over Richard Warren prone in the passageway, delivering a kick to his back as he did. Richard writhed like a worm, too worn by the night to even call out.

William gritted his teeth and rose to go to Richard's aid, but the ship tilted and he tumbled sideways onto old Moses. Harlock and his companions turned.

"Well if it isn't my friend William Bradford," he nudged William with his boot. "If you are in charge here, sir, I suggest you clean this filthy deck before the Master sees it. He don't allow the ship's deck to be covered in excrement and filth. And by that I mean you lot." Harlock dug the toe of his boot deep into William's ribs.

Continuing to apply pressure, Harlock turned to Moses and chortled. "We won't have to worry about this bag of bones much longer. What say you, old man? Got anything of value?" He began rifling through the blankets tucked around Moses, retrieving a square of parchment which he tossed to the floor. "Nothing of value? You may be the first I have the pleasure of helping to pitch overboard. When you're gone, I'll help myself to your treasures. I will. You don't believe me, old man?" he asked, smacking him across the face.

The slap further incensed William, winding him tight with rage. He suddenly unsprung, lunging for Harlock's legs. The deck tilted. Harlock's sea-legs were adept and Harlock moved in time with the floor. William missed, rolling wide, just far enough to avoid the kick Harlock aimed at his midriff.

"I am going to particularly enjoy tipping you over the side, Bradford," he hissed, "You like respect – don't ya? The sharks'll pay you their respects. I like to play a particular game. I take bets on who I can drop right into their gaping maw. They'll jump clean out of the water. Oh yes . . . I've got a way with it. I feed 'em one of the little 'uns first. Gets 'em riled up. Tells 'em what's coming. I bet that little skinny one over there will do quite nicely," laughed Harlock, pointing wickedly at Jasper More who, white faced, cowered against his sister.

William quivered, "Leave us! How can you dare to – "

"I'll drop you straight down the beast's throat. You're my lucky one," he boasted to his companions. "Governor of some kind, are you? Or just the Governor's lacky. I'll tell you what Bradford, your possessions aren't the only thing I'll make merry with when you're gone," Harlock nodded to his friends with a pumping motion of his hips.

William gritted his teeth and lunged again, this time going for his throat. Harlock's eyes bulged. He pried William's hands free and threw him to the floor. Harlock dropped to a knee. Leaning in close, he said, "Did you think it would cost you nothing? I dare you to try anything against me again. If you do, I'll silence her, or one of me mates will for me." Harlock beckoned his companions to the ladder with a nod of his head. The trailing sailor kicked over a bucket of vomit before he ascended.

Shamed by his impotence, William hung his head and turned to Moses, "Are you alright, brother?"

"Yes. I'll do. Don't let him get to you, friend. God sees what he does and has plans for him, I can feel it." Moses turned and shouted, "God has plans for you, Harlock. You won't find them so funny."

When William moved to get up, Ely was at his elbow. "Let me help you, sir. Harlock is bad news." Cocking his head, he added, "but the rest aren't all bad. Quite a few are good spiritual souls – rough, I dare say – but raised with the Bible. They don't wish you ill."

"Thank you, Mr. Ely. I can manage." William waddled duck-like toward the overturned bucket and cast about for something to wipe up the mess. Ely and a few sailors were there to help before he could find a spare piece of cloth.

"None of you are in fit shape, Mr. Bradford. We'll empty the buckets. The Master sent us down to make sure you were taken care of. Unless you feel able to climb a ladder and dump these without pitching yourself over too, why don't you let us do this for you?"

The sailors moved through the 'tween decks taking buckets, mopping up excess water, hanging bedding to dry and securing items that had broken free in the night. William made a mental note of each of the sailors who did so and hoped he could repay them.

October 10th – Forenoon Watch

"They could be anywhere," said Dorothy. "One trunk hit our cabin, one is wedged into the capstan, and the boards from his desk are scattered in front of Christopher Martin's cabin." She lifted a sopping blanket and folded it without wringing it. She plunged her hand into a pile of boots and shoes, stirred them and came up empty.

"All of those papers and maps are somewhere in this debris," said Desire. "Don't even read what you find. We can do that later. And stop looking like you are searching."

Dorothy shook out another blanket. A packet fell with a thud. She glanced around before scooping it up and secreting it into her basket under the petticoat and shirt she had stuffed into it before leaving her cabin.

She got Desire's attention with a hiss and held up one finger. A smile loosened her anxious face.

Prince was striding through the passageway, shaking hands and offering help. Dorothy noticed he was also sweeping his eyes across the boards as he walked. She dropped her smile, but he didn't look at her as he passed. Perhaps he hadn't recognized her in the dim light. She watched as he took one handle of his trunk and Deacon Carver the other. Together they heaved and waddled awkwardly toward the cannon-bay. Prince opened the trunk – and just as quickly slammed it shut.

"We have to hurry," Dorothy said, weaving in closer to Desire.

Prince began lifting crates and bedding.

Desire tucked a folded parchment in her own basket. She kicked aside a large, soggy, leather-bound roll. One of Prince's maps.

"Girls, you need to be checking the cabins as you go," shouted Katherine. "Make sure no one is hurt. I can't do it all. And you have missed a whole pile of bedding behind you."

"Yes, mother Katherine." Desire motioned with her head that they should each check a cabin – if only for appearance's sake.

Dorothy poked her head into Beth's cabin. No one was inside, but her pulse leapt. Plastered to the hull behind Beth and Edward's jumbled crates was a stack of parchment. The water had driven most of the contents of Prince's trunk in through the doorway, and either by the shifting of the crates, the direction of the water, or God's goodwill, the letters had remained trapped here.

She stuffed as many as she could into her basket, a few under Beth's mattress and all that she could under their servant's mattress.

Pulling the curtain as she left, she turned and walked straight into Prince's back. She averted her eyes, spun and retreated. But she felt his body turn with her. Wary of being seen running straight to Desire, she casually bent to retrieve a wet shirt and placed it on the growing pile.

As she stood, he was suddenly beside her. She tightened her grip on the basket, moving as fast as she could toward William without breaking into a run. She felt Prince's long fingers spider-like on her arm. She kept walking. He managed to hook his finger over the back edge of her basket, trying to wrench it free or tip it, but she locked it in place with her other hand.

"William?" she said sweetly, hoping to mask her fear.

"What are you doing out here?" William, left off re-hanging a glowing lantern and extended his free hand. He folded her into an embrace and she returned it gratefully, slowly. When she finally looked again, Prince was back at his half-assembled desk.

Stitching

*T*he sharp salt air stung William's eyes. Sea foam skipped across the wave crests, climbing up the *Mayflower*'s hull like an army laying siege to a lonely castle. Few were on deck, but William kept an eye out for eavesdroppers. As an extra measure, he kept Myles Standish, who had just agreed to take some air with him, between himself and the sea. "I need you to keep this to yourself, Myles," he whispered, his fingers nervously playing along the musket in his hand.

"We are doing another musket drill within the week if we get smooth seas. Can this not wait?" Myles took his hand off the rail to clear hair from his eyes.

"I haven't shot a musket before," said William, beckoning Myles to move further from the edge.

"You ... haven't ... shot ... a musket? You have *never* shot a musket?" Myles spat over the side.

"I need the respect of these men. And although I don't expect I'll ever be able to hit something, I can't look like I don't know how to handle a weapon."

"You're damned right it must appear so. A man is no man if he can't handle a weapon. As far as I'm concerned, your books will be useless in New England," reproached Myles.

"Well, I will quibble on that. Prayer and Love of our fellow man, an understanding of history, these things can prove more powerful than the sword. But – will you teach me?"

"Some situations only answer to the sword – or the musket. Admit that and I'll show you. As a military man I've seen enough to know it's true."

William swung the musket back and forth between his hands like a metronome and then offered it to Myles. "I'll admit it."

October 11ᵗʰ – First Watch

Desire couldn't understand John's insistence that they behave coolly to one another around Katherine and Father Carver. After all, it was they who had arranged the courtship. Of course they must observe a certain distance from one another until the wedding, but he was behaving far too formally still. The night on the floor with him played over in her mind so that nothing short of being in his arms, as she had been then, would ever satisfy her. It was hard to stand an appropriate distance away from him; she wanted to breathe him in and feel the heat radiating from his body.

Priscilla squeezed her waist, bringing her out of her reverie. They had a few minutes to spare and were going to sit and stitch with the other women.

"I thought we were going to die the other night. The ship cracked so loudly next to my ear," said Priscilla, shivering at the memory.

"I hope we never go through another like it," lied Desire. She would go through a thousand more if it meant lying with John again, feeling his hard limbs wrapped around her, touching his face, his fingers, his chest, tasting his mouth. She could still smell him on her dress.

"We had John Alden in our cabin. He asked me a lot of questions about you, when we could hear each other over the storm, that is. Mother asked him to change the subject and said it wasn't appropriate to ask young ladies about other young ladies," Priscilla giggled. It seemed to Desire that Priscilla hadn't found the night completely dreadful either.

"He no doubt was thinking of more ways to insult or otherwise offend me," said Desire.

Priscilla lowered her voice to a more conspiratorial tone. "You are lucky to have shared a cabin with John Howland. I would gladly have switched places with you. I know he's your servant, but I think he is quite handsome, and manly, and I certainly think John Alden would have been just as happy talking to you."

"How can you say it?" she stammered, steering Priscilla to a spot between Sarah and Lizzy and away from the topic.

October 12ᵗʰ – Forenoon Watch

"It can work," said Dorothy. "What harm is there in trying?"

"I think it would be best to have the doctor look at that tooth," said William Button. The twelve-year-old doctor's assistant, whom everyone simply called Billy, squirmed a bit and gestured for her to let him leave his cabin.

"The doctor is busy tending to those with the catarrh," she insisted. "You're his assistant."

"Perhaps one of the ladies," he offered, scratching at his ear. "They've more experience with embroidery and darning and such."

She pressed the threaded needle into his hand. "They can't know my tooth is loose. I'm asking you so that no one will know."

He accepted it and motioned for her to sit on the stool by the door.

"Hold the lantern up higher," he said, lifting her arm. "Now what do you want me to do?"

"Press the needle between my front teeth and feed it back on the other side to make a loop. Then go around the loose one and the one behind and keep doing that until you've got them all tied together."

He carefully pressed the needle between her gum and tooth. She winced. They all hurt.

"Tip your head back and lift the lantern again." He fumbled for the free end of the needle in her mouth. "Coming back through."

He pressed the needle next to the loose one. The bolt of pain almost shot the lantern from her hand, driving through her eye as though he'd jabbed the needle into *it* instead. Blood filled her mouth.

"I'm not sure I can do this, Mrs. Bradford."

"I can't lose this tooth, Billy. I've lost my son. If I lose this, what is next? I'm going to make it to New England in one piece – like my son after me. Keep going. I'm alright."

He lassoed the tooth and she let the tears flow.

"Amen, we need to get there soon." Billy said. "These people that are sick need a warm bed and proper food. Even if we can't plant till spring, we'll have plenty more to eat when we get there. We all need that." Billy narrowed his eyes and circled round the three front teeth again.

"You know, I think this will work. It's steadier already," he said, pressing the silk up to her gums and pulling tight.

"May I have more cloves?"

"I think Dr. Fuller should look at this. Your eye doesn't look right on this side. It's puffy and drooping a bit."

"This is all I needed. Did you make those wood carvings, Billy? They're very good." Small wood carvings ornamented the timber shelf above his pallet – a dog, a rabbit, a bird, a cat.

"Yes. The doctor says it's good practice for steadying my hands. If you ever lose that tooth, I once knew a man that whittled a whole set of teeth out of wood."

"Perhaps you can make me a tooth. You are a fine hand."

"Thank you, Mrs. Bradford. My mother liked my carving."

Retribution

*D*orothy hung her spare shift across the clothes line she had cleverly strung between their bunk and the wall shared with the Eatons' cabin. She reached for William's pantaloons. William had forgotten to ask the Master's permission to do another proper wash above deck. The alternative, rinsing and brushing, hadn't made much difference.

Their cabin was one of the smallest. With neither children nor servants, they didn't need the space, except when it came to drying clothes. William's finer clothes lay flat on the trunk squeezed sideways between the bunk and the wall. She moved the chamber pot to the floor and tossed boots and extra shoes to the top bunk. Standing on the edge of the lower bunk, she stretched her arm out and corralled the footwear to pin down the sleeves of William's wet shirt.

Everyone was on deck enjoying some sun, of which they all agreed they had seen far too little. It was the perfect opportunity to skim through her stockpile of Prince's letters for evidence of who the author really was and what he intended. The letters were stashed behind a loose board at the base of the lower bunk. Desire hid those she'd collected somewhere amongst her things. Since the storm, they'd had no time in private to discuss them, let alone read them.

She popped the nail holding the board and ran her hand along the upper edge of wood, her fingernails seeking a purchase. The curtain rail chimed. She turned guiltily and jumped to her feet, pulling a cloth from the bed to cover the loose nail.

He stepped inside, slowly drew the red velvet curtain and tucked it tight against the door frame.

"You remember me?"

She nodded her head.

"Mr. Prince wants his letters back. He knows you have them."

She squeaked her disagreement.

He traced the base of her neck with a finger, backing her into the corner.

"Get them for me."

"William!" she yelled.

Harlock paused and listened for footsteps.

"You deserve to be whipped and I'll enjoy watching," she said, struggling and failing to keep the tremor from her voice.

His fingers clamped lightning quick around her throat and he lifted her against the rail of the upper bunk. His face contorted with rage as he squeezed. His deep pock marks blanched white against his reddening skin.

Stars flickered behind her eyes.

His voice in her ear softened, "If you were pretty enough I'd treat you to a different lesson."

Her vision collapsed into a tunnel. Her ears rung. Did he mean to kill her? She fought to stay conscious. Her legs kicked involuntarily against the lower bunk. And then he dropped her.

"If I feel one lash on my back I'll cut you to pieces. Tell your husband that." A kick landed in her buttock and she twisted. He stood listening and then pulled the bedding and clothes from the bunks. Finding nothing, he threw open her trunk and dumped armfuls of clothes and books on top of her.

"William?" she gasped. Her throat closed. She couldn't suck enough air.

"Where are they? Does *she* have them?" he said, coming nose to nose with her. He searched her face.

She shook her head and tears rolled down her cheeks.

He drew back his leg and she skittered sideways. His leg flew past her, finding its mark in the loose board behind her. It split, falling in two pieces to the floor, followed by the letters she had tried so hard to hide. He dove for them like an urchin for a dropped purse.

October 15th – First Dog Watch

Her breath clawed its way in and back out again. She lay inert, save the heaving of her breasts.

My tooth?

It was there. She was whole.

But on fire.

From pain, from fear, from anger. Mostly anger.

Why had William not come? Why did he so steadfastly refuse to believe her about Prince, about the jeopardy she was in, that they were all in? None of this would have been necessary if only he believed her.

Why did he bring me? All I want is my baby – my poor, dear boy.

Slowly her anger sublimated, diffusing to an all-encompassing sorrow. If she died, Jonathan would never forgive her for breaking her promise and leaving him alone.

I must see him again.

She dragged herself up to the bunk and lay flat on the scattered, damp clothes. Voices echoed in the common-way.

The curtain parted. William stood for a moment framed in light, "Dorothy, you shouldn't be down here alone. I've been looking. The seas are changing again and we need to prepare."

"William, help," she croaked, trying harder to catch her breath now that her nose was full.

"Almighty! What has happened?" he said, slowly taking in the ransacking around Dorothy, prone on the bare wood of the bunk.

He pulled her to the outer edge and stroked her hair, fussing over her dampness. "You're stiff. What's taken you so suddenly? What happened, my love?"

She cursed him silently without meaning to, wishing he would remove his sycophantic paws and leave her alone. He smelled of beef. He had been enjoying himself, maybe with Prince.

All she had wanted was for him to come, but again he had failed her. Now everything was hurting and it was hard to speak. She stayed mute, conserving her energy. She would likely regret anything she said to him. He would have to figure this out. It wasn't that hard.

"I'm going for Dr. Fuller," said William.

Relieved by his departure, she turned on her side to stop the mucous trickling down the back of her throat, still raw and constricted from Harlock's attack. Too distraught to think or feel, she lay vacant. A line of ants marched into her vision, a column trekking across her floor, up and over the pile of clothes, undeterred by the obstacles placed in their path. She reached down to move a shirt out of their way. How can she and Desire be the only ones to see the truth?

October 15th – First Dog Watch

"Is she still in here?" asked Dr. Fuller. "There's nothing on the bunk but damp clothes." Dr. Fuller motioned for his assistant, Billy, to pass him the lantern.

"No, there. That's her hair," said William. "Raise the lantern higher. She's in shadow.

"Dorothy, its Dr. Fuller. I've come to check on you. Turn toward me, if you will."

Dorothy watched her shadow shrink against the opposite wall as Dr. Fuller raised his light. The instruments in his case rattled as he set it down. He smelled of mint and bitters.

"William, I'll listen to her breathing from the back and then you can help turn her over if you will. Can we please get some of these lines and clothes out of the way?"

The lamp light swayed as he handed it to Billy.

He placed his ear to her back. "No disorder of the lungs."

He counted the beat of her heart. "Strong pulse, quick but regular. Her bodice is damp. Cold with no shivering. No smell of excrement or vomit."

"Ok, William, if you will, turn her at the leg and I'll lift her shoulders. One, two, three." Despite her resistance Dorothy found herself lying on her back.

Dr. Fuller's eyes went straight to her neck. He stared at it, the area where Harlock's hand had strangled her now lit fully by the lantern. His eyes disengaged and moved slowly upward, stopping at her still swollen lip, before moving on to take in the tiny fractured blood vessels around and within both eyes. *There, now you have my testimony.* He would tell the others and en masse they'd march on Harlock and have him whipped.

"My dear Lord in Heaven. She's been *strangled*."

There. It was done. His words reverberated around the room as all eyes fell on her throat. Her shoulders relaxed.

William dropped to his knees and prayed, begging forgiveness of her, asking God to heal her and protect her.

"Who did this?" the doctor whispered sympathetically.

William looked at her over the doctor's shoulder.

She tested her voice, "Harlock. Prince."

The doctor didn't flinch. He passed instructions. William moved to her side, still in prayer.

Dorothy clenched her fists, fighting the pain in her throat. She needed William to believe her. And do something about it. Now.

"We must relieve her humours," said Dr. Fuller. Motioning to Billy for his tourniquet he tied a neat bow around her upper arm. He extended his hand. Billy planted a shining fleam firmly in his palm. Making a flourish with the silvery wand he opened a vein in her arm to let it breathe. The gush of scarlet winding down her opalescent flesh was beautiful, like a painter's stroke of dark on light. As her vein breathed, she breathed less. Stars twinkled in her vision. Her eyelids grew heavy. She slept.

October 15th – First Watch

With a heavy pat of William's shoulder Dr. Fuller took his leave. "I will let you inform Deacon Carver and Elder Brewster of what's happened."

William gave the doctor a pleading look. "What am I to do for her? What happens next?"

"Nothing much can be done. She'll be all right. She is breathing regularly and I don't believe there is any permanent damage to her throat. She will be bruised for a few weeks and then all this will be behind her. If necessary, I can bleed her again tomorrow if her humours remain out of balance. Twice is enough for tonight." Dr. Fuller wiped his fleam and placed it neatly in his satchel.

"You'll be all right. See Deacon Carver while she rests, and let him know. In the morning, if she can speak, you'll find out more."

Dr. Fuller and Billy swept out of the room, taking the lantern with them. Darkness slunk from the corners to claim the room once more.

The violet marks staining Dorothy's tender neck had etched themselves into William's consciousness. Even with his eyes closed he saw them, saw her reproachful stare boring through him. She seemed distant, further even than she had been escaping down that country road. Her silence added to his guilt, the two twisting him into a rage. He must act, but how? Fighting the instinct to lose control, his better judgement pushed him from the room. He must seek spiritual council.

He stumbled down the corridor, the turmoil in his mind multiplying the increasingly erratic motion of the ship. In the dim glow of the low-hanging lanterns the scene flattened into grays and yellows, devoid of definition. He peered into faces and saw only pale reflections; the strength, so visible in their sun-bathed features at noon, reduced to a drawn, weatherworn complexion by the lantern light rising and setting on them with each pitch of the ship. *What is happening to me?* He needed to find Carver.

A hand latched onto his shin in the darkness. He tried to shake it free.

He looked down to find Carver looking up at him, his face a mask of concern. Carver jumped up and steered him to a clear space on the deck near Brewster's cabin. Begging William to sit he signalled Brewster to join them.

"What is it, William?" asked Carver. "I saw Dr. Fuller with Dorothy and assume its more than seasickness. You look shaken." Carver wrapped an arm around him. Carver whispered loudly to Brewster, "Bring some strong water, if you have some to spare," sending him back to his cabin across the rolling deck.

"I wish it were only that. I need your help, as my Deacon, as well as my friend. I'm . . ." William broke off, uncertain whether he was ready to confess what he was feeling. "Dorothy . . ." He swallowed hard. "She's been strangled. The marks are there – on her neck." His fingers automatically encircled his own. "She won't speak to me."

William's face twisted. "It was Harlock. He must have sought to repay me for going to the Master."

Brewster passed the strong water to Carver and kneeled at William's side. Carver asked if he had heard everything. Brewster nodded.

"What was she doing down here alone?" said Brewster.

"I blame myself. *She* blames me," said William, accepting the flask. "I was focused on our discussion about the Adventurers. Prince was adamant we keep our faith in Weston and repair that friendship in case the Adventurers sour against us. He had me worried he knew something we didn't. I promised Dorothy she was safe. But I've failed her. I'm not equipped to keep her safe. What have I done to protect her? I'm no good."

He submerged his grief in the burning liquid speeding down his throat and across his chest. He took another swig before closing his eyes. The weight of Carver's hand on his shoulder kept him steady – but the anguish returned.

He took hold of Carver's forearms, searched his eyes. He found only concern in their brown depths.

"Help me . . . you have to help me. You cannot guess the thoughts that move me to sin." He clutched at Carver's linen; the fabric twisted in his fists. "I'm filled with such violence I can barely confess it. I would take vengeance with my bare hands." His head collapsed on his outstretched arms. He rubbed his brow back and forth on his shirtsleeve as though trying to erase his thoughts, whispering into the muslin, "Have I the strength?"

"Harlock, the sailor you wanted us to watch, slipped down here as we spoke above," said Edward joining them on hands and knees. "Richard Warren said he was watching him but Harlock got away. He saw him again a few minutes later coming up the ladder. Thankfully when Richard ducked his head down nothing was disturbed."

Edward was unaware of the effect he was having. William's head remained on his sleeve. At the news, his teeth fastened in the fabric, tearing at it as he fought to suppress the instinct rising within him.

"He deserves to die," he spat.

Carver looked at him with sympathy. "I'm no stranger to a man's passions. This outburst is nothing more than an outward eruption of the struggle that wages within you. It will soon be won by your better nature."

But William's blind fury strove to keep its advantage. "Brothers, we stood on deck with Myles Standish, only this morning, training ourselves to kill the savages whose only crimes are those we imagine against us. Yet, here is a man, I dare call him a man, for he is the embodiment of evil, who has attacked two of our flock, blasphemed God and the Bible, and what? He tried to kill my wife. Am I am expected to do nothing?"

Edward shook his head confused, "What's this?"

"Another time, Edward," said Carver.

William implored them, "How can God excuse my killing a savage when here before me is a savage much worse, one parading in the clothes of civilized society."

They were his oldest friends. He needed their approval, their consent.

Carver replied coolly, "The savages will seek to attack us without provocation, out of the baseness of their natural instincts. They worship no God but that of their lust and thirsts. You've heard the stories of their barbarism. If we must kill the savage – I hope we do not – but if we must, it will be in war, not revenge. We will do it to protect our colony so that the practice of true and pure worship might take root like sea-grass on a barren shore. If protected, those tender shoots will become a dense, deeply rooted forest."

William could not be swayed from his argument, "This sailor is more godless than any savages. He has been raised on the milk of the virgin Mother, God's word never far from his ear. To know good and evil, yet choose the latter, is a far deeper sin than being born without His hand upon you. The savage, once given the word of God, may still choose salvation."

"Are you hearing what you are asking, William?" said Carver. "You are asking for permission to break God's commandment. I cannot give it to you. God cannot give you the permission you seek. Only the devil will speak to you on this matter. As your Deacon and your friend I assure you that I will intercede."

"As your Elder, William, if you raise your hand against this sailor with intent to murder, you will be excommunicated," added Brewster sorrowfully. "I respect you deeply. Come to your senses, man, come back to the light. You aren't in your right mind."

"Excommunication?" he whispered, not believing the word as it slipped from his mouth. To lose his whole community, when already isolated from all other humanity would be a death sentence. Yet, how could he do nothing?

He breathed deeply, slowly, hoping to stifle his lust for vengeance. Raising his reddened eyes to theirs, he realized how much he loved them, how much their long years of shared sufferings meant to him, how desperate he had become.

"What have I said? It's as if I've committed the act. You've seen my wickedness. How will you ever forget? How will God forgive me?"

"You are not the first to be tempted, William. I admit that I struggled with a desire to see him scourged for his sin. We cannot lose our souls by repaying evil with evil. Remember this, for Satan is sly. He comes for us when we are weak." Carver reached for the other men's hands. "Pray with me now. Tomorrow we'll warn the others to be on guard. God's providence *will* deliver us if we are patient. Keep faith."

October 16th – Middle Watch

William sat with his back braced against the wall, listening to Dorothy sleep. In his fatigue he approached a kind of delirium as the ship rode the waves; he imagined himself riding upon a powerful horse, each rise and fall of the ship the long, purposeful strides of the beast carrying him. He was in search of help, as he had been the night his mother died, when his sister had lifted him onto a horse and sent him galloping for the doctor.

As the night wore on, his ceaseless ride continued. His horse stretched ever forward, driving through the wind and rain in an effort to save Dorothy. He prayed this time he'd be fast enough.

Many times throughout his fitful midnight journey, tears rolled down his cheek.

October 16th – Morning Watch

Dorothy awoke to find that nothing had changed. The lantern above her swung in a steady rhythm. Unconsciously, she matched her breathing to it. William was tidying the tiny cabin, retrieving clothes and books from the floor. He picked up her copy of Markham's *Guide to Housewifery*. "May I take that?" she asked, pulling herself upright. Perhaps there was a remedy for the feeling of having a wizened apple lodged in her throat.

William sat on the end of the bed massaging her ankle. "Tell me again what happened."

"I had Mr. Prince's letters. They prove who he is. They were hidden behind the board Harlock destroyed. Mr. Prince, your friend, sent him to do this. To get his letters back. He almost killed me, William." She breathed steadily to let the dizziness clear.

William waited before speaking, "Where did you get them?"

"We found them while cleaning up after the storm."

"Who is *we*?"

"*I* found them."

"Those were Mr. Prince's property. We've all been looking for his missing maps and papers. He wouldn't have asked for help if he had something to hide. Did you actually see something in the letters to prove what you are saying?"

A tear dropped on her book. She blotted it away.

"I'm sorry, dear, I know you are badly hurt. I just want to make sure before I accuse Mr. Prince of being involved that there hasn't been a misunderstanding. Did you read the letters or is this part of the feeling you have about him? You've made no secret of your dislike."

"We've seen proof in those letters that he is not Mr. Prince; he is a Weston. Proof that he is turning the Adventurers against us. Trying to prevent our resupply in the spring, even though he knows we will starve without it."

"Hmph."

"William."

"Who else saw this proof? If you saw anything, you might have got it mixed around. This is not a place I want you sticking your nose in. You know nothing of what is really going on with the investment or the contract. If you start saying things as though you do, you could damage our efforts. Harlock attacked you because he was given extra duties as punishment for his last assualt. It was a warning against going to the Master."

"This is why I took the letters. You don't believe what I tell you." She slid back down the pillow and rolled over.

A scream cut through the heavy timbers overhead. She spun back toward William wide-eyed as he flew through the doorway.

William leapt through the companionway. Carver was already calming the situation. John Howland, Alden, Gilbert and Brewster were squatting in a semi-circle around Desire, Carver patting her hand. Her blue cheeks were translucent. Priscilla and Mary were talking at once.

"He grabbed her. We were just standing talking."

"I thought he was going to let go of her. She was dangling over the waves."

"He kept asking, 'Where? Where?'."

"She didn't know what he wanted. She was shaking her head."

Carver pulled Desire to her feet and held her in a tight embrace. She tipped her head up to whisper in his ear. William caught none of it.

"Get Prince," Carver ordered John.

John Howland squeezed Desire's hand, "I'll be back. You're safe."

Alden moved to take her hand and direct her toward the safety of the forward cabin wall. Gilbert trailed behind. Judging by the angry expression on Gilbert's face, William concluded that Carver had not yet told Gilbert that Alden was free to court Desire.

"What can I do to help?" said Prince returning with John.

William received one of Prince's customary shoulder squeezes. It relaxed him. He had to smile at the man's affability.

"I'll cut right to it," said Carver. "Did you instruct Harlock to attack Dorothy and now Desire? Both have mentioned your name separately. I know for a fact they haven't spoken to one another since the incident yesterday."

William's smile evaporated.

"What? Absolutely not. Why should I do such a thing? Her fright must have muddled her thoughts. You know I have no love for Harlock. I'm the one that campaigned on your behalf for his punishment. What has he done this time?"

"She says he wanted something back."

"Well she doesn't have anything of mine. Do you?" he said, calling to her across the deck.

"I don't!" she said, narrowing her eyes. Alden and Gilbert each held one of her hands.

"She is no thief and would never keep something that didn't belong to her," said Carver. "If you are such a friend to us, *you* can petition for Harlock to be whipped. After all, you have the Master's ear. We have witnesses. Harlock's time has come."

Sinner

*D*orothy stepped further into the shadows of the cabin and pricked her ears to better hear William and Deacon Carver on the other side of the common-way.

"Dr. Fuller went up to offer a second opinion on the sick early this morning," said Carver.

"What's Harlock's condition? Is he just trying to avoid his whipping? Knowing Harlock was served justice would comfort Dorothy in her recovery. You can imagine how she felt when he complained of illness."

"I only received a general report."

"What of the sailors? How many are sick? What does he think it is?" pressed William.

Dorothy leaned forward in order to peek around the edge of curtain and better-read Carver's lips. William's last question had been pitched low.

"They've a fever, some a flux with it, but one matching Harlock's description has great sores all over with a continual flux. He's been screaming and fussing so much, the other sailors have threatened to throw him overboard."

"That's sure to be Harlock," said William.

Dorothy's hand clenched the fabric of the curtain.

"Dr. Fuller with a few of the women are going up to help. He says he has a few supplies the ship's surgeon could use," said Carver. "He also says we're low on birch bark and mustard seed. He'll run out by November even if no new cases develop. We need to reach land within a fortnight."

"Then stop him from wasting our supplies on Harlock! We should let God finish his work," said William.

"William! You're not yourself."

"Forgive me, John, I am sorry. It's just . . . if he hadn't tried to kill my wife. He knocked her tooth loose. You know there are whispers that I did that to her. We should have told everyone about Harlock from the beginning."

"I didn't realize you were aware – I've been trying to shield you from it. After everything you've borne, you don't deserve this. I tried to stop it." Carver patted William's back and then embraced him. "There is another matter. Prince. I don't trust him. As long as we don't see eye to eye on this, I think it would be better if you kept your own counsel. Let Brewster and Isaac weigh in on matters of the patent . . . let them take over for a bit. We don't want our secrets leaving the core five, even if accidentally." Carver's shoulders sagged as he finished.

Dorothy watched as William began to weep then withdrew her eye from the slit and retreated against the bunk. They were still talking, but her mind was buzzing.

She turned back in time to catch their last words.

"Go down to help Edward and Brewster with the wording of that damn letter to the Adventurers. That would be fine. You're still needed, just . . . you know." Carver's voice trailed down the corridor.

She tied her cap with shaky fingers and lifted the lid of the trunk. William would never know she was gone.

She heard Desire giggling in the corridor. She had not told Desire her plans. It was better she didn't.

"Tomorrow, promise? It's my turn in the morning," Desire tittered.

Dorothy pressed her eye to the slit out of curiosity. Desire and whoever she was speaking to were gone. She spread the curtain. The corridor was deserted at this end. William was just mounting the step to the hold.

She slid the curtains closed again.

Reaching into the trunk, she withdrew her apron and Markham's *The English Housewife*, a gift from her mother. Harlock had come too close to killing her and Desire. She must do this, she must act while she still had the nerve – and the opportunity. Within the book's bound pages she marked two receipts. Mother and Markham would not approve, but a woman must employ whatever knowledge, whatever means available, to keep herself and her loved ones safe. As for God, she could only hope for His forgiveness.

October 20th – Forenoon Watch

With confidence Dorothy swung open the door to the forecastle, determined to look as though she was expected. Instead, she surprised the cook, alone with his pots and pans, who slipped and splattered himself with hot broth from the stove. He aimed a torrent of curses at her and she fled the room.

Leaning against the outer panel, her confidence melted. She felt small, timid, and uncertain of her plan. And it wasn't really a plan. It wasn't much more than a simple *intention*.

How is this going to work? I can't even find them.

A sailor stepped from the general quarters opposite to hurl the contents of a bucket overboard. She caught the whiff of vomit.

In there.

She tightened her apron, re-tucked a loose strand of hair beneath her cap, and hugged the book to her chest, running her finger over the soft papery grooves to ensure her place-markers were still intact. The sailor reopened the door to the right of the poop deck ladder and she slid in behind him.

The room was thinly lit with watery green light. Dorothy kept one hand on the door jamb until her eyes adjusted. With the other, she held her nose. The reek of feces, vomit and illness nearly made her wretch. She didn't know what she had expected, but it wasn't this. Below, they'd had their share of sickness – days in the beginning when scarcely one of them could move without purging, but they'd each waited patiently for Dr. Fuller and handled their misery stoically. Even the little ones hadn't carried on the way the twenty or so grown men were hollering and snarling at one another; each pleading for the attention of Dr. Heale, the ship's surgeon.

She'd hoped to see more women, so she wouldn't be conspicuous. Only Beth, Priscilla and Ann Fuller were visible between the swinging hammocks, carrying cups of water, heroically timing their ministrations to the ailing patients mid-curse. Thankfully, Dr. Fuller was occupied.

If she wasn't back in the cabin by the time William finished his business, he would come looking. She scanned the white spindles of hammocks for Harlock's unmistakeable girth. She didn't have time to search each face.

There was no sign of him. Maybe he'd recovered. Maybe he was dead.

She sidled round the edge of the room toward a trestle table laden with assembled herbals. Here, Ann, Dr. Fuller's sister-in-law, had returned to busily work a mortar. Dorothy nodded a greeting, before standing on tiptoe to check again for Harlock.

There. Moaning and writhing, steeping in his own fetid juice; a weak tea of yellow-brown dripped offensively from the sagging canvas. She clutched the book.

"Dorothy?"

Her heart leapt and she dropped the volume at Dr. Fuller's feet, the page markers skittering free.

"What's this now?" he said, stooping to pick it up. "You won't need this," he said, handing it back. "I'll give you a receipt to follow that'll do better than these common housewives' remedies. I assure you I've more knowledge than Master Markham."

Dorothy nodded and smiled with genuine relief that he'd accepted her presence without comment, all the while worrying her fingers over the pulp of the book where the pages had resealed, thinking how much time was now lost. The light was low and the book thick. She desperately tried to recall the ingredients.

"Take this to the sailor, second from the end," he said, handing her a pewter cup. Then turning to Ann, "If you've got that to a fine enough powder you can use the brazier to steep it in wine and then deliver it to Harlock, that heavyset fellow there."

"It's a little coarse yet," Ann replied, returning to her grinding with renewed vigour.

Dorothy moved quickly, taking the cup down the aisle, holding it to the sailor's dry lips, nearly choking him in her effort to hurry him along. She glanced repeatedly at Ann, still mixing. She needed to get to her before she delivered it to Harlock. She needed to find her receipts. The cup was finally empty. She lifted her skirt and raced to the nearest lantern to examine the book. The thick markers she'd used had opened the binding slightly. Holding the covers loosely she let the pages fall open. They parted simply, as though they'd wanted to be found. She read quickly.

She approached the trestle. Ann was still pounding, a sheen of sweat on her face and neck.

"Let me have a turn at that, Ann."

Ann relaxed her shoulder and stepped back, the pestle extended gratefully. Taking it, Dorothy resumed the pounding while scanning labels on the compounds and herbs carefully arranged on the table. Somewhere among them was stonecrop. She mentally repeated the receipts for encouraging vomiting and remedying costiveness. The latter required fenugreek, powder of peony, and linseed. She also needed aniseed, which she could smell on the pestle. It had to be nearby.

Ann lifted a basin of cold water, slung a wet rag over her forearm and joined Beth and Priscilla patrolling the rows of sick. No one spoke; it was impossible with all of the caterwauling. Dorothy was grateful. Her sudden appearance was bound to raise questions, questions she knew she couldn't answer.

Having located her ingredients, Dorothy glanced over her shoulder. Harlock, for a sick man, appeared to have energy aplenty for swearing, spitting, oozing and heaving. She dumped the contents of the mortar onto the floor behind the table and hurriedly shook the contents of the bottles she'd collected into the mortar. She pounded hard and fast. Then she spied something unexpected, but fortuitous, among the rows of herbs. Something once prescribed for her father's dropsy. Foxglove. Too much of which could be deadly. She took three pinches of the ground flowers and quickly stirred them into the mix. After another glance over her shoulder, she threw in three more.

The wine was already simmering as she emptied the mortar's contents into the crimson liquid. The fine dust swirled before being swallowed up. She let out her breath.

Harlock called out for someone to help.

"Ann? Have you given Harlock his phisick?" asked Dr. Fuller.

"Dorothy's doing it," shouted Ann from the din.

"That's ready, Dorothy, pour half of it in the wooden cup and hold it to his lips. Leave the rest. I've another who needs some."

Dorothy ladled the ruby liquid into the cup with shaky hands, then paused over the remainder simmering in the pot.

She replaced the ladle and forced one foot in front of the other. She had no choice but to leave the deadly elixir stewing in the black pot. From across the room Dr. Fuller encouraged her with nods and smiles. She wiped the sweat from her brow, careful not to tip the trembling bowl in her hand. His expression changed and she quickened her pace. Did he recall her history with Harlock? She forced a smile and kept moving. She must reach Harlock before he called her back.

A patient wailed. Distracted, Dr. Fuller moved off. Her heart beat like a rabbit's.

Harlock's hammock jerked spasmodically. His huge head lunged for the canvas edge as he heaved. Spittle purled down his chin before his head turtled back over the rim.

Dorothy hung over him then glanced quickly around. Across the room she spotted Desire, standing like a lighthouse, staring at her intently. Desire's eyes widened; her head shook back and forth.

Dorothy whispered, "Yes."

"Doc Heale, help me," mewled Harlock.

"Go," she mouthed to Desire. Unwilling or unable to stop what she'd set in motion, Dorothy turned from Desire's beacon toward the abyss hanging in front of her.

"I've something for you," she intoned. Somewhere between the trestle and the hammock she'd left her body; her spirit was now asea. Nothing could intrude on the singularity of her purpose. Harlock must drink – they must be free of him. That was all.

Their eyes met. Bloodshot, crusted, and sunk deep within their sockets, they nonetheless sparked with recognition. His cracked lips parted in surprise. She braced herself for what he might say. An invisible hook pulled one corner of his mouth into a lecherous grin.

She placed the cup to his mouth. Her nerves were on fire. She must return to the pot before Dr. Fuller.

"Drink."

She watched his Adam's apple rise and fall. Two more gulps.

If thine enemy thirst, give him drink: for in so doing thou shalt heap coals of fire on his head. Romans 12:2.

She saw Dr. Fuller working his way closer to the brazier.

"Drink, you whoreson," she hissed, tipping the remainder into his mouth. His eyes widened. He might have been readying a retort – but she was finished with him. What William and the others couldn't do, wouldn't do, she had done.

Then Desire was there, across the hammock. Their fingers encircled as she took the cup from Dorothy. An energy, an understanding, leapt between them.

Dr. Fuller neared the brazier. Dorothy raced for the pot.

God forgive her for killing Harlock, but she had sworn she would see Jonathan again no matter what the cost. She wasn't going to let Harlock recover only to come for her again. Child before husband. Child before God. That was the natural hierarchy as she saw it. God forgive her for that, too.

She was there. Her toe caught her hem and she stumbled forward toward the pot trying to regain her balance. Dr. Fuller was dipping the ladle.

"Slow down there, Dorothy," he said, and then cocked his head. "You're white as the linen cloth."

At that precise moment, the world tipped on its end. She reached for him, missed, and caught the side of the hot pot. Its boiling contents spilled across the front of her cream bodice. Heat seared her as the blood-red stain spread. She screamed and Dr. Fuller doused her with water.

"When will William be back?" whispered Desire as she drew the curtain. She smelled the salve Dr. Fuller had handed her and pulled her stool close to Dorothy's. "Let's peel this off," she said, gently spreading the edges of Dorothy's wet bodice.

"He won't be back for at least an hour."

"Does it hurt?"

"I'm fine. I can do this," said Dorothy offering to take the salve.

The bodice slid to the deck between their feet. "You didn't have to do it," said Desire. She held Dorothy's chin and searched her eyes. "You've damned your soul. We could have found another way." She looped a strand of hair over Dorothy's ear and Dorothy couldn't bear to hold her gaze.

Desire slid her fingers under the straps of Dorothy's shift and eased them gently over her shoulders. Dorothy quickly pressed her hands to her chest to prevent Desire pulling the shift lower. The burn seared anew and she sucked in her chest.

"It's alright," said Desire

Dorothy let her hands fall to her lap.

"It's alright. I won't look at you then, if you don't want. But, I think you are beautiful. And strong. And brave. And I'm brave because of it." Desire stood and lifted the hairbrush from the trunk. The soft bristles whispering through Dorothy's hair loosened her limbs. She began to shake.

"Next time he would have killed us. And I would never see Jonathan again. Yet, we still aren't safe, are we? There is still Prince." Dorothy rocked back and forth, holding her arms tight around her middle. "I'm damned now, aren't I? What if this counts for nothing?"

Desire wrapped herself around Dorothy, holding her until she stopped rocking. "We will prove to everyone who Mr. Prince is. I promise."

Dorothy put her hand over Desire's and turned to look at her.

"Where are the letters?"

"They are safe. I sewed them into my mattress."

"I should be the one to take the risk. Give them to me and hide them in mine." Dorothy pulled Desire around in front of her and onto the stool so that she could look directly at her. "You must marry a man that loves you and will keep you safe. Let me worry about protecting the plantation."

"God will take pity on you. He knows why you did it. Perhaps he acted through you. Perhaps it was predetermined that this should happen." She leaned her brow against Dorothy's and Dorothy could feel her breath warm on her lips.

"I won't let you fall into darkness alone," said Desire.

"We never should have had to. They should have believed us. Protected us"

They parted. Desire picked up the ointment. Dorothy allowed her shift to fall to her hips. Tenderly, Desire smoothed ointment onto her burn.

"I'll never tell a soul the rest of my life. I promise. If you are damned, then I am too," whispered Desire. "But, God will forgive. He is watching us all and keeping us safe. What you did was right."

Apart at the Seams

"William!" Carver shouted, careening toward him, "We need water. I need you to go up and ask the Master. Hurry. They will be shutting us in soon."

"I was going for the animals," said William, trying to keep his feet as the *Mayflower* lurched to starboard.

"I've sent Billy. Go."

William aimed a kiss at Dorothy's forehead. Before he had time to think he was at the top of the ladder without his cloak. Wind whipped his hair with such frenzy that it was impossible to see without letting go. And he couldn't let go. Carver should have asked someone stronger, like Edward or Stephen Hopkins. He went down a rung and then recalled both were ill.

He stepped clear of the companionway and was blown sideways. This storm was already worse than the last. Only mid-day and it was dark as night. The hatch wouldn't be open much longer. He took a few steps toward the rail seeking support, then changed his mind when he saw the speed of the water running alongside. It rose into a great foaming, living, spitting wall that looked sure to overwhelm the *Mayflower*. Frothing crests were all that distinguished sea from Heaven. The sight brought him to his knees. A roar filled his ears. His hair dripped but there was no rain.

On hands and knees he crawled toward the poop deck, gratefully wrapping his arms around the main mast when he reached it. He couldn't believe that sailors still scampered in the rigging, tying down the sails, leaving three bare crosses looming above him. He clung tighter to the mast and eyed his destination – the ladder to the poop house and the Master's quarters beyond. To climb it would mean exposing himself to even stronger winds. Once high on the poop deck he would be tossed about with the greater arc of the ship. He needed to let go of the mast and make for the ladder, but couldn't. He searched the deck in vain for alternatives.

"Master Jones!" he shouted into the storm. Again he yelled, nearly screaming, but could barely hear his own voice before the gale whipped it away. Still hugging the mainmast, with the cold penetrating deep into his body, he realized he would not make it to the poop house, even if he summoned all of his courage.

A faint light glowed beneath the door to the general quarters. As the bow yielded to an oncoming crest, he surrendered the main mast and let himself be hurled backwards along the deck to the door. He flailed for the latch. The ship levelled. He rushed inside and braced himself against the door just as the stern lifted.

The air inside was putrid, the light queer, the energy torpid. He stumbled and slipped among the hunched sailors, asking for the Master. None answered. Swinging hammocks knocked him off balance and fueled his frustration. Down below, they needed water. He was getting nowhere.

The bow tilted and he snatched at the nearest hammock for support, pulling its surprised occupant before his own startled eyes.

Harlock.

He was face to face with the corporeal malice who had wreaked such havoc on him this journey. This rotting creature had cost him the respect of his comrades, Dorothy's love, his very manhood.

Their eyes remained locked in the gloom, Harlock peering through crusted slits sunk deep in his skull. How was it possible they could still mock him? William reached for the knife in his belt.

All Dorothy's fear would be gone.

Harlock deserved it.

Without volition, the knife described a graceful, underhand arc toward the underbelly of the beast. Threads popped like harp strings as the point of his knife split the heavy canvas.

A subterranean shudder flexed the deck and the hammock swung like a pendulum. His knife veered on a tangent, inscribing a gash in the fabric.

Harlock might not call out. The swine was almost unconscious.

No one would know. Not with the turmoil of the storm.

He'd come to something soft; he could feel the yielding of flesh.

He'd been praying for this opportunity. It was as though God was moving his hand. How he hated this animal for all he'd done.

October 23rd – First Watch

Night engulfed the 'tween deck as a sailor snapped the hatch tight. The rough dialect of a dozen or more sailors in the common-way was the first omen of an unusually perilous night. The second was the long shuddering groan that snaked down the length of the ship and reverberated in their spines.

Katherine whimpered. John, sitting on the boards next to the bunk, heard Carver mumble, "Are we to meet tonight, Almighty?" just as another shudder signalled the likely answer.

"John, help me get to the door," Carver said.

John crawled forward, found Carver's groping hand and placed it on the frame. Carver poked his head out of the curtain.

"Ho there! Is there a sailor about? Where is the Master?"

Voices swam in the darkness.

"Someone explain what is about! The passengers are terrified. We need an explanation!" Carver demanded, ill-disguising his own fear.

"We are lying-a-hull, sir." The calm voice from a sailor came from nearby in the darkness. "*Mayflower* can't bare sail, seas are twenty-five feet and building, winds are forty knots sou-sou-west. Master Jones has ordered all below, 'cept his-self and the able body he lashed to the mizzen mast – t' keep him from going overboard. Master's Mate Clarke is working the whip-staff in steerage, best he can, with the help of two more able bodies."

"Give it to us plainly sailor! What danger is there?" shouted Carver.

"We sink or we float," rasped another voice from across the common-way. "Ask your God what it shall be. He knows better than we." A few snickers and hoots overlaid the whistling of the gale.

"Do not mock the Lord! Not a one of us has stopped praying for deliverance since the gale began. Do you seek to reverse our good work by taunting and making jolly with the power that He commands?" Carver ducked back into the cabin and John guided him to Katherine.

The next pitch threw John to the floor, where Desire grabbed him and pulled him in. He wrapped his arms tightly around her waist and did his best not to tense and jump as crest and trough hammered the ship hard enough to surely crack its bones.

They were wedged into the corner. Jasper, Will and Anna lay between them and the door, flat on their bellies. A particularly violent roll knocked Desire's head against the hull with a crack and he raised his hand from her shoulder to cradle it. Warmth enveloped his fingers. She was bleeding. Pulling his sleeve he was able to get enough of it over his hand to try to staunch the flow.

Desire was too overwhelmed or too frightened to feel the gash. She clung to him. There would be no amorous explorations tonight – a mere hour into the storm and it seemed clear they would never reach the far shore.

Terror prevented even prayer as the night wore on.

What might have been morning came and the *Mayflower*'s hatches were still battened tight. Jasper and Will keened as the ship ascended each new wave. Katherine yelled at them to be quiet. When that didn't work she hummed to drown out the noise. It only added to the exhausting cacophony.

Hunger cramped John's belly, but the thought of food made him nauseous. His elbows and knees were bruised and throbbing. Desire repeatedly moaned that she could endure no more and prayed for deliverance by any means. If the end was to come, let it be soon. He held her tighter, kissed her cheek and hair, cried for her to hold on.

Night fell once more, snuffing the weak grey light that had leaked through the cannon ports, shrouding the ship in a pitch so black that John had to touch his eyes to tell they were open.

Everything hurt. Water wicked up his breaches and Desire's skirt was so wet he could fill a bucket wringing it out. His flesh was swollen and what wasn't stinging with the salt was throbbing from the constant assault of hull and inner cabin wall.

"Loosen my stays, John. They're slicing into my flesh," she panted into his ear. She was crying helplessly. "If only I could rid myself of this dress; I can't possibly be any colder and it's too tight. I can't stand it another minute."

John removed his arm from around her back and pulled her down between his bent knees and chest so that he could use both of his hands. He felt awkwardly for the laces along the back of her bodice. His fingers were clumsy, the left digits asleep from resting under her shoulders. Finally he found the bow and snagged the ribbon ends. He pulled but there was no give. The knot had shrunk.

"Please hu..h..hurry John," chattered Desire.

"They are knotted tight." John shook his hands and tried to work feeling back into them. He tried again and picked at the tiny knot with soft fingernails, unsure whether he was loosening or tightening it. Growing frustrated, he grabbed the ribbon again and pulled hard, lifting Desire off his knee. She cried out as the bodice dug into her middle. "I'm sorry, I'm sorry," he cried, frustrated by his inability to complete such a small task.

Renewing his efforts, he clawed at the lacing and the knot. Despite his fingernails ripping, he eventually freed a strand of lacing. It was no more than a thumbnail in length.

"Is it all...mm...most done John?" Desire lay exhausted and faint across his lap. She fluttered in short, shivering breaths.

"Almost." His fingers were painfully sensitive with the return of circulation. The knot finally gave, one bow slipping through the other. He hurriedly spread the edges of the stiff fabric.

She breathed with relief. He hoped that, despite all her pain and the deep chill, she could now endure. At least a little longer. He was exhausted, the knot a labour of Hercules. His eyes drooped.

When he woke, it was raining in the cabin. The upper decking was opening under the strain. Shouted prayers and passionate pleas – *God have mercy, Lord I await your recompense* – had woken him. It was certain they were going down. There was a collective inhalation, a tensing for the blow. Slow minutes passed. Katherine and Deacon Carver said their goodbyes to each other.

The ship rolled to lee, throwing him hard against the beam. Screams tore though the 'tween deck. The ship righted itself then gave a great shudder as another ferocious wave slammed it broadside. The floor heaved upright and let out a deafening crack. The ship rolled to leeward once more and he took a last breath, waiting for the timbers beside him to finally disintegrate, allowing the cold Atlantic to swallow them. Desire went limp.

Labour

*T*hen it was done. Through what they could only conceive as God's special providence, the storm had spared them. The hatch opened to a new morning.

William's curtain hung by a shred. He crawled out of the cabin, wincing as he tried to straighten his limbs. Carver stumbled out opposite him. The crew were gone from the passageway.

Carver called out, "Ho, is anyone badly injured?" before his legs gave way.

Hunched and stiff-necked, William turned sideways to meet Carver's gaze. As their eyes met, the absurdity of the question struck them both. By God's grace here stood two sorry souls – beaten, bruised, shivering and dripping, moving as though rigor mortis had already set in. They broke out laughing, hearty, deep guffaws riding an eruption of relief.

It hurt to laugh.

William shuffled forward and they embraced, wiping tears from their eyes. They looked about, wondering what to tackle first.

Smiles turned to grimaces as they looked aft. The end of the passageway was no longer visible. The upper deck hung low, the main mast passing through at a dizzying angle.

"I need all able men to join me at once!" bellowed Carver. "The main-beam has split and we need to assemble a group to consult the Master. At once!" Carver grabbed William's shoulder and, using it as a crutch, straightened his crooked back. He moved off stiffly toward the mast.

William was relieved to see Thomas Tinkner and Francis Eaton, although unwell, among the men joining them to examine the wreckage. Their experience with carpentry would be useful.

Above deck the damage that met William's eyes was surreal. The main sail, unfurled, lay draped over the side of the *Mayflower*, its lines trailing in the water. Timbers in the sunken, twisted main deck were missing; he could see through to the deck below. Lines limply hanging from the mast-work fell in such profusion that it was impossible to walk without tripping. Everything that *had* been secured to the upper deck was swept clear. He hoped that the missing barrels weren't their beer or water.

The Master ploughed toward them through the debris, hands locked behind his back, nose raised to the topsail.

"Don't bother asking. My boatswain and carpenter are still deciding what can be done. It is too soon for me to give you a report." He ran his eyes over them. "I will have beer and water brought down directly. I advise you all to eat something if you can. I'll inform you of the situation at six bells." It had just rung three. The Master turned to go and then spun back around. "Any dead?"

William was shocked at his cavalier attitude, but said nothing, shaking his head *no*, in time with Carver. They looked around at the others for confirmation, realizing no one actually knew the answer.

October 25th – Forenoon Watch

"Is there something I can do, Mary?" asked Dorothy, keeping her hand to her mouth. Mary Brewster's hand was on Stephen Hopkin's chest. She was trying to prevent him from re-entering his cabin.

"It's Lizzy, the babe is coming," said Mary tersely. "She's weak. It's the worst time. Stephen, you must let us help her."

"My mother used to swear that for a hard labour you should take four spoonfuls of a nursing mother's milk," volunteered Mary Allerton. "Should we get Sarah Eaton?"

"It can't hurt," said Mary Brewster. "Someone ask her."

Lizzy howled.

Dorothy peaked inside. Lizzy had enough help for now.

Dorothy knelt and resumed sweeping her hand across the uneven boards. She lay flat and squinted with one eye down the length of the deck as far as she could see. Too many people were in the way. She sat back on her bottom and leaned against the outer wall of Lizzy's cabin. Her tooth was gone, knocked out sometime in the night.

Lizzy moaned then cried out ferociously. Desire hurried past and ducked into the Hopkin's cabin. Suzanna White, her pregnancy almost as advanced as Lizzy's, stared ashen through the doorway and then slid down the jam onto her bottom beside Dorothy. They nodded to each other, then Dorothy closed her eyes. Her tongue vainly probed the socket and its dangling threads.

October 25th – Forenoon Watch

William stood with the handful of men well enough to meet with Master Jones and his chief crew.

"The ship's carpenter has judged the main-mast to be beyond repair," announced the Master. "He hasn't the right tools or means of support. The buckled deck will be impossible to seal and if we meet another storm, the pumps won't be able to keep up. We can fasten the mainsail to the deck to try to seal her up from the rain but a heavy sea will carry the sail over and take us down. I am giving orders for us to put about. We are barely halfway over the seas and it will be a miracle to make land. I am not willing to hazard the ship by continuing. I've the return trip to consider." He turned on his heel.

William's knees buckled and he gripped Carver's arm; what they had endured already would come to nothing.

"This can't be!" shouted Carver. "This will be the end of all hope. We have nothing if we return. We have spent it all on this venture."

The Master's mate spoke, "the ship is not sufficient. She cannot take another storm and the main mast is in peril of cracking and capsizing us." He gave them a hard look. "It is not just *your* lives which you ask us to risk."

The crew affirmed it, but William perceived a hint of dissent among them. "What say the opposition?" he asked.

"There is great concern among the able-bodied sailors, sir, that despite the voyage being more than half over, their wages may not be paid. But they won't risk their lives either, sir," offered the ship's carpenter, speaking as much to the Master as to them.

"And what is needed to fix the cracked beam?" asked Thomas Tinkner.

"I've nothing to jack her up. She is bowed too badly and all the weight of the main sail is keeping her in that condition. We would need a powerful jack and then something to secure her. Even if it could be done, the decks may not hold their caulk. We'll be a very wet ship and, as I said, unlikely to weather another storm like the last."

Tinkner beckoned them to lean in for private council. "We have the iron jack screw we brought from Holland. The Master likely doesn't remember it being transferred from the *Speedwell*. I think it could work."

William didn't remember an iron screw either, but nodded his head. *Anything to keep us from turning back now!*

Francis Eaton, who'd helped purchase the screw, shook his head. "We'll need it in New England. What if Master Jones tries to keep it for himself for the return voyage?"

Carver considered the idea. "We won't make New England if we don't use it," he said. "Besides, he has treated us fairly thus far. Has he not?"

William and the others nodded.

"Thomas, tell the Master, and take the carpenter," directed Carver. "Show him where the screw is stored. Render all assistance required."

William followed Master Jones as he picked his way through the fallen rigging back to his cabin. There had been more than one crack in the night. Even before the beam broke, water had sloshed along the cabin floor. "How do you judge the ship otherwise," William asked. "Will we still be in serious peril once the beam is fixed?"

"The ship holds underwater. I'll agree not to put about until we've tried this screw of yours. As for peril, if you believe it will help, I'd ask you to pray for good weather."

October 25th – First Watch

Dorothy snapped to attention at the sound of Lizzy's scream. She closed her mouth, embarrassed it had dropped open in her sleep. William didn't know about her tooth yet. Even if she found the tooth, it was unlikely to go back in. The socket was closing.

The boards beneath her shook and she opened her eyes.

"Dorothy, quick, give me a hand." Beth dragged her to her feet.

"I can't. I'm too tired."

"It's Billy. He was in the manger throughout the storm. He is trapped in the goat's netting. I can't wake him. Come. Come!" said Beth, desperately.

Dorothy grabbed Beth's hand and outpaced her, tugging her to keep up.

They found Billy's twisted body hanging from the netting, arms and legs dangling like the rigging on the deck above him. Several goats, almost equally imprisoned, were nipping at him in irritation. Dorothy pushed them away and urgently felt Billy's body for signs of life. He was cold as the sea, blue as the winter sky.

"Untangle him."

They laid him on his side and bent over him, listening.

"Nothing. Do you feel anything?"

"No," said Beth with a sob.

"Help me lift him. We have to get him to Dr. Fuller."

Dorothy put her arms under his shoulders and Beth lifted his knees. He was heavier than he looked.

"…amma," he mumbled softly.

"Praise Lord. Praise Lord. Praise he's alive." Tears flowed down Dorothy's cheeks. "Billy?"

"amma."

They rubbed his cheeks and his back.

"Mama?"

"You're safe, Billy."

"Dr. Fuller!" yelled Beth.

Revelation

*T*hey worked through the day in silence. Even the sailors were stone-faced in reaction to Lizzy's anguished cries. It was worse when the screaming stopped and still no baby was born. By nightfall, the beam was raised and a post secured beneath it, both in the lower and the 'tween deck. Exhausted, William dragged himself off to finally find Dorothy. He hadn't spoken to her since first crawling out of bed that morning.

As he sat down by the brazier, he heard a thin wail and breathed a sigh of relief.

"It's a boy, Oceanus," Stephen called out. "Lizzy's safe. She's sleeping."

Desire and the other makeshift midwives stumbled to the brazier for a bite to eat. The women hadn't refreshed themselves once through the long day. With the storm's privations, that meant none of them had eaten for nearly three days. Desire could barely raise her spoon.

William was struck dumb when he saw John Howland sit down beside her, take the spoon from her hand and lift it to her lips. William glanced quickly around for Carver – or Alden.

Edward, sidling over to him, looked as shocked as he was.

"Have you heard?" he said.

"Heard? I'm watching it right now."

"Harlock is dead! They've just dumped his body over the side. I saw it with my own eyes."

William fell to his knees, shaking. "Thank you, Lord."

What had he almost done?

"Romans 12:19, avenge not yourselves, but give place unto wrath: for it is written, 'Vengeance is mine: I will repay, saith the Lord'," intoned William.

"Amen."

"Dorothy?" he called. She emerged from the cabin looking sunken. He rushed to her.

"Billy was all alone, half drowning, for two whole days. Alone," she said, wrapping her thin arms tight around his chest. "Will he will be alright?"

"He will be fine, dear. Dr. Fuller won't risk losing such a good assistant. He will have the best care." He rubbed her back.

"Look at me, Dorothy," he said raising her chin. "I have news. Harlock is dead. God has finally given him his just reward."

"Dear heavenly God," She gasped, nearly slipping through his arms.

"I thought you would be relieved. You are safe now."

She lifted her lip and he saw the gaping hole. "Ahh, Dorothy. I'm sorry. I love you regardless, you know that."

"God is punishing me," she whispered. "He didn't just take my tooth. He nearly split the ship because of what I did. I had to do it though, William. And I have to keep doing anything I can to save our plantation. Everything depends on it." Dorothy pulled away, falling to her knees just inside the cabin door. She clawed at the stitching of their mattress. She seemed spent, almost delirious.

"I'm helping those I love, no matter what you say this time. God save me, forgive my soul, and reunite me with Jonathan."

"Stop that," he said, taking her wrist.

"It's in here. Let go."

She stuck her hand in the opening and pulled out a fold of paper. "This is proof, William. This is the letter I saw Mr. Prince writing that will prove he is trying to turn the Adventurers against us. He says here, in the middle paragraph, that we never intend to repay our debt to them and they should not supply us." She waved the letter around and marched over to Deacon Carver. He was half-asleep by the brazier. She placed it in his lap.

"Dorothy. It's inappropriate. Here, I'll take that back. I'm sorry about this," he said to Carver. Beside him, Brewster and Isaac stared at Dorothy.

William plucked the unfolded letter from Carver's hand and scanned it. It was … everything she said. He was wrong. *She did know something.*

"Prince!" he bellowed.

Prince came immediately.

"What is the meaning of this?" said William, showing Prince the letter. "Is Dorothy right? Do you betray us?" William handed the letter to Carver.

"Excuse me for saying it, but your wife is hysterical. The doctor should see to her. She's lost more than her tooth."

Carver grabbed William's elbow, but he shrugged it off. He didn't intend to be held back this time. He stepped nose to nose with Prince, indifferent that Prince could read the hurt in his eyes.

"William, stand down," said Carver. "It's not his. Look at it. It's signed by Christopher Martin and John Billington."

"Martin's signature?" William backed down, flabbergasted.

"Destroy the letter," said Brewster.

"Dorothy!" said William, furious.

"It is not Christopher Martin's," hissed Dorothy. "Mr. Prince, or whoever he really is, wrote that. We watched him. It was with his letters."

"You can turn in, Dorothy. We will speak later," said William. "Do nothing with the letter yet, Brewster."

October 26th – Afternoon Watch

Desire stooped to stir the beef and onions then ladled the stew into a bowl Priscilla held ready.

"I can't believe I was jealous of your looks," Priscilla said mischievously, touching Desire's bandage. "You're more ragged than an urchin."

"Hey!"

"You know, now that Mother and Joseph are as sick as Father, I don't think I could conscience courting Mr. Alden if he asked."

"*Mr.* Alden is it? You talk of him so often I thought you were in love."

"I have a duty to them first and it was only competition with you that spurred me into flirting with him," said Priscilla.

Desire handed another full bowl to Priscilla, gave a nod toward Joseph and picked up the next. She'd made enough for Priscilla's family, Moses Fletcher, Mr. Crackstone, John Goodman, and a few of the others who were too ill to rise. She set two more steaming bowls on the deck. Priscilla retrieved them gingerly by the rim.

"Priscilla, I told you I wasn't interested in John Alden."

"You said that, but it's clear he was interested in you."

"Can you keep a secret?" said Desire.

"Of course. Let me take these to Mother and Father first."

Priscilla hurried back and settled in front of Desire.

"John Howland and I are in love. But Father Carver wants to confirm the details of our engagement, so it is a secret." Desire grinned and let out an excited squeal.

"How could you have kept this a secret? All this time I thought you were after John Alden." Priscilla pouted. "And can you imagine how jealous your John was of Mr. Alden, with all of his wooing ... before he began calling on me?"

"I honestly don't think my John would have noticed," Desire laughed, "*I* didn't notice!"

"Well, I suppose that is love. It was quite plain to me."

Desire handed Priscilla two more bowls and motioned toward the men on pallets. After handing one to Moses, Priscilla looked back at her and playfully rolled her eyes. Priscilla's reaction was a relief. Keeping the secret felt like lying.

When Priscilla returned, Desire motioned for her to kneel in close. "That's not everything. Can you keep a very deep secret ... one unmarried woman to another?" Desire's eyes sparkled and a sly smile played along her lips. Priscilla nodded.

"We have been meeting, secretly. He kisses me so passionately," said Desire. Priscilla's face remained passive but her eyes flickered. Desire leaned in closer. "And I could tell you the contour of *every* muscle in his body," she added, aware it would shock Priscilla.

"Desire! Are you saying what I think you are saying? Can he say the same of you?" Priscilla's tired eyes widened.

"We had our clothes on! It is not as bad as you think," said Desire, regretting her confession.

"Still, could you not have waited? What if he decides not to marry you?"

"He would never do that. If you could see how tender he is with me and how earnest."

"Men can be fickle. Have you not heard it often enough? How do you know he doesn't say this to every young woman?" warned Priscilla. "You might be ruined."

"What other women? Only you, me, and Anna are eligible for marriage. Mary Chilton, Elizabeth Tilley, and Constanta Hopkins are still only fourteen. He *couldn't* be chasing anyone else." Desire unstacked two more bowls, anxiety at her free tongue growing within her. "Promise me this will be our secret."

"I will." Priscilla squeezed her round the waist and then extended two more empty bowls as Desire drew another teeming ladle of stew.

"Mmmm – mmm."

Their expressions slackened.

A sailor hovered over them. "Sure looks good. I'd like a taste of that," he said.

Desire's tension melted as she recognized him as one of the friendly sailors who had helped them after the storm. Unlike the others, he kept his straight blond hair in a neat que and his clothes in good repair.

In a barely audible voice Priscilla said, "It's not for you." She was as still as a rabbit.

"It's just that we don't have enough," apologized Desire.

He leaned over the pot and sniffed. "Maybe next time."

October 26th – First Dog Watch

"We've shown you the evidence. What say you for yourselves?" said Carver.

"I'm innocent." Martin crossed his ankles and leaned against his doorframe.

"We have never seen that letter before and have nothing to do with your Adventurers," added Billington.

"You're trying to ruin their good names, but it won't work," cackled Eleanor Billington subsiding into a coughing fit. She burrowed into her bosom, withdrew a grey rag, spat into it, then buried it again. "Ain't that right, Mr. Prince? You know my husband's good character."

"I'm afraid they aren't taking my word for it, good wife Billington."

"You say it was Mrs. Bradford that accused them? How dare she?" said Mrs. Martin, appearing suddenly at Eleanor Billington's elbow.

"You can go, ladies," said Carver.

William, Edward, Brewster and Isaac had Martin and Billington cornered. Prince had wandered down uninvited. William felt angry at himself for accusing Prince without reading the full letter. Yet despite his blunder, Carver and the others still trusted him enough to include him in the questioning of Martin and Billington.

"You have both been trying to undermine the plantation. Are you telling me these are not your signatures?" said Brewster.

"They are not," said Martin.

"Produce a document with your signatures and we will believe your assertions," said Edward.

"We are being framed. You don't like that we have the support of so many, some of them your own men," said Billington.

"We have proof," said Carver.

"I'll get you a copy of my signature," said Martin. He disappeared into his cabin and drew the curtain behind him. After a lot of ruckus within he thrust a neatly tied roll of parchment through a slit in the drape. Carver took it.

"What is it?" asked William.

"His Will. The signature doesn't match."

Martin poked his head out of the curtain, smiling broadly. He snatched the parchment back and redrew the curtain.

"Billington?" said Carver.

"I have nothing to show you. And that's not my signature." He crossed the deck to his cabin. "Bradford's put his lunatic wife up to this. He's too afraid to accuse us himself. I'm done."

"You're not done," said William.

Billington drew his curtain.

"Dorothy never mentioned your name. She accused Prince," said William.

"Leave him, William," said Carver, stepping over Peter Browne's bedroll. "Prince, leave. This is a private meeting."

William was the last to follow Carver down to the hold. In the darkness, Carver cleared his throat, "William, are you here?"

"Here."

"As one of the five council members I need you to fall in line if we are to keep you involved," said Carver. "Despite Prince's name not being on that document I must make it clear to you that Andrew Prince is not one of us. Share no information with him. Remember your loyalty."

"My loyalty is firm. You know that."

"We do," said Brewster.

"And you must speak to Dorothy. She lacks respect for Church authority and steps out of place too often. As her husband it is your duty to manage her. I should not need to tell you that. Remind her of the hierarchy and her duty to obey it. She has her role to play, but it does not, in any part, involve our business with the Adventurers, or the discipline aboard this ship."

"I will speak to her. You won't have to worry about it again."

Exposed

*D*esire stripped off her jacket. With trembling fingers, she reached behind her back and undid the lacing of her bodice so that she could shimmy it down. The goats looked at her curiously, their grain-dusted mouths opening and closing in unison. She would have to remove her sleeves or she wouldn't be able to get the bodice low enough. The silky slither of each one down her arms made her shiver. She could hear her heart beating. The tumult in her belly left her knees weak.

She stepped behind one of the upright deck supports and waited with her back pressed to the course wood. Her naked breasts were now free above the upper edge of her bodice. She glanced down and surveyed their fullness. Her nipples had stiffened in the cold, the skin goose-pimpled as though dusted with snow. Her waist wasn't flattering with the bodice pulled low. She retrieved her scarf and had time to hastily arrange it round her middle before she heard his footsteps in the narrow corridor. They'd been meeting here secretly for a week – but not like this.

An embarrassed flush rose to her cheeks as he drew near. She got up her nerve and swung out from the hiding place. "Surprise!"

Beth screamed, narrowly escaping the unexpected offering.

Desire's eyes sprung wide.

Beth stumbled. Her hand gripped her chest as her face iced in confusion. The pail of water she'd been carrying lay on its side, empty.

Desire spun, pulling at the stiff bodice while simultaneously shielding herself with the scarf, hoping to retain whatever dignity remained.

"I'm so sorry! I was hot. I thought I was alone."

"Your breasts were out to the wind, for pity sake. Don't think for a minute that I believe you, Desire Minter," said Beth, looking around. "Who were you *surprising*? It wasn't Gilbert. He is studying the Bible with Edward and William this morning."

"No one, Beth. I wasn't expecting anyone. I wasn't doing anything wrong. Believe me," she pleaded. Her eyes welled up. She heard a clang nearby and hoped it wasn't John. She talked louder just in case, "I was just feeding the animals and I got hot. I don't know what you are thinking, but it is wrong. What? Why Gilbert?"

"I thought you were innocent in what happened with Harlock. Have you been meeting the sailors here, playing the hussy?" seethed Beth. "These ..." She drew circles around Desire's breasts, "suggest that you don't deserve Gilbert."

"Harlock *attacked* me. And nothing happened. I was rescued." She batted angrily at her tears. "And I'm not marrying Gilbert. I'm not playing at anything."

"If I find out otherwise, whatever you are up to, you will only have yourself to blame for your ruin," said Beth, shaking a finger in her face. "Get dressed."

She stepped past Beth in shame and hid behind the pillar to retighten her bodice and attach her sleeves. She hastily pulled on her jacket, straightened her skirt and sailed past Beth, her chin in the air. She paused on the threshold of the common-way to warn John away. The click of a door closing beside her made her jump. It came from a small door she hadn't noticed before, a door with no handle, just a small key hole. The space within would have to be narrow. She pushed on the door, but it wouldn't give.

"Are you still here?" demanded Beth.

"I'm going."

John approached with long strides and she shook her head. Her face was doubtless still red for he gave her a worried look.

The rest of the day she waited in turmoil for Beth to tell of the encounter. Only after Beth closed her curtain for the night did Desire's tension begin to drain.

Tossing, unable to sleep, she rolled carefully down from the bunk. Katherine and Deacon Carver breathed heavily. She pulled the curtain and slipped out. John was against the outer wall, his head near the doorway. She stroked his cheek and he stirred. Looking to see if anyone was watching, wakeful, she eased herself under his blanket and let him pull her in close.

"I was mortified today, John," she whispered, "Beth discovered me waiting for you with my bodice down and my breasts bare."

John turned his head and found her ear. "I am *very* sorry I missed that," he said, catching her lobe between his teeth.

The tickle of his warm breath made her sigh. "I missed you. It was meant to be a surprise." She moved her hands down the rounded muscles of his back and slid them under the waist of his breeches. He sucked in his belly to make more room. "I'm worried she is going to tell. She suspects I was there to meet someone. She might try to ruin me. She still thinks I'm engaged to Gilbert."

Someone coughed.

"We will just have to be more careful," he said, planting a kiss on her nose. "I love you."

"I love you," she whispered, nuzzling into his chest.

His leg jerked in sleep. Afraid she would fall asleep too, she rolled out of his arms. A whorl of cold air filled the void.

October 27th – Second Dog Watch

"Nothing new," said Desire, looking into the pot. "He hasn't spoken with anyone all morning, nor written anything. He just sits, chewing his nails."

Dorothy tipped ground herbs into the simmering wine, dusted her fingers on her apron, and stirred until the last of the powder disappeared. A malaise had fallen on the ship. Above, Master Jones ran a skeleton crew. Below, Katherine, in consult with Dr. Fuller, moved the fevered single men aft, Billy among them.

Dorothy studied Prince. His desk was a mere ten feet from the capstan where Dr. Fuller set up his apothecary. "He knows we are watching," she whispered to Desire. "He's gotten away with it anyway, hasn't he?"

"No. He hasn't. We are going to stop him."

"There is no point. Nothing we've learned, or will learn, can make any difference. No one is going to listen. Worse, we'll be punished for trying. We just have to trust the Deacon and Elders to figure this out on their own," said Dorothy, absently stirring the wine.

"No. We can't give up," said Desire.

"Nothing will come of anything we do; we will just get hurt trying. We go back to looking after everyone in the way we always have. You focus on getting married, to whomever they choose, and start a family. That is how we will survive." An amber whirlpool was now riding the edges of Dorothy's pot.

"But, he can't hurt us now. And we've already … "

"Shh." Dorothy let go of the spoon which continued its rapid circuit while she fished through Dr. Fuller's supplies. Martin dropped a stool next to Prince's desk. Prince spat and leaned in.

"Take this grease over to Mr. Crackstone, quickly. Find out what Martin is saying," said Dorothy.

Desire squatted next to Mr. Crackstone and lifted the lid to the pungent grease. "It's time to rub a bit more on your chest, Mr. Crackstone. Take your time." He was slow, but still capable of doing it himself. She tucked her hair behind her ear and strained to catch the conversation above her.

"How did my name get on that letter?" asked Martin.

"It wasn't me who put it there," said Prince.

"Don't lie to me. You've been encouraging me to oppose the Leydeners from the beginning. And rumour is, that letter was found with others from your desk."

"Where did you hear that? Crazy wife Bradford?"

"You hide behind false gentility. I know a heady man, a violent man, when I meet one. And I know I'm easily your match. You won't use me to further your own aims again."

"How do you know it wasn't John Billington who put your name on that letter?"

Mr. Crackstone tugged on Desire's sleeve. He was done.

"John can't write," hissed Martin.

With difficulty, Desire refocused her attention on Mr. Crackstone. His eyebrows were raised. Apparently bad hearing was not among his many ailments. She put the lid back on the ointment and tucked his blankets under the thin mattress to clear a pathway to Richard Warren.

"Do I get some of that too?" said Richard.

"Of course." She lifted the lid again and waited, watching Priscilla spoon soup into Billy's mouth three beds down. Richard dug his fingers into the grease.

Prince bumped the edge of his desk and cursed as he came out from behind it. He squeezed between Mr. Crackstone's bedding and the stool left overturned by Martin. When he was gone, Richard leaned toward Mr. Crackstone.

"You don't know whom to trust anymore," he said.

"Some business that is."

Desire looked from one to the other. "Deacon Carver should be told what they said, shouldn't he?"

"Eh, sorry?" asked Richard. It was as though he had forgotten she was there. She smiled and walked back to Dorothy. She had an idea.

"Dorothy, we need the letters I gave you."

"We might as well dump them over the side. I'm not showing them to anyone again. It didn't work." Dorothy ladled another bowlful of simmering wine and handed it to Desire. "Why? What did Martin say? No, never mind. I don't need to know. I don't know why I asked you to go over there."

"Give the letters to me. I know what will work."

"Please don't. It's over. We can do more by nursing the sick."

"Dorothy Bradford, you give me those letters. They are mine as much as yours. I believed in you. Just because you've given up, doesn't mean I have to. Now, where are they?"

October 29th – First Watch

Desire counted the letters. Some of them had nothing to do with the plantation or the Adventurers. She would use them anyway. They bore Prince's signature and the handwriting matched that on the letter Dorothy showed William and Father Carver. The remainder hinted at Prince's plans, his hope to buy a Lordship. More than one letter was for Thomas Weston. None of the correspondence had anything to do with cartography.

Katherine would be back any minute. Desire folded her mantel around the eight remaining letters and tucked the bundle down between her trunk and the wall. With her eyes closed she practiced walking from the bunk to the corner and bending to find the mantel. Then she rucked up her shift and climbed into bed. Eleven sick men in the common-way. Perhaps seven she could trust to be loyal to Father Carver.

The ship lurched to starboard and righted itself again. Water whisking alongside, slapping at the ship, signalling the arrival of another round of bruising weather.

October 30th – Evening Watch

Desire handed Moses his broth. He hacked up some phlegm and spat into his handkerchief. She tucked his blankets round his toes and kissed the top of his head. "Are you any better?"

"Oh, so much better my dear. Dr. Fuller will move me back to the forward common-way soon, I suspect."

She lifted another bowl from her tray and handed it to Peter Browne. His dog licked her hand. "May I pet her?"

"Of course."

She made idle chatter and scratched the mastiff's huge head. The dog rolled on her back, inviting Desire to scratch her belly. Next to Peter's bed, she spied the letter she had tucked under his mattress in the night. It was unfolded, probably read. She looked down the line of mattresses. More open letters.

Pleased with herself, she handed out the remaining soup and returned to Beth for six more bowls. "It worked," she whispered, leaning across Beth to wink at Dorothy.

Beth tossed her ladle into the pot, where it landed with an ominous clang. "You are a hussy, Desire Minter! I knew you were up to something. I couldn't sleep last night after Jasper woke with a bad dream and I saw you sneaking down the common-way. So it's Peter Browne is it?"

"No."

"You're awfully close."

"I'm engaged," whispered Desire.

"You won't be anymore. There is no way he is marrying you now. You don't deserve him."

"You don't know what you are talking about," said Dorothy.

"You don't know what I know, Dorothy. Does she, Desire?"

Desire looked around. The other women were listening.

"You've been meeting men all over the ship. I've kept your secret. Shame on me. You and that disgusting sailor. Dorothy lost her tooth because of you!"

"Quiet, Beth!" said Dorothy.

"One of them in the manger. Your top down! Flirting with John Alden. Now, Peter Browne. You disgust me. My Edward and the others have been trying to protect your reputation. Do you not care about that at all?"

"I didn't do any of those things," said Desire.

"That is what makes me so mad. I caught you. Twice. You lie so boldly."

Desire turned, branded by the heat of a hundred eyes. She burst into tears and ran for her cabin, catapulting into the upper bunk.

She tried to recall whether John's eyes had been among them.

If he had been there, he would come. She knew that at least.

But how foolish she'd been to think that Harlock's assaults would die with him. Her relief at his death was premature – she saw that her reputation would continue to suffer, as though he still lived.

Katherine peered in.

"Father Carver will be out for a while yet. Do you want to tell me what that was all about? And for goodness sake come down from the bunk. It's too early for bed," said Katherine in a gentle voice.

"Everyone thinks the worst of me. I can't go out there again."

"No one thinks the worst of you," said Katherine. "But, tell me why she said what she did. I can't pretend I didn't hear."

"I can't. Father Carver knows. Please don't abandon me if he tells you. I couldn't bare it," she said, sobbing again.

"Come, come my child," soothed Katherine. "Everyone knows Beth is just resentful that Gilbert wasn't chosen above John."

"Does everyone know that, or think that?"

"Yes, anyone who matters, and knows you, will be inclined to think nothing more of it. Do you agree, Dorothy?" said Katherine, looking up at Dorothy now hovering in the doorway.

Dorothy nodded and Desire kissed Katherine gratefully on the cheek.

"Now let me loosen your stays so you can lie your head down after all. It will do you good."

Desire let Katherine tuck her in.

"Tomorrow, we'll have the engagement settled. A respectable engagement will overshadow any rumours," Katherine resolved.

Lightning

*J*ohn found an errant cask and pulled it up to a board balanced between two barrels of salted herring. He straddled the cask, seating himself at his new desk. A lantern swung back and forth overhead, its light playing over the parchment he'd spread before him. He began copying William's finished letter to the Investors. The winds had been rising all day and it was difficult to hold the inkwell and write, but he persevered. Normally, he had a fair hand.

A month ago a change in the wind would not have caused alarm; it might even have been welcomed. Now . . . another storm like the last could tip those struggling with illness to the brink of death – if the weakened ship didn't give way entirely and take them all down.

"I was told I'd find you down in the hold," said Alden, appearing out of the darkness. He dragged a trunk over to the opposite side of John's makeshift table and sat down.

"Take this ink for me please. The roll of the ship will soon have it on the floor," said John. "I suppose you heard what happened to Desire yesterday?"

"I did," said Alden, "but I didn't put too much stock in it. Beth is feeling resentful and it has nothing to do with Desire." Alden lifted a boot to the table edge and reclined against the slope of the hull.

"Can I trust you?" ventured John cautiously, "because I need your advice."

"Of course."

"Keep this to yourself."

"Yes."

"I'm in love with Desire. If you already suspected as much, I thank you for not saying anything. The problem is, I'm doubtful Carver will let me marry her – not while I'm indentured." He put the quill down. Alden gaped at him.

"Is she in love with you?"

"Yes – and she's been expecting a proposal."

"I won't challenge you, I'll give my word on that."

"Well, no. Why would you?"

"I won't. I'm in love with Priscilla. She is the superior girl, no offence. I intend to let Carver know I have feelings for her."

"Yes," said John slowly, trying to figure Alden's meaning. "Carver?"

He picked up his quill again and copied another line, then set the pen down and frowned. "Your advice – should I ask Carver for her hand? She keeps speaking of it as though it is a done deed."

"Well . . . you haven't much chance he will agree, have you? I mean, on paper, you're not a very attractive suitor. Carver takes his responsibility seriously. Though, if her reputation's been damaged, this is the time."

"That's a poor way of looking at it," said John. He blotted the line. "Now give me a hand by reading out the original of this letter for me, starting at … *since you conceive your selves wronged as well as we, we thought meet to add a branch to our 9th article that will almost heal that wound….*"

October 31st – Last Dog Watch

Desire finished her fish, securing the plate under the edge of one foot while reaching for the cup trapped between her knees. John was still in the hold and probably hungry. She hadn't spoken with him since yesterday – before the incident. After a moment to consider the sway of the ship she decided to risk the sloping deck and take him his supper.

She drained the rest of her beer. Over the brim she watched Carver bend to whisper something to Katherine, something shocking enough to elicit a gasp. Desire looked around wildly for John.

Katherine stood as Carver repeated his disclosure, this time to William. The pitying look that creased his face unnerved her. She felt her dinner work its way back up her throat. Katherine strode over, took the cup from her hand and steadied herself as the *Mayflower* slid down a trough. Desire looked into Katherine's face, trying to read her expression. "Is it John?"

Katherine shut the curtain and directed her to sit.

"We've had some disappointing news. John, I am afraid, has taken advantage of your feelings. He has decided to marry someone else. I am very sorry."

Desire felt a knot weave itself around her throat. But still she managed to give form to her incomprehension. "Some … someone else … Who?"

"I'm sorry, Dear, this pains me as much as it does you." Warm with pity, Katherine delivered the blow nonetheless. "Priscilla Mullins."

Desire went numb. *Priscilla? And John?* Her numbness evaporated, chased by the anger coursing wildly through her. Words flew like hornets from a threatened nest. "He couldn't! That deceitful wench! It's Beth's fault! What – are – you – saying? YOU'RE WRONG!"

"You will get over this. There are others. Hush now." Katherine held her hand and rubbed her back. "Best not to show you are too upset."

She stood, ready to bolt from the room, tugging against Katherine's grasp. Then, unable to face anyone ever again, she threw herself onto Katherine's bunk and buried herself in a pillow.

"I'll leave you to have a good cry. While you do, Deacon Carver and I will consider how to repair this." Katherine tiptoed out of the room.

Next door, Edward was shouting at Beth. Desire caught her name in the maelstrom. She mashed the pillow to her ears.

How could he do this to me? How could Priscilla listen to me talk about how in love I was, all the while betraying me?

The room spun, a motion altogether separate from the pitch of the ship. *John and Priscilla must be laughing at me behind my back.*

What is the point of living? Everything I have ever loved has been taken from me. God's special providence? What a lie that is.

What was it she had said to Priscilla? *There is only you, me and Anna that he could be chasing.*

She beat her fists into the pillow. Allowed the linen to smother her. Wondered how long it took to suffocate. *Too long.* Quicker to toss herself in the ocean. Her life had been nothing but pain. *I've been such a fool thinking John could love me.*

And she had shamed herself with him.

She trembled with horror.

"God, why did you take him from me?" she sobbed. "Don't kill me slowly with shame. Take me now. You are the only one to love me."

Gathering her strength, she rolled out of the bunk, straightened her shoulders and stepped into the corridor. Katherine tried to take her hand, but she kept walking. Eyes were averted as she passed; hands feigned busyness with invisible tasks.

There was no sign of John. A small blessing as she made her final walk of shame.

She stared straight ahead. Reaching the ladder, she mounted its lower rung, hesitated, then stepped off. Bending, she carefully removed her shoes and tucked them neatly beneath. Then slowly she climbed, barefoot on the sodden wood. Her bowels melted. The sky above whirled in a cyclone of grey.

God, if all You can offer me is suffering, smite me now. She climbed higher, smelling the quicksilver of lightning. The topsail snapped loose; she heard with strange clarity the strangled cries of sailors scrambling to gather it in. As she neared the deck, the gale sucked at her, pulling her hair through the hatch, clawing at her with static, bitterness, and portent.

"Desire! Desire!"

She ignored whoever was calling her name. No one could stop her. She would climb to the railing and if God chose to take her over it, so be it.

Then a hand was on her ankle, gripping it fiercely. She couldn't shake free. She turned with fury to see Priscilla's gloating face looking excitedly up at her. The wind was so high she couldn't hear. Something about John.

"Oh God, must you punish me to the end," she yelled into the wind.

Priscilla climbed behind her, and yelled again, "Come down, Desire. It is too dangerous up there. I must tell you my news of John Alden! I *do* care for him." She cupped her free hand to her mouth, "He has refused to marry another. He is in love with me! John Alden is in love with me! Come down! You'll catch your death."

Inches from Priscilla's face, Desire's toes turned to their target. She steadied herself on the ladder, drawing her leg back. And then Priscilla's meaning stuck.

She quickly descended the ladder, grabbed Priscilla and shook her. "Repeat that. Say that again!"

"John Alden has refused a marriage proposed by Deacon Carver. I've heard the rumour that he's in love with me," she said, frowning at Desire's angry expression. "Let go of me. Your nails are digging! What's wrong with you? I'm happy for you and I expect the same, regardless of what I said the other day."

Desire gasped and sunk to the floor, her knees turned to water. "Help me to your cabin," she pleaded. "I can't stand."

October 31st – Last Dog Watch

John sat down, a wrinkled cold fish in his bowl. Before he could take a bite, Katherine tugged him up again. Wringing her hands, she spilled the news of Alden, of Desire's fevered reaction, and of Anna's inability to find her.

He went cold. "Which way? Where did she go?" He moved a step in one direction and then the other, trying to guess from Katherine's eyes which way to travel.

"She went that way, aft. We've looked. Anna's looked."

He'd just come that way but hadn't passed her. After several strides, he grabbed Richard Warren by the arm. "Which way did Desire go? Did you see her come this way?"

"Yes, she was on the ladder."

He saw her little shoes and leapt to the deck above. Violent gusts punched at him. The seas, streaked with white, thundered past in great swells. The sailors still fought to contain the unfurling topsail, the twisted rigging squealing under the strain.

Why hadn't the hatch been closed? He scanned left then right before staggering across the deck, calling her name. His heart raced. Was he too late? Had she fallen overboard?

"WHAT HAVE YOU DONE?" he bellowed. "DESIRE!" There was a shout from above. He looked up.

His head split. His vision went white. He was weightless and then a shock of cold turned his blood to ice; he was in the water, sinking fast.

He stroked desperately, beating hard at the cold; the ship was slipping away. His chest ached with the effort of holding his breath; stars filled the black sea around him.

His fingers snagged something and he held tight. Abruptly his lifeline jerked, racing through his palm and flaying his flesh. He closed his hand against the searing pain, then with every ounce of energy remaining he stretched his other hand toward the line. His head suddenly whipped back and he sliced through the water like a hooked Marlin.

Kicking furiously, he broke to the surface. His first gulp was through a wall of spray – more seawater than air. He instinctively lowered his arms and took another breath. He gagged, gulped and held, gulped, and held as the line dragged him like a plow through the massive swell. He forced his head down to keep water from jetting up his nose.

The rope went slack as a large wave crest caught him and rolled him under. Sinking again, he climbed the limp rope hand over fist.

Something large moved beneath him and struck his foot.

It struck again. A grey shape warped the blackness. The urge to draw breath was acute. He kicked harder and took one hand off the rope to stroke. His knuckles scrabbled over something solid. Sail. He was trapped within it, his lungs growing more desperate! What if he was swimming sideways? He lost his bearings. He kicked wildly at the void. He needed to breathe. His head pounded as he pushed himself along the sail one-handed, a death grip on the rope.

The edge. The surface. He gasped. Thumping in his ears. Shouting. He went under again.

The cold numbed his muscles. His arms and legs were lead.

The rope stretched and yanked him. He breached, took a quick breath and was under again.

A bubble of air escaped his compressed lips and then another as water filled his nose. When he broke the surface again, he was coughing and spluttering too hard to take another breath. He prayed to God not to put him under again.

A stabbing pain shot thought his buttock and he wriggled like a speared fish. His vision was watery. He was warm and tingling. His head smacked something hard. Another sharp bite and he screamed. His arms stroked furiously in an effort to escape the beast.

"He must have a charm on him – unbelievable."

"E's alright if he can scream like that. Git him below."

He lost consciousness.

October 31st – Last Dog Watch

William slipped between the gasping women, then flattened against the capstan as two sailors, John's body draped between them, struggled past. The deck was slippery with blood.

Katherine broke from the group and took John's head in both her hands. She swept the blond hair from his brow.

The sailors ignored her. "Where's your doctor?" they shouted.

"Here," said Dr. Fuller striding up the passageway. "Put him in here, quickly," he said, waving the sailors into the nearest cabin. It was the Tilleys'. Young Elizabeth Tilley jumped off the lower bunk to make room.

"What's happened? Why is he bleeding?" said William, helping to roll John into the bunk.

The sailor shook his head, still unable to believe the rescue. "He went o'er board, sir, when the top'sl was swept off. Must ha' grabbed onto the halliards trailing behind – underwater a long time, he was. I though he was lost a'sure, then we spotted 'im. Dragged 'im in with effort, the sail bein' attached and pullin' hard against us. Got 'im though di'n't we. Caught 'im with the boat hook round the waist and hauled 'im aboard."

"That's a strong man, that is," nodded his companion. "Not many could 'a hung on like that."

Through all the clamour, Dr. Fuller had been poking and prodding his patient. He shooed Elizabeth, her mother, and her aunt from the room and began tossing John's wet clothes to the floor.

"Give me a hand, William."

Turning John onto his belly they found the gash from the boat hook that saved his life – a three-inch cleft in his buttock bleeding freely.

"Thankfully the hook pierced his buttock and not his abdomen or kidney. If it had, he'd of died a worse death than drowning. Get me hot broth," Dr. Fuller hollered into the corridor, dismissing the sailors with a wave. "And bring me hot water for bathing."

He covered John with a blanket and sighed. "Once again I don't have the necessities. Stay with him. I'll retrieve my bag."

October 31st – Last Dog Watch

Roused from Priscilla's cabin by the commotion, Desire wandered into the corridor. Katherine, outside the Tilleys' cabin, was alternately wringing her hands then bunching them in her skirt. Her face was wet.

Seeing Desire she beckoned her urgently. "Oh Desire. It's our John in there. He was swept overboard. He went looking for you. Who knows what possessed him to go on deck. I'm frightened. He looked dead when they brought him down."

"Dead? No! No, no, no." Desire wrenched her hands from Katherine's and threw open the Tilleys' curtain.

Desire's entry startled Dr. Fuller, who was in the midst of bandaging John's buttock. William tried to steer her back into the corridor. She struggled past him and managed to grab the edge of the bunk near John's head, "John? John? Oh please. John, can you hear me?" she sobbed. "Don't leave me."

Dr. Fuller eyed her curiously, but being presented with the hot broth and boiling water, carried on with his work.

Katherine's eyes widened in sudden recognition. "Our John?" she said, full of accusation.

John regained consciousness, reviving thanks to a barrage of kisses from Desire. She smiled down at him, murmuring a prayer for his deliverance.

"That's enough," sputtered Katherine. "I'm going for Father Carver. Come with me, Desire."

John raised his hand weakly and she caught hold of it. His familiar hand felt uneven and rough. She turned it over, drawing a sharp breath. "Doctor, his hand. It doesn't even look like . . . ."

Dr. Fuller leaned forward and swung the lamp toward John's hand. She turned away. It hurt to imagine the pain. "Please help him."

"You cannot stay here, Desire. I don't pretend to know what you're about, but I can't tend him properly with you in the way," said Dr. Fuller.

"I can't go. I can't. I'll do anything to help, but I won't leave him."

"We'll both go, Desire," said William.

"I'm not going."

Dr. Fuller shrugged, "If you're staying, then wring these hot cloths out until they are almost dry. Lay them on his chest and under his arms. Careful, they're near scalding. As they cool, remove them and replace them with more." He placed one over John's leg and tucked it into his inner thigh. "Don't leave the flesh bare or it will cool again.

"Did anyone bring a warming pan?" he shouted out into the hall. "Go and retrieve it; we are in need."

"If we don't raise his temperature, he'll die. He's cold as ice."

Desire continued to mutter prayers as she busied herself wringing the hot cloths and arranging them on John's chest. They cooled quickly but she developed a rhythm. She worked furiously to warm him. When he lapsed into unconsciousness she redoubled her frenetic pace.

"This broth's gone cold!" Dr. Fuller complained loudly. "Warm it again someone. I'll need it the moment he wakes."

"I'll warm it, Dr. Fuller, I'm right here for whatever you need," said Elizabeth Tilley from the door jam.

"Go and find Billy. You women shouldn't be here with John lying undressed on the bed, both of you unmarried!" He scowled and shook his head but continued with his work.

"I am not leaving him," Desire repeated with conviction.

"I fear these cloths aren't working. The air is too cool." He drummed his fingers on his knee. "Where is the warming pan. Did anyone find one?"

Hearing no reply, Dr. Fuller turned to Desire. "Keep trying to revive him. We need to get some broth into him." He turned and shouted, "Where is that broth, Elizabeth?"

"Here sir, here. You wanted Billy and he's coming too, though he looks poorly," said Elizabeth.

John mumbled, his body twisting. "He's coming around. Prop him up if you can, lass. Talk to him while I try to get some of this into his belly."

John's head lolled but he smiled dreamily in response to Desire's words of encouragement.

She ignored more than one curious look from Dr. Fuller as she poured her heart out. She was beyond caring what anyone thought.

Dr. Fuller muttered to himself, not satisfied with John's condition. Then he exclaimed, "Bring me that Mastiff, the Terrier too." He slapped his knee. "My first thought was of William White, with his fever raging, but this is better."

The dogs jumped onto the bunk and, seeming to sense their purpose, lay their heads across John's body.

Dr. Fuller stepped out into the corridor.

Desire leaned over quickly and kissed John on the lips. His eyes came into focus.

"Desire? You're alive?" he said weakly.

She took his face in her hands, "John, it was you who almost died – because of me. It is my fault you were washed overboard. And if you had died, I would have thrown myself in after you rather than live without you."

She perched herself on the doctor's vacated seat and lovingly spooned broth between his smiling lips.

They were alone in the universe, Adam and Eve.

The mark across his nose where it was split by Harlock was still pink with new flesh. She was amazed. How could their love be that fresh? The scar was maybe a month old, yet he was her whole life – as though she had sprung from his flesh and spirit. Sin and death, hunger and despair were meaningless. There was such promise in their togetherness.

"Desire. My beautiful Desire." His eyes brimmed with tears. "I know why you went to the deck. You thought it was me who wouldn't marry you. I'll marry you this second to prove how wrong you are. I have loved you from the beginning." He coughed and took a rattling breath. "I will never stop loving you." He struggled to free his arm from the blankets and reached up with his bandaged hand to clumsily stroke her hair. "It was only instinct that made me hold on. I thought, as I stood on deck, and saw you nowhere, that you had already been carried away." He started to cry and she soothed him, tucking his hand back into the blankets.

"I love you more than myself, John. I will never do anything to harm you again."

"John! Good to see you revived," thundered Deacon Carver, making John jump and bite his tongue.

Desire rubbed the back of her head where it had smacked the top bunk.

"I can hardly believe it, John. The account of your strength and the desperation of your rescue impresses us all." Carver gave John's calf a firm squeeze. "How do you feel?"

His pulse was pounding beneath Desire's fingertips. "I'll live, though I'm terribly cold and my lungs are aching."

"But you've no trouble speaking. I couldn't help overhear." Carver dropped his joviality. "Don't misunderstand my joy at seeing you alive. It is a miracle you didn't drown. I don't believe another of us could have held on and survived." Carver looked at Desire's hand cradling his head and frowned.

"Leave us, Desire," he said tersely.

Desire slowly removed her arm. She picked up the discarded bowl and cloth and stepped past her guardian, meeting his eyes with equal parts fear, apology and defiance. She didn't close the curtain behind her but stepped away, only to turn and hug the outer wall so she could eavesdrop at its opening.

"John you know I have respect for you. I am grateful to the Lord for sparing you and know it was with a higher purpose that he did so. No man could survive such peril otherwise. You may think that purpose was to marry our Desire, but I disagree. You are indentured. I wish I could free you of your commitment but we have a contract between us. You are my servant."

He opened his mouth to speak, but Carver raised his hand to stop him.

"It has come to my attention that things have become inappropriate between you and Desire and that may have been the result of a misunderstanding between her and Katherine. But you, you knew better. You've abused your position. I cannot give permission for you to marry her. That is final."

"I'm in love with her. I've told her I will marry her and if you say no, I might as well throw myself overboard again. I cannot live without her."

Desire peaked around the door jam. John had dropped back on the pillow, an arm covering his eyes.

"We're in love, Deacon, I know it is God's will that she be my wife. He would not have created a love this strong without purpose."

"It's lust, that is all. And this is uncharacteristic drama. Time away from each other will lessen your passions. We're nearing the coast. If you want to do what is best for Desire, you'll stay away from her and not encourage her in what she confuses with love," said Carver, oblivious to the torment he was causing.

She rushed back into the room and, giving Carver a wide berth, pressed herself to the head of the bed.

John struggled to sit up and with all the assertion he could muster said, "I have never been surer of being in love in my life. I will not be parted from her for one day, for she is my life! She is the breath that sustains me! We must marry, or be forced to live in sin. I cannot stop what I feel just because you order it to be so!" Perspiration beaded his forehead and he slumped back.

Desire clasped his arm, sinking with him. Pleading, she turned her eyes to Carver. "If you love me, you will bless our marriage. We will never find a stronger love. John is a great man, better than any man you may force me to marry. Please. Reconsider, Father Carver."

Carver's face softened but his lips remained resolute.

"It is impossible. You cannot marry a servant. It is beneath you." He reached for her hand, but she clung to John, unyielding.

"I'm never going to stop loving him and I won't marry anyone else!"

"Leave us!" Carver barked. "You disgrace yourself."

"But he needs me," she implored, gripping John's arm tighter. "I won't stop loving him. You must allow us. I'll die of heart break if you don't."

Carver grabbed her elbow, but she struggled free and locked eyes with John.

They were as tortured as hers.

Tears ran down her cheeks. They formed little rivulets that merged at her chin and in a last moment of freedom splashed on John's upturned face.

He reached up with his bandaged hand to touch her cheek. His tongue reached for the tears pooling above his lip as Carver lifted her from the stool and ejected her from the room.

Young Billy waited outside with more broth, stooped as an old man. He glistened with sweat.

"You don't look well, Billy," Carver said, still gripping her round the waist.

"Doctor needs help, sir," said Billy taking a seat in the cabin.

"I should be nursing him, Father. Billy needs his rest. You can see that. Let me, for Billy's sake." She couldn't loosen Carver's hold. Everyone in the common-way was staring.

Carver didn't answer her. He turned to John, "Let this be on your head."

"I would marry her. There's no better way to protect her honour than that."

"There is no path to that day," said Carver with a slow shake of his head. He gruffly marched her back down the common-way.

He nodded to Brewster, whispered something to Katherine and thrust Desire into their cabin.

October 31st – First Watch

"It's better to get it over with," said Katherine.

"Get what over with?"

"Your punishment."

"Punishment? No, Mother Katherine! I'm suffering enough." Desire backed into the corner with her hands behind her back, afraid Katherine was going to drag her out.

"Don't make this harder on us, dear. You know Elders Brewster and Allerton don't relish it. But it has to be done. You can't behave that way and be given special treatment just because you are our ward. Everyone has already seen and heard you."

"But you told me we were engaged. I thought you gave me permission. I wouldn't have done it if I thought it was wrong," begged Desire.

"Strip down to your shift. You won't be bare. Not with the sailors and the likes of Billington and Martin about," said Katherine, coaxing her forward.

"No. Don't do this. I'm already suffering," she said, swiping at the tears on her cheeks.

Katherine spun her around, yanked her laces loose and pealed her bodice open. Desire crossed her arms in a vain attempt to hold it secure. "Now the skirt and petticoat."

"Would you really shame me like this? Is this what Father Carver told you to do?"

"The skirt, Desire."

She shook her head. Beneath the skirt her legs began to wobble.

"Anna!" hollered Katherine.

"Yes," Anna said meekly, from just outside the door.

"Help me remove Desire's skirt."

Seeing Anna's tortured expression as she timidly loosened the drawstring, Desire stopped resisting. There was no way out of what lay ahead and she would not spread her suffering to Anna.

Clad now in nothing but her shift, Desire was towed by Katherine into the common-way. She had cooked and tended the sick here, laughed and taught the children, carried out every task asked of her on behalf of the congregation. Her neck and face flared hot. She turned her back, mortified by the feel of so many eyes probing her thin fabric, trying to expose her further. Katherine jerked her violently, forcing her face forward.

"Over here please, Katherine," Brewster said. He and Isaac were standing at the forward end of the common-way near the passage to the manger.

She kept her eyes on the smooth planks, trying to imagine she was not at the centre of this terrific chaos where everything was upside down, the opposite of what it was. She wanted so badly to preserve the respect so suddenly forfeit. She prayed she would not fall apart. Was she to be forever remembered in her shift, weakened and shamed before them like this?

Brewster leaned in and spoke to her quietly. "Will you submit to the strap willingly or do we need to tie you to the post?"

"Please don't do this!" She lost all composure. "Katherine said I could court him."

"I did not!" said Katherine, letting go of her hand. "You must have deliberately misunderstood."

"Move back," Isaac said to the pressing crowd.

She risked looking over her shoulder. All eyes were on her. Lizzy with her baby. Mr. Crackstone and John Goodman, whose fevered brows she wiped. Mary, John Alden. Peter Browne and Richard Warren whose meals she always cooked. William. And Dorothy, her mouth firmly set. Disapproval from her friend, after all they had come through? She should have been honest with Dorothy. She lowered her eyes then raised them again. What of Priscilla?

Priscilla's brows were cinched with worry. Her face was wet with tears. Their eye met. Desire willed her not to reveal what she and John had done.

"Desire, it has been made known to Deacon Carver that you have been carrying on with his servant in an inappropriate manner. You will receive twenty straps as a lesson to yourself and any unwed woman tempted by your behaviour," intoned Isaac. "Do you have anything to say for yourself?"

"I *did* believe we were allowed to court." She looked at him hopefully. "We are in love."

"I am sorry, Desire, that is not an excuse," said Isaac.

"Do you want to stand and accept the strap or will I need to bind you?" asked Brewster again, gently.

"I'll stand," she said, looking from one to the other, still hopeful for a reprieve.

"You will have to turn around."

She turned awkwardly, unsure how to stand. It was hard to raise her eyes to the crowd. Their expressions were grim; grim and expectant. Among these friends she suddenly found none. She stretched tall and braced herself. Isaac accepted the wide leather strap from Brewster. Her stomach lurched with fear.

A sharp intake of breath as Isaac's arm drew back. She was determined not to give them the satisfaction of her pain. The strap landed, propelling a cry from deep within her. Sobs followed, in spite of herself. The pain sunk deep into her buttock. It was unjust.

They all stared in silence.

The second blow landed on top of the first and she lurched forward. Brewster placed a hand on her shoulder to draw her back. He kept it there and nodded to Isaac.

Another blow just below the last. It hit her tailbone and she screamed.

"STOP!" John roared from down the passage. "STOP. SHE DOESN'T DESERVE THAT!"

As the crowd spun she saw John dragging himself, naked, out of the Tilleys' cabin, fighting to stay upright.

"Stay there, John," she called, "I'm fine." She tried to regain her composure.

"It's not her fault. Punish me, Isaac. I'll take her punishment."

"John!" she cried, as his one good leg crumpled and he rolled forward. He was whiter than snow.

The Doctor, William and Edward rushed to him, pulling him up and back into the cabin. He fought them off.

"John – I'm fine." It hurt far more to watch him trying to stand. "I'm fine," she said, wiping her tears.

"You're still cold and bleeding. You must get back in bed," said the Doctor firmly.

John couldn't keep up the struggle. He was forced through the doorway. Desire fell to her knees.

"You must stand up," said Brewster, taking her arm.

"I can't," she said.

"You must. We have to finish." He nodded, encouraging her to rise.

She cried silently and stiffened her spine. She locked her knees and kept her eyes trained on the Tilleys' cabin. She clenched her teeth tight as each blow struck. Only one of them needed to feel this pain. She winced and grunted as the strap snapped eleven. Isaac was going lighter on her. She knew he was, but it still burned within and without.

The twentieth stroke fell and she stood stiff. She didn't trust herself to move without falling over.

"Do you ask forgiveness for your sin and loose behaviour?" asked Isaac gently.

Desire remained mute. Her silence stiffened the strap in his hands. He looked at her expectantly, almost pleading for her to speak, but she was still. She looked again to the Tilleys' cabin where John would be listening. She measured the pain she would inflict on him by pronouncing their love a sin against the pain he would experience if another blow cracked her flesh. She was in too much agony to sort out the answer . . .

"Three more straps," Isaac said.

What? Twenty. I was to get twenty.

He didn't hold back this time. With the first hit she lost her balance.

Billington's snicker stripped her bare. She heard him murmur to Martin, "No one will want her now, but if they pay me enough I'll take her off of Carver's hands and use her to keep my bed warm."

Martin laughed.

"Look at the size of those nipples," said Billington.

She felt like her eyes were bleeding shame.

She willed Isaac to get on with it. What was he waiting for? She opened her eyes just as the second blow found a fresh patch on her lower back. She wiped her nose and clenched her teeth harder. She wouldn't give them satisfaction.

"Make her sweat more," Billington hooted.

She heard a scuffle and opened her eyes. Dorothy had stepped in front of Billington and Martin and spread her shawl wide, obscuring their view. Billington swatted the shawl down. Again she raised her screen. The tension in the room, already high, became electric. Now all eyes were on Dorothy. Billington swatted again, this time with force enough to wrench the shawl from Dorothy's hands. Mary moved beside Dorothy, drew her own shawl from her shoulders and raised it in front of an incredulous Billington. Priscilla raised hers. Eleanor Billington lunged to snatch one of the uplifted shawls, but Mary Allerton stepped in her path. She was quickly joined by Elizabeth and Suzanna. Anna raised her shawl. Soon a fleet of shawls billowed in the room. Katherine raised her shawl. She looked at Beth. Beth pulled her shawl tighter around her shoulders. And then she loosened it and raised it high above her. Desire sobbed.

Isaac stepped back, the strap limp at his side.

"Do you ask forgiveness from God for your wanton behaviour?"

She knew he hadn't lost count.

"I do." She fell to the ground and wept.

Dorothy's arm swept under her.

Katherine kissed her cheek. Mr. Crackstone patted her shoulder and old Moses lifted her hand to his mouth and gave it a gentle kiss. "You did bravely, dear," he said. John Goodman and Peter Browne nodded and then dropped their heads. Returning to the cabin she was touched by unseen hands. Gentle hands.

She fell into bed and cried, wishing for the day to finally end.

In Sickness

J ohn wiped a drop from his forehead and turned on his side. Seized by a coughing fit, he wrapped his arms around himself to contain the splintering pain in his ribs. If only Carver would take pity on him. Surrounded by other men calling out or moaning in their fevered dreams, he wondered at his chance of recovery.

Young Billy, who had tended him for two days, had collapsed after lunch the day before with his own fever and was taken to Dr. Fuller's cabin. Priscilla, Elizabeth, and a number of other women came in Billy's stead to swab his brow and help him eat. But the one woman he needed was kept away.

Desire wept as she worked, separated from him by a gulf of thirty feet, but a lifetime if Carver would not relent. His eyelids sagged with fatigue. As soon as everyone was asleep he would drag himself to her side and reassure her that nothing had changed. He would once again feel her gentle touch.

He opened his eyes to darkness. Behind the doctor's curtain a candle blazed to life, the doctor likely preparing to make his midnight rounds. But the lantern never left the cabin and John wondered whether it was too late to crawl to Desire. The doctor might appear with his herbal at any moment.

He woke again with a start. Keening filled the 'tween deck.

William's lanterns bobbed past his head. He set it down nearby and grasped the hands of Edward and Stephen.

"Dear God in heaven. So young," said William. "It will crush his mother." William looked over his shoulder. Dorothy peered through a slit in their curtain. Her face glistened with tears. He lowered his voice. "We'll send word gently to let her know."

Brewster blew his nose and pocketed his handkerchief. "Billy's mother had cause to be proud of him – a doctor's assistant. He was a hard-working and caring lad and shall be rewarded now with God's great care and keeping."

Sorrow ripped along the corridor.

"I tried my best," sobbed Ann Fuller as she emerged from the cabin. She stretched an arm out to her son, just two years younger than Billy, and locked him in a tight embrace.

Dr. Fuller retreated into the shadows, refusing to be consoled.

Within earshot of John, Carver murmured to Katherine, "Let's hope this isn't all of our fate. So many are sick. How many are children? Look at the mess and filth we live in."

"The children just have sniffles and coughs. Little Ellen's fever isn't any worse. And the men are strong. Aren't they?" said Katherine, wanting to believe it. "We're almost there. We'll get dry and warm when we arrive and have fresh food."

"Not soon enough." He added limply. "Please help Ann prepare Billy's body for a service at daybreak." He crumpled into Katherine, who bore the weight of his shaking shoulders. "I hate to do it – he should have a proper burial."

John sat up. *He's a good man, despite what he is doing to me and Desire.*

November 3rd – Morning Watch

Impossibly slight and wrapped in cotton, William Butten was borne across the companionway into the glowing light of dawn.

The sunrise was more glorious than any they had seen yet. A stained-glass morning reflected upon the sparkling sea. Dewy lines twinkled with rosy light and great columns of ruby and amethyst stretched from horizon to gilded heaven. So much beauty, too late for Billy's eyes, made Desire sob anew.

The Master insisted he pay the honour of presiding over the funeral.

With all her might, Desire willed him to finish and let them worship in their own way. His rote seaman prayers and speeches, delivered with stern monotony, grated on her raw emotion. How little he understood the general tide of reluctance they shared at the thought of casting Billy overboard, how vulnerable they felt at this moment, how much it cut at their hearts to lose one of their own.

Seizing on one of the many lengthy pauses in the Master's sermon Deacon Carver leapt to his feet and invited Elder Brewster to lead a prayer.

Then it was time to say goodbye. One by one they made their way to Billy's body.

When it was John's turn, he stumbled badly. In obvious pain, he needed help to return to his place. He then collapsed, shaking within his blanket.

It was her turn. She stood and came forward to touch the shroud and whisper farewell. The damp linen chilled her already numb fingers. On the way back to her place Desire tugged little Love Brewster's collar up round his ears and pulled his cape snug.

Deacon Carver spoke. It was time. The men who had carried Billy to the deck reluctantly stepped forward and, lifting his little body, brought him to the rail.

A tightness developed in her throat and the involuntary cry escaping her lips echoed around her. Adam's apples bobbed as the men sought to contain their grief. The burial party raised their small burden higher, shared a look, and let Billy slip from their arms. Everyone stepped forward as though to catch him, but at the sound of the splash they sank to their knees. He was gone.

The lines of the ship sharpened, returning to the sombre palette known for so long. Desire waited with the Carvers, her feet numb in her boots, as some of their weaker friends were helped down the ladder. Katherine urged her to get some sleep. She nodded, but had no intention of lying down. She might get to John, unseen, if she stayed awake. Just before Billy's death, Carver had announced that she would marry Gilbert. Her new suitor acted as though he was doing everyone, especially her, a favour by relieving her of her shame. John must know that despite the rumours, she would never marry anyone else.

November 3rd – Forenoon Watch

Katherine and the Deacon disappeared behind their curtain. One by one, everyone shuffled to bed. The children and a few single men rustling in their blankets along the walls were the only ones likely to be awake when John came down. Desire stood by the capstan where she could see the ladder, fully aware that Anna, instructed to chaperone her, knew why.

John was taking a long time. Nearly everyone had returned.

A boot appeared on the top rung.

She stepped forward and unclasped her hands. She recognized Alden's green hose above the boot. He was giving instruction. Her pulse quickened with anticipation.

Suddenly Alden's left arm arced back and his foot flew off the ladder. A blur tumbled past Alden, landing with a thud on the deck.

She screamed.

John had fallen through the open hatchway.

She tapped his cheeks and begged him to wake.

He wouldn't.

"Don't die, John." To the thin slice of heaven visible above, she yelled, "Don't take him!"

Everyone was with her. Deacon Carver pulled at her.

"Check to see if he's breathing," said Carver. Edward's hand apologetically rooted between her and John's chest.

"He is."

"What if Billy was just the first?" said William.

"No. Father Carver, help him," she sobbed, "I'll do anything. Let me care for him."

"Out of the question," he dismissed. In the cramped space both he and Dr. Fuller were trying to pull her away by the shoulders.

"Open your eyes, John," she said, struggling to stay close. "It's me. Wake up."

"Desire, move out of the way. You are making things worse for him, and yourself. Let the doctor do his job. Go sit with Katherine. You are forbidden to be here," said Carver.

"We can't leave him alone like before," she pleaded. "That's why this happened."

"The answer is no. You will stay away from each other."

"I'll marry anyone you say if you let me look after him. Please, Father. He has to live . . . I can save him . . . I know it," she said, barely able to catch her breath through the tears.

Dr. Fuller lifted his hands in surrender. "Don't put all your faith in me, Carver. First Billy, now John. Almighty, they'd just the catarrh. And now I'm low on necessary simples." He shook his head. "You decide, but we have to get him off the deck."

"Obviously you are the best person to care for him, Doctor," said Carver.

"Please, Father. I promise I'll do as you say. If he lives, I won't ask again to marry him. This happened because you wouldn't let me look after him." She was on her knees begging him and he looked at her stonily.

"We need to move him and get him warm," urged the doctor.

"Alright. Move him to our cabin," said Carver. "You will marry Gilbert, Desire. I have your promise."

"Just help me save him, Father. I will."

Poison

"What do you think of that business between John and Desire, William?" asked Isaac, "I sorely hated to beat her for it."

Wind snapped the sails and whistled between them. William pulled his cloak tighter and glanced over at Dorothy sitting with the other women on deck. Desire wasn't among them but, oddly, Eleanor and Martin's wife were. They were each sipping a warm drink.

"Carver is uncompromising when it comes to hierarchy and position. I can't say I disagree with him. We can't all be equals or else there'd be no order to society whatsoever," said William.

"But you know as well as I do that John is of good blood. And if he had been anyone else's bond servant, Carver would have agreed to the match," said Isaac.

Brewster joined them and stomped his feet against the cold.

"We're talking of John Howland," said Isaac.

"How is he?" asked Brewster.

"Recovering. Thanks to Desire, I'm sure," said William. "Carver's not pleased with her. Gilbert, seeing what's going on, is having second thoughts."

"All this talk of marriage and there is no civil body set up for the performance of one yet," said Brewster.

"Yes, occasions will arise," said Isaac. "Now that we are nearing the coast we need to discuss governance. A new election perhaps and the appointment of more assistants to the Governor."

"As Church Elders, neither Isaac nor I should run for civil government," proposed Brewster. "It'll muddy things if we're disciplining on behalf of the Church and the state."

"True. And those outside the congregation, those most likely in need of discipline, would never allow it. We were wrong to think Martin was our problem. It's Billington," said Isaac.

The children ran rings around them, laughing in the cool sunshine. William glanced again toward Dorothy. She was wrapped in the blanket he had brought for her.

"Billington?" he said, returning to the conversation, "Yes. John Goodman just told me Billington is still agitating for others to forget the agreement with the investors and make for Virginia instead. He has been trying to rally support among the single men, but with everyone so sick, he hasn't gotten far."

Brewster hollered for Carver, who immediately came loping across the deck.

"Tell William what you were given," Brewster said to Carver.

"I've had several letters turned in to me, written by Prince. As we feared, he is trying to drive a wedge between us and those we once thought of as strangers. He has been corresponding with Weston too."

"Billington's attempt to garner support for Virginia, and the attempt Martin made early on, are clear efforts to divide us," said William. "But their efforts started before Prince got involved."

"That we know," Carver growled. "We need to stop talk of Virginia. We don't have a patent with them and we don't want one either. We need to make this clear. The Virginian government won't tolerate the practice of reformed faith. We'll have given up everything only to be worse off than we were in Leyden."

Brewster gripped Carver's arm. "Prince or Martin or Billington, whoever is behind it, won't get the support they expect. We'll do as we discussed and start our own campai – "

They turned to starboard as a volley of ear-splitting screams broke across the deck.

November 4th – Afternoon Watch

"Grab her!"

"Bring her down!"

William wondered if a fight had finally erupted between Eleanor and the other women. Then he saw Dorothy, one leg over the rail, struggling against Beth's attempts to pull her from the edge.

"Dorothy!" he shouted, sprinting to help Beth and the other women now holding Dorothy's skirt and sleeves.

"Dorothy! What are you doing?" He grabbed her around the waist and tore her from the rail.

She looked at him with uncomprehending eyes; eyes that bulged with fear and confusion. "Answer me!"

She turned away, mumbling incoherently, struggling to reach the rail.

"Find the doctor," he said as calmly as he could to Beth.

Dorothy's face came alive. She startled them all with a sudden yell. "They are coming for me! He knows! He knows!" Then an octave lower, "Get off quick. For Jonathan. We must get away."

"Dorothy. Dorothy speak sense!" William shook her roughly.

"The doctor is busy, William," said Beth, poking her head through the companionway, out of breath.

"Help me get her down to the cabin," said William.

"She was fine until a few minutes ago," said Mary. "Just sipping her tea. All of a sudden she got a funny look and started swatting the air before her nose."

"Doctor!" William called, his voice breaking under the strain as he lifted and dragged Dorothy toward their cabin. "Dorothy's tried to throw herself overboard. Help, please!"

"Get her settled and I'll be there directly. I'm finishing with Moses' leg."

Dorothy lapsed again into nonsensical muttering, but her struggle against his hold was undiminished. Her energy shocked William.

"There, there, dear," he repeated mechanically.

"You'll be alright now, will you, William?" said Beth.

"I need you, Beth. She trusts you."

"That is exactly why I can't do this," hissed Beth.

He gritted his teeth and spoke over his shoulder. "And how am I to do it as her husband? But I must, Beth. If we don't hold her down, she will try it again."

While his head was turned Dorothy kicked his leg, then pulled a wrist free and struck him clumsily against the side of his head. She giggled at her success, as though it were a game. He lost his patience and twisted the flesh on her arm. She cried out, the surprised look on her face filling him with instant regret and shame. "I'm sorry dear. Please stop fighting me and just lie down on the bed."

Though he held her with all his might, he couldn't stop Dorothy's gyrations, her arms and legs running amok in every direction.

Keeping her distance, Beth watched him struggle, then suddenly gave in with a sigh. She spoke to Dorothy in soothing, cheerful tones and managed to get Dorothy to sit still on the edge of the bunk.

"Doctor!" shouted William.

"I'm here." Dr. Fuller's face worked with unvoiced concern. But he hesitated only a moment before springing into action, stirring the contents of his bag purposefully and extracting his fleam.

"We'll bleed her. She has too much of the hot tempers within her blood. She suffers from inflammation of the cauls of the brain and for that I shall have you, Beth, go and get me some beet juice."

Beth quickly disappeared in the direction of the hold.

"Beet juice?" William asked

"Syringed into the nose, it settles the frenzy."

Dr. Fuller sat at Dorothy's side. He gave William a look of pity and then took Dorothy by both of her upper arms and forced her to lie backward. "When Beth returns, have her get ten long strips of linen bandage," he mumbled so that only William could hear.

"He wants to kill me. Stop him." Dorothy grunted, wriggling to twist free of Dr. Fuller's grasp.

"She is hot. Her heart races," said Dr. Fuller.

She threw William such a pleading look that he wanted to dismiss Dr. Fuller. But his better judgement told him not to interfere in what was to come.

"If we had lettuce and violet leaf I could boil her a draft with posset ale that would calm her to such a mild temperament that we wouldn't have to bind her. If she stays like this, she mustn't be free until we are off the ship," said Dr. Fuller, planting his forearm across her chest to prevent her rising, "for her own safety."

William took a seat behind Dr. Fuller and held Dorothy's ankles, afraid that if he looked her in the eye, he would see reflected all the ways he had let her down – how he was this moment betraying her trust in him.

"Thirst, I'm thirsty," said Dorothy jutting her tongue out again and again.

After long minutes Beth returned from her second errand of collecting long linen bandages. "I'm done. I can't help you anymore," she said.

William hated himself for persuading her.

She twisted linen around Dorothy's flailing legs, occasionally grunting with frustration in company with the curses and scolding remarks of Dr. Fuller who was having little success binding Dorothy's torso to the bunk.

William busied himself wrapping Dorothy's wrists, but, cowed by his failure to be a better husband, he was making little progress against the hurricane that was his wife.

"William! Are you helping man, or not?" berated Fuller. "We'll be all day at it if you don't haul her arm in! I can't do it all. Do you want her bound to the bed or not?"

William's heart answered in the negative, but he increased his efforts, apologizing profusely to Dorothy. For his pains, she bit him hard on the hand.

Her shrill screams seeped throughout the ship, which bit by bit took on a dreadful silence.

Nearly an hour later, Dorothy's face, Beth's apron and both Dr. Fuller and William's hands were stained red – the majority of the beet juice never having made its way into Dorothy's nose. She was bound to the bed, the mysterious electric currents inside her still alive, still forcing her head to strain skyward from the pillow. From her bound right arm, blood trickled onto the yellowed linen.

Beth stood watching in the door frame, curtain pulled around herself so fully that only her glassy, reddened eyes were visible. When Edward touched her shoulder, she slouched. He led her away, sobbing. William sat alone and frightened.

After a time, the curtain slid open a hair. Desire peeked in. "William, was Eleanor with Dorothy earlier?"

"Yes," he stated morosely.

Dorothy spasmed against the bed.

"It's just that I saw Eleanor with Mr. Prince yesterday. He gave her something and she pocketed it and he made a note in his little brown book. He makes notes in that book every time he asks someone to do something. I've seen him do it many times. I know you trust him, but I'm sure whatever is wrong with Dorothy is his fault. He probably thinks *she* gave Father Carver his letters. But it wasn't her."

"How do you know about the letters?"

"It just isn't her fault. But Mr. Prince thinks it is. That's why they gave her something."

November 5th – Forenoon Watch

"How is she, Mary?" asked William.

"Almost back to normal. No fever and the vomiting has stopped. I checked on her after you left and she's had plenty of visitors since. Whenever we get a break, we go in to see her."

"Does she remember anything yet?"

"Not a thing recounted to me. She may have said something to the others."

"I'm just going to take her some beer and then I've got to go back to the hold. We aren't finished taking stock."

William knelt by the bed and lifted Dorothy's blanket from the floor. She was struggling in a dream. He stroked her head and soothed her. She was burning up.

"Dorothy. Dorothy!" He shook her but she wouldn't wake. "Dorothy!"

He ripped the curtain aside. "Mary, get Dr. Fuller." The binding round her wrists was stained with fresh blood. She'd been struggling for a while.

"Dorothy, wake up."

Dr. Fuller rushed in and tossed his bag on the bed. He elbowed William against the wall, bent to listen to her breathing, felt her head, placed his hand on her heart, smelled her breath and wiped something from around her mouth. He licked it and spat.

"Datura stramonium," said Dr. Fuller, spitting again. "Dorothy? Wake up. It's Dr. Fuller." He pinched her arm hard.

"Get Billy," he said.

William gaped at him.

"No. I mean . . . I've got to check something. Stay with her."

William squatted on the floor next to her and undid the binding round her wrist. "Mary?" he called through the doorway.

"William, I swear she was alright," said Mary, looking aghast as she peered in through the doorway.

"Who has been here?"

"Priscilla, Desire, Suzanna, Elizabeth, Beth, Mary Allerton, Sarah, the old hag Eleanor, and myself."

"What was Eleanor doing here? Did you not think that odd?"

"She said she felt badly for her. She's been trying to make amends before we arrive. She's been doing so ever since that night with poor Desire and John Howland."

November 5th – Forenoon Watch

Billington, Martin and Richard Bitteridge were seated by the mizzenmast, sharpening their swords. The ship pitched beneath William's feet as he approached, but he was oblivious. He charged straight at Billington, grabbed the larger man by the stock and hauled him to his feet. Billington's sword dropped with a clang.

"I have had enough of you and that viper you call a wife." William gave the stock a twist and yarded it back and forth. Billington's head bobbed.

He grabbed William's fists to loosen the choke hold. Unsuccessful, he took a hard swing at William and they both fell to the deck, rolling back and forth in the narrow space between the rails.

William, blind with fury, pinned Billington down.

"What kind of husband are you? You've no control over your wife. Who's idea was it to poison Dorothy?"

He pounded Billington's head against the deck and Billington, freeing an arm, wrestled to get hold of William's neck.

"What'd you do it for? If she ever comes near Dorothy again, you'll answer for it."

William puffed hard. His body drew the last drops of adrenaline from its reserve. He suddenly became aware of his proximity to the short port side rail, and the foaming sea below. A slip, or a counterattack by Billington and he would be swimming. His arms turned to jelly.

Billington saw his advantage and flung him. William slid, clamping his arms tightly around the spindles of the railing when he struck it side-long. Through the turned oak, he watched the dizzying sea rise and fall.

Billington flew at him, spitting profanities, his eyes berserk with rage. William clung tighter as the gargantuan grabbed one of his legs and tried to lever him overboard. The incoherence of Billington's litany did nothing to mask his murderous intent.

William placed a well-aimed kick into Billington's midriff then scissored his legs to prevent being re-caught.

"Stop!" he heard. "Stop, or I'll push it through your bloody gorge!"

Billington froze.

William turned from the frothing sea below toward Billington's wide, startled eyes. Martin's sword dug nastily into the flesh at Billington's throat.

"Leave him! He's right. Your wife is a brute and you know it, man. This can't be the first time you've been called out for it."

"No man who insults my honour lives!" roared Billington, neck still balanced on the point of the blade. Despite his declaration he let go of William's ankle.

William took the opportunity to scramble away from the edge and back toward the foremast.

"I'm lowering my sword and I don't expect you to make any more trouble. You haven't many friends on this ship, so don't cross me. And your wife will apologize to Bradford's, in front of everyone."

"She will not. How do you think I'm supposed to make her?" growled Billington, pushing Martin away and clutching his bleeding neck.

"I believe that was Bradford's point." Martin hooted, turning to Richard Bitteridge. "That was his point, man," laughed Martin even harder.

Billington glowered. William moved toward the hatchway.

"Hold up there, William," Martin said, almost behind him. William tensed, but knew he had no energy for another brawl.

"Hold up! Just a word."

He stopped and turned squarely to face Martin. There was no guile in Martin's face and he relaxed a hair. "What is it? Keep your distance."

Martin stopped and held up his hands, dangling the sword by its hilt. "I want you to know, we have both been fooled. I know nothing of your wife's predicament and, Bradford, *I* am not your enemy."

His adrenaline was spent and fatigue weighted on him. He struggled to keep his emotions in check.

"Thanks for pulling him off." William's despondence turned to giddiness. "I don't know what I was thinking. The man is all muscle. Look at me." He began to laugh and couldn't stop.

"Yes, what were you thinking? You finally showed some backbone though, didn't you?"

William caught himself. He was sharing a laugh with Martin; he'd never thought it possible.

Land Ho!

*J*ohn allowed Desire to cradle his head in her lap. Her body curled protectively over him; his cheek pressed against her stomacher.

Carver and Katherine were above deck.

One by one, Desire swept the stiffened strands of hair from his brow.

"You have no idea the affect of your touch on me," he said.

"Yes I do," she smiled.

She hadn't bothered to put her hair up today. He pulled a curl and let it spring back. He ran his hand down the side of her bodice. "Often when I was lying in the common-way, I imagined you in my bed alone with me, free of these layers, and ties, and bows, and pins. Just you, in the raw."

"You have to save your strength, John. Just lie quietly."

"Why do you put me off? Your touch is so loving, yet you're not you. We should be cherishing this time alone."

"I am, John. I am. I love you," she stroked his cheek and pulled his head close against her again. "I will always love you. Never doubt it."

He wrapped his arms around her and closed his eyes, savouring the feeling of her fingers in his hair. "I'd marry you without his permission, even if it left us outcasts."

"Hush, John. Don't talk. Let's enjoy this, while we're alone. You're so much improved and tomorrow he may put you back to work."

"What's that?" said John. There was a loud sound above them.

"I'll go look." She lifted his head and slid off the bunk.

At the foot of the ladder, she deciphered the shouts echoing above.

She rushed back.

"John! It's land! They've spotted land! I'll help you stand. We must see it together."

November 11th – Forenoon Watch

"Land ho! Land ho! Land three points off the lee bow." The cry
reverberated with triumph through every crevice of deck and hull.

"You see that, Katherine!" William said, wishing Dorothy were up
here to share this moment.

Katherine straightened her skirt and squinted in the direction the men
were gesticulating. "I see nothing but a thin, grey scratch on the horizon."
Katherine looked harder at the distant seascape. "Where is it?" she asked,
grasping his arm.

Brewster leaned over to get Katherine's attention. "That is surely it
Katherine! God be praised we made it." Seeing her hesitation, he added,
"Aren't those the biggest mountains and greenest trees you've ever seen?"

Those on deck hugged each other with joy. Katherine rubbed her eyes.
"Oh yes, the prettiest trees," she said with conviction.

Brewster let out an explosive roar of laughter and slapped his knee.
"Katherine, I'm jesting. You see what we all see, but that little speck on
the horizon is land sure enough. Oh, am I glad to see it!" He grabbed
Mary round the waist, turned her, and kissed her deeply. "We made it,
wife."

"We made it and we'll soon have a pretty little village next to
Katherine's pretty little trees," said Mary.

Behind Katherine, John, ashen from the climb to the deck, pulled
Desire closer. William steered Katherine toward Carver, lest she see.

He was thankful John had made it above deck under his own power.

William looked around. So many of them still sported bruises from the
storms. Most coughed. Hunger and long bouts of sleeplessness had, like
the effects of frequent storms upon their ship, cracked their skin and
opened their seams. But the time of healing and repair had come.

Carver cleared his throat. The congregation quieted, knelt in prayer.
The others, equally inspired by their arrival, knelt with the congregation,
Billington and his family among them.

"Psalm one hundred and seven," Carver began, "Does it not say, they
that go down to the sea in ships, and occupy by the great waters; They see
the works of the Lord, and his wonders in the deep."

His head swung low and then rose in time with his hands, which
ascended to the heavens. "For He commandeth, and raiseth the stormy
wind, and it lifteth up the waves thereof."

William felt Carver's words reach deep inside him. He reached for a
hand on either side.

"They mount up to the Heaven, and descend to the deep, so that their soul melteth for trouble." Carver rocked back and forth. "They are tossed to and from, and stagger like a drunken man, and all their cunning is gone."

"Amen" called out several of the congregation, some of the others nodding their heads.

"Then they cry unto the Lord in their trouble, and he bringeth them out of their distress. He turneth the storm a calm, so that the waves thereof are still. When they are quieted, they are glad . . ." He shook his outstretched hands, lofting them skyward before finishing softly, "and he bringeth them unto the haven, where they would be."

Carver pointed, over the seascape, to the thin shadow of their promised land. William hugged those next to him and joined the now unanimous chorus. "Amen!"

William remembered Dorothy. He shook the hand thrust in front of him and hurried below.

November 11th – Afternoon Watch

"It is all trees. Trees as far as I can see. Right to the water's edge," said Mary Allerton.

"How are we to live here?" said Katherine, dropping to her knees. "I imagined we'd have shelter and food. We've looked forward to it. Depended on it." The coast line was clearly visible now, a sheer cliff rising before Katherine's eyes. Trees sprouted randomly from its vertical face and clustered thickly at its crown.

William understood their fear. A hungry, weary imagination had long fed their expectations, his included. His promises to the congregants relied entirely upon stories recounted by the Adventurers and on rudimentary maps of the coastline. He realized with a start that the uninterrupted fecundity of this land, the very richness that had underwritten their dreams, could, perversely, lay waste to their hopes of survival. How are they to cultivate without proper tools or sufficient physical strength? And, without cultivation, how can they claim the land as a true settlement in the name of King James?

He broke from his thoughts as he realized Katherine was still waiting for an answer. "Don't worry," he soothed. "The Indians have lived here for centuries. The Dutch at Long Island Sound, close to our destination, are engaged in profitable trade and have good land. Thomas Dermer on his maps has marked many good rivers and an exceedingly fruitful coast at North River. They have good relations with the Indians there and we are sure of the same welcome."

In truth, on that last point he was anything but sure. A good reception by the Native people, upon which so much depended, seemed as much subject to their control as the weather or the current beneath the *Mayflower*.

Carver drifted over. "What William says is true. This is the northerly coast and hasn't yet been populated by Christians. It will be different heading south toward the river," he said, lifting Katherine back to her feet and rubbing her back.

"We can all see, with our own eyes, what it is here," said an eavesdropping Billington. He raised his voice. "The coast is too rugged. We are spent. One in ten of us is well. We can't build until we clear the trees and that brush is as thick as your wife's thatch. Well, not your wife's, Bradford."

Brewster, Edward, William, and Carver stood shoulder to shoulder.

"Leave Billington. You're not wanted here," said William.

"Hear that everyone? *I'm* not wanted here. Maybe that goes for all of us Londoners. Should we tell the Master that the ship is to continue on to Virginia?" How many are with me? You've seen the place these men have brought you to. Is it what you expected?"

"Now hold on, everyone," said William, "We head south toward Long Island. There will be clear land there. And remember why we chose not to go to Virginia. We came for freedom. The Virginia company refused to grant it. Besides, we have an agreement with the Adventurers. Our investment is with them."

His words hit like a spark to the priming pan and the upper deck exploded with argument and speculation. Camps formed, each side lobbing invectives at each other.

"Quiet!" shouted Carver, bewildered by the dissent. "We will discuss this in an orderly manner."

William whispered to Brewster, who dashed off to retrieve a quill.

"As your Governor and assistant Governor, we will put this to a test of reason," said Carver.

"We should be heading for Jamestown, Virginia!" shouted Billington. "They are farming tobacco with indentured labour from Africa. We can all be rich like them if you follow me."

"We will keep this discussion reasoned," Carver declared. A sidelong look at William asked him if he was keeping score. "We have one vote for Virginia."

"How many more of you are for Virginia?" shouted William. "An error worthy of Satan," he added, muttering.

Carver counted hands. "Twelve. Billington, I assume that includes your wife and children?" Billington nodded. "The rest of you, are you with us?"

"We are for New England and the patent to which we all consented," said old Mr. Chilton, grasping his wife around the waist and laying his hand atop his daughter Mary's shoulder. "We left Holland for a place of our own. You know how much we've gone through to be here."

"We are too," said John Tilley and his wife Joan together. "Virginia is out of the question. We were promised freedom to worship the reformed faith."

"I must have a level of society that will suit my needs," shouted Eleanor Billington, her giant bosom shifting dangerously as she spoke. "Most of the women here wouldn't be fit for my table," she sniffed.

"On that, we will agree, but for different reasons I am sure, Eleanor," said Mary Brewster with her hands on her hips. She took a step forward, daring her to speak again.

"Ladies!" Carver shouted. "Settle down! We have important matters to decide." He motioned them to sit.

"Are there any other questions?" asked William taking the pen and parchment Brewster offered.

"Do we have a right to land at New England since the agreement wasn't signed?" said Francis Eaton.

"Yes," said Carver. "The King granted the patent. All we need to do is lay claim and show that we are a permanent settlement by farming the land. We'll plant in the spring," said Carver.

"But . . . there is a *small* chance we may not be supplied by the investors as originally promised," said Edward. "If so, we must be honest that this could mean we have neither seed nor fresh supplies to sustain us, despite our industry. If this comes to pass, I fear the land may not sustain us."

The volume of argument swelled.

Edward raised his hands apologetically to William and Carver.

"Men!" said Stephen Hopkins, "After surviving a year marooned on The Isle of the Devils, I sailed to Jamestown anticipating long-hoped for sustenance. What we found was disarray. The palisades were destroyed, the gates barely hanging on their hinges, and the few people still alive were barely so for want of food. There was no order. No leadership. The Indians were hostile and likely still are. No, you don't want to go to Virginia, tobacco farming or not."

"They have a legislative assembly. There is civilization there," said Martin.

"We, too, can have a body politic!" countered Carver. "We've been discussing it."

"And a letter to the Adventurers has been drafted," added William. "If they agree to the terms, which I am sure they will, there will be no doubt as to our resupply."

"Well, what of Virginia?" said John Turner, who, like Thomas Tinkner, was undecided.

"What have you left to offer the Virginia Trading Company as investment?" asked Brewster. "We've thrown our lot in with the Adventurers. They got us this far. We lose all of our shares if we quit now."

Billington was still restless. "All you have said so far has nothing to do with us. Your congregation is all you ever speak of, yet yours is not the only voice. *We* have no fear of persecution. *We* have no shares with the Adventurers. Is our voice never to be heard among the majority?" He focussed his gaze on Carver. "You say you've been discussing a government. Were any of us consulted?"

It was a fair accusation. Carver was in the habit of only considering the needs of the congregation, though he'd been making efforts to include those he still referred to as strangers.

"It's true. It's been us and them from the start," said Martin. "If it's not going to change, we can leave them in New England and continue on for Virginia." He looked around defiantly before lapsing into a coughing fit.

"Now hold on there, Martin," said Richard Warren. "Speak for yourself. I am happy to stay in company with this honourable group of men. Can you say you've been treated unfairly? Have you had less than them in any way on this voyage? You hold yourself apart and that is your fault – as it is yours, Billington. A more welcoming and caring band of men I have never had the pleasure to share company with. As for the investment, it is true that not all of us are party to it in the same way, but we owe the Adventurers a debt for getting us here. We agreed to repay it with our labour."

"I agree," said Peter Browne. John Goodman nodded his head beside him.

"Martin, you've been plain about your feelings from the start, but I've come to count Leydeners among my closest friends," said Stephen Hopkins. "They've become brothers to me. And who was it that delivered Lizzy's baby?"

"I meant no offense to any of you," Martin said quietly, offering an olive branch. "William, have we not made peace?" Before William could reply he went on. "It is only that as the appointed spokesperson . . ."

"Self-appointed spokesperson," snickered Billington.

Martin shot him a contemptuous look, one that affirmed to all who saw it that the two now shared only enmity.

"As I was saying, as the appointed spokesperson for the passengers boarded in London, I ought to speak to their interests, which would be better served in Virginia. Carver, you speak of persecution, but you persecute us for our gambling and high spirits when they are but harmless fun."

"Gentlemen. We are not making progress," barked Carver.

Billington shuffled impatiently. "We are for Virginia!"

"*You* are for Virginia, Billington! Of that we are well aware," barked Carver, turning to the others in the group. "Those of you who were intent on Virginia, what say you now?"

"I am satisfied with New England," said John Turner.

Stephen Hopkins gave his servants Edward Doty and Edward Leister severe looks. They shot their hands up in assent.

Prince pushed off the rail and stepped forward confidently. "Forgive me for intruding, as this doesn't affect me, but I can sense your uncertainty about this place. As a cartographer, I know all too well the shape of the challenges before you. This is a truly wild country, not the gentle woodland of home. Are you truly prepared to be alone here? To carry on insignificant before this vast land? Ever at the mercy of her savagery? I plan to continue on to Virginia by another vessel. You don't owe the Adventurers your lives."

"You are not part of this," said Carver.

"I've made up my mind," called out Martin, vehemently. "I am for New England."

In an instant, the wind was gone from Prince's sail.

"Is everyone . . . else," Carver nodded warily at Billington, "still for New England north of the Hudson?"

A great cheer went up among them. William slumped with relief. Unity, finally!

They would be there before nightfall.

Compact

"*W*ind shifting to sou-sou-west, sir," shrilled the Master's mate.
"Breakers ahead, sir," shouted the lookout.

Master Jones took up his eyeglass and scanned the coast uneasily.
"Begin sounding!" he ordered. With surprising dexterity, he scrambled to
the poop deck and swivelled his glass out to sea.

"Mark twenty!" came the call.

"Bring her round to starboard, establish heading east-nor-east. We'll
put some distance between us and the shore."

William could see whitecaps off the starboard bow. He moved to the
rail to watch a sailor feed out the sounding line.

"The Master won't risk the slow beating out to sea by plotting a course
to windward on the port side," explained a kind, neatly dressed sailor
nearby.

"Mark ten!" called the sailor feeding out his line on the starboard side.
William leapt back from the rail to avoid the spray from the lines as they
played out and were hauled back in. Tensions rose quickly. William had
the distinct impression that they were in serious trouble.

"Mark ten!"

Master Jones uttered a silent curse. He had counted on having more
sea beneath him on the starboard tack. Soon the *Mayflower* would be
running with the wind, at the mercy of winds now strong enough to drive
her aground if he couldn't complete the turn in time. "Bring her hard to
port!" he bellowed. "Change course to sou-east!" Pipes shilled amidst
these orders and the ship was brought hard around. "Give me a new
Mark!"

"Mark twelve!"

The crease in his brow eased imperceptibly.

"Mark twenty!"

He would not get comfortable yet. They had a hard beat into the wind. A rogue wave battered the windward side. She was parallel to the shore now but still in the middle of her tack.

"Mark five!"

"Damn!" he growled, startling his mate beside him. "What do you see from the beams? I want eyes on the shoals. Get me a second sailor on the lead! We are feeling our way out." Master Jones began pacing the poop deck, any effort to appear calm forgotten. "Report! Report, God damn you!"

"Mark seven to starboard!"

"Mark ten to port!"

"Adjust course east one point!" he called.

"Shoal to port side. We are running in the channel Sir," called the sailor from the fore-top mast rigging.

"Ease her another point to port." He would have to risk it. The breakers were building on the starboard side and he was running out of room to manoeuvre.

"Mark five, sir!"

Just a little over twenty feet stood between the keel and the ocean floor. Jones' lips moved in silent prayer. "Bring her round heading east-sou-east and begin beating into the wind. Keep all eyes on those shoals. Reduce sail to one half."

"Mark ten!" Another wave battered the port side. The *Mayflower* trembled.

"Mark fifteen!

Master Jones' fevered pacing slowed. "Malabarr!" he cursed. He had driven the ship straight into its dangerous shoals. "A foolish mistake."

"Mark twenty!"

"Join me on the poop deck, Governor!" called Master Jones, peering down at his cargo of nervous passengers. "Governor Carver, a word, quickly!"

Carver mounted the deck apprehensively. William joined him. It was obvious they'd had a narrow escape, but they were free and clear of it now. Were they not?

"Carver, inform your company that we are heading nor-nor-west and I intend to put anchor at Cape Cod. I will not risk the journey south. These shoals stretch all the way down the coast and with the day beginning to wane I will not risk being driven into them by the contrary wind. You will disembark at Cape Cod or the nearest suitable harbour. Give up on the Hudson."

"But we had an agreement!" blurted Carver, purple with rage at the sheer caprice of this off-handed treatment. They ought to be discussing another route south.

"I'm not risking the ship and one spot is as good as another in my opinion. Prince has already confirmed that Cape Cod will suit you as well as the Hudson. I'm tasked with planting you in New England, and I will. It is a broad coastline."

"But you cannot decide on matters of which you have no knowledge! Nor is our fate to be in the hands of Prince!" said Carver.

Heedless of the eyes upon him, Carver stepped within a nose of the Master. His fists quivered by his side, barely restrained.

William leapt forward to lay a soothing hand on Carver's arm. He felt steel. Carver remained apoplectic.

"Are you threatening to mutiny, Governor Carver?" queried the Master. "If so, I suggest you get on with it so that I might have you secured in the hold. If not, leave my deck and inform your party of my intentions."

"This is unspeakable!" frothed Carver. "I expect to discuss the matter once we are anchored. It's not settled." He spun and headed for the ladder.

William followed in shocked silence. The stress of Dorothy, and now this – to be dropped so far from their goal. It was too much.

Congregants and Londoners swarmed Carver as he touched the deck, expressing sympathy at his treatment and outrage at their own. Against this common oppressor the alliances so recently made were as good as struck by a blacksmith's hammer. Wounded, yes, but also forged into one.

They returned to their familiar cabins and the smell of unwashed bodies, urine, and smoke. Each was anxious over what their new destination might, or might not, offer.

The *Mayflower* arced north. By nightfall, the heavy rattle of the anchor echoed round the bay of Cape Cod. Despite the circumstances, upon hearing that sound, William felt the return of his excitement.

November 12th – Morning Watch

Dorothy woke to a burning pain in her ankle. She reached out, only to be pulled back. She tested the binding round her chest and wrists.

"Help! William, help me!" she cried. "My ankle."

"Dorothy?"

"Desire," said Dorothy, collapsing back onto the pillow. "Help me. My ankle is on fire and I can't reach it."

"Tied again? I've undone you twice, but William and the doctor keep rebinding you." She lowered herself to the stool beside Dorothy's head and held her swaddled hand.

"Oh, Desire, this is not how I thought it would turn out."

"Let me look at your ankle. Try to calm yourself, you'll breathe easier. I'll stay. I've been checking on you while you slept. Do you remember anything?"

Desire's stool scratched along the deck. Her eyes widened. "It doesn't look so bad. I'll get the doctor to put something on it. I'm sure he can move the bandage so it doesn't bother so much."

Desire returned to her place by Dorothy's head and helped her sip some beer. She felt her brow. "Still hot, but less so now."

"Are you sure it's not too bad?" Dorothy asked. "It's paining so badly."

"Not so bad." Desire changed the subject. "Did you hear that we have arrived? We are anchored. There is land all around us. A wild and weather-beaten place, for sure, but solid land."

"Untie me. I'm not going to jump off the ship. You know I'm not."

Desire frowned. "As I say, I've done this before. The problem is keeping them from tying you up again." She tugged on the knot at Dorothy's wrist with her teeth until she got it loose. "Promise me you won't look at your ankle until the doctor dresses it."

"You said it wasn't bad." Dorothy sunk back into the pillow. "Tell me the truth."

"It is bad."

Dorothy sprung upright as soon as Desire pulled the binding from her chest. She felt faint when she saw it. The ankle had opened into an angry sore where the bandages had, with her struggles, worn through the skin and muscle. Bone appeared at the centre like a small, iridescent pearl.

"This is what I get for trying. And you are no further ahead. After everything, you still have to marry Gilbert."

Desire cast her eyes down.

"I heard," said Dorothy rubbing her wrists.

"It wasn't for nothing, dear Dorothy. Prince is no longer trusted. If we can just find the final proof we need about who he really is, he will pay for his betrayal. And Deacon Carver will be able to warn the Adventurers of his plan against us."

Desire carefully undid the binding of Dorothy's ankle. When she pulled the linen from the right leg, a deep impression remained.

"Perhaps Pastor Robinson, Deacon Carver and William are right. We must obey our husbands and trust that God is helping them to see what is best for all," said Dorothy. "Perhaps they would have discovered the truth about Prince without us. We should return to doing what is expected of us and save ourselves further pain."

"I don't believe that. I won't go back to believing it. Don't give up on us."

"Do you think God might be punishing me for what I did?"

"You were protecting me." Desire leaned forward and kissed Dorothy's brow.

"I think He is. God is taking everything from me. I should have trusted God to strike Harlock, but instead I broke His commandment. I am a murderer, Desire."

"God wasn't protecting us. The men weren't protecting us. What was left, but for us to protect ourselves? Don't give up, Dorothy. No matter what, God can't break the love we have for each other."

Shade was cast upon the room and they turned. Annoyance flicked across William's features seeing Dorothy unbound. Then he saw her ankle and retched.

"You untied her?" he said unevenly to Desire.

"Yes. You see what the binding has done? She isn't going to hurt herself. You are doing that for her," said Desire.

"Don't be mad at him," said Dorothy anxiously.

"I told you," said Desire, annoyed, "Eleanor gave her something. There is nothing wrong with Dorothy. You must let her up."

There were voices in the corridor. William peered out. "Doctor Fuller? Can you see Dorothy, before Suzanna?"

Doctor Fuller slipped in, hovering over Dorothy's ankle. "It's nothing but a wee sore. With the poultice on you'll hardly notice it, Dorothy." He eyed William. "Why is she untied?"

"She is recovered," William answered quickly. "I thought it best. Her fever has broken, has it not?"

The Doctor felt her head. "Only a mild fever. I am inclined to say it is a quartan fever, the most enduring variety. I'll bring a lemon slice covered in mithridate to bind to her pulse. Keep her warm so that we might encourage sweating. Difficult, I know, with this chill and damp."

"Does she need anything else?" asked William, stopping the doctor before he could leave. "A julep maybe? You gave me a julep with strawberry leaves once for my fever. Will that help?"

"I'll bring a salve of plantain and alum and a plaster of red lead for the ankle. As for the fever . . . I have worse cases and am running low on supplies."

November 12th – Forenoon Watch

Everyone able was on deck, welcomed by the call of gulls nipping at the crisp morning air. Whales splashed in the distant corners of the bay. Near at hand, the soft white tide tumbled against a crescent shore rimmed with trees. Autumn gold and red leaves shimmered in the breeze and took flight. Further inshore evergreens waded knee-deep in colour. William couldn't take his eyes from the scene before him, nor Brewster. They spoke without turning.

"Have you completed the social Compact I suggested?" said William.

"I've got it here. I want the four of you to look it over," said Brewster.

"Are we not continuing to the Hudson?" jeered Billington loudly. "You made such a fuss, Carver, getting us all to agree."

William finally turned from the view, the magic spoiled by Billington's sarcasm. Carver took the Compact from Brewster's hand and unrolled it between them, ignoring Billington.

Carver spoke quietly, his lips barely moving. "Should I press to raise anchor and go south?"

"No. We cannot risk further delay," said William. "We had good accounts of the land at North River, but we've heard equally of the bounty of fish here at Cape Cod. Let's find a settlement before infirmity cuts us down entirely," said William.

"This social Compact will do more to unite and legitimize us than even the agreement with the Adventurers. It is proof that we have formed a Christian government," said Brewster.

Carver whisked the parchment closed. "Gather round!" he trumpeted to all on deck.

Shuffling and scuffing, a wide semi-circle of listeners formed around him. "It is late in the season. The leaves have long since turned on those trees. The Master refuses to venture further south. As unwanted as that decision was, time itself has now played its hand. We must settle here and gird ourselves for the coming winter. I propose therefore that we unship, mend the shallop and begin searching for suitable habitation, a harbourage and sources of food."

Brewster chimed in, "Carver has in his hand an agreement that all men over twenty-one may sign. Our covenant to one another shall be delivered to the King. It will leave no doubt as to our intentions as his subjects and our right to claim this land in his name."

Carver squinted, shielding his eyes from the watery sunshine as he began reading.

"In the name of God Amen. We whose names are underwritten, the loyal subjects of the dread sovereign Lord King James by the ... you read it, Brewster," said Carver, rubbing his eyes and passing the parchment.

Brewster stood erect and held the document up. He stepped forward a pace with each line he read.

Having undertaken, for the glory of God, and advancement of the Christian faith and honour of our King and country, a voyage to plant the first colony in the Northern parts of Virginia, do by these presents solemnly and mutually in the presence of God, and one another, covenant and combine ourselves together into a civil body politic, for our better ordering and preservation, and furtherance of these ends aforesaid; and by virtue hereof to enact, constitute, and frame such just and equal laws, ordinances, acts, constitutions, and offices from time to time, as shall be thought most meet and convenient for the general good of the colony; unto which we promise all due submission and obedience.

Brewster rolled the parchment closed. His audience remained silent, each listener digesting the import of the document.

Billington broke the spell. "Which Christian Faith?" he asked cynically. "Your Reformation, Brownism, Calvinism, whatever you are calling it?"

Carver cleared his throat and opened his palms. "We welcome you to practice our faith. We are seekers of truth, through whatever instrument God chooses to reveal it, but above all through His holy written word. To call it by a name would limit it. We don't claim absolute understanding. Full and perfect knowledge cannot break forth all at once for the Christian World, coming out of a period of such long darkness as it has. Truth was revealed to Luther and more to Calvin and so it will be to you, if you are open to receiving God's light."

William could see this wasn't the answer some were looking for. He spoke up quickly, "We remember the jailings, the beatings and the fines we endured in England. We've founded this colony to escape persecution; we will not persecute any man for his faith or the manner of its practice, but neither will we tolerate persecution for our own. There will be no pursuivants here, no corrupt church wardens. The great promise of this new world is that you may keep your faith in the manner you choose."

"Church and state are separate," Brewster added. "When you sign this Compact, you are signing a pledge to maintain civil peace and submit to an elected government."

"And what if some of us won't sign?" asked Soloman Prower, Martin's stepson.

"Don't try to stir the pot, son," Martin said calmly. "Even Billington must see that no man can be allowed to stand outside the law. We can't have some amongst us that are unanswerable to the rule of state. And if you mean to go against this, you, or Billington if it's in his mind, must either go live with the savages, or beg the Master to take you on to Virginia."

Carver pressed on, "Are there any other questions before we proceed? Once the Compact is signed we should begin to unship the shallop and make her seaworthy. Meanwhile, the longboat can take some of us ashore to investigate and gather firewood."

"If we agree, will every man, woman, and child be given a share in the venture? Will even my little Oceanus be given a share?" asked Stephen Hopkins.

"Everything will still be as you agreed originally with the Adventurers – if they honour our bargain," said Brewster.

"I'll sign," said Stephen.

"I will too," said Richard Warren.

"Will you sign, Martin? Are we, from this point on, no longer two bodies but one – the first planters of New England?" asked Carver expectantly.

Everyone turned to Martin, waiting for his answer.

"I will sign!" he said to cheers. He strutted in front of the men, puffing his chest in a challenge to Billington, before resuming his place.

"Are there any opposed?" asked Carver.

Necks stretched right and left.

"No? It carries! Edward, pass me the quill," said Carver, jubilant. He patted Brewster on the back so hard it almost toppled him.

William pumped Carver's hand. Together, he, Carver, Isaac, Edward and Brewster had managed to shepherd these friends and strangers alike across the Atlantic. Now they were poised to plant the seeds of freedom. He thought of Robert Cushman, who chose to stay behind, and wished him well. They would have need of him again, and of his friendship with Weston, if they were to get their supplies come spring.

The Smell of Earth

William marched behind Myles Standish, matching his gait and the set of his musket as they moved through the wood. He tried to discern the advantages – and disadvantages – the land afforded. He also stayed mindful of Isaac behind him, who would probably not welcome a second inadvertent blow from his musket.

The undergrowth was sparse, revealing a forest floor carpeted in a pungent quilt of leaves and needles. They stopped earlier and, with a spade, discovered excellent black peat to its depth, underlaid with sand. Francis Eaton, professing some knowledge of planting, claimed it was better than the downs of Holland.

There was no sign of native habitation as their fifteen-man foray marched silently inland, moving perpendicular to the shore. Regardless, William was acutely aware of the quick pulsing above his collar.

He fiddled with the match of his musket, afraid it would either burn out or go off by mistake. "Myles? Am I to keep this burning? We haven't seen any sign of hostility. How likely are we to fire at the savages on first contact?"

"There have been other white men here before us. We don't know what the savages' reaction will be," Myles cautioned. "If we encounter thick brush we will need to be on guard for ambush. If they attack, we must show we are fearless. Any sign of weakness and we'll be done for."

"He is right," said Stephen. "It is the same in Virginia. The Indians must respect you, and they respect you if they fear you. At the first sign of advantage, they'll attack a neighbouring tribe – we don't want to be a weak neighbour."

Edward Winslow changed the subject. "This here is ash, this one is oak and over there a stand of pine. Wood aplenty and no end of sweet-smelling juniper."

Stephen amiably joined Edward's musings. "There are birch in the distance there, and all around, plenty of sassafras. A good variety here for sure. Edward, watch yourself around that hole."

"We'll load up with juniper for the fire when we return," said William. Following another long silence he said, "We don't want to be the first to strike. We don't want to provoke their wrath."

"Of course not. I wasn't suggesting it," said Myles.

"I think I'll extinguish my match," said William. It was too hard to concentrate, beset as he was with the worry he might accidentally shoot one of his friends.

The woods thinned. Myles suddenly stopped.

"What is it?" whispered Richard Warren.

"Beach," shouted Myles, waving them all to move forward and witness the discovery. "We are on a long spit of land. Shallows on this side as well."

"This won't do," said Isaac. "There is no point continuing. We can see it is the same for a mile. Tomorrow is the Sabbath, but Monday we'll follow the beach on our side and head inland. Find a stream and follow it. We need a fresh water source."

"Shall we head back? I saw a walnut tree on our way. We can stop and collect nuts, gather oysters in the bay and have a celebration tonight," said William.

November 13th – Morning Watch

The oysters were delicious and full of fat pearls. Unfortunately, those that ate them cast and vomited through the night and woke, after little rest, to find they were no better. A cold wind, whipped up in the bay, slid its icy fingers through the loose outer planking of the ship. It keened in sympathy with Dorothy.

"William, it's a blessing I am sick. If I was well you would have left me again today," said Dorothy before vomiting into the basin balanced on her knees.

"I am so sorry. I thought they would be a treat. I wouldn't have given you my portion had I known."

"When I'm better, can you please take me above deck? I haven't seen the land. I am so hungry for fresh air and the smell of earth. If the Lord takes me, at least I will have made it to see the New World."

"You aren't going to die. It is only the oysters. I'm helping to oversee the unshipping of the dismantled shallop tomorrow. We shall be back and forth with the pieces and tools all day. I'll worry if you are on deck alone."

"Just for a bit. Someone else can help me down," said Dorothy, "I need the bedpan – quickly, William."

She resisted getting back in bed so he resettled her next to the bunk.

"I have a confession to make, William. It has been weighing on me. Everything is going so wrong."

"You are already forgiven." He pulled the blanket from the bed and wrapped it around her shoulders. "Carver has appointed me to go on the first major exploration when the shallop is mended. He wants Stephen Hopkins, Ed Tilley and I to go with Myles Standish. I am to provide counsel and advice. Myles, though an unequalled soldier, has no skill with diplomacy. Stephen is familiar with the Indians and Ed Tilley has experience with planting."

"Deacon Carver can go instead of you."

"He's chosen me. Carver wants to stick close to Master Jones. He doesn't trust him. He fears the Master is too eager to have us disembark."

"If you are going to be gone soon, you must please take me up the ladder tomorrow."

"I'm not sure, Dorothy. Tomorrow is Monday. The other women are going ashore to launder now that they have fresh water. I'll be ashore assembling the shallop. Even if I can get you up the ladder, I can't get you over the side and into the longboat. A few more days of waiting to let your ankle heal won't matter."

"I can make it ashore with them. I can help with the washing and you won't have to worry about me getting hurt. Let me off the ship, William, I beg you."

"I'll get you some beer and something for the lax. The doctor has a concoction of prunes and powder of wood rose. Suzanna White swore it worked."

He gave her a warning look to stay where she was and didn't close the curtain. At once he was seized by a coughing fit that took his breath. He hacked and spat into his handkerchief. His chest was tight and full.

Come Clean

*D*esire reached up for one more basket of laundry from Katherine's arms. The pitching of the longboat threatened to toss her into the water. Priscilla held her waist, guiding her to her seat the moment she had both handles. There was only room to ferry ten of them at a time. Their feet rested on sections of shallop arranged along the bottom of the boat.

The men dug their oars deep. She and Priscilla yielded to the strokes, swaying with the motion of the boat until it abruptly thudded against a hidden sandbar. Desire looked about, uncertain. The men, nonplussed, stored the oars.

"The boat draws too much water to get within one-hundred yards of the beach," said one of the sailors tonelessly.

Ed Tilley, shivering and pale, jumped into the frigid water with a splash. He held up his hand in invitation to Elizabeth, his niece, to do likewise. She squealed at the icy touch of the water on her feet. Desire, still unsure, suddenly understood that she, too, would make the journey to shore knee-deep in water, the laundry hoisted above her head.

Desire glanced to see if any of the men were watching and then carefully removed her stockings and tucked her skirt into her waist band, exposing her lower thighs. The men tactfully kept their heads turned and busied themselves unloading. *If only John* ..., she thought, then reprimanded herself for thinking of him.

She had made a bargain. He was well again, but it had cost her her soul.

She wiped her nose, handed a load of laundry to Priscilla, already in the water, and then took Ed Tilley's hand. The icy water set fire to the soles of her feet. She immediately felt ashamed for making Ed wait. She lifted the last load of laundry. The others laughed at the difficulty of walking on their sea legs and the shared flinch of the cold, but guilt over John lessened her mood.

Mary had the fire going by the time they reached her. There wasn't another woman who could start a fire faster than Mary Brewster. Flames licked the bottom of the cauldron. Watching tiny bubbles rise in the simmering water, Desire ached to plunge her feet in.

"When the laundry is done, let's set-up a bath house between the drying sheets." Desire clapped excitedly. "Imagine the feeling of fresh, warm water running across your scalp." Giddiness momentarily shouldered out her sadness over John. "We're on land – land! And might finally be clean."

"Stop that jumping around, Desire," said Mary with a broad smile. She winked. "I had the same thought. I've saved some of my special lavender soap for this occasion. I swore if we ever made it safe, we would all have a special treat."

Priscilla grabbed Desire by her hands and spun her around, squealing with joy and falling in the sand in an explosion of laughter.

"Are you sure, Mary? We won't be sorry if you save it for yourself," said Beth. "It may be the only luxury you'll have. There is nothing here but sea and sand and wood." Her mood clouded over. "I'm frightened."

Mary bent to add more wood to the fire. Looking up and down the coast, she said, "That sea will give us supper; that wood will give lodging."

Desire shielded her eyes to search for John among the men sawing, hammering and chopping at the far end of the beach. They were a slow, ragtag group compared to the brightly dressed men of vigour who had begun the voyage. What must she and the other women look like to them?

They hadn't long to wait before rendering an improvement to their situation. By midday the laundry snapped in the breeze round a makeshift bath house about three paces in length.

Carrying a pot of steaming water, Desire took her turn behind Priscilla, Beth and Anna, sliding through the narrow opening in the sheets.

She stripped down and lay her clothes across a juniper bush. Goose pimples sprung from her flesh. She tiptoed through the dewy grass, brushed the sand from her toes, and stepped into the small basin. She crossed her arms over her breasts and vigorously rubbed her upper arms.

"Ready?" said Priscilla

"Uh-hmm." Warmth hit the top of her head and flowed like cream through the roots of her hair. It bubbled over her lashes, caressed her neck, slid between her breasts, and then plunged down her belly in a final paroxysm of delight. The sensation nearly brought her to her knees. Her muscles liquefied. And then the snap of wind on wet flesh brought her to attention once more.

They took turns pouring water on one another, the four women luxuriating in the smell of Mary's fine soap.

Working the soap into a thick lather Desire scrubbed her hair and skin, dislodging a residue of filth nearly a hundred days in the making. Beth poured another ladle of steaming water over her scalp.

When they were done and the laundry folded, Desire sat down to shell nuts, watching lazily as two men approached. Their cooling breath obscured their faces. Something large dangled from each of their hands. As they drew nearer she recognized John. Unthinking, she grabbed Priscilla's hand and ran toward him.

"They have caught some foul!" she shouted. Katherine waved her back. Desire recalled her new situation and continued at a walk.

"Shouldn't you go back?" asked Priscilla.

"Katherine is too weak to follow and we are halfway there already."

John turned to Alden and they both stopped and waited.

It was impossible to suppress her smile as she drew closer. Priscilla pinched her arm with disapproval.

"You look nice," John said stiffly as he handed her the birds.

Alden beamed at Priscilla.

"Did you shoot these?" Desire asked, hoping John would smile too.

Priscilla took Alden's hand.

"No," said John, not looking at her. "Your father asked they be prepared and cooked over the remains of your fire. We'll be finished soon."

"Well, thank you for them," she said

"Gilbert shot them. He's a good shot," said John, his face unmoved.

Alden sniffed Priscilla's hair.

"It's lavender. Do you like it?" she said leaning into him.

"I'm sorry, John," said Desire, close to tears at his refusal to look at her directly. "If you knew why I did it."

"We have to go back."

Alden, sensing John's urgency to leave, turned to Desire. "We'll need that meal. Ed Tilley can hardly stand and Gilbert and the others have been doubled over coughing so much it's a wonder they didn't scare all the game away."

"I'll see you back there, Alden," said John, turning and limping off without waiting.

"Look after yourself," said Priscilla as Alden backed away, holding her fingers until the last moment.

"Yes, do," said Desire to John's retreating form. She hefted two turkeys and turned back toward the fire. Katherine was walking down the beach in her direction.

November 14th – Forenoon watch

The t'ween deck was eerily quiet and unnaturally cold. The braziers had long since gone out. Dorothy rubbed her hands together and dragged the blanket from the bed to pull it tight around her shoulders. Even though the longboat had bumped alongside a few times in the last hour, the ship was deserted, except for her. She lowered her bottom to the deck and began the slow process of scooting toward Prince's desk. She had given up too easily against him. Every look he shot her proclaimed his inviolability. She could not let him win.

She reached up and shoved the top plank of his desk, letting it clatter to the deck. She could make as much noise as she liked. No point wasting her time with the rolls of parchment she could see. What she looked for would be well hidden. She lifted the lid from the first trunk and let her eyes roam over the slippery silks and embroidered vests. Her hand hovered. Everything connected to him repulsed her. She plunged, eyes averted, stirring and pinching the contents. She felt something hard and yanked it free: parchment. She looked over her shoulder and listened. The wind whistled full-throated over the open hatch. She held her breath and listened harder. No one. She broke the seal and scanned the loopy script for something important. It concerned a rendezvous with a fishing ship, nothing more. She tucked it under her knee. She dove in again, elbow deep. Her fingers slipped inside the rim of a boot, continuing, landing on a solid mass. She dug for the boot and pried free a bounty of letters. She thumbed through them as quickly as she could.

Her heart leapt at the sound of the longboat bumping alongside. She held the stack of letters to her chest and listened. Her nerve failed her. Not waiting to find out who had returned, she closed the trunk. The plank proved too heavy to lift back in place. She had to leave it.

Aside from the echo of activity above – Dorothy reasoned that the sailors were transferring provisions to the longboat before setting off again – the ship was still. She didn't get back in bed. She positioned herself in the doorway using the dim light of the companionway to read letter after letter. Every few lines she glanced at the ladder, but no one appeared. At least fifteen minutes passed before the longboat pulled away and she relaxed. Against her chest she clutched the letter she had been looking for all along. The outside of the letter was addressed to Andrew Weston, and began, 'Dear Brother'. It detailed the scope of their plans and was signed 'Tho Weston'.

She started for Deacon Carver's cabin with the remaining letters tucked in her bodice. Desire had the right idea with their last letters. To come forward with this evidence themselves was useless. She had to put it where Carver would find it himself.

Crossing the common-way, she paused to listen. Nothing. The ship was still deserted. She pulled Carver's curtain aside and knelt next to the Deacon's pillow. She slipped the letter under his blankets.

The evidence was now safe under the Deacon's very head, she crawled from the cabin. The cold was biting. She made her way to the brazier and unlatched the oven. Its larger coals were black and lifeless. She fed small twigs to the embers, hoping to coax them back to life. The ladder creaked. She spun.

Prince looked at his desk, then at her, and charged. She had nowhere to go. Quickly she turned from him then slammed the brazier shut.

She screamed into the empty ship.

Instead of striking her, Prince undid his cloak and threw it over her head. He dragged her bodily to her feet and wrestled her down the passageway. Her ankle skittered against the deck, overwhelming her with ever-intensifying pain. She could hear the scattering of goats – they were in the manger. She let loose a scream as deep and frightful as she could manage, but heard only anxious bleats in return. Under the cloak, heat built round her mouth and nose; combined with the unrelenting pain, she felt faint. A door clicked. He threw her from him, pulled his cloak free, and slammed a door behind her with a heavy thud.

Darkness lie in the room like a hibernating animal. Under her hands she felt salty coils of hawser and spools of line. From her knees she reached out to feel the walls of her narrow prison. She swept them with her palms, hoping for a latch.

Nothing.

"Help!"

This time, not even the goats would answer.

November 14th – Last Dog Watch

The mood was jovial when Desire boarded the ship at dusk. They had been renewed: they'd washed, laughed, danced, warmed themselves by a roaring fire, and feasted on fresh meat. Desire walked arm in arm with a smiling Beth. She felt and smelled every bit a woman at court.

A thin, wavering cry trailed their laughter. So thin they weren't sure they heard it. Then it came again.

"Dorothy?"

She and Beth rushed for the manger. She wasn't there. They listened again.

"Where are you?" yelled Desire.

"In a cupboard. I can't see."

Desire followed Dorothy's voice along the corridor between the manger and common-way. "Come help us," she called, spying Edward and Father Carver.

"Help," cried Dorothy again.

Carver found the keyhole, called for the keys and applied his shoulder to the door. It flew open and an overpowering smell of waste and putrefaction wafted out.

Desire dropped her eyes to Dorothy's ankle. The plaster had come loose, the ballooning flesh it once covered mottled like a rotting cucumber.

"I need ale . . . and food," whispered Dorothy.

Desire took Dorothy's hand, but couldn't catch her when she fell from the cupboard. A yellow smear soaked the back of Dorothy's skirt and trailed across the floor behind her.

"I tried not to ... I tried to hold it."

"We're going to help you. Is anything hurting?" asked Desire. She couldn't help glancing down toward the ankle, even though doing so made her stomach turn.

"I'll get her something right away," said Beth, covering her nose.

"How could William insist that you stay here alone all day?" fumed Desire.

Beth returned with pickled egg, nuts, and a tankard of ale so full it slopped on the floor.

"Where is William?" Carver yelled.

Dorothy took a long draw on the beer. "Deacon, Prince put me in there. Look under your blankets. · Please. Right away. I found them. I can't do this anymore."

"You can leave us," said William, dashing to Dorothy's side. He pulled her head into his shoulder.

"I'm staying with her," said Desire.

"I did it," said Dorothy, faint with exhaustion. "I found the letters. Proof he is Andrew Weston. Proof of what they are doing." Her knees buckled.

"I pray you don't think less of me – I love her," pleaded William.

Desire knew he was as desperate as she, desperate to keep family safe, desperate to finally get off this ship, but she said it anyway. "I do think less of you, William. She would have been safe had you just believed her from the first. She would not have gone through any of this; neither of us would have."

Carver returned. "There is nothing there," he said gently to Dorothy.

"I put it there," said Dorothy, uncomprehending. "He is Andrew Weston, not Andrew Prince. Ask him. He is going to starve us." She was weak with exhaustion.

William helped her up. Desire took her other side.

"It is over, Desire. We can't win against him. I had him. I had the proof. What can we do against such evil? Nothing."

Prince walked past, smiled, and nodded his head.

"You did this!" Dorothy yelled. She lunged for him. Everyone watching fell silent.

"You are still trying to blame everyone else for what you do to yourself," he said.

"I believe her," said William, stepping in front of Dorothy to shield her.

"I've supported you time and again, William," chided Prince. "You can't tell me you really believe her over me. I know she is your wife, and I have nothing against her, but she suffers from grave delusions."

"I'm calling for a search of your possessions."

"Go ahead." Prince gave William a sober look. "I'm disappointed in you. I thought you a wiser man."

"From now on, you will not be out of my sight," said William.

"Take him above. Bind his arms to his legs behind his back," ordered Carver. "Andrew Prince – or Andrew Weston – it matters not to me. I've enough proof you are against us."

Edward and Brewster seized Prince's arms. But Prince would not submit. He wrestled free and swung at Brewster. "Who believes me?" he shouted. "Can you believe this lawlessness? Taking an innocent man!"

Edward struggled to pin his arms. "Get some rope!" he ordered.

Escaping their grip, Prince rushed to his trunk, lifted his sword and swung it in a broad arc.

The men fell back, shielding the women as they gathered their own weapons, the lantern light glinting dangerously from the blades. Prince swung again, but instead of retreating, the men advanced in an ever-tightening circle. He yielded swiftly, and tossed his weapon to the floor.

As soon as Prince was tied, Desire lifted Dorothy's arm around her shoulder for support and helped her down the passageway. Desire was anxious to get Dorothy cleaned up. She didn't deserve to be seen this way.

In the middle of the t'ween deck, Mary went back to work, preparing to puff the brazier to life. Dorothy spun around. "Don't light that!"

Pursuit

November 15th – Morning Watch

*D*awn came bright and cold. William checked for the tenth time that he had his powder and shot with him. He lifted his corslet, tried it on again, and gave it a few knocks with his fist. His mind was half on Prince. The odious schemer was gone. He was nowhere on ship and none of the sailors would admit taking him ashore. If Prince was out here with them, without food or weapons, it may have been less a kindness to him than a death sentence to be set free.

Shame burned in William for his role in Prince's plot. Hotter still, for his failure to support Dorothy. He re-examined his musket and tried to recall the drills Myles had put him through. This was it. Ready or not, they were relying on him to act when called upon.

As repairs on the shallop would take weeks, not days, he and the others were setting out on foot. Master Jones' own hesitancy to approve the reconnaissance did nothing to allay his fear – especially since all knew the Master wanted them gone from his ship.

It wasn't just fear of attack that troubled William. In his pack, he carried little more than Holland cheese, a few crackers and a length of dried salt-beef. There was room for little else. They would have to forage and hunt for sustenance, perhaps in snow if his nose was right. Not one out of the fifteen of them had cloaks or breeches adequate to the task.

He, Stephen Hopkins, Ed Tilley, and eleven others fell in, single file, behind Myles and marched down the beach. Several times he glanced over his shoulder to check for Dorothy's figure among the others until eventually the women grew too distant to recognize. He wondered how Prince had gotten away. After reading the evidence against him they had secured him in the forecastle with his wrists and ankles behind his back. By morning he was gone, though his possessions and maps remained.

William trained his eyes on the sand and trees ahead. The charred parchments pulled from the brazier were Prince's letters to the Adventurers. He worried about those sent before their departure. They had no way of knowing what false reports the Adventurers might have received already. Dorothy was right. An arrest warrant must be issued for Prince and conveyed to England, either on the *Mayflower*'s return voyage or via one of the fishing ships frequenting the coast.

"Looks like we're to meet Master Jones and some of his crew," called Myles. "How they got so far up the beach ahead of us I don't know."

Round the curve of the beach William could see the Master and five or six men – one likely John Goodman. His mastiff was with them.

"He's probably trying to find a place to plant us himself," laughed Stephen. "Though he claims he is scouting supplies for the return voyage."

William's legs were aching. With each step, it became harder to lift his foot out of the shifting sand. He was already thirsty and light headed. Behind him, Ed Tilley coughed hard, weak with exertion.

They had a long way to go yet.

"Ho – that's not the Master! Indians – Indians, men! PORT YOUR MUSKET," ordered Myles.

William's heart tripped. He jerked the musket across his chest. His hands were moist and the smooth finish was slippery in his grasp.

"Into the woods! We may be ambushed!" bellowed Myles.

William's feet would not move fast enough. He scanned the tree-line, unsure of what to look for. Some sinister movement? Some sign of attack?

He threw himself behind a large oak. His cheek kissed the tree's girth. He inched his way around. The others were doing the same, all silent, all waiting on Myles for further instructions. He could see from this vantage point that the Indians had taken to the trees as well. Were they at this very moment creeping toward them?

Behind him, someone fell in an explosion of snapping branches. He dropped swiftly to his knees, the men behind him ducking to the ground as well. Myles shouted something he didn't understand. He prayed and it calmed him. The woods returned to focus. A yard behind him, Ed Tilley lay on his back in the undergrowth, helmet askew, face ashen.

William crawled through the dry grass on his belly. He grasped Tilley's ankle and used it to drag himself forward. Catching Tilley's hand, he pulled. Tilley's shoulder shifted and he pulled again. Tilley's body rolled toward him. He slid his hand into his tunic searching for signs life.

At his touch, Tilley curled and vomited. "Thank you God!" William exclaimed with a shout, too relieved to catch himself. He turned to see Myles glaring at him.

Fainted.

He had only fainted.

Still shaking his head, Myles stood and scanned the forest and beach for signs of attack. Cautiously, he ordered everyone back on their feet. "Careful now, stay behind the trees for shelter. William, help Tilley up."

"He needs a moment," said William.

"I'm recovered. We can go on," said Ed.

"Shoulder your muskets, men," barked Myles, "we follow them in the woods. Be as stealthy as you can."

William worked his arm under Ed's shoulder. Even without shepherding his friend, the choking undergrowth made graceful forward movement impossible. There was no way of being stealthy. They were a herd of oxen.

"They are taking to the beach! We'll give chase," yelled Myles suddenly.

William hitched up his belt and obediently raced with the others onto the sand. As soon as his feet sunk into the soft grains, his limbs turned to lead. Within thirty strides, he knew they had no chance of catching the Indians. He could see their easy sprint in the distance; sand kicked from their bare heels in a steady rhythm. One by one the men stopped, hunching over for breath, their hands on their knees and their muskets in the sand.

"They are running from us," said William between laboured breaths. "Maybe they think we mean them harm."

"Or maybe they're getting reinforcements," countered Myles. "I say we follow them. Show them we're not afraid – OH MY GOD MEN GET THOSE MUSKETS OFF THE SAND!" He moved from man to man, picking up their weapons and pushing them forcefully into their hands. "Your weapon is your life out here," he said with diminishing vehemence. "They will not work if the match goes out and you've clogged them with sand. Now, as I was saying, we should find their camp and gather what information we can. Perhaps we may better determine the threat they pose."

"I agree," said Stephen, fingering grains of sand from the muzzle of his musket. "We should try to talk with them. If they are friendly, we may be able to truck with them for supplies, test for good relations."

"If the weather holds, we can follow their footprints," said Myles. "Gather up men. Keep moving and watch the trees. And keep your ears open. No talking."

They began the slow march down the beach.

They soon discovered clear footprints, showing the natives had retreated the way they'd come. Hope of discovering the village rose.

"Myles, I suggest we move to the treeline," offered William. "The walking will be much easier there and I won't have to stop continually to empty this wretched sand from my boots."

Myles nodded his agreement and they altered their course for the forest edge. Instantly they made better progress, although Ed Tilley occasionally placed a hand on William's shoulder for support. Focussing on the path and fearing ambush, no one spoke as they plowed ahead, although the chorus of coughing, spitting, and nose-blowing meant their approach would be no secret.

They had spotted no game and had been too busy tracking to stop and forage. William's vision blurred. It became worse as twilight descended. His stomach growled loudly. They had cheese and crackers, but no water. There'd been no sign of a creek.

"Should we set up camp and gather what we can while we have the light?" said William.

"We should keep going," said Myles.

"I agree with William. We'll have an easier time constructing a barrier and setting sentinels if we stop now, don't you think Myles?" said Stephen.

"As you wish," said Myles.

"We need water and food. Ed needs rest," William said. "I propose we search the tide pools – but not for oysters." They laughed, despite their exhaustion.

"Some can go in twos and threes to look for water, the rest for firewood. We have enough driftwood to construct a defensive barricade and cut this wind," said Stephen.

"I can keep going if that is what everyone else wants," said Ed. His face was blue and slicked with sweat.

William undid his corslet and laid his musket on top, careful for it not to touch the sand. His fingers quaked with hunger. Every few minutes he tipped his head below his waist to spill the stars clouding his vision.

"I'll go for water," he volunteered. He thought without pleasure that sickness and life at sea had levelled the playing field in terms of strength and stamina. He no longer felt physically inferior. They were all struggling.

"Before you go anywhere, put your helmet and corslet back on," said Myles.

William was beginning to detest the sound of that voice.

November 15th – Afternoon Watch

Dorothy sat on a large driftwood log and watched as Jasper and Richard More played in the sand. A steep range of mountains had sprouted in a tidy row along the high-tide line. Love Brewster skipped away from the water with a bowl of water cradled in his hands – half of his would-be river sloshing over its side.

Her first day off the ship had been wearing. For as long as she could, she helped the other women launder. But when the throbbing in her ankle became too intense, Beth moved her to the log. The new bandage applied by the doctor in the morning hung wet and heavy with sand. She unwound it to look at the ankle. She'd only caught a quick glimpse in the shadows of the cabin when it was applied that morning.

As the last slip of cloth peeled away she wasn't surprised. Her ankle didn't feel right, it didn't smell right, and it looked positively ghastly. She needed to examine it, but the sight made her head swim.

"That is disgusting," said a small voice at her elbow.

She looked up and met Jasper's eyes. He stood very close, leaning over her arm to get a better look at the ankle. He raised his head again to study her face.

"I'm not crazy," she said matter-of-factly. "I can tell the other children are scared of me, but I'm not crazy."

"I don't know." Jasper scratched his bottom. "How did you get an ankle like that?"

"I was sick and the bandages cut it."

"Then why did you wear them bandages?"

Dorothy wasn't sure she wanted to explain. She opened her mouth to try, then closed it again. She shrugged instead.

"I am sick too," said Jasper.

She looked at him closely and realized that his normally deep complexion looked pale. A sheen of sweat glistened on his brow despite the chill.

"That is why I have to sit over here with Love and Richard instead of hunting nuts with Ellen. She took Bartle and Remember," said Jasper.

"Are Love and Richard sick too?"

"Some. Not as bad as me."

Dorothy looked past him to little Richard. He was the same age as her Jonathan. Despite being sick, he seemed content pushing the sand around. He talked to himself and made animal sounds as he ran his fingers around the sand mountains. It dawned on her that little, motherless Richard and

Jasper had made it. Jonathan would have made it too. William was wrong.

"Why do you yell and cry so much?" said Jasper curiously.

Dorothy forgot he was beside her. Her thoughts had drifted home. She turned to look into his wide brown eyes. He fiddled absently with the edge of her apron and it reminded her of the way Jonathan used to do the same.

"I miss my son. Do you miss your mother?"

"Yes, but I'm old enough to look after myself now. Richard and Mary miss her and ask about her still, so Ellen has to look after them. I help."

"Your mother would be happy to know you're such a brave lad."

Dorothy felt an urge to hug Jasper and lifted her arms, but he suddenly scampered away shouting to Love excitedly about their brimming bowl of water. Her shoulders slumped again and her ankle began to throb anew. She ached for Jonathan.

Closing her eyes, Dorothy listened to the sounds around her. The boys argued over how to improve their village. Jasper ran back and forth to the water with the bowl, collecting enough to form a lake between the mountains. In the distance, she could hear Katherine giving orders, and the strong voice of Mary Brewster contradicting her. Seagulls called to one another. Overhead she heard the occasional flap of a wing. The ocean lapped at the sand, sluicing in, rolling the pebbles with a sound like heavy rain and then sluicing out. The rhythms made her sleepy. She lowered herself to the sand and reclined.

When she woke, the boys were gone and the sand hills flattened. Her neck was stiff. She pushed herself upright and gingerly rolled her neck side to side. Her head pulsed in time to her ankle.

The smell of roasted fowl reached her. As she pulled herself up, a splinter of the log broke off in her palm. Balancing on one leg, her knees against the log, she tried in the dusky light to root out the white needle. Failing, she scratched hard at the heel of her hand.

She looked longingly down the beach. Why hadn't anyone come to wake her before eating? She hobbled forward. The pounding of her diverse aches salted her self-pity. As she neared the fire, she wiped her tears away. She wouldn't allow the others to see her cry, especially after what Jasper had said. Did everyone really believe she cried all the time? No wonder they didn't come to get her.

"Dorothy! You're up. Why didn't you call me?" said Desire, jumping to her feet.

"I'm fine. Just tired."

Beth slid an arm under her shoulders in an instant, and she fought back a new wave of emotion.

"We've put a bowl aside for you. Come and sit down. The doctor's been waiting to look after your ankle. He has a new plaster of *fresh* herbs."

"Thank you," said Dorothy sitting in the space Beth offered and accepting a still warm bowl smelling of meat, garlic, and fresh onions. Heaven.

As soon as she picked up her spoon, everyone stood in unison and walked to the far side of the fire. They couldn't stand to be near her. It must be the smell from her ankle. Perhaps it was her outburst or the image of how she had looked last night emerging from the closet covered in her own excrement. She lowered her eyes and stirred her stew. All at once, the silence cracked. Clapping. Her spoon fell from her hand. She looked up in bewilderment.

"Thank you, Dorothy!" Desire, Beth, Priscilla and Lizzy – all of them, those she had doubted – were on their feet, speaking as one, clapping for her.

She quickly swallowed the broth she'd been savouring. A wave of emotion surged inside her. She half-sobbed, half-laughed with joy.

Katherine placed a crown of bright red maple leaves on her head and the women pressed kisses on her forehead and cheeks.

Desire knelt before her. "Everyone knows what you did. I told them everything. How brave you were and what Prince tried to do to us all."

Dorothy put her bowl down and threw her arms around Desire. "It was you! You should all be thanking Desire!" she laughed, covering her face self-consciously with one hand and then kissing Desire's cheek.

"As a special treat we've got warm water for you to bathe in. It was Desire's idea. We'll help you wash when you've eaten," said Mary excitedly.

November 16th – Morning Watch

William was awake and shivering before first light. The sleepy eyes of the sentries, Stephen Hopkins, William Mullins and Richard Warren, glowed in the firelight. He roused himself. There was no point trying to get back to sleep. He was too uncomfortable.

He rose like an old man, every joint stiff, his feet chafed raw from his thin leather boots. He shuffled past the sentries with a nod. A low, grey mist hovered offshore, here and there reaching with lazy tendrils into the hollows of the forest at their back.

He returned with an armload of driftwood and fed it into the fire. A fizzle of sparks and a cheerful new flame spurred him to find more. He wandered in expanding circles gathering wood. When his arms were full, he joined the sentries and added his haul to the flames.

The sun broke on the horizon.

"Everyone up!"

William jumped at Myles' order. The man must have sprung to life the second the sun hit his eyelids.

"Have some courtesy, Myles," said William, "It's been a rough night."

"The Indian's won't be so soft. We need to be moving the moment we pick up their tracks. Otherwise we may lose them."

"All the same Myles, surely you can grant a man a moment to stretch before having him armed and marching down the beach."

Myles grumbled and fastened his corslet. Ignoring him, William rummaged through his pack for cheese. His stomach was a hollow gourd. He could easily devour his whole day's ration.

After the first bite, he changed his mind. The cheese rolled in his dry mouth, turning it mossy. "We need water before we march."

"We can search for it on the way. Myles is right, we should get moving," said Stephen, dressed and ready.

Minutes later, following a bend in the beach, they spotted where the Indians had run up a hill, perhaps to check whether they were being followed. They would know, then, that they were coming.

Several miles further, they happened upon a creek. William dropped to his knees and swallowed a handful of water. "Ekk, brackish," he coughed, spitting it out. "Maybe it will be cleaner further up."

"Over here! The tracks follow the creek," said Stephen.

William pulled Ed Tilley, who had seized the chance for another rest, to his feet. The tracks they followed were of long, healthy strides. William worried, as Myles no doubt did as well, whether they would be fit enough for a meeting with the natives, if they were hostile.

The trail narrowed. Myles slowed his pace, giving William time to pluck whatever dried berries he could find. He stuffed them into his cheeks hoping to stimulate saliva flow. When this didn't work, he chewed the berries and forced them down his parched gullet.

"Halt!" Myles dropped to his hands and knees. Lost again.

"My feet need a break," William said, shifting uncomfortably under the weight of his musket and armour. He sat and unfastened his boots. Large, crusted blisters covered his toes and the backs of his heels. His hose had torn and snaked half-way up his feet. Steering them into place, he tried winding the material around the ends of his toes, but it refused to stay put. Desperate for comfort, he freed several patches of moss carpeting the trail edge, pulled out the twigs, and wrapped one section over each foot before shoving them back in the boots.

"Found the trail. Let's go," said Stephen, tapping Myles on the back.

Branches stabbed William under his corslet and threatened to pull it from his chest entirely. The path dipped into ravines strewn with boulders that caught his tailbone when he slipped. The morning was a never-ending struggle with undergrowth he could barely see. He kept his head down and eyes narrowed as he threaded his musket through the brush.

There would be no surprising the Indians.

"Are we lost?" he asked. "If this is the way to their encampment they have hidden it well. No one in their right mind would go this way."

"Do you doubt my abilities?" Myles' face grew darker than his russet hair.

"I've no doubt the Indians are in their right mind. What they've done is lead us on a wild goose chase," mused Richard Warren. "This would be easier going without our armour, muskets, and packs. Very clever of them."

William was glad at least to have his pack. He slipped a hand into it, fishing for a morsel of cheese. He was growing testy.

Only by late-morning had the brush thinned enough to allow them to stand upright. Before them opened a broad, grassy valley criss-crossed with deer trails.

"Men, over here!" Myles shouted.

William groaned involuntarily. Just when nature had seemed to offer them respite!

The sound of trickling water in the direction of Myles' voice gave him pause. Turning, he spotted Myles crouching down and eagerly lapping water out of his hands. William ran over and knelt beside him. The water was the sweetest he had ever tasted – better than beer. If only he could bring some back for Dorothy. The fifteen of them drank long and greedily. William relieved himself for the first time since leaving the ship.

Afterwards, he laid in the tall grass and sighed, his joints relaxing.

Something whispered in the grass.

He clutched his musket. It wasn't lit. He rolled over and drew his knees up. The others did the same. He settled his helmet securely and then raised his eyes above the tall blades.

"A deer!" he gasped and fell back down on his belly, his heart hammering. He heard a shot ring out. Myles had fired at the deer but missed. Just as well, as none of them could carry the animal, and there was no time to eat.

"The ship will soon be looking for a sign of our whereabouts," said Stephen.

"If we head due south, by my reckoning we should hit the beach on the other side of the spit. We've been so turned around in here that if we head in any other direction, we are likely to be lost," proposed William. "We have a better chance of building a signal fire from there too."

Myles raised an eyebrow at William. "Yes, I agree with William's reasoning. We shall abandon finding the native village for now. Instead, we move south and locate the beach we discovered on our first exploration. From there we can search for the river I thought I spied in the distance."

The sun was just past its zenith when they found the beach. Their signal fire flaring, they heaped fresh bows on it and left it to smoke.

Marching west, they came upon an open wooded valley richly matted with sweet smelling leaves, and headed inland to explore. At the top of a rise, they stepped out onto a golden plain of about fifty acres, fit for ploughing, with corn stocks wilting among the grasses. For the first time since leaving the ship, William felt a quiver of hope.

"This is promising. And the pond we passed could be a good source of fresh water," said Ed Tilley breathlessly.

"It is indeed," enthused William. "But what kind of harbour does it have? Is it deep enough for ships? And the pond, could it be dry come summer, and frozen in the winter? A river would guarantee us year-round water, if we find one."

"Agreed," said Stephen.

They returned to the beach and continued west. In the slippery sand, their line looked more bedraggled than ever, with Ed trailing far at the back.

"Halt!" William yelled up the beach. William waited for each man behind him to catch up. Myles, Stephen, and Richard retraced their steps.

"It is too hard going on the sand and we see nothing of the land from here. I propose we step inland, keeping an eye out for the river and for habitation at the same time," said William.

Ed vomited.

"We may miss the river if we do that," said Myles, turning back down the beach.

"Not if it is a sizable river," called Stephen after him, "Let's do as he suggests. We can't leave anyone behind and half the group aren't fit for this."

Judging from the look on Ed's face, struggling further through either wilderness or sand was less appealing than being taken by Indians.

William picked up Ed's musket along with his own. He suspected that Ed lacked the strength to use it anyway. Back on his feet but unsteady, Ed nodded his thanks. William hadn't done it for praise, but the remarks from the others buoyed him.

They resumed their march, only to suspend it after a quarter of a mile when Myles halted. "What have we got here?" he said, waving the rest of them past. They had been following a beaten path and arrived in a clearing dotted with sandy mounds.

Richard stepped forward, stamping lightly on a mound with a mortar overturned at one end and a bowl at the other. It gave slightly. "This might be a hidden cache of food," he said.

"Dig it up. Who has the spade?" said Myles.

"I do, sir," said a sailor, excitedly biting into the earth, clearing the sandy soil from end to end. He worked steadily but soon slumped forward, pale and sweaty, and begged another to take over. No one stepped forward. William sighed and put his weapon down. He took the spade and dug down into the centre of the cleared area until he heard a crack. Stephen probed the sand with his fingers, eventually pulling out a long piece of wood with what appeared to be string hanging from one end.

"It's part of a bow."

They soon unearthed several arrows, all in poor condition.

"This may be a grave," said Stephen, "Indians often bury loved ones with their possessions."

"Keep digging, there may be treasure in here, or something useful," said one of the sailor.

"Wait!" ordered William, motioning for the digging to stop. "If we violate the graves of their loved ones, the Indians might see this as an act of aggression. We need to establish good relations. What will be the cost of taking things that are sacred? Think how you would feel if your relative's graves were looted."

The men agreed and reburied the rotten bow and arrows. They replaced the soil and turned the mortar over at its head, or toe – they weren't sure.

The discovery invigorated them; the village must be near. They found a second trail, leading to another field. It was smaller than the last, but with signs of recent harvest. Although the finds had put William on his guard as never before, he was deeply excited to see signs of civilization.

Despite his stupor, Ed was the first to spot the settlement.

In a clearing beyond, William saw the outlines of at least four dwellings. But there was no sign of activity. Approaching with caution, their matches lit, they soon determined that the site was deserted. William revised his expectations of civilization. Each dwelling was no more than four or five planks laid together.

"The village is clearly abandoned," said Richard. "And look, they left an old ship's kettle behind. I wonder where they found that?" He rolled the kettle back and forth on the ground with his toe. "To leave it, they must not have valued it. Should we take it?"

"If we do, we must give them compensation when we meet. We can't set an example of stealing from them if we hope not to be looted ourselves," said William. He picked up the kettle to check for holes or other defects. "It looks sound."

"Who is going to carry it? Its weight may have been the reason they left it," said Stephen.

"We could hide it and return for it with the shallop," suggested Richard.

"If we hide it, are we not admitting that someone may return looking for it?" said William.

"I suppose so, yes."

William put the kettle down and continued exploring the clearing. "Look, this is a new mound of sand. You can still see the hand prints where they've patted it down. We're gaining on them."

The others hurried over. The sailor split the mound with his spade.

"Stop, you've got something." William dropped to his knees and carefully cleared away more sand. He pulled a small, beautifully woven basket from the ground. It was shaped like a gourd. He lifted the lid and peered inside. "Corn."

"You five, that side, you five the other side, form a ring with your muskets ready and stand guard," said Myles excitedly. His whiskers quivered. "The rest dig it up. They may be watching us from the trees."

William set to work with the others, digging with his hands. They unearthed several similar, but larger, baskets of corn – so large that they had difficulty lifting them from the hole. The baskets were made so cleverly and so artistically that William had cause to reconsider his opinion of the Indians once again. Whoever was capable of this artistry with so few materials at hand was clearly no savage.

"We can't carry all of this and we can't leave it behind," said Stephen. "We need this corn. We have no seed for spring and we are low on meal for this winter." He wiped his hands on his breeches.

"We can use the kettle to carry some and then put as much as we can in our packs," suggested Myles.

"Is it edible?" asked one of the sailors, "It is blue and red in spots."

"If the Indians have gone to the trouble of burying it, it is undoubtedly edible," said Edward Winslow. "What's more, we have proof it will thrive in this climate."

"When we meet them, we can give them satisfaction for the corn with the beads we brought," said Stephen. "The kettle we can return or trade for, as they wish."

They loaded all the corn they could carry and reburied the remainder.

The party continued west, taking a route that led them to the river they had been searching for. On the way, they stumbled on the broken remains of an old Christian fort, a reminder that, even as newcomers, they were walking in the footsteps of other Europeans, evidently less successful than they hoped to be.

The trek was now wearing heavily on all the marchers. William struggled to keep his eyes open. Finally, Myles agreed to return to the ship, delaying further discoveries until the shallop was seaworthy and they could collect the remaining corn. As it was, Carver expected them back within two days.

It rained hard when they stopped for the night. Their hastily erected barricade barely kept back the wind. Though they were exhausted, Myles insisted that four sentries keep watch through the night. They now had proof that an Indian encampment was near, and they had just stolen their food. They slept fitfully, cold and wary.

November 17th – Morning Watch

When morning finally came, William was the first ready, anxious to get back to Dorothy and the shelter of the ship. The dark had been a barrier keeping him from her. The moment it lifted, he was ready to run. The others must have felt the same. There was no talk. They gathered nuts as they walked through the field and opened packs without pausing.

By mid-morning, they should have come to the beach in view of the ship. Instead, they stared down brush growing increasingly dense in all directions. In trying to skirt the hills and quagmire of branches that had tormented them the previous day, they had seemingly lost their way.

Despite his eagerness, William lagged. The moss stuffed in his boots had failed to cushion his blisters. He now walked bare-foot on the icy brown slush, keeping an eye out for twigs and sharp rocks.

When he glanced up, the others were waiting for him, standing in a circle examining a bent sapling. He joined them to offer his opinion.

"No, don't!"

The world slipped beneath him and he was whisked off his feet. His eyes clouded with blood and the faces of the others laughing at him blurred as he bobbed up and down like a fish on a line. Memories of childhood taunting by other boys flooded back. Once again, he was a clumsy, awkward object of ridicule. He felt the admiration he had gained on the trek slide away.

"Get me down," he implored, twisting and trying to lift his body up to his ankle. He could not even lift his head.

Half of the men pushed on the sapling, bending it low again, while Myles sawed at the rope around his ankle. "Stephen was just explaining how this contraption works to catch deer. Thanks for the demonstration, William," said Myles. His lips twitched and he guffawed.

William reclaimed his leg as soon as it was free.

While he tugged to loosen the noose from his ankle, the others praised the contraption and the make of the rope. They wouldn't find it quite so fascinating if they were trying to get the damn thing off their own leg. "It is just an ordinary rope," he grumbled.

"That's what is so fascinating." Stephen held up a long length of it. "It is as good as any roper in England could make, and as like our own that you have to wonder whether they copied our example. Perhaps they came up with this independently. Even more fascinating."

"Bring it back with you then if it is so *fascinating*." William tossed the circle of rope from his ankle into the forest and regained his feet. "Let's go."

He ill appreciated the chuckles behind him as he limped the rest of the way to the beach.

Spy Glass

*D*esire savoured her nakedness; the feeling of the breeze tickling between her legs. Gulls craned their necks to peer at her over the sides of the bathing tent. She slid her palms down the clean, smooth curve of her breasts and past her belly, chasing the warmth of the steaming water. She bent to scoop more heat from the basin and tipped the brimming ladle over her shoulders once more.

"I overheard the Master say we'll have snow within the week," said Priscilla, cracking a walnut between two beach rocks.

The hanging sheet billowed outward, enveloping Priscilla, before sucking itself back in toward her.

Desire peeked at Priscilla over the top of the sheet. "I may have to give up my baths. The water cools too quickly in the basin now. It was nice while it lasted." She stepped out of the basin and reached for her shift. The pale sheet, thrust inward, clung to her wet body like a second skin.

"You know I can see every contour of your body," said Priscilla, picking a piece of shell from her mouth with a dainty finger. "Don't let Gilbert see you do this."

"You know I don't bathe with the men around."

"I'll confess to you Desire, I wouldn't mind tormenting the men. Perhaps it would make my John get up his nerve to ask father for my hand. It's been weeks. He hardly pays attention to me lately."

"They are busy. And they are sick," said Desire, the lightness gone from her voice. "Since the men returned from their exploration, they've been working harder than ever to finish the shallop. He probably doesn't have the energy. I doubt there is one who doesn't cough twice for every swing of his hammer. William Brewster and Captain Standish are the only ones not affected."

"Maybe that's it." Priscilla said sceptically. "But he doesn't pay attention to me the way your John used to."

"Used to. You know it hurts me to talk of it," said Desire.

She cinched up her bodice and stepped out from behind the blind. "Help me tighten this, will you? And pass me my mantle."

"Can we go and sit by the fire now with the others? I'm freezing."

Desire laughed. "Of course. You are a good friend, Priscilla." She caught the billowing walls of her bath, pulled them down, and folded them neatly.

Mary Brewster, Beth, and Suzanna huddled around the fire, feeding fresh herbs into a broth. The children were foraging in the grasses and trees nearby.

Suzanna stood, rubbed her back, and then moved closer to Beth, making room for Desire and Priscilla to squeeze onto the log. Suzanna's belly stretched tight against one of Mary's borrowed dresses.

"Why haven't I seen Dorothy?" asked Desire.

"She's resting," said Suzanna. "Dr. Fuller insisted she go back to the ship with some of the men."

Smoke drifted into Desire's eyes. She rubbed them and tilted forward to smell the broth. "Fresh fish and herbs. I'm sick of the dried rations. Now, if only we had shelter to keep back the wind and cold, we wouldn't need to go back onboard."

"We need those dried rations," said Mary. "What the men and the children are catching isn't enough." She raised her eyes heavenward. "Lord, may the Adventurers bring supply." She nodded to Desire. "I hope what you and Dorothy did will be enough. I curse that man Prince . . . Weston."

"How are your parents, Priscilla?" asked Beth, changing the subject.

"Not well. Mother can't recover her breath. She wheezes and gurgles in the night. My brother Joseph too. Mother stayed in bed today, but Father insisted he and Joseph do their part and work on the shallop. I'm worried."

"Your father and Joseph are noble, like the rest. I feel guilty sitting here while they work," said Beth, coughing.

"Let's take broth down to them, rather than making them come for it," said Desire. She was doing it for John, even though he wasn't talking to her, but Father Carver would think it was for Gilbert. She had barely spoken to Gilbert before the engagement was arranged. Now that he was sick, he was even more introspective and every conversation centred around the Church.

"Is it ready, Mary?" asked Beth.

"Yes. Take the pot carefully, you and Desire, and I'll get more water in the other. By the time you've returned, Suzanna and I should have another started. Someone see if Love and Bartle have caught more fish."

Desire took one handle, Beth the other. Priscilla followed with a stack of bowls.

Setting the steaming pot near the work party, Desire helped Priscilla fill bowls and pass them around. Handing John his portion, she whispered with as much meaning as her volume could imbue, "I miss you."

He said nothing, downed the hot liquid, and picked up his hammer.

She squeezed back tears and carried on serving

November 21st – First Dog Watch

Since her bath in the morning, the wind had continued to strengthen, dragging an ominous line of clouds from the horizon and scattering them rudely overhead. The men continued their work, the shallop key to their prospects. Desire had hoped to stay until John finished, so that she could be in the same longboat, but after his reaction on the beach, she changed her mind. Besides, Mary and Priscilla needed her help. The children needed carrying from the beach.

Bartle Allerton, seven and spindly legged, happily climbed on Desire's back. His feet dangled in the water despite his valiant attempts to keep them wrapped around her waist. Even with her dress tucked impossibly high, his legs splashed in the water, soaking her. Twice, she almost fell forward when he shifted his weight. In contrast, Priscilla and little Richard More appeared perfectly dry from mid-thigh up. Thankfully, Mary carried her two children, Love and Wrestling. Through Mary's careful ministrations, they had both managed to stay round and hearty.

When they reached the longboat, Bartle scampered from her back and curled into the hull. Desire headed back to collect Remember Allerton. She quickened her pace, her feet threatening to fall off with cold. Ashore again, she ran to sink her feet in the hot sand by the fire.

Her comfort was short lived. Remember hopped on her back and Desire braced for the sawing cold of the breakers. Coming alongside, Remember hopped aboard and snuggled in next to her brother. Mary was helped in by a sailor. Desire reached up to take his hand.

He winked and puckered his lips at her.

She withdrew her hand so quickly that she stumbled backward. Only pin-wheeling her arms saved her from falling under the water. He was the neatly dressed sailor she had met while making stew with Priscilla. Though she had thought him not unhandsome, his face now made the hair stand on the back of her neck.

To avoid the hand still hanging ready to help her, she grabbed the side of the longboat beyond. She pulled mightily but the gunwale proved too high and her feet found no purchase on the boat's slick exterior. Kicking vainly, her grip weakening, she slipped, plunging breast-deep under the hull into the icy water.

In a flash, the sailor reached over, grabbed the back of her bodice and hauled her aboard, flashing her a mischievous grin. She scuttled away from him and found shelter behind Mary. Safe, she rubbed her back hard against the hull to remove the feel of his hands.

To erase the sailor's leering face from her mind as well, she closed her eyes and counted each stroke of the oars. She risked a look and regretted it. He held a spy glass, winked, lifted it to his eye, spun it toward the shore and then back in her direction. He stowed it in the leather case at his belt, picked up his oars and resumed rowing with exaggerated effort. She squeezed her eyes shut. *One-fifty, one-sixty, one-sixty-two.* Surely they were almost there. When the boat finally bumped the ship, she scampered out of its belly, not bothering to help the little ones.

She wanted to wrap herself in the security of the overcrowded, smelly 'tween deck. There were places to hide; she could go to her cabin and pull the curtain. A hundred sentries would guard her door. As she wove between the cots, around the capstan, then past the brazier, each up-turned face pleaded for help. But she had none to give. She needed *them.* Even Moses, pale and sweaty on his pallet, won only enough time for a brief word and tuck of his blanket. The warning bells in her mind would not let up. She wanted desperately to hide. Was her fear irrational? Had the sailor simply been teasing her? Still, the adrenaline in her limbs propelled her forward. She needed to be alone, to be safe, and above all, to be free from the suffocating feeling of his touch that clung to her skin like her soaking dress. Finally, reaching her open curtain, she dove inside.

November 30th – Last Dog Watch

"The shallop is fit. We leave again tomorrow." William announced the news gently as he smoothed the blanket over Dorothy's hips. He kissed her forehead before resuming his assault on the pile of implements tangled in the narrow space between the hull and their trunk.

"Must you go again? I need you," said Dorothy, patting the bed beside her.

"I must." He returned to the bed and laid a hand on her brow.

"I felt so strong and triumphant a fortnight ago. Now I'm so weak. Maybe it's my ankle. Maybe it's the chills. I look haggard without my tooth and I can hardly walk. None of my clothes fit. I have diminished so much."

"I confess, I neglected you as your husband. I should have kept you safe and I *will* make it up to you. But, to do so, I have to leave. The weather is getting worse and the Master doesn't plan to spend the winter with us. He'll be gone as soon as his crew is healthy."

"Can he not see that we, too, are sick? Would he leave us?"

"As soon as we have a settlement, yes. He ordered his mates, Clarke and Coppin, to accompany us tomorrow, along with the master gunner and six other sailors. They're all he can spare of the healthy, yet he risks them for our benefit – his ultimately, I suppose. The longer he stays, the fewer supplies he will have for the return."

She pushed off the blankets and swung her legs over the side of the bunk.

He supported her as she hopped into the common-way.

"The Master might be coming with the sole intention of planting us wherever he feels is fit, regardless of our wishes," said William. "I pray we are guided to a safe and bountiful harbour. So far we've seen nothing."

"What if you fall ill like the rest? What if the Indians capture you, or kill you? I'm afraid for you. We are so close to settling and finally having Jonathan come to us. But something isn't right." They passed the gunport where Prince had once sequestered himself. All evidence of Prince was gone.

"What of Prince?" she added. "What if he returns?"

"You worry too much. And you've proven you can protect yourself."

"No. I haven't. Look at me."

He spun her and drew her close. His lips touched hers warmly and lingered. He looked deep into her eyes.

"I don't want to protect myself," she whispered. "I just want to be safe. I want to heal. I want to see Jonathan again."

"You won't be alone. A few of the men are staying behind."

They turned at the capstan and headed back to the cabin. He helped her to sit on the edge of the bed and then wrestled his pack from the corner.

"God plans to keep Jonathan from me and rob me of those I love. William, I need to confess something to you."

"There is no need of that. Besides, I've got to meet the others in the hold and fill this." He hoisted his pack onto his shoulder and kissed her again, swiftly. "God is looking out for us."

Recovery

A blast of wind twisted William's cloak behind his back, tightening it against his throat. Nearly choking, laden with pack, musket and sword, he struggled to balance on the ratlines. His foot tangled in the ropes momentarily and he thought he would fall, but he shook it free and cautiously moved the fingertips of his right hand one rung lower. If his grip gave way, he intended to throw his musket and sword into the waiting shallop and pray they didn't hit anyone. It was that, or let himself fall and land on someone himself.

He winced as a fresh gust drove ice crystals into his cheek. He smelled snow.

Thirty-four men. Twenty-four of their own and ten ship's crew, including the Master. Only twenty of their own men to protect the women, and of those, not even a handful were well enough to rise from bed. More than likely, the women would be looking out for the men.

The plan was to rediscover the river, sound the harbour and return to the Indian camp to collect the remainder of the corn. They would be back by nightfall, travelling swiftly under sail to the mouth of the river. The longboat, following, would eventually catch them up.

William knew nothing of sailing. Ely and Thomas English, familiar with handling the shallop, had control, though their interchange was marked, he thought, by a worrying and increasing sense of agitation. When ordered, he pulled on a rope, but otherwise hunkered down out of the wind. It was pre-dawn and frost gilded the gunwale and mast.

Despite their experience, Ely and Thomas seemed to be making a mess of things. The shallop, to William's unpractised eye, was making little headway and continually turned shoreward. He twisted and hoisted himself up to see over the aft beam. The longboat was close behind. "Do you need assistance?" he shouted up to Ely. The wiry little man pulled hard on a rope.

"Crosswinds, sir. We are having the devil of a time keeping the water." The boom swung overhead and Ely ducked just in time. "Forgive my language, sir."

"Can nothing be done?" shouted Brewster.

"You can pick up oars and try rowing, sirs," said Ely, pulling his ears into his collar as though the suggestion would win him a cuff.

"Pick up the oars," said Isaac with resignation. "I'd rather row to the river than walk. My feet are too sore."

William and the others retrieved the oars from the shallop's hull, snapped them into their locks and began to pull on the lee. He couldn't believe they had spent weeks assembling a craft to take advantage of the wind and here they were rowing as though this was simply another longboat. But, they put their backs into it, determined. After thirty minutes they were exhausted.

"Keep her on course as long as possible, Mr. Ely," said William as he collapsed against the hull.

As long as possible proved a very short time. They felt a shudder through their seats and the shallop came to a halt. They had run aground.

"What do we do now?" asked Brewster.

"We could take cover and wait for it to improve," suggested Isaac.

"If the wind doesn't change, we'll freeze to death here before night comes," said William. "I say we get ashore, continue on foot and have the shallop come to us when it may."

Ely sounded the water on the lee side and held the line against his legs. "You'll be in above your knee."

The consensus was for going ashore.

"Mr. Ely, you and Thomas will wait here with the shallop and then come to us as able," said William. "Look there, the longboat is doing the same. They're making their way to the beach already."

He held his breath as his legs slid into the icy water. His boots filled instantly. Thank goodness he had thought to bring spare hose. He splashed ashore, his musket lofted high above his head. Tears came to his eyes and they weren't just from the cold.

Once ashore, the men did what they could to be comfortable, draining their boots and wringing out their wet clothes. On a command from Myles, they waved to the two boats and fell into line along the tree-line, mindful of their earlier difficulties in the sand.

William marked the difference in mood from their first adventure. Though perhaps they had more fear in their hearts on that initial outing, they were also somehow happier. They had been freezing on their last expedition, but today, every fibre in every appendage of his body felt as if it could snap if touched. He ignored Myles' directive to shoulder his weapon, clutching it close to his chest instead so that his hands could shelter within his cloak.

It began to snow. Five miles on, they were covered.

William was mesmerized by the icicles jumping up and down on Brewster's beard whenever he spoke. And confused. Brewster's lips were so numb he was having trouble articulating. "What was that? What are you saying?" William asked.

"Matter Jo's sez we muz top and may camp."

The wind unchanged, they had no hope of seeing the shallop today. As the temperature plummeted, their first priority now became survival. William dropped his pack and weapons and joined in the effort to collect wood for a simple shelter and fire.

They slept in groups of ten, each man tucked in as closely to his neighbour as possible. Chilled, William found sleep nearly impossible.

We set out late from England, he thought. *We should have been in proper shelters by now, with ample food stored for winter. How will we make up for lost time now, when we are frozen and hungry?*

The wind howled, menacing them with the chill of winter.

December 2nd – Morning Watch

When dawn came they built up the fire and scanned the beach for movement. The shallop and longboat held the shore a few miles away.

"We'll be warmer if we get moving," commanded Master Jones.

William scowled and stood a little closer to the flames, letting the heat penetrate deeply through his leather boots. Only when his still-wet hose began to scald did he step back. He dared not get his cloak too close. Francis Eaton lost six inches of hem, melting the wool away to nothing before he could react and put it out.

As they marched, William let himself be lulled by the cadence of the man in front and tried not to dwell on his fatigue. He hoped that today they would have more luck by sea, for he was not sure his legs could withstand another day's march. His relief at seeing the shallop and longboat now maneuvering freely was tempered, however, by the flood of freezing Atlantic seawater into his boots as he waded out to them. It faded further as they learned the rivers they'd been so excited for proved to be only twelve feet deep at high tide – not deep enough for ships. All they could now expect to accomplish was the retrieval of the corn.

"Assemble and check your match," boomed Myles, as they disembarked and prepared to set inland again.

Ostensibly, Master Jones was in charge, but Myles ignored this. It was Carver's idea to have the Master lead the expedition, a token of gratitude for volunteering so many of his crew. Yet Myles saw the Master for what he was: a ship's captain. On land, they needed a commander.

William and Isaac moved up the beach to join Carver, Brewster and Edward.

"I propose we call this Cold Harbour," said William, through numb lips, his words slow and muffled.

"What say you fellows, should we christen this Cold Harbour?" shouted Carver above the wind.

"It's done. Congratulations William, you have named a harbour," said Edward with a mock sweep of his arm from beach to horizon.

"Well, I propose we make for Warm Harbour," said Brewster.

"We make," the Master snapped, "for the corn. We will follow the larger arm of the river. The shallop can sail beside and we'll see how far she's navigable. Keep your match burning in case of ambush."

"I have already said the same," said Myles to the Master. He turned to the assembled men, "Remember your drills. Do as *I* had instructed and we will be ready for anything."

The march continued, the terrain generally flat but covered in several inches of snow. William's feet burned with each step. The ground began to slope upward into thickening brush. Before long, they were in the same hampering thickets that had threatened to tear their armour from them on the first exploration. Except this time was worse: slippery on the inclines and peppered with hidden potholes.

Their line thinned. In the hush of the snowy forest, every sound amplified. William could hear the hiss and crunch of boots and the dull clank of steel from far ahead and well behind him.

Branches disturbed by Carver's tall frame swung back, plopping wet snow down William's back. He lagged further. He was soaked and the temperature continued to drop.

"Halt," whispered Carver, "Pass the message. A sailor has collapsed."

December 2nd – Afternoon Watch

Dorothy took her time dressing. She hardly felt stronger than the rows of sick men outside her door, yet couldn't stand to see her friends wearing themselves out by nursing on top of preparing meals and caring for the children. No one was truly healthy now.

She lowered herself between two of the men's cots and wrung cool water from the cloth at Peter Browne's head. When she placed it on his brow, he pinched his nose.

"I can do it myself. Thank you," he said.

"Your bedding is soaked with sweat. Would you like me to change it?" she said.

"No, no. No need."

The other men refused her help as well, so she scuttled back to her doorway to watch the children. She wondered at the men's reluctance. It might have been the foul stench of her ankle – or her reputation. Those who hadn't known her in Leyden might have taken her delirium aboard the *Mayflower* as her norm.

Her talk on the beach with Jasper and her time watching the other More children, who had come without parents, comforted her in the belief that, when it was time, Jonathan could travel to her safely. When the time came, she wished she could be with him, to quiet him and reassure him through the storms, but knew that if he was cared for as these children had been, he would have arms around him in time of need. And soon enough, he would be in her arms again. She had to believe it.

She watched the children play another minute and then working her fingertips between the planks of the cabin's outer wall, she hauled herself up. She still needed her injured foot to steady herself, but doing so brought stars to her eyes. She lurched forward as gently as she could, fighting to keep the pain from her expression.

The children were using Isaac Allerton's chess pieces to play soldiers. The two older boys, Bartle and Jasper, hoarded most of the figures. Their younger siblings, Remember and Richard, kept their meagre pieces penned in behind a barricade formed of their small arms.

"You are sharing, aren't you, Bartle and Jasper?" she asked.

Jasper opened his mouth to answer but was struck by a coughing fit that left his lips and cheeks blue.

Bartle answered for him. "These are my father's pieces and we don't want his brother and my sister to wreck them. They are just allowed to have the pawns."

"We want some of the captains too," whined Richard. "Our men can't fight a war without a captain."

"There, there, Richard. Can you boys please give the younger ones each a knight? I am sure they will be careful – won't you?" she said.

Bartle and Jasper put their heads together to sort through their armies and agree on which men they would surrender. Bartle handed Remember and Richard each a new piece and looked at her for approval. She nodded and leaned back on her hands, letting her eyes drift over the common-way while enjoying their babble.

"Jasper, where is your sister, Ellen?" asked Dorothy. "She is usually nearby."

All four looked at her, their mouths tight slits.

Something was wrong.

"What is it, where is she?" she said, trying not to sound as unsettled as she felt.

The older boys pointed down the corridor, but remained mute. Her heart hammered. They were pointing in the direction of Billington's cabin. *What was she in there for?* Already she was on her feet, shuffling along the wall. Eleanor Billington hated the girl.

Halfway there she heard the cackling of Eleanor's voice up on deck. Dorothy released the breath she held. She didn't know what she'd been expecting, but the expressions and silence of the boys had unnerved her. She slowed her pace and peaked through the curtain of each cabin as she passed. They might have been pointing at any one of the cabins at this end.

Ellen wasn't in any of them. The pain in her ankle renewed. She rested a moment and then shuffled past the last cabin before Billington's. A man's voice, unnaturally soft and coaxing, filtered through the curtain.

She might have hesitated. She knew to avoid Billington – all the good women did, but she heard Ellen's name and adrenaline shot through her.

She ripped the curtain aside and stood agog, hanging on it for balance. Billington had been caught off guard and backed from her like a cornered animal, the whites of his eyes huge, his lips bared in a grimace that exposed a serrated line of broken molars.

Ellen, her thin chest bare, knelt on the floor at his feet, tears streaking her little cheeks. Dorothy returned her attention to Billington. He composed himself; his pupils were dilated. She let go of the curtain with one hand and extended it to Ellen. The hand still clenching the fabric was stiff and in the back of her mind she hoped her legs would still work. Dual belts – rage and fear – cinched her chest.

Billington feigned nonchalance against the bunk. She pulled Ellen behind her and pressed her into her skirt, daring him to make a move.

"NEVER go near these children again." Her voice was resolute and strong.

Billington's expression slipped. "Just a game, woman," he chuckled. "I don't know what you think you saw but it was nothing. Just a little game this wee one wanted to play." He smirked in Ellen's direction. Thankfully Ellen's face was buried in her skirt.

"I'll kill you, John Billington, if you touch one of these children. If I so much as find you alone with a child again, you spawn of Satan, your life will be forfeit." She'd done it once and would do it again. She knew it as a fact, despite everything. "Think of harming a child, think of speaking to one, and I will *kill* you."

"Oooh wee, you are insane. You stupid wench. Do you think anyone would take your word over mine?" He gave a breathy laugh. "I can pop you like a flee. Hopping here and there . . . stomp! I'll crush you."

Her eyes glassed over with rage. She let go the curtain and turned on her good leg, cloaking Ellen from his view. Her ankle felt the best it had in weeks.

Before reaching Beth's cabin, Ellen tugged on her dress, looked up at her inquisitively and then down to where the passageway wall met the floor. Ellen bent to retrieve something and they continued. As soon as they crossed the threshold, Dorothy's legs turned to water and she collapsed to the mattress. Ellen rushed to her embrace and burst into tears.

Dorothy patted Ellen's back, the pleasant weight of a child in her arms recalling a song from happier times. She murmured a few bars and soon felt Ellen's convulsions soften. She sang a little louder. Ellen pushed herself from Dorothy's shoulder and looked into her eyes, a slight smile forming on her lips. She brought her hand up and unfolded it, revealing her discovery from the passageway.

A tiny gift from God.

Yellowed, sticky with hair and detritus, but wonderful all the same.

Her tooth.

Stepping in to stow her sewing, Beth started in surprise at the tableau. "What happened?" she said gently.

Dorothy compressed her lips, shook her head slightly and nodded toward the doorway. She lifted Ellen off of her lap and pushed the tooth up under her bodice.

Beth settled Ellen into the top bunk with a kiss.

Out of earshot, Beth looked at Dorothy expectantly, a gentle smile lingering on her lips.

"Billington, *John* Billington, had Ellen in his cabin on her knees. She was crying."

Beth gasped and turned to go back to Ellen. Dorothy caught her. "He was dressed, and so was she, partly."

"Partly!"

Dorothy lowered her voice. "I told him I would kill him. I know it was wrong, but I will never let him harm the children."

"Oh, Dorothy." Beth wrapped her arms around her. "Thank you. Thank you."

When Beth let go, Dorothy slid down the outer cabin wall and pulled her knees up to rest her head on her arms. She watched the children with their soldiers, watching her.

Dear God. Thank you for this sign that I am not forsaken. She pressed the tooth hard against her body. *I will atone for my sin, but am ready to sin again if You ask it of me. I will protect them all.*

December 3rd – Morning Watch

Arguments for and against continuing along the river volleyed over William's head. He feigned sleep. It was early. His huddle beneath a copse of sheltering pines would likely be the only sanctuary he would see that day. Some were for continuing up river to seek its source, others disliked the area in general; the ground too hilly, the harbour too shallow. Among those to argue its unsuitability was Master Jones. William was reassured. It was a sign the Master truly cared for their situation and would not simply abandon them at the first opportunity.

He opened his eyes. Myles and the Master continued to argue.

"My sailor cannot travel further," said the Master.

"The shallop's too far behind now. It's too dangerous to separate," insisted Myles.

"Would you risk one of your own?" said the Master.

"There is no risk to him. He seems quite recovered," said Myles, gesturing to the sailor curled around himself by the fire. "We need that corn. Stick to naval tactics, sir. We are on land, now. I will not be challenged on land. If we separate, you put us all at great risk."

William rose. He was in a world of snow and ice. Even his cloak was covered, the winter alchemy having transformed the fabric from wool to wood. He cracked the ice from its folds, but the garment remained cantilevered at odd angles. His gloves were likewise frozen, pinching his fingers when he bent them.

He knelt to their sputtering fire, adding the remaining fuel they'd scavenged. The argument continued; he ignored it, focussing instead on coaxing a little heat from the flames. He dangled his gloves over the blaze then shoved his hands into them while they were still hot.

"Who are we missing?" It was Stephen, breathless, his legs rasping with frost as he cut through the snow toward them. "There are boot prints heading northward from our camp. I followed them some way but thought best to turn back. Who are we missing?"

Stephen counted bodies. He counted a second time. Oddly, all were present. As a group they examined the prints, a single track snaked from the camp into the trees.

This is certainly not the trail of an Indian," said Myles. "Not unless they've pilfered a pair of boots – and surely their owner would have said something by now. Look, too, how the track wavers, as though its maker was unsure of his destination.

"A mystery, yes, but we have weightier matters," said the Master, still eager to resolve their day's agenda. Slowly they drifted back to the fire, colder, yet thankfully, thought William, in a more conciliatory mood.

By the time the ice had melted from his cloak they'd reached a consensus. Nothing further would be gained by discovering the source of the river. With the temperature so low and so few men fit for heavy trekking, they would turn toward the smaller creek. From there, they could navigate to the abandoned village and collect the remaining corn.

Despite the snowfall, the morning's march proved easy going. Three geese idly picking through snow fell victim to their musket balls.

On reaching the creek they discovered an abandoned canoe.

William eyed it skeptically. "It's too narrow. It will tip." He glanced up the creek and assessed the odds of finding a better way across without turning around and returning to the shallop. If they fell in the water, even waist high, they would freeze to death before getting another fire going.

"It looks to be a solid enough craft," said Brewster, testing its buoyancy.

"I'll go first," said Myles. "It would be foolish not to attempt a crossing and it could shorten our journey considerably."

"No, it should be me. I'm lighter," said William.

He stepped in, gripping the sides. Edward and Brewster nodded and bent to slip the canoe into the water. The pair took up paddles at either end of the canoe while William kept as still as he could in the middle.

He was surprised by the ease with which their borrowed craft reached the far shore. The comparison of the light, maneuverable canoe with their plodding longboat rankled him. Again he was struck by the ingenuity of the Indians.

"Well done," he said, climbing out.

"It's pretty steady with the currents," said Edward. "We should be able to take several at a time."

After they were all landed, the group moved on, leaving the canoe high on the shoreline. They reached the clearing with the reburied corn only to find it blanketed in fresh snow. Dozens of soft, white mounds dotted the landscape; William and Stephen looked around trying to recall which one held the corn.

Myles walked confidently to a mound on the far side of the clearing and pointed. "This is it. Lets get the snow cleared and start digging."

"Who has the spades?" asked Edward.

Blank faces swivelled in silence.

"Bloody fools!" cursed Carver, kicking at the mound and whipping up snow devils in the quickening breeze. "How could we forget the spades?"

"Well, we have knives and cutlasses," said the Master. "We can use some of those planks from that hut to scoop the looser dirt. You three," he said, pointing to his sailors, "help Captain Standish and Edward clear snow from that mound. Double quick! A fresh storm is moving in. I taste it."

They cut and stabbed at the frozen earth, scrabbling a foot deep before they could begin removing the soil. When the baskets were uncovered, they proved to be full of beans, not corn.

"We've got the wrong mound," said Edward in disappointment, until the import of the find struck him. "There must be more buried here!" he said excitedly. "Start digging in the others."

Everyone hacked at the hillocks. Soon the village resembled the scene of a great massacre. The snow was trampled and churned; its pristine whiteness marred with dark gashes.

Depositing a heavy basket in the centre of this misery, William stretched, feeling a sharp pain shoot down is leg from his lower back. He hobbled to a log and sat. They had managed to lever up ten bushels of corn, a bottle of oil, three big baskets of wheat, more of wheat ears, and the bag of beans. The cache could be presumed empty.

"We must give them satisfaction for this food. I won't have it any other way," William said.

"Of course we will," said Myles, grinning broadly, "we can bring beads from the ship and leave them here in one of the shelters."

"As long as we do. I won't be responsible for bad blood between ourselves and the Indians."

"I am no thief either, William," said Brewster. "But this corn, beans, and wheat are going to ensure our survival. We haven't enough of our own left to get through the winter. I took stock and calculated the time till harvest. With a hundred mouths to feed, we won't make it on what is left, even at half rations."

"We have what you came for," said Master Jones, "and weather is moving in. I order that we march to the ship directly and board these supplies. We've taken too great a risk as it is, with so many in failing health."

William examined the sailor collapsed against his log. He was tempted to check to see if he was still breathing. He'd stopped shivering. Relieved, he saw the man's chest rise.

"I agree," said William, getting to his feet. "Divide the bags between us. Some can carry the geese and we can switch part way through." At last they were heading back. He'd been away from Dorothy for too long already.

"I'm for staying and continuing," said Stephen. "We've come this far. We may be within half a day's walk of the Indian village."

"I would stay and continue," volunteered Edward.

"I as well," said Carver. "The weak and ill can go back with the Master while the rest of us continue. I haven't seen enough yet and there may be more promising land ahead. Certainly this corn is proof the land is fertile."

Eighteen were appointed to continue. William was not among them.

With the loss of man-power and only the weakest left among them, it was anything but a smooth trek back. They stopped often to set down the heavy bushels of food.

When finally they reached the beach and spotted the *Mayflower* in the distance, he laid his head on the frozen sand and slept. The shallop would be a while coming.

The smell of roasting goose and a tingling warmth against his boots roused him an hour later.

Cold Welcome

$\mathscr{D}$esire scanned the returning shallop anxiously. The temperature had dropped again and John didn't own a heavy woollen cloak like most of the others. If he froze to death she would never forgive Father Carver for the misery of the past weeks.

Gilbert remained with her, too sick to march. She nursed him. She wished for his recovery. But she felt no love for him. She loved only John.

Below in the shallop, the men sat with bowed heads. Knees were tucked up to shoulders. John's red coat wasn't visible. She stepped back as they started up the rat-lines and swung over the rail. Another blast of wind stung her cheeks and she buried her face in her mantle, huffing into the wool to warm herself before peeking over its edge again. The Master shouted from the shallop for a rope. She hurried back to the side to see why.

A line slithered past her and the remaining men in the shallop wrapped it under the armpits of a limp sailor. His head nodded as though he was asleep. The Master barked and the rope jerked the sailor upright, working his body like a marionette. His hands moved feebly to grasp the ratlines, but failed. As he neared the rail, the master gunner hauled him by his breaches, up and over, and dropped him with a thud at Desire's feet.

"What's wrong with him? Is he wounded? Where are the rest?" She looked from face to face. They nudged her aside.

William stepped forward and handed her a soggy goose so that he could get his hands under the sailor's shoulders.

"Not wounded. Sick. When I left John, he was safe. The stronger men stayed behind." He lifted, grunted, and nearly toppled as he and another sailor shuffled to the aft steerage cabin with the man's body swinging between them.

Desire exhaled and sunk to her knees. Katherine reached for the goose forgotten in her hand, tisking at her with disapproval.

"Let's move below," Katherine ordered.

Priscilla, expecting to see John Alden, began to cry and Desire hugged her hard. They scanned the distant shoreline in vain for a fire or any sign of the men. Beneath them, the water reflected a heavy pink blanket of cloud. Snow was coming again. And John was out there without shelter.

"I have to talk with you, Mother Katherine," she said, kissing Priscilla's cheek and following Katherine to the hatch. Its rim was decorated with the long icicles of a thousand frozen sighs.

Katherine ushered her into their cabin and drew the curtain.

"You know how much I love John and you know I've tried hard with Gilbert, I've kept my promise . . . but, really Mother, I feel nothing for him but kinship. How am I to marry him when I suspect he does it to please Edward and Father Carver? And I'm doing the same, denying my true feelings and injuring John, who will probably never forgive me. Is this truly what is best for the congregation?"

Katherine sat down and laid the goose at her feet. She patted the bed and Desire felt a pang of hope. "You are in love with each other. Father Carver can see it too. Trust me, I have advocated on your behalf."

She studied Katherine's face. Was there a *but* coming? She wasn't going to let her say it if there was.

December 3rd – First Dog Watch

William parted company with the other men and dragged himself off to his cabin. A buzz intensified in the common-way behind him. He stored his musket and undid his pack. The buzz grew louder. He parted his curtain to find a party of women at his door accompanied by the husbands with whom he had just returned.

"I see you all missed me," he chuckled, "what have you done with *my* wife?"

"I'm here."

William craned his neck around the door frame.

"Dorothy," he said, extending his hand to help her into the cabin, "we have guests." He planted a kiss on top of her head, relieved to see her.

"While you were gone, something happened," said Beth, "Deacon Carver didn't come back with you so we need you to deal with it."

"It's John Billington," said Dorothy.

William groaned. "Let me sit down." He didn't want to hear the rest. *Why Billington again?*

"I found little Ellen in his cabin. With him. She was on her knees. Billington was dressed. Her chest was bare and she was crying."

"Dear God," blurted William. "Who else saw this?"

Heads shook. "I need all the men with me. Where is Billington now?"

"He is up on deck, sharpening his sword," said William Mullins ominously, leaning on his daughter for support.

"Good to see you up," he said, shaking Mullins' hand gently. He took stock of the men he had. Francis Eaton, Richard Warren, and Dr. Fuller were the only men left with any strength. The rest were too weak to challenge Billington. "Where is Christopher Martin?"

"Abed in his cabin."

"Will someone get him?"

"Are you sure, William?" said Richard Warren.

William had forgotten that no one knew of his rapprochement with Martin following the fight on deck with Billington.

Before anyone could go, Martin approached wrapped in his blanket.

John Tilley's voice shook, "I won't have him threatening the children with his perversion."

"He will have to come with us on the next expedition," said William. "But what of his punishment? And what of his crime? Accusing him of frightening the child isn't enough."

"I daresay his crime was worse than frightening a child, William," said Moses. "If not for Dorothy's vigilance, we all know the evil that man could have unleashed in his cabin. I say we put him ashore and leave him there to fend for himself. Keep everyone safe."

"It might be more fitting to have his hands and feet tied behind his back. As we did with Prince. Leaving him ashore in this cold might kill him," said William.

December 3rd – First Dog Watch

"Is this some crazy story his wife concocted?" said Billington, raising the point of his sword and leveling it at William. The newly honed edge glinted in the lantern light. "I can't believe you are taking her word over mine. She can hardly walk. Did any of you see her come to my cabin? That bastard girl is probably in on it with her. She's a clever, scheming child who is set against my good wife for no good reason."

"Tell your lies to the wind," said Richard Warren. "I've heard with my own ears Eleanor abusing the child and her siblings. Little Ellen is innocent and you won't touch her or any other child again."

"Who says I touched the child? Can your wife prove that, William? I paid the child to polish my boots."

"So you admit she was in your cabin – on her knees?" said William.

"She was there, but I did nothing to the little waif. Perhaps you accuse me of something you wish to do yourselves."

William White, father of five-year-old Resolved, his wife Suzanna ready to give birth within days, lunged forward. He broke through the group and swung his fist at Billington. But his weakness betrayed him and he stumbled on the deck before he could land the punch.

William picked him up. He could feel the man's fever radiating through his cloak.

Billington snickered, "I guess we're done." He pushed past William.

Observing from behind the others, Christopher Martin had remained silent, save for a hacking fit of cough that double him over. But as Billington passed, Martin whipped a hand out from beneath his blanket and yanked Billington back by his collar with surprising strength.

Billington lost his balance. He shot an arm out to brace his fall, but too late. His wrist snapped with a loud crack as he landed on the deck.

Oblivious, Martin leapt on top of him, ploughing his fist deep into Billington's face. Billington was in too much pain to defend himself.

"Enough!" shouted William. "We won't have violence."

He pulled Martin off, still swinging. "Enough. We needn't do more today." He brushed Martin off and draped his fallen blanket back around his shoulders.

Beneath his stern exterior, William offered a prayer of gratitude. "The man's broken his own arm. It's God's punishment. Billington will be with us on the next expedition and each step will send a jolt of pain through his arm. A frequent reminder of his transgression. God had a plan."

They left Billington cradling his arm. Dr. Fuller could attend to it if he felt it his duty, but none of the others would help.

The Promise

The ships bell clanged three and fell silent. Too early to be awake. A discordant lapping of waves against the hull kept Dorothy from falling back to sleep. She rose and quietly limped into the common-way. Desire, awake, was huddled around the glowing belly of the brazier. On seeing Dorothy up, she sprang to her feet to help.

"Let's go to the manger so we don't disturb anyone," whispered Dorothy.

Desire lit a lantern and hung it from the beam near the goat's pen. It cast a warm glow that roused the goats. They bleated once then tucked their heads again. Desire scattered some fresh straw under the pool of light and helped Dorothy onto the soft mat. She knelt beside her, scooting in close.

"Why are you up so early?" asked Dorothy.

"John hasn't returned. Every time I hear a thump, I hope it's him and can't sleep."

Dorothy took her hands. "He will be back soon." After a moment of silence, she added, "you shouldn't marry Gilbert. I meant what I said about him."

"I gave my word to Father Carver."

"And yet here you are anxiously awaiting John."

"I know."

They reclined, knees pressed against each other.

Dorothy wiggled closer. Their breath formed one cloud. "I'll do anything to help you, you know that."

"I do." Desire wove her fingers into Dorothy's and smiled.

"Then promise me you will do everything you can to help yourself too. You can't be afraid to stand against Deacon Carver when it comes to John."

Desire lowered her gaze. "I'm not afraid. It just may be too late. John refuses to talk to me."

They silently held each other, listening to the soft bleating of the goats and the chickens stirring in their nests.

"And you must do everything you can to heal," said Desire. "Jonathan is going to need his mother strong and healthy."

Dorothy turned onto her back. "The day before yesterday, when I helped Ellen, she found my tooth. I think it was a sign from God that I am forgiven for Harlock."

"I never believed God would damn you anyway. It was a selfless act. You were protecting us."

Dorothy pushed herself upright. Desire wrapped her in her arms and rocked her back and forth. "I love you, Dorothy. I'll always be grateful for what you did."

"I love you, too."

Desire leaned her head against Dorothy's. "I think you are right. About the tooth. He does approve."

Dorothy closed her eyes. "We are safe from men like Harlock now. And safe from Prince's lies. I could never have asked for a better friend by my side. Things can go back to normal. We can rebuild the happy life we once had."

December 4th – First Watch

The shadowy silhouette of the *Mayflower* vanished against the night sky. Thin cracks of light stealing from the edges of battened gunports were the only clue to her presence. The ship was eerily quiet. Only the sound of the wind strumming the halyards and tinkling the shackles dappled the silence.

John hoped for a more fulsome welcome. Only the image of Desire kept him upright and helped him pull the oars when the wind and his arms begged him to give up.

He got his boots in the ropes and reached down to grasp gear from Edward. He passed it above to Stephen who dumped it with a clatter on the deck. He heard rumblings from within the ship and then the creak of the ladder.

When he came up over the edge, she was there. Her loose hair lifted in the wind to frame her face. She'd been sleeping. The tracks of the pillow were clearly visible on her cheek. She began to cry.

He dropped his load and took two long strides toward her. He caught himself just as he was about to pull her into his arms; he took her delicate fingers instead and ran his thumbs over the backs of her hands.

"I still love you," he whispered. Her eyes flared like a candle nourished with oxygen.

Aloud, he said, "I'm sorry we're back so late and that we've woken all of you." And then quietly again, "I'm grateful to God for getting us back in one piece and for the sight of you."

"Was it bad? I worried when you didn't return." Her voice was strangled with emotion.

"Where is Gilbert?"

"Asleep."

"Come here quickly while your father is still in the longboat," he said, motioning her to the far side of the main mast. "It was deathly cold and I'm desperate to get below. Take this package, but don't open it until I can sit with you and see your face." He reached awkwardly under his cloak and fumbled with the buttons of his vest, finally pulling free the tiny gift wrapped in leaf and straw. "I've thought of nothing but you. It kept me alive."

The warmth of the t'ween deck felt hot against his chafed, cold skin. He deposited his armour, sword, and musket by the cabin door, unhooked his cloak, which he then spread wide over the pile, and then stiffly lowered himself to the deck next to Katherine and Desire. He was grateful to Katherine for fussing. He needed the care right now.

Desire's eyes glowed in the soft light from the coals. Surreptitiously, he explored every inch of her.

Katherine finally got up and ducked back into her cabin to check on Carver.

"Can I open it now?" she said excitedly, looking right and left to see that they weren't watched. "What can it possibly be?"

She took her time slipping the knot he had made with beach grass around a large, yellowed maple leaf. When it fell loose, the leaf unfolded to reveal a bracelet of woven hemp and tiny blue and yellow beads.

"How very strange and uniquely made," she said, lifting it gently and turning it in the faint light. "If it was made by savages, how savage could they be to wear such pretty things?" She extended her arm so that he could tie it round her wrist. "What did you trade for it, John? It must have cost you something dear."

"We never met the Indians. We found this and other treasures just as we were coming from the woods this morning. It isn't much, but it is all I have to give you so far."

"It is a gift of great value to me and I will never take it off." She turned the bracelet back and forth, admiring it and bathing him in a deep, radiant smile. She yawned and he yawned in turn.

"I could stare at you all night," he whispered. "Wherever you are, home is. It is so good to be home." He took her hand. "Promise me you won't marry Gilbert. Promise me, Desire. We love each other. Until you can marry me – marry no one."

They sat in silence, falling in and out of sleep. When suddenly he jerked awake, she made an excuse that she was too tired to stay up any longer.

He didn't have the heart to tell her he was expected to leave again in the morning.

December 5th – Morning Watch

William shivered as his damp breaches settled against his skin. He walked bowed-legged to the brazier, hoping to reduce their sting. Edward and Carver were already warming their backsides. The three spoke over their shoulders.

"How are Brewster and Isaac?" asked William.

"Not well. They both faltered shortly after you left us. By the middle of the day, they needed to stop and catch their breath every thirty paces. Myles lost his patience with them," said Edward.

"We'll leave them and William White behind. He wants to be near Suzanna for the birth," said Carver, turning to face the fire. "I hate to leave Alden behind but he caught his ankle in a hole and had to limp back last night leaning on a branch. He is likely to slow us down."

"I'm packed and ready. When would you like to leave?" asked William.

"The seas were too rough when I checked at six bells. Sleet's coming down hard. We can wait until after we've eaten to recheck."

William rotated to warm his side in the weak heat. "Delaying our start will not improve the weather. If the rivers freeze over, we won't be able to find them under the snow. I've packed enough for a week, but I suggest we bring more dry rations if they can be spared, just in case."

"Prince is out there somewhere in this," he added. "I'm convinced those were his footprints we found. He'd have fared better had he stayed on the ship as our prisoner. Regardless of his fate, we will still send letters to the Adventurers warning of his plot against us."

"I fear we don't know the full extent of what he has done or will do," said Carver.

"Excuse us, husband." Katherine squeezed in next to Carver with a pot of water. She settled it on top of the brazier and waved her hands for Anna and Desire to stop hovering and push their way forward to get the cooking started.

William took the hint and retreated. His steaming breaches were still damp but at least now more comfortable.

He heard Dorothy sliding along the wall behind him and rushed to her aid.

"Where can I take you, love?" He kissed the top of her head. He could imagine now the anguish she had been wrestling with regarding Prince.

"Just over to the brazier. Beth is bringing our supplies with her own. I'm going to make you some porridge with raisins. It's the last of the raisins, so enjoy them."

"How have the women been? Did anyone new fall sick while I was gone?"

"Little Jasper has been moved closer to the doctor's cabin. Dr. Fuller wants to keep an eye on him." replied Dorothy. "Mary Allerton has taken ill, but their daughter has recovered. I'm hopeful Jasper will do the same."

"He will. And *you* will bounce back as soon as we get you into a warm house with plenty of fresh food." William helped to lower Dorothy to the deck by the brazier and exchanged nods and smiles with the other women.

"How are you holding up, Desire?" he asked, noticing the exhaustion in her face.

"I would sleep better if Father Carver could take time to talk with me," she said, loud enough for Carver to hear.

Carver grumbled and called down to John, "Are you almost ready with those packs?"

"We're ready, sir. You likely have time to talk to Desire after all." John laid the muskets on the deck and innocently examined his armour.

"Please, Father Carver. I'm not entirely going back on my word," she said in a whisper.

He softened, "I'm not avoiding you. You just aren't seeing the important tasks in front of us. I don't blame you for that. You're young and you have your own troubles here with the cooking and laundering. Your wedding is not a priority. Gilbert isn't going anywhere."

Desire threw down the spoon she held and stomped off to the cabin, angrily wiping tendrils of hair from her face. William saw John give her a look of affectionate sympathy. Moments later they heard her sobbing.

"What have I done now?" Carver said to Katherine.

She rolled her eyes at him.

William smiled at the expression on her face that said, 'If you don't know, I can't help you.' How often had Dorothy served him that look?

There was a mighty crash and howl of agony above them.

William, Carver, and Edward dashed for the ladder. It was probably a sailor, but there weren't many about to offer assistance, even if it was. Most were as sick as they were.

Carver poked his head through the hatch. "Not you!" he said angrily.

William was anxious for him to move above so that they could all see.

"It's Billington – the fool," said Carver, peering through his arm pit.

When Carver moved, William climbed into the driving wind and skated across the deck toward Billington's rolling, thrashing body.

Carver, Edward, and William stood over Billington, trying to suss what was wrong with him. William looked above and couldn't imagine that he'd fallen from the main mast. He was rolling around too much to be seriously injured.

"What have you done then?" asked Edward

"My leg," winced Billington in agony.

"I'm freezing out here. Can you stand on it?" said William.

"I slipped on the ice. I've broken it, like my arm. I can't stand," he said, resuming his howling. William eyed him with suspicion.

"Well let's get you below to the doctor. He can have a look," said Carver offering his hand.

"Aghh," he cried as he tried to sit up. "Help me."

William exchanged a look with Edward. They were thinking the same thing. Bending together, they grabbed Billington's cloak. They spun him round and dragged him roughly back to the edge of the companionway. He sputtered and howled the whole way.

"You'll have to swing your legs over and get yourself down. I'm –"

BANG!

The boards shook beneath William's feet. He rushed to the hatch and plunged his head through the opening. Smoke purled from one of the aft cabins. The stillness lingering over the sick and weary ship was gone. Raw panic lined the faces hurrying to and fro beneath him.

"Get down there," said Carver, pushing past him.

William followed on his heels. He caught the acrid whiff of gunpowder in the smoke.

"Has someone fired their musket?" Carver's voice boomed. "Hurry now, is that what we heard?"

"It's Billington's cabin. The smoke is coming from Billington's cabin," cried Edward marching past him and throwing open the curtain of the smoking cabin. It was impossible to see. He waved the curtain back and forth. A shadow leapt from the darkness and tried to duck past him, but William caught it by the arm.

The shadow was young Francis Billington. His sooty face glared at William as he squirmed to get free.

"You take your hands off 'a me or my father will cut your throat," the boy said, now digging his long nails into William's wrists. William gave him a shake and shoved him away.

"He will, will he?" he said. "Shall we invite him down here?" His disgust with Billington began to override his cautious fear of the man. "Billington! I'm sure you can manage the ladder. Your son seems to feel you are fit to run me through. You'd better get down here and explain why he's been firing pistols on the ship."

Edward spread the curtain wide, and they searched for the musket.

"God keep us safe!" William exclaimed. "He's made little piles of the gunpowder and set a wick to them. Billington's left a half-full barrel of gunpowder open in here, with powder over everything. With all this flint and iron lying about, an explosion here could have killed everyone sitting by the fire."

"What exploded? What did you fire off?" Carver demanded of young Francis.

The boy glared at him and crossed his arms.

"The fouling piece is hot," said Edward.

Billington limped to the cabin doorway. "You have no right to be going through my things."

"Your son just loaded and fired a gun in the middle of a crowded ship. We are lucky he didn't kill anyone or blow us all up," said Carver.

"Did you do this, son?" he asked, bringing the boy under his wing while giving the rest of them a challenging look.

"No, I did not. It was already loaded. I picked it up and it went off by accident," Francis raised his chin, gave William a smug expression and then moved even closer to his father.

"You left a loaded fouling piece lying around in your cabin. You have gunpowder everywhere. Clean it up before we leave!" he said to Billington. He glanced at the boy and back to Billington again. "You'll be on the shallop with us as soon as the weather clears and your musket and every grain of gunpowder better be put where this child can't reach it."

"I can't go anywhere. I've broken my leg. I need the doctor."

William's hands shook with fury, but he held his tongue. Carver's anger would suffice for now. Their eyes met and he was grateful his feelings were understood.

"If you've injured yourself – if you've done it on purpose, its not going save you from coming. Pray the doctor splints you well," said Carver. He nodded to William and Edward. They were done here.

"I slipped on the icy deck. I was checking the weather. Of course I intended to go until this happened," said Billington to their backs.

William dreaded the thought of travelling with Billington, but he also couldn't leave him behind. He promised he would keep the women and children safe.

Figures on the Beach

*W*illiam crouched as low in the shallop as possible while still working his oar. They had been rowing for an hour, the sail above them luffing with disinterest. Every lazy flutter mocked his aching back and freezing joints.

John Tilley and his brother Ed had both volunteered to join the exploring party but neither was well. Ed Tilley's oar jumped from the oar lock again and he fell backward against William's knees. William reached a hand out and pushed him back to his seat. Steam coiled from Ed's collar despite the icy stiffness of his coat.

The search of Corn Hill and Cold Harbour had sapped his strength, as it had the rest of the party. Physical exhaustion, a sparse diet, the cold and damp, or all three, had severely weakened them. Half the volunteers for this voyage were fainting with fever. William felt fortunate to feel better than most.

Billington should have been with them.

He was convinced the leg injury was an act, but Dr. Fuller couldn't prove it. Regardless, Billington wouldn't be moved from his bunk. He moaned and fretted as the rest of them boarded the shallop. They had delayed an extra day for him, but it had made no difference. The weather was still foul and Billington still fouler.

They had to find a deep harbour and level ground fit for cultivation. He vowed not to return until they did.

The sail gave a sigh, sucked in, then suddenly filled. The men held their oars and looked up hopefully.

"Keep rowing. If we get clear of the sandy point, we shall have the weather shore," said Master's mate Clarke, puffing.

"How far is this Thievish Harbour and the great river?" William asked of Robert Coppin, their pilot.

"Not above eight leagues, I imagine. It was right over against the headland there, if I am remembering right. It's been some years. We done some trucking with the Indians there and one of them stole our harpoon, so we called it Thievish Harbour. I'll know it when I sees it."

The sail caught and an invisible hand yanked the shallop forward.

"Ship and store the oars!"

William dragged his oar out of the water and glanced behind him to be sure he wasn't going to butt Edward Winslow in the head. Water purled down the cracked wooden surface and landed in his lap. He tried to shake it off but it froze too quickly, thickening the heavy, milky sheet that already gilded his coat.

"If we can keep this wind, we may reach it before we freeze. John Tilley, you should have stayed onboard the *Mayflower*. We could have done without you," William said, not unkindly, as Tilley slid again from his seat.

"I had to come. There are many closer to death than I on that ship. If we don't return with good news, there won't be another chance. It would be Edward, Myles and Stephen alone well enough to raise their heads." He coughed and his brother lifted him upright again. "What those men do that no sickness touches them, I should like to know...they must have the hand of God upon them."

It was true. They had neither coughed nor fevered the entire voyage despite the general sickness around them. Brewster, too, with the exception of the last two days.

"I worry you're right. We must find a settlement if it means scouting the entire Bay," said Carver behind him. "There were only twelve of us well enough. With the six men Master Jones has supplied we're a small company. How many next time?"

"Do you think it a bad omen that we've seen so few Indians?" asked John Howland, coughing and raising his collar to cover his ears. "The villages have all been abandoned. This land is populated with graves, not people. You missed it, William, but we uncovered a rich grave on our return from Corn Hill, not far from that old Christian fort. There was a babe all wrapped in bracelets of fine white beads. With it were the bones and unconsumed flesh of a man – with golden hair."

"You didn't say anything about this, Carver. Was it a Christian grave? Was there evidence of a Christian settlement?" said William.

"Not really. It was an Indian burial mound much like the rest. Some of the men saved a few of the prettier things from the grave. We supposed the man to be a sailor of some kind that did well among the Indians. He was bound up in a sailor's canvas cassock and wore breaches. Ask Edward. He brought away a pretty tray and bowl."

If Edward Winslow wasn't blue with cold, he would have coloured.

"Why didn't anyone mention this before?" said William.

"Truthfully, I didn't want you to think less of me, William. I know you don't keep with disturbing their graves – let alone taking things from them," said Edward.

"I don't. You're right. But this is important."

"I thought so too," said John, "that's why I brought it up. Perhaps the land is too harsh or too impoverished to settle. Where we find the Indian's thriving, we might also thrive."

"Perhaps," said Stephen.

The conversation lulled. The wind whisked sea spray onto their coats and boots until they appeared glassed. William's beard grew heavy with icicles. He tried to pull them free, but they were stuck fast.

"Look ahead! Speak of the Devils," said a surprised sailor.

He followed the sailor's gaze. There on the sand, about a league distant, a small band of ten or twelve Indians were hacking at some great black thing on the sand.

"Do you suppose it's a whale?" said Stephen. "We've seen them sleeping and playing by the ship often enough. Perhaps one's beached itself. It may be this water is too cold for them."

"Let's go past them a league or two and then come upon them once we've warmed a bit and made ready," said Carver.

It was hard work maneuvering through the shallows. William refused to have anyone wade to shore. They were too sick already.

Once on land, Stephen and Myles took charge of assembling a barricade and starting a fire. The cold and the lateness of the day made it too dangerous to explore – especially with the Indians so close and their own numbers so few.

"Tomorrow, we split up. Eight of us shall stay with the shallop and ten of us will scout the shore," said Carver, reclining against a log and pulling his cloak to his chin.

The sound of snoring echoed from the back of the lean-to. William pulled his legs in under the driftwood overhang and watched the snow. It had begun to fall shortly after dark. If it got much thicker, the fire could go out. He added a heavy piece of driftwood and trained his eyes on the fringe of trees above the beach. One more hour of sentinel duty and he and Carver could turn in.

"Do you intend to let them wed?" he said quietly, shaking himself when he realized he had been staring into the fire instead of watching the trees.

"She's betrothed to Gilbert. I suppose it's him you mean? The other is my servant."

"She and Gilbert aren't in love. She did it to please you. They won't be happy."

"She was left a great sum of money for her dowry. John is beneath her."

"Where is that money now? It won't be of any use to her here."

"Hmph." Carver hunched his shoulders and readjusted his cloak to cover his boots.

"She and John are in love," pressed William. "Marrying her off to another man won't change that. You are inviting trouble. We are a small community."

"What has being in love got to do with it?" asked Carver. "She's a good girl. She'll grow to love whomever we choose for her."

"Don't be so sure. You are a stubborn, prideful fool. I tell you that as your friend," said William, tapping snow off another piece of wood before laying it across the fire. The fire sizzled and began to smoke. He gave it a quick stir.

"We've got to be sensible about this marching around," said Carver, changing the subject. "Firstly, we must find a good harbour for ships, as trade and payment to the Adventurers is paramount. Secondly, we must have a good source of fresh water that we can depend on year-round. Thirdly we must have good level ground that will not be too hard to clear and prepare for planting."

"I agree. We've found plenty of cleared ground the Indians have abandoned."

"The area near Corn Hill was neither defensible nor close to fresh water. What water we could find was in ponds, liable to dry up. We don't know the climate well enough to depend on them."

"So we won't waste effort tramping through the woods if we don't find a river or good creek tomorrow. Do you agree?" William stirred the fire and then scanned the forest. They both listened intently for a few moments.

"I thought this harbour was good – sheltered and broad. They can sound it further tomorrow while we explore," said William.

December 8th – Forenoon Watch

William looked up from the enormous fish at his feet and watched the far off shallop pull in the sounding line and recast it. The vessel was too far out for him to guess the length of the line as it was reeled in.

His attention returned to the fish. He had thought it a whale, it was so large; five or six paces long with thick fat under its dark, swine-like skin. Stephen told him it was called a Grampus.

It appeared to have been tossed by the tide and stranded. Thick white ice rimmed the shore, preventing it from sliding back into the sea.

The Indians had cut great slices of it a pace long and two hands wide. One had been dropped in haste on the nearby sand. Retreating footsteps gave them a direction they might follow next.

Until they could establish whether the harbour would serve their purpose, however, there wasn't much point exploring further.

A quarter of an hour later, the shallop sailed within hailing distance.

"What's your news?" yelled Carver.

"Five fathoms!"

William nodded happily to the others.

"We found two more of those great fish deep in the harbour," called Robert Coppin from the shallop.

"We'll call this Grampus Bay," said William.

"As we follow the Indian tracks down the beach, follow us by water," called Carver through cupped hands.

They picked up their packs and muskets and shuffled down the beach. William moved to firmer ground. The rest gradually joined him.

The brush to their left cleared and they could see a pond of clear water that came almost to the shore. The Indian tracks led inland at the far edge of the pond. William waved to the shallop as they moved out of sight.

John Howland thought he saw a dwelling on the far side of the pond, but when they reached it, it was only brush. They marched again following a well-worn path deep into the forest.

"The ground is level," said William at length.

"But not very productive. No nuts, vines, nor fruits," said Edward.

"The creek is also too narrow. We could jump across," remarked Stephen. "The pond is too small and might be salty at high tide."

"Should we turn back? We shouldn't wear ourselves out if it's no good," said Carver.

"I can go further," said John Tilley, his step faltering despite his words.

"A half mile further then?" said William. "It looks as though the brush is thinner ahead. If we find nothing, we turn back."

Walking kept him warm but they had brought nothing from the shallop to eat. There was nothing on the ground and no game in the bush.

Five hundred yards on, the wood opened on a broad, previously planted field. Just beyond, they came across another graveyard.

"This is a sad and lonely place," said William, "Is this what is to become of us? Not a living soul in every village we've found."

"It reminds me of a churchyard. All these saplings ranged so close together like a picket fence round the whole thing," said Ed Tilley.

"Let's go back," said Myles. "It will be getting dark soon and I'm not fond of this place." He had been subdued the whole day. Fatigue must have been plaguing him too.

On their return, by another route, they happened upon the remnants of more long-abandoned dwellings. But with the light dying and their energy all but gone, they passed through without stopping.

The Indians had eluded them again.

Screams in the Night

*T*he ship was in mourning. Not long before noon, Jasper took his last breath. As hope of his recovery failed they kissed his brow.

At the end, Ellen held him in her arms and counted the space between each breath. When the last one came and she had counted beyond her ability she collapsed on him and cried over and over that she was sorry.

Reluctantly, Dorothy removed Ellen from Jasper. Had she not, she knew the faithful child would have held him until he stiffened.

They held the funeral as soon as Jasper was washed and wrapped. William Brewster led them in prayer aboard ship and then he and Isaac took Jasper to shore in the longboat. Jasper would, at least, have a proper Christian burial.

Grief overwhelmed Dorothy the moment the longboat pushed off. Jasper's death might easily have been Jonathan's.

Beyond her grief she was grateful that Jonathan was still safe in Holland. Understanding toward William welled inside her. She would rather Jonathan remain there forever than risk his life with this fickle crossing. William was right; Jonathan would not have been strong enough. She wished she could tell him.

Her eyes softened on Ellen, Richard, and Mary clasping each other, inconsolable, and she prayed. *Is this why I have come? Is it to care for these lost children? William and I will raise them, Lord, and I will love them as my own. Please protect my Jonathan and send him to me only when he will be safe.*

December 8th – Afternoon Watch

Desire felt wetness seep into the fabric under her knees while Elder Brewster led the prayer.

She slowly lowered her hand to her skirt and lifted the edge of the fabric – it *was* wet.

It dawned on her that Suzanna beside her was in labour. Her water had broken. If she was in pain, she hid it well.

She reached for Suzanna's hand and Suzanna grasped hers tightly. She *was* feeling it then.

Elder Brewster finished.

"Amen," Desire said clearly.

Desire waited while Jasper's body was gathered up and Ellen, Richard and Mary said their final goodbyes to him. Jasper's death tore at the fragile weave of her sole. She was thinned and warped. She couldn't take much more . . . she didn't want to take much more.

Suzanna gripped her hand again. She had to remain present, as much as she would like to lie down and sleep for an eon.

"When did the pain start?" Desire whispered.

"An hour ago, or so. I didn't want to make a fuss. Jasper deserved to be mourned first, the poor ba....aggh."

"How long was your labour with Resolved?"

"Long. I've been praying for this babe to come easy."

Suzanna rose to her feet and knuckled her back. With her other hand, she pulled Desire in close and whispered, her eyes wide, "I've had a superstitious thought. When Lizzy delivered Oceanus, we lost Billy. Now we've lost Jasper and my babe is coming. What if He is giving one and taking one away? Am I to blame for Jasper's death?"

"Don't be silly. God does no such thing. How else would you account for the increase of our families?"

Desire looked to Mary Allerton for support, but Mary looked as frightened as Suzanna.

December 8th – First Watch

William stumbled onto the beach and tore off his pack. He couldn't take another step. Carver stepped past him and waved his arms. William looked up with effort and spied the shallop some way off, riding at anchor in the bay. Carver waved again and the sail went up at once.

William pulled off his left boot and rubbed at his ankle and toes. He couldn't feel the touch on his skin.

"Don't rest yet. We still need wood for a fire."

William's head snapped. It wasn't Myles' voice, but John Howland's. Unexpected. He checked Myles for a reaction. Myles sat in the sand, his face pressed against a log. *Even he is human.*

No one moved. He knew the wisdom in John's words. They needed fire. He slowly pulled his boot back on, bartering with himself that if he could close his eyes for a few minutes, he would be willing to stand.

He drifted off. Of course he did. It had only been a moment. He stood, chastising himself for his weakness. Now that he was up, he only needed enough inertia to propel him forward until he met with a piece of wood.

Before long, he had collected five. The pile grew as others, marching dead on their feet, returned with their own collections.

"Hello! You are safe, praise God," said someone on the approaching shallop. "We began to fear. We lost sight of you this morning and with no word where you were going, we feared you were attacked."

"Come ashore, warm yourselves," Edward yelled back.

The shallop had been kept from coming ashore all day by the tide and the men onboard were likely as cold, if not colder, than William.

William handed Isaac's brother, John Allerton, his aqua vitae. "I'm sorry we were so long," he said.

"When it grew dark and we still hadn't seen any sign of you we began to worry. If we'd come ashore to look for you, dividing our numbers further between the shallop and a search party, we might easily have been ambushed," said Robert Coppin.

William shivered and passed Robert his drink. "You did right remaining with the shallop. We never did make contact with the Indians. We followed their bare feet as far as an abandoned village and then gave up. Bare feet, can you imagine?" he said, contemplating the toughness of the Indians.

He faded. His eyes closed despite his best efforts. "Who takes the first watch? he mumbled to Carver.

"I will, William," Carver answered, patting him on the shoulder.

"I'll keep it with you," William heard John Howland say, before drifting off.

December 9th – Middle Watch

Desire wiped the sweat from her eyes with the back of her hand.

"Breathe with me, huff, huff, huff," she coached Suzanna. Now in her twelfth hour, Suzanna was starting to panic. It was close to midnight and Desire was nearly as drained as she was. It was hard to be encouraging.

"Help me get her on her hands and knees, Beth. Ready Suzanna. One, two, three."

"Naa…ah," Suzanna complained.

"Now breathe with me again when the next one comes. Rest your head down on the pillow."

"I can't do it. I'm too tired. Oh plea…….se." Suzanna's body tightened and she held her breath with the pain.

"Huff, huff," encouraged Desire. She tried to remove the note of frustration in her voice. "You are doing great. You can do this, Suzanna."

Like a ship on the sea her body sensed the subtle changes in Suzanna's as the contractions came on. She rose to meet them and collapsed against the bunk when they passed.

The contractions hastened and she called to Mary to bring the lamp. She waited for a contraction to finish and quickly brought the light low to check the cervix. "Still only four fingers," she whispered to Mary over her shoulder.

She didn't get her hand out in time and Suzanna screamed as the next contraction came on. When it was over, she shared the disappointment with Suzanna. Still a while to go.

Suzanna screamed with each new contraction. As Desire worked to calm her and make her focus, it became clear that Suzanna was either too tired or too frightened to control the animal instinct driving her to howl. Desire felt her own urge to howl.

December 9th – Middle Watch

William woke with a start and reached for his musket. Full dark. Screaming shred the night's mist.

"Arm! Arm yourselves men!" barked Myles.

William rolled on his belly and felt for his shot pouch. His fingertips quivered as he tried to pick up the ball. He'd made the mistake of not preparing his musket before falling asleep. Where was his damned wadding?

A hideous howl followed a chorus of yips. William's blood chilled another degree. He worked faster, probing for his powder horn.

A musket fired close by. His ears rang; acrid smoke caught in his throat. The ball struck a tree with a heavy thwack; branches cracked.

All went quiet. He held his breath and watched the dark shapes of the trees sway, Edward and Carver breathing hard on either side of him.

"Woah, woah –yip– yipyip," shrilled in the forest to his right. He pivoted his musket on the log and yelled as he pulled the trigger. The match snapped forward and the musket swung back at him with such force that he fell on Edward.

He had fired. Adrenaline coursed through him. The pounding in his ears and the ringing aftershock made it impossible to tell whether his shot had hit anything, but at least he had fired.

He waited and listened with the rest. All was quiet. At the sound of snapping branches, his body stiffened again.

"What do you suppose it is?" he whispered after what seemed like a long silence.

"It sounded to me like wolves, maybe a fox with that *yip* sound. I heard them once up in Newfoundland," said Master's mate Clarke.

"Not an Indian ambush then?" he said, the tension releasing a little.

"I wouldn't say so. No Indian can sound that much like a dog. I'm sure it was a dog of some kind." Clarke reassured them by laying down his own musket and stretching out his legs.

William laughed with relief and the others joined in. Before long they were guffawing and slapping each other on the back. When all settled, William was too keyed up from shooting his musket to go back to sleep.

"I'll take the next watch. What time is it?"

"Just after midnight, by my guess," said Richard.

He threw another log on the fire and stood to warm his muscles. The weather was easing.

One for One

*D*orothy had to get some air. She gripped the rung above her head and, with a hop, painfully made for the deck.

Suzanna screamed. Mary and Desire were both with her now. She was fully dilated, according to Desire, but the baby wasn't coming. As hard as it was to climb the ladder and as cold as it was above, she needed some peace.

The deck was slippery. On hands and knees, she crawled toward the two water barrels fastened to the outer wall of the steerage cabin. There was just enough space between them to sit out of the wind.

With so many sailors sick, the deck was deserted. The ill were being cared for by the cook and ship surgeon in the larger aft quarters. For those well enough, there was nothing to be done in the rigging and it was too cold for regular duties. She settled deeper into the crevice, covering her ears to block out the screams from below.

She tried to rest. The sky brightened in the east and a soft glow dusted the ship mauve. Gulls swept low overhead and turned their heads to eye her curiously, before drafts lifted their pearly wings aloft. Sleep eluded her. She couldn't keep her mind from replaying Jasper's death, little Ellen's grief, Suzanna's pain and Desire's impending marriage to Gilbert.

Her ankle thumped rhythmically. She turned it against the icy surface of the deck, shuffling a little to tip her knee sideways.

She caught a movement to her right. Desire stretched by the rail. Heaving a deep sigh, she flopped her forearms onto the frosted wood. She wasn't wearing a cloak; she wouldn't be here long.

Dorothy shut her eyes and tried to picture the settlement they would create. Perhaps William had already found a suitable spot and was on his way back. She imagined spring coming, their new house smelling of fresh cut timber, the grass turning green and spring flowers growing in the fields.

Next winter, they would have wood stacked and a warm fire glowing in their own hearth.

She heard a scuffle and opened her eyes.

A handsome sailor had his arms around Desire.

Dorothy lunged, only to fall heavily back. Her woolen skirt was frozen to the deck. She yanked at it and Desire's wild eyes found her.

Desire twisted, trying to drop through the sailor's grasp. But he was too strong. His hand closed over her nose and mouth.

Dorothy yelled, but the sound seemed to travel no further than the puff of breath that accompanied it. Must she go to the hatch, or pull Desire from his grasp? He hadn't yet seen her.

"Help!" Dorothy yelled again.

The sailor dragged Desire toward the forecastle, kicked open the door and tried to toss Desire in. She flung arms and legs wide to prevent him. He let go of her mouth to pin her arms and she screamed.

No one was coming.

"Dorothy, go!" Desire hollered, before her words were cut off with a yelp. He smashed her head against the door jamb.

The skirt came free. Dorothy scrambled to her feet only to slip and fall back down. She slithered on all fours toward Desire. The door slammed. It rattled as Desire thrashed against it on the other side.

Dorothy grabbed the door handle and pulled with all her might. Blood pounded in her ears, her whole being focussed on this one effort. She yanked, yanked, then fell against it in defeat – it swung inward under her weight.

She fell against the sailor, now on top of Desire, trying to stuff his neckerchief in her mouth. He froze for an instant and Desire took the opportunity to scratch his face, before twisting beneath him.

Dorothy stood, without pain, and tried to throw him off. Desire twisted and kicked like a mad animal. In a strange state of heightened sense and narrowed focus, Dorothy fixated on his swaying pale hair, loosened from its ribbon. She reached out and yanked.

He threw her backward with one push and her head smacked the hull. She held still until she could see straight and then crawled for him again. She pulled Desire's legs trying to free her.

A gag sunk deep into the soft flesh of Desire's cheeks. Her legs were now stiff and tight, her eyes restless.

The sailor leaned forward and ran an unhurried tongue across Desire's cheek. Dorothy begged Desire to fight. She let go of her legs and threw herself at him. He raised an arm to fend Dorothy off, but she managed to unbalance him. Desire immediately came to life and crab-crawled away.

He lunged to recapture her, but Dorothy restrained him with an iron grip around his middle. He lost patience, gave up on Desire, and turned on her instead, spitting and cursing violence. His face was ugly, unmasked.

He squeezed her throat. She panicked. The berserk energy she used to protect Desire left her as quickly as it had come. She whimpered. Her body froze like an animal grabbed by the scruff.

A heavy pan rose above his head. Dorothy's gaze followed its assent, betraying Desire before she could swing. The sailor turned and kicked Desire backward with such force that a great *whoosh* escaped her now unbound lips. Her head ricocheted off the edge of the long wooden table and hit the brick stove. Her body thumped the deck, eyes closed, soul inert.

His hands left Dorothy's neck, but he was on her again the instant he was satisfied Desire wouldn't move. He knocked Dorothy to the ground, pinned her arms with his knees, and gagged her with a towel. The cloth sliced the corners of her mouth. He cinched it tighter, knotting it by her ear. She tossed her head side to side in an attempt to drag it free. She was choking.

She tried to buck him off, but his crotch just moved closer to her face. His stench was overpowering. He was excited. She tried to scream through the gag but her lungs were depleted. He wrestled her arms together and, pulling a rope from his waist, bound them together before tying her off to the bunk above.

She twisted like a snared rabbit. He sat on his heels examining her struggle and then shuffled back to Desire, whose chest rose and fell rhythmically. She was alive. He bent and kissed her before walking to the door to ensure the deck was still deserted.

He flipped the latch in place and grinned at Dorothy. Unhurriedly, he approached her first. A cold tide of fear ran through her from crown to toe. She looked away. He bent to lick her chest then stood; his breaches pressed her cheek. She twisted and pulled against the hammock enough that she could get her feet under her and backed away from him.

"Ah, the beast has legs," he said. "As little as I favour you, you'll get yours when I'm finished with her." He swept a leg under hers as he turned, catching her ankle. She screamed into the cloth and fell once more to the floor, her arms jerking up behind her.

Tears streamed down her cheeks as she was forced to witness him lift Desire's skirt. His fingers stroked the pale flesh of her flaccid legs.

She shouted, "Don toosh heh!" over and over again. It was no use.

Desperation pulled her to her feet once more and she tried through hazy eyes to see the rigging of the hammock, searching for some way of freeing it or cutting the rope. She grasped the hammock and shook.

He pulled down his breaches.

She saw the hook in the ceiling. She shook the canvas as high as she could, flapping up and down. Once. Twice.

He eased himself in and began to pant, thrusting in and out.

The hammock fell heavily off its rig and dropped her to the floor with it. She was awash in hammock and rope. Her knuckle grazed the handle of the iron pan.

He panted, his mouth was soft with bliss.

She held the pan and swung it with all her might, spinning herself toward the table. The heavy iron landed with a satisfying crack across his skull, just before her own head hit . . .

December 9th – Morning Watch

William stood at the opening to the barricade and appraised the sky; high cloud, the rising sun a narrow sliver in the east. Inside, the party stirred. They moved stiffly round the fire, hacking, coughing and spitting their greetings to the new day.

They had camped for the night on a dune just above the beach grass. Bleached limbs and waterlogged branches littered the sand, detritus from the massive oaks crowding the high tide line. Building their shelter had required merely untangling and straightening the larger of these, covering the whole with thick pine bows and hanging their coats within. The heat of eighteen bodies and the fire burning within had kept William warm all night.

"We needn't linger this morning. A bite of breakfast after prayer and let's be off," he said. The breeze felt warmer, but perhaps it was only the result of being dry.

"I agree. We haven't had clear sky like this for a while. Let's not waste it," said Carver. "I'll start taking the muskets and armour down to the shallop."

Carver struggled to the opening of the barricade with his arms full. "Who is coming with me?" he said.

"I don't think it's necessary. We can take them down when we go," said Stephen.

"We will have an easier start if we're already loaded," Carver countered. "Whose can I take down?"

"I'll come with you," offered William, "Tilley? Can I take yours?" Both Tilley brothers were still pale and feeble. William wondered again why they had been so stubborn about coming along.

"Sure, thanks," said Ed Tilley. "My stomach is griping. I'll be in the tall grass there. Start prayer without me." William lifted Ed's musket with his own. "I'll come back for your malle and cutlass."

"John, will you give the fire a stir and boil the oats?" asked Carver, hitching up his pack and starting down to the shoreline. William followed.

"You needn't ask him to do the menial tasks," said William. "He is an equal member of the company, in my opinion." The muskets and armour were heavy; he was grateful the shallop was only half a musket shot from the shelter.

"Any of us might have made the oats. Who says it is menial?" said Carver defensively. "The tide's not quite high enough for the shallop to get off the sand. Drop your stuff here and we can go back for more."

William made another trip, joined by Edward Winslow and the sailors, some of whom had thought to wrap their muskets in their coats to keep them dry.

Returning, he relieved himself in the grass and gazed at the swaying forest. It had seemed so menacing in the night. Yet now in the half-light of dawn, it rematerialized as timber, moss, and leaves.

He ducked inside the shelter and accepted a hot bowl of porridge from John.

"Thank you, John. Are you taking a load down to the shallop?" he asked.

"No. I'll eat then carry my gear as we leave," he said, sitting down to check his musket. "I think this got wet in the night. I might just have a go with it – if the rest of you don't mind?"

John carried his musket outside, knelt, and steadied it on the far end of a log. Aiming high into the brush, he checked the match was lit, adjusted its length, then shouted, "Ready!" and fired.

There was a jovial round of applause.

"I'll have to try mine," said Stephen. He took John's place at the end of the log and aimed at the trunk of a thick tree.

"You'll have to aim at something bigger than that if *you* hope to hit it," joked Richard Warren.

"Shows what you know!" said Stephen, pulling the trigger. A solid thunk echoed from the tree. They cheered. Being warm and dry did wonders for the spirit.

"Let me try now. Watch how it's done," said Richard going for his musket at the back of the lean-to.

"No more wasting shot," barked Myles. "Ready your weapons. We aren't on a lark."

William tossed a pebble at him. "It's a beautiful morning Myles, don't be such a grump."

Carver stirred the porridge. "Anyone not had any? Let's eat and get to the shallop. Tide's coming in."

"Save some for Ed Tilley. It'll bind up his bowels for the day," said Richard, scooping a generous mouthful and swallowing hard.

"Woach woack haa haa hach woach." The air reverberated like the skin of a drum, powerful, strong.

They turned right and left and dropped to the sand confused, peering out through the cracks in the barricade.

Ed Tilley burst though the brush to William's right, one hand holding up his breaches and the other waving and pointing at the trees.

"They are men! Indians! Indians!" he yelled.

Arrows flew from every corner of the wood, whistling past them or sinking into the barricade with soft thunks. Shadows shifted in the half light.

"Arm!" bellowed Myles.

William reached for his musket, felt his chest. His armour and musket were on the beach.

Myles fired his snaphance, followed quickly by Richard, his musket already poised.

"Defend the shelter!" yelled Myles.

"I'm going for my musket!" yelled William over his shoulder. The whir of arrows buzzed past him. He dropped beside a log, afraid to move forward and afraid to stay put, exposed on all sides. He gathered his courage and dashed from his meagre cover, his legs churning and sliding in the sand. Carver and Edward were right behind him.

He could see John and Ed Tilley poised to follow like runners on a start line.

"Stay there! It's too risky. You won't make it!" he yelled, trying to remember the sequence for loading his musket. An arrow stuck in the sand at his feet.

He looked over his shoulder. Two sailors and Robert Coppin were firing from the shallop.

"Make you aim count!" bellowed Myles.

"My match is out!" called Carver, kneeling nearby blowing on his match.

William leapt to him ready to light it – only to discover his wasn't burning either. Edward was half way up the beach again.

"We are both out!" He started to run back to their fire. An arrow flew at him and he ducked just in time and then dodged back for the Tilleys' muskets. "Help me carry one of these!" He thrust one at Carver, who was still blowing and fussing with his match.

He looked up again to see John Howland sprinting across the sand, a lit log from the fire flung across his shoulder, showering sparks behind him. It was a beautiful sight, a brave and dangerous sight.

John threw it at his feet, grabbed Carver's musket, lit his match, handed it back and did the same for William's and the Tilleys'. Only then did he bury his burning hand in the cold sand. He picked up a great, wet fistful of it, then with the other hand snatched one of the Tilleys' muskets and launched himself back to the barricade.

William sprinted behind him, uncertain he had really witnessed the deed. When he looked back at the beach, the log still burned bright, surrounded now by a smattering of failed arrows.

Arrows flew like angry hornets past William's ears, yet miraculously he hadn't yet been stung.

He spotted a lusty figure behind a tree not half a musket shot from them. The Indian made a beastly sound, then shot three arrows in quick succession before calling out in that same terrible menace to the others. William took aim and landed a ball in the tree – too high.

"That one there!" he called to Edward. Edward swung and fired, his ball skittering through the foliage, showering leaves and branches on his target. The Indian stood his ground and raised his bow to William.

William fired without thinking. Bark exploded beside the figure, rocketing the Indian's face with debris before he could loose his arrow. A great shriek rent the air and he called again, "haa, haah, Woach, Woach, Woach," and the wood shook as the Indians folded back into the forest. The man he'd hit leapt a bush. He wore a wool cloak – Prince's cloak.

"Stay with the shallop! Be of good courage!" Myles yelled down to the beach.

"After them!" he called to the rest of the company. They gave chase, hollering and cursing at the fleeing figures, their fatigue and sores momentarily forgotten. But soon, tiredness overcame them. They fired a final volley in the direction of their foes to show they weren't afraid.

As they retraced their steps to the beach, Myles called out, "Here! Letters and a brown notebook. Who dropped these?"

"Let's see those," said William, racing over.

He scanned the first letter. "Mercy! She was right . . . about everything." He blinked and reread the signature.

Carver reached for the notebook, moving quickly through the pages and then fanning them, just to be sure of what he saw. It was Prince's, the one he used to record his debts and promises. "There is nothing on these pages."

December 9th – Morning Watch

Dorothy slowly recovered consciousness. At first, hazy outlines emerged, then came clearer shapes, but only through a narrow tunnel. Memories emerged from the fog and she scrambled to her feet. She twisted her head side to side. Something was in her mouth. She rubbed it against her right shoulder but couldn't remove it.

More of her senses returned. Gagged – she was gagged. Her left shoulder throbbed cruelly and hung at an odd angle. She couldn't lift it. Looking around desperately, she spotted Desire on the floor at the end of the tunnel. She knelt and tried awkwardly to shake her awake with bound hands. Lightening shot through her shoulder.

"Aake ub," she urged.

Desire moaned. She was alive. Dorothy had to get her out of here.

Fear prickled down her back as more memories ignited in the gloom. She took in the pile beside Desire: breaches below pale kneecaps, exposed buttocks, a leg still resting over Desire. She looked at his face. Blood had trickled from his ear into the pool of red beneath his mouth.

She had to hurry. Shuffling to Desire's ankles, she pulled as hard as she could. Her left hand sprung wide with pain. She grasped harder with her right, but she couldn't do it. She shuffled back up Desire's body and kicked the sailor's leg free. She gripped Desire's hand and began scooting toward the door. Desire remained motionless.

"Aake uuuu!" she shouted through the gag. It was no use. She would have to go for help.

She rolled to her knees and leaned forward in order to get to her feet. Her first step, on her right foot, rolled her to the deck again. She landed hard on her left shoulder.

A scream so jagged parted her lips that it could have sawn straight through the cloth. All that emerged, a whimper.

She crawled across the boards. She flipped the hasp on the door and lifted herself over the sill.

"Hep – hepp!" she called, but the words were whisked from her. She tried standing and this time struck out on her good leg. She gripped the outer panels of the forecastle and slid along. If she could reach the deck rail, she could use it to guide herself to the hatchway. It would only be a few short hops from there.

She tipped her head back, peering through the narrow window that framed her vision. The railing. It would be her road home. Her vision collapsed further. She had to hurry. She put weight on her ankle. The pain was unbearable, yet she launched herself forward, hand out expectantly, her world now irretrievably dark.

She tumbled. She reached out to stop herself. Cold slapped her cheeks and brow. Cold folded her in half and sucked her into its embrace, filling her mouth with ice. Tiny rivers threaded their way round the gag. The Atlantic filled her and choked her. She writhed in its icy grip.

Her vision cleared and brightened. Jonathan looked up at her, smiling, his hand on her skirt. Brilliance enveloped her.

December 9th – Morning Watch

Desire reached up and felt her head. Her fingers came away sticky. She had a terrible headache. She opened her eyes. A brick wall loomed above.

She gasped. Fresh, cold air filled her lungs. "Oh God. Dear God." She crawled backward, kicking with her heels. She curled up and rocked back and forth, transfixed by the scene.

His pants were down. "Oh God. Please God," she cried aloud. Her hand dropped between her legs. She was wet. She lifted her fingers and stared at them. Bloody. "Oh God." Her hand shook. Her body began to quake. She grasped the brick stove with one hand and the overturned table with the other and stood.

He wasn't moving. Keeping her back to the table, she sidled around him, expecting him to grab her at any moment. She stole a quick glance to either side. Pots and pans strewn everywhere, a hammock torn from the ceiling. She backed toward the open door, moving faster now. When she was free of it she ran for the hatchway. She jerked to a halt so suddenly she slipped.

They'll know; they will know if they see me. Her mind worked furiously. She scooted to the water barrels and squeezed out of sight. She took quick stock of her gown; nothing torn – just dirty. She eased up the hem of her skirt and risked a glance between her legs, then turned sideways to wretch. There was nothing to bring up; she hadn't eaten in at least twelve hours. She ran a hand over her face and brushed the hair out of her eyes. It was matted above her left ear. She ran her fingers through the strands. They were sticky and crusted with blood.

She glanced around. She was alone. Someone would come soon. She couldn't stay here and she couldn't go below looking like this.

She tried the lid of the water keg. It wouldn't budge. She tried the other and her heart leapt when it shifted. She threw her shoulder against it and it cracked open. She wriggled her fingers inside, pulled them out and slapped her hair. Loose tendrils spilled drops of blood on the deck. This wasn't going to work, she thought, frustrated.

She pulled her petticoat off. Hurrying, worrying someone, or her attacker, would appear, she fed the end into the barrel and let it drink up water. When it grew heavy, she pushed it under her skirt and scrubbed violently between her legs. Then she scrubbed at her crusted hair, ringing the bloody cotton onto the deck and wiping again and again until her head was dripping and hopefully clean. She wiped her face, twisted the petticoat into a ball, skated to the side of the deck, and threw it over.

As quietly as she could she descended the ladder. A newborn mewled. Everyone crowded around Suzanna's cabin. Safe then. She walked briskly to her cabin.

December 9th – Morning Watch

William took his coat down from the barricade and shook it.

"Look at this. Its been shot right through," he said reverently.

"Mine too. Look here, *two* holes," said Edward. "There must have been a hundred of them. Not a single scratch on any of us." He raised his hands in supplication, "God, thank you for our deliverance."

"Amen," said William.

He was wobbly, his legs moving like rubber as he stepped to examine Edward's coat. Something cracked under his boot and his heart leapt. He was on edge, but he had never felt more alive and enervated than during the battle. He stooped and pulled two halves of an arrow from under his heel.

The arrow was beautiful, almost artistic. It was beaded and splendid, the craftsmanship mesmerizing. "What is this on the tip?" he said, passing it around.

"That's an eagle's claw," said Stephen, whistling. "Here, let's find some more. We'll send them back to England with Master Jones. I'm going to keep one for myself, too. One landed right by my foot – that one's mine."

"Good idea. Take a minute, but we need to be off. The wind is picking up," said Carver.

They had to rifle through the leaves and grasses but they managed to find eighteen to send to England and a few more to keep as souvenirs. William stuffed a copper-headed one in his pack. He knew for a fact it was fired by the chief Indian, the one *he* had succeeded in scaring off. With *his* shot he had ended the battle.

"The tide favours us. Time to go," ordered Carver.

Away from shore the wind grew in strength. William was wet and cold again. After sailing for several hours with no sign of a river or deep harbour, they agreed to make for the place at the other side of the bay that Robert Coppin called Thievish Harbour. Robert guaranteed it would have all they needed.

It was now mid-afternoon. William was caked in ice and longed for their snug barricade. He reached into his pack and pulled out a handful of nuts. They hadn't brought any water and eating would make him thirsty, but the stabbing in his belly was one discomfort too many.

Perhaps it was the three-foot swells, or the fever, but they were now down three men. A sailor had joined the Tilleys on the floor of the boat.

"Did you all notice the great shot I had?" said William, testing the unfamiliar sensation of making a boast. "I scared off that brave young Indian after he stood his ground against all other shots." At first no one replied. The silence made him rue his foray into braggadocio. But then Edward spoke.

"You were very impressive, for sure," said Edward. "You hit him where I couldn't."

Carver put his arm around John's shoulder and gave him a hearty shake. "If you want to talk about bravery, you need to talk about my son-in-law to be." He stretched taller, winked at John, and then smiled at the others. "Did you see what he did? Carrying that fire brand down the beach in his bare hands. He saved William and me. Did you see that? I'll bet that gave the Indians pause for thought – seeing a man like him, afraid of nothing, thinking only of saving William and me."

John looked embarrassed … and then turned to Carver. "Future son-in-law? Not Gilbert? No disrespect, Edward."

"Very near future." Carver nodded to William. "It is long overdue."

"Here, here," said William, his frozen beard chiming.

William hugged his arms tighter around himself and leaned toward John. "That was the most remarkable thing I ever saw. A Roman warrior could not have done better. Your hand must be raw under those gloves, yet you sit here uncomplaining. You're a tough man, John, surviving the fall overboard in the storm, and now this. Carver's a lucky man to have you as a son-in-law."

The boat abruptly swung round, throwing them sideways.

"What's? –" said Carver.

"The hinge on the rudder has come away – grab it – grab it!" yelled Master's mate Clarke. He lunged past the tiller and gripped the rudder with both hands. "The seas are too rough. We can't steer without her and the wind's pushing us toward the breakers."

"Grab an oar," said Coppin. "You there, grab an oar – we'll make a rudder." Coppin stood, pushed past William, and began wrestling one of the oars out from underneath their feet.

"We can help," said William, shoving the packs out of the way and feeding the oar along the hull. "We'll take turns with her. Just tell us what to do."

Their makeshift rudder worked. Two hours and William was ready for his third shift, though his arms had barely recovered from the last effort to steer the heavy shallop.

Now the light was failing, reducing the already poor visibility.

"We've got to pick up speed," said William, "or we won't make it by nightfall. There is nowhere to put in. It's all breakers. Can you do something Master Clarke?"

"We can increase the sail but it's risky."

"Do we have another choice?" he asked, looking from Coppin to Clarke, the most experienced sailors. They put their heads together and muttered.

Extra sail was hoisted and the shallop responded immediately. The wind gusted. The strain on the rudder worsened.

"Be of good heart! I see it! I see it!" Coppin shouted bouncing on his seat and pointing northward. "Over there in the mist. That is the harbour."

William moved into position to steer. He grabbed the oar and strained against the black sea's efforts to force the oar toward him. The sailor, formerly at the tiller, pressed down to help William hold it under the water.

They were almost there. He prayed under his breath and thanked God for their deliverance thus far. Providence was with them.

CRACK!

William looked up, instinctively raising his arm as the top third of the mast came down heavily on him. He grabbed hold of the splintered wood to stop himself from falling overboard. Canvas whipped his face. Only when he'd batted it down did he see that the mast had broken in three places. Edward, Carver, and John were hauling the rest of the sail into the boat and shouting for help. If the sail went under they'd capsize. He let go the makeshift tiller.

The boat swung hard to port. He clumsily leapt for the oar and with heart pounding he wrested it into place and resumed his fight with the sea.

"Get that sail down!" barked Clarke above the general melee. "Grab the oars. We're almost there – we row, we row!"

William's arms burned but he kept hard on the rudder. Sleet cut his face, sweat stung his eyes. He couldn't shield himself.

The flood picked up. They were accelerating. They were safely beyond the breakers.

"Steer for that island!" called Clarke from the head.

The island advanced, its dark boulders menacing in the gloom.

"We'll be dashed to bits," yelled Edward.

"No, there, to port, ten-o-clock, steer for it, there's an opening in the rocks." Clarke shouted orders William couldn't follow.

"I can't see it," he yelled. It was too dark and there were too many bodies in his way. He steered blind.

"Tiller five degrees to starboard. Now ten … hold it … hold it … we're nearly there," directed Clarke. "Now stroke, stroke, stroke," he urged the others.

Gravel raked the hull. William pitched forward, collapsing across the dripping oar.

December 10th – Forenoon Watch

The island was deserted. In contrast to the violence of their arrival, they slept at ease. In the morning they relaxed by the fire, drying their boots and coats and reminiscing about their first encounter with the Indians – the first combat most had ever seen. Embarrassed by the adulation heaped on him for his role, William changed the subject and proposed they hike to a lookout.

The top of the island provided a panoramic view of the harbour and its sparkling bay. A jade green perimeter dropped precipitously to a cobalt blue that William knew without sounding was deep enough for a ship – a hundred ships. Through Master Clarke's spyglass he could see a brook emptying into the bay. The gently rising terrain was crowned by a hill that must, like their current vantage point, offer a commanding view of both land and sea. Myles was so pleased he'd already made plans to plant their cannon upon it.

"It's Saturday. Tomorrow we rest," said Carver addressing the party from the west facing rocky bluff. "What do you say to a march today? We can explore the land up along the brook. If it proves as good as it looks from here, we can keep the Sabbath safe on the island and then head back the next morning."

"I'm more than game," said William. "We can row across now and fix the mast in the evening."

"We've proposed to name this Clarke's Island. What do you say to that Mr. Clarke?" Carver shook the startled sailor's hand. "It was you who spotted the island and brought us safely ashore last night."

"Thank you," Clarke bowed, "It's a great honour."

"Glad you're pleased. Now let's get on," he said to the others. "We're rested and dry just in time to get wet again."

William lingered to take in the landscape once more. In imitation of the eagles above he soared down the hill, exalting in an unfamiliar sensation of lightness. December 10th. They'd found their new home. He already knew it. He couldn't wait to tell Dorothy and see the smile on her face.

December 10th – Forenoon Watch

Desire woke to the clanking of a spoon. Her head still throbbed. She'd fallen asleep, still in her clothes, on Katherine's bunk. Someone had put a pillow under her head and tucked a blanket around her. She peeled it off and reached for her hairbrush.

Wincing as the bristles passed over her left ear she recalled everything too clearly.

"Dorothy!" She stood abruptly. *Where is Dorothy?*

She checked the impulse to rush to Dorothy's cabin. She could not panic. She undid her dress and put on a fresh one, spun her hair up neatly and washed her face, her toe tapping with suppressed urgency the whole time.

Who knows of it? The sailor. And Dorothy. No one else must ever know.

John!
Gilbert.
She can't *even* marry Gilbert. He would discover it.

She straightened her back and opened the curtain. Everything was quiet; the few that were up moved at a languid pace. Mary stirred the pot, Katherine beside her. Beth brushed Ellen's hair. The men lying on their pallets stared glassy eyed at the doctor and Priscilla passing them bowls of broth. Bartle and Love played a game on a blanket, with Wrestling jealously watching.

"Good morning, Mother Katherine," she said as naturally as she could.

"Oh, you're up dear. You were dead to the world. We wondered where you'd gotten to when Suzanna delivered her little boy – Peregrine, she's calling him. Then we found you asleep in the cabin."

Katherine's arm wrapped around her waist and she bent to let Katherine kiss the top of her head. Tears – of guilt, of unworthiness – sprang to her eyes.

"I'm sorry. Have you seen Dorothy this morning?"

"No. I guess she's still sleeping. We were all so worn out we went straight to bed after the birth," said Katherine, looking at her softly. "What happened to your face?"

"What?" said Desire, raising fingers to her cheek.

"Your lip is swollen and your cheek is blue. You're bruised!"

"Oh, I slipped when I went up on deck for air. It doesn't hurt."

"Well where else are you hurt? Should we get the doctor to look at you?"

"No. I am perfectly fine, Mother. Do you think the men will be back today?"

"Only if they're successful." After a pause she added, "I dread telling Father Carver about Jasper."

She'd forgotten about Jasper. She felt sick.

"Dorothy was very upset about Jasper," Desire said, "I should check on her."

Desire parted the curtain an inch and squinted at the crumpled linen of Dorothy and William's bed. It looked empty. She pulled the curtain open a little more and stuck her head in.

"No one is here," she said, turning to Katherine. "Have you seen her this morning at all?"

Katherine shook her head and resumed her conversation with Mary.

"Could someone come up on deck with me and look for her?"

"I'm busy at the moment, dear. Perhaps Anna can go," said Katherine "Anna?"

Anna shook her head. Desire knocked at Beth's cabin. "Will you come up with me? I can't find Dorothy anywhere."

Beth took her time getting ready and then followed Desire up the ladder. The sun shone brightly. Surely Dorothy would want to be up here on such a beautiful day.

Desire reached for Beth's hand on the pretence that the deck was slippery. She eyed the forecastle warily. The door was closed. There'd been no news of a sailor found dead. Their eyes roved over the whole deck. From bow to poop deck there was no sign of Dorothy.

"Lets get below. Maybe she's in someone's cabin," said Beth.

Desire's fear mounted. The image of Dorothy, pinned by the sailor, looking at her over his shoulder sent a chill through her.

Who had killed the sailor?

By the time she stepped onto the 'tween deck she was in full panic. "Who has seen Dorothy?" she demanded in a shrill, unfamiliar voice.

They looked at one another, then back at her, shaking their heads.

"Probably chucked herself overboard. Good riddance," hollered Billington from the far end of the corridor, snickering. She ignored him, but her stomach cramped.

"I saw her go up on deck yesterday," said Ellen in a little voice.

Ellen, yes, thought Desire. She would know where Dorothy is. "When did you last see her, Ellen?"

"Yesterday morning, before Peregrine was born. She said she was tired and needed some air. She said it was too cold for me and that I should try to rest."

Yesterday morning. Had it been that long? How long had she been asleep?

"Thank you, Ellen," said Desire.

"Everyone help me search! What will William say if something …" She started pulling curtains aside. Her obvious anxiety finally roused the others, the Billingtons excepted, to begin a search of the ship from top to bottom.

Even ailing Isaac Allerton rose from his bed to search the steerage cabins and knock at the Master's door. On his return he whispered something to Elder Brewster and Dr. Fuller. Desire couldn't bear to see their faces; neither could she turn away.

She continued her search, scouring every place twice. Then, steeling herself to the only remaining possibility, she approached the upper rail. It was a bright day and the water flat and crystal clear. Beth and Katherine joined her.

She reached for Katherine's hand, afraid of what she might see. They looked together. William Brewster and John Alden did the same on the port side.

She scanned the sandy bottom. Moving shapes and reflections glided in and out of view.

"There's something here!" yelled Brewster. "Get the boat."

Sailors hauled on the lines tethering the longboat, bringing it alongside to starboard where Isaac, Brewster, and Alden waited to climb in. Two sailors passed Alden a gaff hook before jumping aboard themselves. They rowed out and disappeared around the stern. Desire raced to the port side.

The longboat re-emerged, the half-submerged gaff hook in one of the sailor's hands cutting the surface like a shark's fin. The sailor grunted, suddenly raising the hook hand over fist. Nauseous with foreboding, Desire forced herself to watch. Brewster bent to catch hold of a what looked like fabric.

He held it aloft. A lady's petticoat.

Desire sat down hard with her back against the rail.

A piercing shriek exploded from Katherine's lips.

Everyone watching wept and moaned. She covered her ears.

She recognized it, even at this distance – her own petticoat. The relief that washed over her as she saw what Brewster held, was short-lived. In the seconds before she recognized it was not Dorothy, she knew it might have been, and she had desperately wanted to look away. She was a coward. Dorothy had died for her, yet she couldn't even look? She stood and opened her eyes, willing herself not to turn away from whatever the men found next. The friends around her were not mistaken in their grief. Dorothy was down there, alone, somewhere.

Katherine convulsed in tears. "I promised William. I promised William to watch over her. What will he say? She snuck away and jumped overboard when we were all busy. He'll never forgive me."

"There was nothing you could have done about it," said Mary. She lowered her voice and shook her head, "It is a terrible sin."

Sarah Eaton and Lizzy held hands and put their heads together. "Remember how nice she was back in Dartmouth?" said Sarah. "William never should have brought her."

Desire turned from the scene below. "Dorothy did not jump! How dare you accuse her of such a sin," she said sharply. "She loved Jonathan and no amount of grief or pain would ever cause her to abandon him."

"She's tried to do it before. You know that, Desire," said Beth. "Just because we wish it wasn't so doesn't change the fact."

"That is a lie!" said Desire, boiling with rage. "Dorothy endured far worse than you can know simply to stay alive. I myself slipped on this deck yesterday. Look – look at my cheek," she said, pulling her hair back. "You know how weak she was, hobbling around on that ankle. She could have rested, taken time to recover, but instead she tended the sick, cooked, watched the little ones and remained our tireless advocate. The least you can do is honour her with your sorrow."

Mary and the other women shrugged with non-committal gestures.

She wanted to shout that Dorothy had saved her. She wanted to tell the story of Dorothy's heroism, of the battle to the death Dorothy had waged to keep her safe. But she couldn't. Her rape was not only a hideous violation, it was a stain never to be removed. It was a life sentence; its first, but by no means only, cost the freedom to sing the praises of the woman who had saved her. The woman she had loved. It was selfish, perhaps, but she had to think of herself now. All must remain a secret.

She turned back toward the rail. The men worked silently stroking and then gliding, studying the deep water in ever growing circles around the ship. They kept it up hour after hour. The bells kept tolling. They kept searching. The women took their gossip below.

She was frozen despite the sunshine. Unable to get up, she peeked between the rails. The men were half standing in the boat and working together with the hook and one of the oars. Had they found her?

She held her breath.

They sat back down and continued rowing.

She let it out.

The bell clanged again. They would be getting hungry.

They bobbed at a distance, leaning on their oars. Snippets of their conversation carried clearly across the water to her.

"have to . . . William will think . . . I can't . . . blood on the water barr . . . Master Jones said . . . do we keep . . ."

How much did they know? What did they suspect? Dorothy didn't deserve their suspicions. Desire didn't want the sailors in the longboat to know any of it. She wanted them to stop searching, fearful now that they would find Dorothy's body, spear it with that awful hook, tumble it at their feet like flotsam. Far better that she remain safe below.

What had happened to her? Was she sullied too? Is that why? It had to have been Dorothy who killed him. Did guilt drive her overboard? Shame? No. Jonathan. For him, Dorothy could withstand anything. They were all wrong!

She rocked back and forth and surrendered to her grief.

I'll love you forever, Dorothy.

The boat swung around. They were heading back.
She felt her wrist – it was gone. The bracelet was gone.

December 12th – First Dog Watch

William leaned back in the shallop at ease, his feet on the seat ahead of him. He passed his flask to Edward. "How many varieties of tree did you count? And the plums, the cherries, the walnuts. Never mind," he laughed, "too many to count!" He merrily waved Edward's hand away. "Pass it behind you. Celebrate. We have found our new home."

"And the brook – the sweetest water I've drunk yet," said Carver. "I wager it will be full of fish in the spring."

"And then we can plant straight away," chimed Ed Tilley. "There is more corn ground cleared than we have seed for. We can use our time building homes instead of clearing the land." He slapped his brother on the back. "Aren't you glad we were here for this? I wouldn't have missed it. This is the new beginning."

"I drink to that!" said William. "We shall look back on this moment and tell our children and grandchildren. This is the new beginning."

"It's damn cold here," said one of the sailors.

"You're a part of history today," said William, laughing. "Watch what you say."

"Hail the ship, they can probably hear us from here," said Carver, standing up and waving. William grabbed Carver's leg to steady him and then hollered with the others.

"We've done it! We've found it!"

"Look there, the longboat's out. Head for them, they'll be the first to know," said William to Master Clarke. "You can tell them about your island. I can't wait to tell Dorothy about the land we've found. It won't be long till we're settled and our Jonathan can come."

"I'm telling Desire that we're to be married right away," said John beaming. "I have your word, don't I?" he said turning to Carver, who nodded.

Noisily, they hove to by the longboat. "Catching anything?" said William to Isaac, who stood with the gaff hook deep under water. Brewster leaned over the gunwale beside him.

"William, we've sad news," said Brewster, choking back tears. "Terrible news."

December 12th – Last Dog Watch

William lay down in the bunk, brought Dorothy's shift to his nose and inhaled deeply. Not conscious of breathing out he breathed in again, remembering. He feared he might use up her scent, but each time it was there. *Would there come a day when it was not?*

What was he to think? Desire had rushed to his side when they boarded, insisting that Dorothy had not jumped. That she must have slipped. That Dorothy was brave and strong.

Then Isaac had whispered something about finding blood on the deck. That a sailor had been found dead. What on earth was he to make of that?

Brewster suspected Billington. *That made the most sense.* He never should have left her here alone with him. *I failed you again, Dorothy.* Billington's leering face burned in his mind. *If it was you, I'll have you hanged.*

He wept, burying his face in her pillow. Billington, Prince and his lies, Harlock – how could he defend her against this legion of ills? But he knew. He knew who shouldered the blame. He brought his knees up to his chest and a howl of grief escaped.

Did you . . . jump? I promised to find you a home. What of Jonathan? How am I to tell him his mother is gone? Dead. You were afraid . . you tried to tell me . . . if I'd listened. Dorothy, my dear little Dorothy.

From his vest he pulled the neatly folded poem he had penned and forgotten to give to her the morning of their parting. It was damp with the sweat of seafaring and combat. He didn't have to unfold it. He pressed it to his heart.

Faint not, poor soul, in God still trust,
Fear not the things thou suffer must;
For, whom he loves he doth chastise,
And then all tears wipes from their eyes.

Above deck he heard Master Jones bellow commands to his crew. *Mayflower* was getting underway. In the morning they would be anchored in Thievish Harbour, by nightfall treading the shore of the New World. A new home.

He fell to the floor and gathered her things to him and rocked back and forth willing them to fill with her body once more.

O Lord, this heavy cost. We must succeed. Or what have I done?

Acknowledgements

The author's profound appreciation to . . .

Kate Furnivall for invaluable advice over cups of tea in beautiful English gardens; for honest criticisms and unwavering encouragement; for reading the first version of this novel and remembering every detail a year later; for invaluable brainstorming sessions; and for being an all-round marvellously generous and talented woman.

Norman Sharam for reading and for sharing his creative spirit.

My wonderful compuserve (TheLitForum) friends: Julie Weathers, Beth Shope, Rose Phillips, Diana Gabaldon, Jerusha Bloyer Greenwood, Theresa Kiihn, Rebecca Johnson, Donna Rubino, Claire Greer, Martha Williams, Becky Hopersberger, and Carol Krenz, for lively conversation, writing insight, scene reading, more scene reading, and the all-important prop up when things got tough.

Jan Knecht and Meghan McPhee my dull-pencilled first readers.

June Manney for introductions, encouragement, tours of Dartmouth and Kingswear, and for demonstrating what it is to be a true Lady.

Uncles Gary and Richard Blaikie for inspiring my love of history and for preserving generations of family heirlooms, letters and photos. My beloved history keepers.

The rest of my four-quarter family, talented writers and intellectuals each, for the kind of support that can be found nowhere else. Their editing and technical suggestions have been as valuable as their patient acceptance that every available surface in the house was to be littered with books, papers, notepads, and computer charging cables.

Author's Note

While this is a work of fiction, it draws heavily on the first-hand accounts of the passengers aboard the *Mayflower*. In letters and journals, William Bradford and Edward Winslow documented the events surrounding the voyage and the many setbacks they faced on reaching the New World.

Our villain Andrew Weston is indeed Thomas Weston's brother. He appears in the diary of William Bradford in April 1621. A letter addressed to Bradford and fellow pilgrim William Brewster describes Andrew Weston as 'a heady and violent man'. The same letter warns that Andrew and Thomas Weston are working to sabotage the plantation and the Adventurers alike.

It must be mentioned that the term 'Indian' is used in this novel for historical accuracy only. The term "indigenous peoples" was not in use in 1620. The novel also takes place before the *Mayflower's* passengers befriend the indigenous people of the region. Their biases had hitherto led them to view the non-Christian inhabitants of the New World as 'savages', an offensive term that is repeated here to accurately reflect the mindset of the pilgrims.

The book also deals with several incidents of assault. There may be a perception that, in the past, women endured assault as a normal part of their experience. But even in 1620, women refused to accept it.

In the 17th century, women came forward to charge their attackers. Isaac Allerton, the Elder responsible for punishing Desire over her relationship with John Howland, was in real life accused by an Irish girl of beating her for having "carnal conversations" with his servant. And Artemisia Gentileschi, a well-known 17th century painter (and whose father, Orazio, is behind the artwork on the cover) brought charges of rape against her art tutor. She was subject to several hours of torture with thumb-screws while testifying in court before the jury decided she was telling the truth. She went on to become a leader in a popular art movement that depicted women as equal to men, both in their power and their violence. Dorothy and Artemisia would have gotten along fabulously.

Manufactured by Amazon.ca
Bolton, ON